BORN OF WAR

Also by the Author

A-18

A Piece of This Country

BORN OF
WAR

Thomas Taylor

McGRAW-HILL BOOK COMPANY

New York   St. Louis   San Francisco
Hamburg   Mexico   Toronto

The following quotations have been used with permission:

Quotation on page 390 from *The Second World War*, vol. 5, *Closing the Ring*, by Winston S. Churchill. Copyright © 1951 by Houghton Mifflin Company. Copyright © renewed 1979 by Lady Sarah Audley and the Honourable Lady Soames. Reprinted by permission of Houghton Mifflin Company.

Quotation on page 389 from *The Turn of the Tide* by Sir Arthur Bryant. Reprinted by permission of Doubleday & permission Harold Ober Associates, Inc. Copyright © 1961 by Field Marshal Sir William Slim.

1 2 3 4 5 6 7 8 9 DOC DOC 8 9 0 9 8

ISBN 0-07-063192-1

LIBRARY OF CONGRESS CATALOGING-IN-PUBLICATION DATA

Taylor, Thomas, 1934–
   Born of war / Thomas Taylor.
   p. cm.
  ISBN 0-07-063192-1
    1. Wingate, Orde Charles, 1903–1944—Fiction. 2. World War, 1939–1945—Fiction. I. Title.
PS3570.A955B6 1988
813'.54—dc19

It is well that war is so terrible—or else we would get too fond of it.

ROBERT E. LEE

Contents

Prologue

By day the jungle is a place of fleeting motion. Birds on the wing dart warily among the branches and often alight to reset their bearings. Below there is even less movement. The predators are nocturnal, so by day the jungle floor is ruled by the elephant, and even it does not much disturb the habitat. Though its passage is ponderous and destructive, the foliage rises from under its weight almost as the sea reclaims the wake of ships.

For all its strength the elephant respects the constraints and contours of the land. Though relatively invulnerable, the elephant watches more than it moves. It seems to know the message of the jungle, which is to wait—to watch and wait—for something is always about to happen, or something may.

In the fortieth year of his life a man was crashing through this jungle. He fought it in long spasms, resting to pant and suck his sweat, then crashed on, glancing at the treetops for glimpses of the dappling sun. In a few more hours the double canopy of teak and mahogany would filter only a dim light; then the descent of night would be sudden and complete. Till then the glow of the afternoon was his only guide, for but one direction concerned him—west. He would follow the low luminescence of daylight until it expired.

He was close to expiring himself. His khaki uniform was slashed to rags, his grimy toes poked through holes rotted in his boots. Somewhere along the miles behind him his canteen had been torn from his shoulder as he waded humpbacked through brush and bramble. He was succumbing to dehydration.

Though he was a soldier he had lost his weapon—a memory blurred by utter fatigue. All he remembered was the final volley fired by the enemy as he bolted off the trail, the last trail he had seen in two days. It was there he heard his last comrade die at the end of a bayonet.

For the first time in his life he was fleeing. That shock had sub-

1

sided; the humiliation no longer burned him but clung like the darkness soaking his uniform. He was fleeing the fate of three thousand men famous as "the Chindits." He had left them in the jungle to be hunted down as he was hunted now. If he was the most desperate of the quarry, it was because he was the biggest game—the general with a price on his head.

Denser jungle pushed him into the margin between fatigue and collapse, an involuntary zone where the body stops and sleeps when it must, as when he collided with trees, leaning against them to sleep a few seconds, never realizing he had been anything but awake.

Sometimes rough bark against his face awoke him; sometimes the fury of ant stings sent him stumbling on. He was losing his race with the afternoon, for the sun was blurring into pearly half-light. His thoughts of survival began to ebb, replaced by images from five years of war.

From the deepening shadows a branch reached down to gouge his head, reopening a wound of an earlier war. He touched the oozing blood and licked it from his fingers. The taste brought back a time that merged with the present so that the pressing jungle rolled back to become the flat horizons of a sea—the Mediterranean—as seen from afar through the hospital window in Haifa. Remembering, his cracked lips formed a name. He repeated it, starting to explain why he had sacrificed others for an ultimate end.

But now the answer would not return to memory. Only the name remained, the name of whom he asked forgiveness, of whom he had asked if forgiveness was necessary.

"Lorna...."

PART I

The Captain: Special Night Squads

1

Finally Lorna went to the nightstand, picked up the alarm clock, and set it squarely in front of the phone. It was 6:45. Officers Call was at 7:30 and her husband should be seated by 7:15; yet he had sat naked at the desk for twenty minutes, the receiver at his ear, listening for the most part, except to interject clipped questions.

"Hacohen?" she had whispered when he answered the phone. Wingate nodded. As he listened he seemed to fall into a calculating trance: he doodled, tapped his fingers, then slowly loaded a revolver.

She brewed tea, but he took only a sip. She handed him his uniform piece by piece; he managed to put it on with one hand. When he hung up she knew there was time for only one question:

"Why did you load it?" she asked as he darted for the door.

"He thinks they'll hit Tiberias." Wingate turned and opened his arms to her. "A kiss, my bonnie sweetheart, I'm after a prize!"

"Don't become one yourself," she cautioned as he bounded down the stairs of their flat, gnawing an onion as if it were an apple.

Outside, the morning markets of Jerusalem were gathering Bedouins, Jews, Lebanese, Syrians, camels, and donkeys. Through streets anciently narrow he dodged through the flow, his coxswain's size and rumpled uniform receiving respect from no one; only the crumbling onion in his mouth drew glances. He returned them with a private smile, for he felt the day would bring the sudden excitement that sometimes rewards the patient intelligence officer.

The crowd thickened; he was jostled. He noticed each contact, the draft of spice and sweat as faces pressed by him, but he glanced at none of them for he could not reveal a sign of recognition, knowing that someone in the crowd would slip a note in his pocket, a note with instructions from Hacohen. The traffic and scents thinned as he approached the government offices; he emerged from the population into his official identity.

He was hurrying toward a graceful stone building, a legacy from the Ottoman Empire. Koranic scripture wove around the giant entrance in carved filigree, a delicate backdrop for the stark wooden sign: "Headquarters, British Trusteeship for Palestine." Swagger sticks in hand, crisply uniformed officers strode up the marble stairs. The sentry's salute vibrated at his forehead.

There was a self-conscious bustle in the main corridor that morning—a little extra wax on the floor, polish on the brass, and rank in the air. Wingate arrived at an intimidating door lettered in gilt, "Commander's Conference Room." Underneath was a removable sign cautioning "Silence. Conference in Session."

The other officers—nearly a hundred of them—were already seated. Wingate eased open the door and slipped into the rear row among the other captains, none of whom greeted him. General Ritchie called the room to attention.

"Gentlemen," he announced, "the commander in chief, Middle East Theater, General Sir Archibald Wavell." He offered the podium to a squarely built general, a stolid Welshman who pondered the message he was about to deliver.

"Take your seats please," said Wavell, as if the invitation gave him time to collect his thoughts.

"I didn't want to end this little visit without, ah, speaking to you as a group. No doubt you suppose I know a great deal more about what's going on in Europe than what you read in the papers. I wish that were true, but the prospects of war are as hidden from me as from any lieutenant in this room. Mr. Chamberlain does not seek my counsel, and it's not my job to suggest or to speculate, even among fellow professionals, what our nation's course should be. Mr. Chamberlain is the prime minister, our elected leader, who will answer the questions of war and peace. Your job and mine is to prepare for war. Other than that, the affairs of the continent are the province of the politicians. That is my standard answer to the inquiries of the press in all the many nations of this theater. I find it a short and serviceable answer. I commend it to you whenever you are asked about a war with Hitler.

"Meanwhile there is war aplenty to concern us here in Palestine. A war small in size but large in its consequences. Here again my admonition is the same: We are *not* to take sides." Wavell paused to let his emphasis be appreciated. Wingate retrieved the planted note from his pocket. It was written in Hebrew. He read it as Wavell continued:

"We are not here to make historical judgments as to whom this land originally belonged. We are here by mandate of the League of Nations to reconcile the conflicting claims as best we can. To put this in military terms, our mission is to *maintain the peace*.

"I have come from Cairo to reiterate that very point. We have received disturbing reports that there is a faction...no, that's probably not fair...there are *individuals* among the British officers here who have taken it upon themselves to interpret the Balfour Declaration as an endorsement of the Jewish claims in Palestine.

"Let me assure you there is no such endorsement.

"It is His Majesty's current policy that Jews be allowed to immigrate into Palestine in reasonable numbers. That means if they can buy land from the Arabs they can hold it just as any other purchaser of real estate. It has never been and is not now British policy to set aside certain areas for exclusive Jewish settlement.

"What we are here to do is prevent armed hostility between disputants for the land. In this policy we must be evenhanded and strictly impartial." Wavell looked around the room to see if there could be any misunderstanding. "Can there be any question on his point?" Expecting none, he looked back to his notes. "Now I would go on to say..."

Wingate sprang to his feet. "I do have a question, sir," he shouted across an aghast silence.

Ritchie's head turned to him like the turret of a battleship. "Identify yourself, Captain."

"Captain Wingate, sir. Intelligence."

"Yes, Wingate," Wavell said evenly.

"Earlier you said our mission was to maintain the peace. Yet your last words were that we are not to take sides. The terrorists are on one side, General, and the settlers are on the other. To drive back the Palestinian terrorists, we must take the side of the Jewish settlers. Could you reconcile this contradiction, sir?" said Wingate and sat down.

"Wingate—yes. I recall your name from the dispatches. You got into a scrap with the terrorists at Dabburiya, am I right? What did you call your Jewish force?"

Wingate rose to answer. "Special Night Squads, General."

"I'll use that little action at Dabburiya as an example of how the peace can be maintained without taking sides between Jews and Arabs. Your notion, I believe, was that with British training the Jewish settlements could provide their own security, especially at night, rather than call upon our troops for protection. That's praiseworthy. If the settlers can defend themselves, this tends to maintain the peace. As peacekeepers we would then be providing advice on security to anyone who needs it, both Jews and Arabs. If you had stopped there, Wingate, no 'contradiction,' as you put it, would have arisen. But you went a crucial step further. You *participated* in the fight at Dabburiya. You took sides. Suppose you had been killed? I might have had to go to your funeral." An uncertain laughter rippled across the room. "I say that not to embarrass you, Wingate—I'm only using your experience as an example of how zeal in performing our difficult duty here must be tempered by the requirements of diplomacy. Thank you for your question. Are there others? Very well, then: General Ritchie."

"Atten-shun." The officers came to their feet. "Dismissed."

Wingate broke for the door. Ritchie's voice halted him like a dog on a leash. "Captain Wingate..."

The departing officers made way for his return. Hands clasped behind his back, Ritchie waited where his voice would not be overheard.

"In twenty years' service, Captain, I have never heard such impertinence. You will report to me..."

"Oh, Ritchie." Wavell had remained at the podium to answer some individual questions.

"Yes, General." Ritchie glanced at Wingate, a signal that the matter would be resumed. Wingate made for the door. Wavell's aide ducked beside him.

"Good question, Orde."

"Thanks, Malcolm."

"Only you would have asked it."

"Can you come over tonight? Lorna's making *tabbouleh*."

"What's in it? Last time, you know." He coughed as if to cover an indiscretion.

"You what?"

"I reeked of onion for days."

"Best thing you can eat."

"Agnes wouldn't let me near her."

"How is she?"

"Impatient to see you again. Are you catching a train?" That seemed to be Wingate's purpose as he accelerated down the hall.

"Appointment in Samara."

He felt Finley tug his arm. "Haven't you been in enough trouble today? For God's sake don't..."

"Try to keep the general around today, won't you, Malcolm? Wouldn't be surprised if there's some action in Galilee."

2

He glanced at the note as he skipped down the marble stairs. It directed him off the main thoroughfare, down an alley, and across a square where he looked for a battered car. Its engine started before he opened the door; its driver was Isaac Sadeh, a leader of the Jewish guerrillas.

"I'm not convinced," said Wingate as the car hurtled down the back streets.

"Zobi is in Tiberias. Believe it."

"Hacohen can't be sure."

"They've already infiltrated."

Wingate removed his tie and dress cap, tossing them in the back seat. Sadeh smiled as his captain donned an antique pith helmet.

"Isaac, Ritchie moved a battalion into the fort outside Tiberias yesterday."

"The British will not stop Zobi."

Wingate opened the glove compartment, took out a binocular case, and slipped it around his neck. "Where did you get these?" he asked as he discovered two hand grenades.

"American friends. Do you have a plan?"

"Not until I see for myself."

"See what?"

"Zobi's men."

"In Tiberias? How could we recognize them?"

"Only when they leave."

Sadeh careened around a curve as they roared through the Galilean countryside. "When they *leave?* Zobi will leave only when he completes his slaughter."

"Think with me. Who do we have available? Two squads can't stop them if they've mixed into the townspeople. We can only take revenge."

Sadeh gripped the wheel in frustration. "If we go in armed..."

"Their weapons are concealed. They would know who we are but we could not identify them. True?"

"The truth is too cold."

Wingate reached under the front seat. He began to assemble a Sten gun. "Didn't I warn? Didn't we offer to train them? Watch!..." The car skidded around a bearded Bedouin and his pair of donkeys.

The road spiraled down a crease in the ridge overlooking the placid Sea of Galilee; Tiberias was a town of sun-baked stone perched by the shore. Trailing a plume of dust, Sadeh turned down a dirt trail along the ridge and stopped. From an olive grove six men, their pockets bulging with grenades, converged on the car. They saluted Wingate by brandishing carbines. Their weight bowed the running boards as the car bounced on to a distant farmhouse.

Toward the Golan Heights was an old Turkish fort. On a rampart the Union Jack hung limply in noonday heat. "How long have you been watching?" Wingate asked the owner of the farm.

"Since sunrise." He was one of Sadeh's twelve men who stood in smoldering silence.

"Not even a patrol," Wingate muttered as he studied the fort through his binoculars. "Isaac, are you sure Zobi commands this raid?"

"It is he."

"Then he'll have the fort covered. Probably mined the road last night. What do you think?"

"I think you're right."

"Then the British are out of it."

"What do you mean?" a man asked in Hebrew. Sadeh translated, setting off a sputter of rage among the guerrillas.

"There must be something!" Sadeh demanded, voicing the consensus.

"If I had a mortar..."

"What would you do?"

"I'd shell the fort. Wake the British before Zobi strikes."

"I will attack the fort myself—with my pistol!" exclaimed the farmer.

Wingate answered in Hebrew. "You will do as I say. We ambush Zobi when he leaves."

"The Jews in Tiberias are defenseless!"

"My sister..."

"What use are we?"

"I did not choose this sacrifice!" Wingate answered them. "I can only help avenge it. The blood will be on Zobi's hands."

"And on the British!"

"Yes, and on the British. Enough blood may even soak into the minds of generals."

The market was the center of Tiberias. By noon awnings over the stalls dappled the milling Jews and Arabs in a checkerboard of shade. Cool shadows also attracted men to the high arched doorways. The merchants had been most active in the morning. Now, as activity subsided under the strength of the sun, the desert people dressed for the heat, which, in contrast to western notions, meant adding rather than removing garments.

Cloaks and robes blurred the contours of men's bodies and whatever they were carrying. Some raised their *wafras,* the cloths that protect the face in sandstorms. Slow in other movements, the Arabs' eyes darted around the market.

Lorna had gone back to bed, for Wingate rarely slept more than five hours at night, preferring to nap during the heat of the day. The phone was silent all morning. When it rang, Lorna was sure it would be her husband, but it was Finley.

"Malcolm, are you coming over?"

"Afraid not. Sir Archie's in with Ritchie now. Looks like they're winding things up; then it's off to Cyprus."

"Did you see Orde?"

"Both saw and heard him. What's he up to, Lorna?"

"What do you mean?"

"He was in quite a hurry to get somewhere." ·

"Oh."

"Can't you tell an old friend?"

"Not on the phone. It's so complicated. And so unfair what the British are doing here in Palestine. Do you understand what I mean?"

"Orde expressed himself on that point this morning. Didn't go over well with Ritchie."

"It's been that way for a year."

"You're with him in this, are you?"

"Absolutely. Malcolm, could you possibly arrange an evening with us? If we could just talk, you'd learn what's going on."

"Why don't you ever come to Cairo?"

"I know."

"I'm not sure you do. Either of you. You're so caught up in this Arab-Jewish imbroglio. Doesn't the rest of the world concern you?"

"Hitler you mean?"

"Principally. The world turns around Europe, my dear, not Palestine. Orde should be seeking transfer to the U.K. Get back to the gunners. Find a regiment going to France. There's where the main event will be. You know what I mean?"

"He's found a mission here. A cause."

"And enemies. I don't mean the Arabs."

"He defies them all."

"Careers are not built on defiance. Lorna, to say the least he is defiant."

"Don't you find that endearing? I do."

She heard him sigh. "An army's highest value is in obedience, not defiance."

"He's not an army, he's a person. Malcolm, why take the collective view? Individuals do matter."

"Lorna, if individuals didn't matter, would I have stayed so attached to you both?"

"Forgive me, my mind is very much on Orde today. When he gets back, we shall take his calendar and circle the dates for a visit to Cairo."

"I have your promise?"

"Yes."

"And just in time. Here comes Sir Archie. Till Cairo."

"Yes. Cheerio, Malcolm."

Finley caught up with Wavell in the hall. "On to Cyprus, sir?"

"Tomorrow. Ritchie feels a quick visit would be appreciated by the mufti." Wavell glanced at his watch as they walked. "I'd like to see a bit of the countryside. Inquire if we can motor to Amman."

"Very good, sir."

Zobi's signal was the noon call to prayer. The falsetto chant quavered over the marketplace summoning Muslims to the mosque. Curtains rolled down. The Arabs drifted away, though some loitered in doorways. More quickly than usual, the square emptied, leaving it to the Jews.

Wavell's small convoy included his sedan and two armored cars. Ritchie was pleased that he was traveling overland to Amman, for Wavell would see for himself the security of the countryside. Reports of terrorism, Ritchie stated, though serious, should not be exaggerated. He was interrupted by the duty officer sprinting down the marble steps.

"General Ritchie!"

"Yes. What is it?"

"The line to the fort outside Tiberias, sir. Went out while our battalion was reporting sniper fire."

"Get a plane up," Ritchie snapped. "What's wrong with their wireless?"

"Well, this is opportune," said Wavell. "Let's get on up to Tiberias. Tell Amman we'll be delayed. Care to come along?"

"I certainly would," Ritchie answered. Finley moved to the front seat, and the little convoy was on its way, sirens howling.

"Not like the terrorists to attack a battalion in garrison," Ritchie stated. "This could be a wild goose chase. We've had lines cut before, sir."

"Just as well. Always wanted to see Tiberias. Wasn't that where Jesus walked on the water?"

"Somewhere offshore."

"Malcolm, was it Tiberias?"

"That's where he and the apostles went fishing, I believe."

Four children, as they happened by a doorway, were the first to scream under flashing knives. Grenades lofted over the Jews standing paralyzed by the cries. They buckled under the blasts, falling as awnings collapsed around them. Fruit and flesh splattered the dry walls and hung there.

Zobi's men leaped into the street, turned their backs to each other, and sprayed the scattering crowd with fire from their Sten guns. Ricochets spurted plaster in crisscross patterns between the walls.

Hatches clanged as the fort's sally port creaked open and three armored cars roared out into the countryside, but within a half mile the first one set off a land mine. From within the fort British mortars searched the hills for invisible snipers whose shots puffed dust along the battlements. He was under siege, said the battalion commander, as he radioed Jerusalem for reinforcements.

Herding Jews in front of them, the Arabs converged on the schoolhouse, the newest symbol of Jewish presence in Tiberias. Many of the women fled to its safety. That was what Zobi expected. He ordered gasoline poured along the wattle walls and sloshed under the door. The fumes puffed into a hair-singeing flame.

3

The dirt road made two loops as it climbed the ridge from Tiberias. Half a mile above the town at the second curve, Wingate's men were burying a land mine. They had darted between rocks and crawled down gullies to reach the site, which was the only stretch of road that could not be seen from the fort. They feared British mortars as much as Arab snipers as the two dueled since noon.

The mine, a relic from the First World War, would detonate under five hundred pounds of pressure. When it was buried, Wingate had a rock half that weight placed over it.

"Why?" Sadeh asked.

"Zobi always steals donkeys. They'll come out first. We must let them pass." He repeated that command in Hebrew to the other Jews. "The mine is for his truck."

"He could steal many trucks."

"If we stop the first one, the others are exposed to fire from the fort. It's the best we can do."

The Jews silently agreed. But when Sten guns stuttered in Tiberias, they turned on Wingate once more.

"We cannot wait here!"

"Better to die attacking!"

Another man drew his pistol and Wingate's attention.

"You can die with bravery or kill with cunning," he said softly. "The choice is yours. Am I right?"

The question forced a tiny nod from Sadeh, who stayed crouched behind a rock, his eyes on the town. Between bursts of fire they heard sounds like a crowd in a faraway stadium.

"Understand our feelings, Orde."

"Later."

Over the town wall, a puff of flame became a black roll of smoke.

His face masked by a black *wafra,* Zobi watched the window frames crumble in flames. For a few moments a frenzied pounding thudded within the walls. His men stood fascinated until Zobi shouted for withdrawal.

Sadeh first saw the donkey train pass through the gate loaded with candelabra and silver. The Arabs' robes were streaked with soot.

"Lock your weapons," Wingate commanded. One by one he heard the safeties click.

He had to look away as the loot of the slain swung by. The donkeys disappeared around the bend and over the ridge. Wingate signaled for the rock to be removed as two trucks began to climb the hill with Zobi's men on the running boards.

"What are they dragging?" Sadeh hissed.

Wingate focused his binoculars. Six Jews were tied by their ankles, hands clawing above the dust. Their cries were faint over the grind of gears and laboring engines.

Another sound droned above them. A British observation plane cautiously circled the fort, then went into a shallow dive to investigate the trucks. The ropes were cut. From the back of the trucks, Sten guns furrowed the ground and left the Jews writhing. Free from their tows, the trucks accelerated around the first bend.

Over the radio Ritchie and Wavell could hear the observation plane guiding a pair of Spitfires. The targets were two trucks.

"Roger. Description please."

"Civilian. Three-ton lorries."

There was a pause as the pilot considered the situation. Ritchie turned to Wavell: "That's the problem, of course. Those could be people fleeing the village."

"Jews?"

"Most likely. RAF policy is not to fire unless fired upon."

"Wait a bit!" the observer's voice exclaimed. "One hit a mine!"

The front wheel disintegrated, its rim bounced down the hill, the shattered axle dug into hard dirt. The driver's head stuck through the windshield as though he were in a pillory. Bullets jerked the trucks' tarpaulins. Six Arabs crumpled from the running boards.

The ambushers hurled their grenades. They finished the first truck, but the second braked and received only a hail of fragments. The Arabs spun to the ground. Several charged the ambush while Zobi shouted to the others. Bullets cracked wildly from both sides as targets became invisible; then the fight turned into a blind exchange of grenades. Overhead the Spitfires banked in long loops.

"I think I saw him," Wingate whispered.

"Zobi?"

"A black *wafra*."

"Yes!"

"He's controlling his men from the second truck." Sadeh raised his head to fire a furious burst. Sparks and glass showered from the truck. "No! He's *under* it. I've got to cross the road."

"Why?"

"To see all four tires. Keep him covered."

Over ribbed hills and thin valleys named in the Bible, a pall of smoke ascended from Tiberias. A company from the fort was examining the devastated town; a detachment began to climb the road when Wavell's convoy arrived.

Wingate was unconscious from a grenade concussion so close that it bounced his helmet onto the road. Sadeh had bandaged his shoulder wound, then retreated with his men when the British approached, for guerrillas on both sides were outlaws.

Wavell, Ritchie, and Finley stepped among the bodies which had been dragged behind the trucks. The officers were shocked into silence until they came upon the second truck. Arab corpses strewn nearby clutched British carbines. Wavell radioed Jerusalem, canceled his visit to Amman, and ordered an investigation of the serial numbers on the carbines. Ritchie returned the futile air patrol to its base. Hands clasped behind their backs, the generals proceeded up the road.

"Isn't that a British helmet?" asked Wavell.

Finley stiffened. "Orde..."

"Who?"

"Captain Wingate, Sir Archie. He said..."

"What did he say?" Ritchie demanded.

"Appointment in Samara."

"This isn't Samara."

"An action in Galilee. Today." Finley searched the roadside.

"He told you that?"

"Orde!"

Slumped behind a rock, he had watched the party approach. Wingate stumbled by the generals to the second truck. It was collapsed on deflated tires. Wingate squatted to look underneath. Zobi's leg was crushed by the undercarriage. Pinned to the earth, he had killed himself with his pistol. Wingate undid Zobi's *wafra* and stuffed it into his pocket.

"Howard," said Ritchie to his driver, "radio the fort for their ambulance."

"It's in the town, sir."

"Bring it here. A British officer's been wounded."

Wingate steadied himself against the truck. "The donkeys got through us. Headed for the border. Those Spitfires can intercept."

"What happened?" Ritchie demanded.

"They're going to get away, sir!"

"Who?"

"Zobi's raiders! That's him under the truck."

"You ambushed him?"

"No, we were playing croquet..."

Finley took his arm. "Orde, come on. You need to lie down."

"And who were your allies?" Ritchie called after him.

Finley was asked to ride in the armored car so the generals could be alone as the convoy raised dust on the road back to Jerusalem.

"Who was this Zobi?"

"A notorious raider, General. In the pay of Sheik al-Abad, we suspect, who will be quite upset with us. Nevertheless, we're well rid of Zobi."

"And Wingate too, I gather."

"I can't say enough for his courage."

"Quite so. That action today is worth a DSO—however awkward the presentation might be."

"I very much agree, sir. Any decoration should not be presented to him in this theater."

"No?"

"Every officer in the headquarters heard your admonishment about taking sides. Hardly an hour later Wingate is out here fighting alongside the Zionist guerrillas. No matter what the circumstances, such flouting of authority is intolerable. To award him a medal for disobedience would be a military mockery."

"Perhaps he's in need of home leave."

"I was thinking rather of permanent transfer, sir."

"Apparently a first-class fighting man. What an idea—to shoot out those tires and crush that Zobi."

"Quite. Wingate's just the sort of fellow we should have ready for the Germans."

"Would there be a problem removing him from Palestine?"

Ritchie nodded. "He's quite chummy with the Zionist leadership—

very thick with Chaim Weizmann. These Jews have political influence at Whitehall, you know. If Wingate wants to make political trouble, there's no doubt he could."

"That's something I'd like to find out about him."

"Absolutely. No matter how brave or resourceful, the man's not an asset if he cannot obey his superiors."

"There are people who would disagree with you. They would cite Lawrence of Arabia as an example of how independence can be a military virtue."

"Around the Officers Club they provoke Wingate by calling him 'Lawrence of Judea.'"

"Do they?" Wavell chuckled. "Do they indeed."

"Yes. What's more, I've heard he and Lawrence are cousins."

"Ironic."

"Isn't it. Each a Christian—one the champion of the Arabs and the other of the Jews. Wingate thinks as little of Lawrence's tactics as he does of his politics."

"He seems a loner like Lawrence."

"That he is. Married though. Quite an attractive woman.... Howard." He tapped the driver on the shoulder. "When you drop us off, go right over and fetch Mrs. Wingate, please. Take her to B.A.H., Haifa."

"I'll have Finley go along," Wavell added.

4

The doctors operated at once, removing grenade fragments from his throat and head. Propped in bed, Wingate smiled faintly at Finley and Lorna. His first question was whether the donkey train escaped. It had.

"While the RAF cruised the bright blue sky," he sneered. "I hope Sir Archie saw that futility."

"He was observing Ritchie throughout," said Finley.

"Why didn't he overrule him? Wavell's as responsible for aveng-
ing the massacre."

"He's not nearly as direct as you. A perceptive man, though. Don't
underestimate him."

"Malcolm says you've gained an admirer in Sir Archie."

"Is that so?"

"The Spitfires reported the donkey train scattering north," said Finley. "Requested permission to attack. Wavell refused—for a reason
quite complimentary to you."

"But no compliment to your character, if he's right."

"What are you two saying?"

"Dear, why didn't you take your men into Tiberias? Wouldn't they
go?"

"Hardly. I had to restrain them." The taste of blood rose in his
throat. He coughed.

"Then why?"

"I'd like to hear what Sir Archie said."

Finley stepped over to the bed stand and flipped the corner of the
black *wafra* that had become a tablecloth for a vase of flowers from
Menachem Begin. "The Spitfires asked permission to strafe," Finley
said, watching Wingate's expression. "Ritchie was waiting for a cue
from Sir Archie."

"What did he say?"

"Something like: 'Strafing isn't really necessary now, is it? The head
of the snake is severed, so the tail can only thrash.' Very poetic for Wavell.
Was that your plan from the start? Your appointment in Samara?"

Wingate looked at Lorna and dropped his eyes. She sat down on
the bed and asked again if he could have stopped the massacre.

"Orde couldn't have stopped the raid. He did more than that. He
stopped the raider. Stopped him for good."

"Was that your plan?"

Wingate fidgeted. "That's the way it developed. I did not intend
to sacrifice the Tiberians."

"This morning when you talked to Hacohen."

"We certainly did not agree to sacrifice Tiberias."

"It was a nasty choice," said Finley, "but the best one in the long
run."

Lorna walked to the window. "For once I agree with Ritchie," she
said under her breath. Wingate looked at her blankly. She glanced at

Finley, who averted her eyes. "We're leaving, dear. We're leaving Palestine."

His head came forward, leaving a small spot of blood on the pillow. "We're what?" Lorna gestured to Finley.

"You're to be posted to England," he said. "With honor. The citation for a DSO is being prepared."

"What scoundrel..."

"Your doctor says you won't be fit for duty in less than..."

"It wasn't any doctor!"

"All right: it was Ritchie. And Sir Archie concurred. Furthermore..."

"It's the Arabs!"

"Furthermore, I concur. You've become too emotionally involved here, Orde. Get back where you belong. England itself is threatened."

"Can't Wavell...?"

"No. And I wouldn't ask him."

"Accept it, Orde. Some day we'd have to leave. It may as well be now."

"I must talk to Weizmann. Ben-Gurion."

"I have already," said Lorna. "They agree."

"You've given the Jews confidence. I think they are a long way toward defending themselves."

"They think I should leave?"

"It's not that they want you to, dear. It just seems best right now."

"And I must go now myself," said Finley. "Sir Archie wishes you a speedy recovery."

"When's he leaving?"

"This afternoon."

"Could I see him?"

"If it's to ask him to overrule Ritchie—no."

"Ask him if I can go to Cairo."

"Write me from London if you still feel that way. Well, dear friends, I must get straight to the airfield. How Agnes would love to have seen you."

"In London," said Lorna. "You'll be back before too long, won't you?"

"Hopefully. My worry is just the opposite of Orde's. If there's war, transfers are frozen. Especially with the Italian threat in Libya."

Finley and Lorna kissed. She closed the door behind him and returned to her husband's bedside. "Are you bitter?" she asked.

"Yes. Aren't you?"

"At first. But I see how this may be for the best. Eventually Ritchie would have thrown you out. Or you'd get in another scrap like Tiberias. You know I suffer when I see your bandages."

He took her hand and drew her closer. "What did Ben-Gurion say?"

"Very much what Malcolm said."

"What else?"

"Yes, I sensed something else. No matter how grateful he is to you there's this underlying fear that you could become..." She paused.

"Out with it."

"A liability."

"An embarrassment is what you mean."

"It's a level of politics that's...above us, Orde. There are always repercussions. Look what happened at Dabburiya. And now Tiberias. You upset the politicians' games."

"And now I've upset you."

She dabbed her eyes. "I find Tiberias very hard to understand. Even realizing that in the end it..."

"More Jews will be saved than were lost. The position of my soul rather depends on that assumption, doesn't it?"

"Few could have made such a decision. I should support it fully."

"I'll never know for certain whether I was right. My instincts rule me, Lorna."

"This morning. You weren't agonizing—you were almost light-hearted. 'A kiss, my bonnie sweetheart....' Remember?"

He nodded. His head slumped back on the pillow. "The prospects were exciting. Planning for me is adrenalin. Once the insight flashes I'm blind to all else."

"I'm glad we're leaving."

"Look at the window. What do you see?"

"The flowers on the sill."

"I see the horizon."

"We'll be crossing it soon. Ritchie has booked us on the *Dorsetshire*. Our second voyage together, Orde. I want it to be like the *Cathay*."

On the *Cathay,* they had fallen in love. He was thirty years old, returning from an off-duty expedition to Libya, while she, sixteen years old and escorted by her mother, was returning from a visit to Australia.

After several months at sea Lorna was bored. By the time they

Wingate about the time he met Lorna.

reached Alexandria she knew all the passengers on the second deck, the reading matter they circulated, the schedule by which they strolled the deck, their habitual arrangement in the dining room. She was ready for some novelty even if only a new face.

Wingate's appeared at the dining room door. He regarded the passengers suspiciously as the women examined him from the corners of their eyes.

He was studiously unkempt, his sun-bleached hair dry, intractable, and low.

"Enter Cyrano," Lorna whispered, teasing a reproachful smile from her mother. His nose seemed driven between the eyes like a wedge-drawing them together. In shorts and shirt of cotton khaki, he resembled the customs inspectors who had just left the ship.

He slouched toward Lorna's table, his sandals flapping as if he were still trudging through sand. With a nod he sat down, ignoring how his presence inhibited the Patersons' conversation.

He asked for an onion, a big one. "With vinaigrette?" the waiter inquired. Wingate shook his head. He felt Mrs. Paterson's stare as the giant bulb was placed on his plate.

"You're going to *eat* that?" Lorna blurted.

"Of course. It's the perfect food."

Mrs. Paterson offered tentative praise of a vegetarian diet. Lorna asked if it caused the skin to molt, as Wingate's was peeling from his arms, and if onions turned muscles into cables, as his appeared to be. This led him into a laconic tale of his search for a lost oasis of antiquity.

"So did you find it?" asked Lorna pertly.

"Regretfully, no."

The conversation continued cordially, but Wingate realized he had been teased by a teenager. During the months of the voyage she had grown confident of her liberties. Raven hair set upon a deep tan and the figure of a sylphid had already attracted shipboard flirtations with men twice her age. Lorna quickly learned that men were flattered by the slightest attention from a beautiful woman no matter if she was young; indeed, perhaps all the more if she was.

This truth led to a second—that once launched, a man can talk tirelessly about himself. Thus Lorna had become a sophisticated listener as she roamed the decks, and now recognized the intriguing captain from the desert to be a quiet contrast to the other men on board.

Soon she became Wingate's guide, at first with her mother, then alone when the Mediterranean heat was high and a nap more appealing than the duties of a chaperone.

"We're not allowed on the first deck, you know," Lorna confided to him as they approached the ladder, "but here we go. It *is* quarter past one, isn't it?"

"Right you are. That's important, is it?"

"Miguel's on duty now. He's OK."

The first-class steward winked at them as they strolled along the white, sanded deck. As luncheon music drifted through the decks, Lorna referred to each stateroom as if it were a picture at the Tate.

"Lady Haig's suite. Have you heard of the whiskey?"

"Very favorably."

"She's a widow. An awful bother with her yorkies. Miguel has to... you know."

"Yes."

Suddenly she took his hand and swung him to the rail. Their thighs pressed close as they feigned rapture with the seascape. "Don't look up," she whispered, "or we're discovered!"

"I won't."

"Viscountess Bolton-Jones. A horror. She'll have us sent below."

Wingate felt her pulse in his hand as a shadow slowly passed their feet.

Her eyes ached from sideward glances when Lorna said, "All clear. I hope she doesn't find Miguel or she'll report us for sure. We haven't long, Captain. She'll be coming back soon."

"So let's follow her and cut through the middle passage before she returns."

"Good thinking, Captain."

They scurried away, seldom to part for the rest of the voyage.

Wingate felt utterly unique—part knight-errant, part uncle, part playmate, part schoolboy. Lorna was as sudden and fleeting as a citral fragrance, as distracting as the ship's dance music after the silence of the desert. They first kissed tight-lipped while the moon flickered on the sea. They kissed; yet Lorna still called him "captain."

Religious and family insularity had locked him out of normal boy-girl infatuations during his own teen years. The shipboard romance was therefore an unexperienced delight—but one mingled with guilt. For seven years he had been affianced to a sensible, sensitive woman who was his complete companion. His return to England was to have brought him into marriage with Peggy, for finally the engagement had been announced.

But Lorna was his first love even though she appeared out of sequence in his life. With her Wingate could enjoy teenage romance
from the invulnerability of maturity. It was nothing less than love without pain: no jealousy or painful shyness, no fragile feelings or irratio-
nal arguments.

But he had to tell Lorna about Peggy.

She reacted like a Brontë heroine. She would go ashore at once, by
lifeboat if necessary. He belonged to another, engaged, betrothed, in
every sense but physically married. The intimacy of the voyage must
become a memory. She hoped she had the composure to explain this
stunning development to her mother.

Lorna extended her hand in farewell. He took it in both of his.

"Have I acted dishonorably?"

"Captain, we must part. Please don't make it impossible."

"Then let us part with a kiss."

5

Tense guilt hovered over the reunion with his fiancée. This was England in the 1930s when relationships were not expected to remain
inconclusive. Two years at most was the period for a couple to determine their compatibility and prospects; then their commitment to each
other was expected to be formalized in an engagement.

Peggy crossed the grain of convention with him because he did not
lead her on. Consorting with him for seven years, she was prepared for
the hints of disapproval their conduct drew from time to time. Formal
betrothal would have been a social buffer for her, but she waived it
without visible regret.

"But you regret it," Wingate had thundered. "And if you don't, I
do in your behalf!" This outburst was the result of another complicated weekend where Peggy and Orde had to be invited concurrently
but separately to a country estate for a tennis party where they could

not be quartered under the same roof, a privilege accorded to an engaged couple at the same party. It was typically so—delicate allusions to propriety, the soft clearing of throats as the subject reemerged in many contexts: sailing on the Irish Sea, cycling through Cornwall. Inns were closed to them; friends' houses seemed always to require difficult arrangements while Wingate was loath to ask favors of anyone. At the tennis party it was Peggy who again became the conciliator.

As she changed courts she could see him pacing the grounds; he was easy to spot in his knickerbockers and Shetland sweater while the other dozen guests were turned out in tennis whites.

"Now who have you offended?" she asked, leading him toward the refreshments.

"Offended?"

"Mrs. Frothingham."

"The elephantine lady? You're much mistaken."

"What was all that about rubber?"

"You heard that?"

"There's not much conversation during a match, Orde. Yours was the only voice I heard."

"She has an abysmal knowledge of Malaya. Thought tennis balls 'grew' there."

"Her family is connected with Dunlop."

"So I learned. Incredibly ignorant. Thought the balls sprouted out of the ground like berries."

"Did you *have* to instruct her?"

"Not offensively." She was silent as they walked. "Should I apologize?"

"No, dear." She tried to catch Mrs. Frothingham's eye. In time she did, and with an ingratiating smile Peggy made right with her.

"You've smoothed things over again," he said with simple gratitude.

They sat apart on a grassy slope, the kind of controlled terrain that reflects the groomed order of English manors.

"Are you enjoying yourself, Orde?"

"In my way."

"A well-shaped pond, don't you think?"

"Tidy. All is tidy."

"Except your inner life."

"Do you think it shows to others?"

"You compensate for your oddness—sometimes."

"But you compensate for me much more. You interpret me to the world. Always in the kindest terms."

"I may be Chapman but you are Homer."

"You are nothing short of an angel."

"Waiting to roost."

The "subject" arose once more, this time raised by her but as often it had been he in his bluntness who had brought it up as though every context of life was an aspect of prospective marriage.

"Angels do not roost, they alight, and not on the shabby tin roofs of army garrisons."

"Remember Ruth: 'Whither thou goest, I will go'...Orde, tell me again about Ruth's devotion."

"Ruth's fate was not a happy one. You deserve better."

"Isn't that for me to decide? Free agents, and all that?"

"If there were a way to describe for you, to let you sense the Philistine tedium of an army garrison, then such a decision might be possible. Compared to the life I could offer you there, this party is lively and populated with ravishingly interesting people."

"You make any surroundings interesting."

"The army is beyond me. Introverted, stultifying, enervating."

"Yet you've never considered leaving it."

"The army is a poor curator for the art of war. I must be patient while waiting admission to the gallery. But I practice in my mind; I know I can do work that could hang with the masters."

"A strange metaphor. When did you conceive it?"

"While walking the grounds. Conceited, isn't it?"

"Not coming from you."

"There you go again..."

"I'm not protecting you, dear heart."

"You *are!*"

"Please, Orde, no more unwelcome attention." His exclamation had attracted glances from elsewhere on the lawn.

"Yes, you'd be a great helpmate in the army. You would mediate for me in the military culture. Or the lack of it. I would be such a fret for you. I'm really much worse in army environs than here."

"'Whither thou goest,...'" she said, rising as she noticed the guest of honor departing.

"I'm well placed here at your feet," he said looking up at her.

"Don't look at my legs."

"I'm looking at you, Peggy. The legs will come later."

"Get up, Orde. You look like I'm about to knight you."

"Marry me instead."

She sat back down so inelegantly that he laughed. "Orde, did I understand you to say..."

"You know my love for you. Now there is only this concession to convention."

"You know what you're doing?"

"I was about to ask you that."

So the engagement was announced. But the date put off. Unexpectedly, the Royal Geographic Society informed Wingate of their interest in his treatise that an oasis of antiquity corresponded with reports from recent trans-Sahara travelers. Wingate was referred to some prospective backers, and in a remarkably short time a small expedition was financed and put under his leadership.

The army and Peggy both granted him leave. The expedition put him in such a happy state of mind that she rejoiced with him. Besides, their marriage would be delayed for only a matter of months.

The expedition was inconclusive; so too had been the interlude with Lorna. They had parted with such fervent finality that he knew nothing could keep them apart—unless it was his sense of honor.

He and Peggy were reunited in London. The occasion was lunch at the Army & Navy Club at 46 Pall Mall. He met her at curbside. They kissed ardently; then he buried his face in her hair.

"Was there an accident?" she asked.

"How do you mean?"

"You're tanned—but you're ashen. Did you see an accident?"

"No. Let's walk."

There was something in his grip that was more than love. She strode with him in a silence that reached a crescendo.

"Something has happened," she stated.

"Yes. Quite unbelievable."

"I know you. You'll tell me. So tell me now. You've met someone..."

In his confused state he was not sure what that "someone" meant. Peggy had proved her love; Lorna had only professed hers. Support and understanding were with ·Peggy while Lorna was a vanished fragrance. The choice seemed to be between what he needed and what he wanted, a choice between security and adventure. All that Wingate knew was what he wanted—Lorna.

But he had entered into a covenant with Peggy, one so large that it amounted to a major expression of his honor. For men of Wingate's era, honor was not a quaint concept but a quality of greater stature than masculinity.

Thus it did not trouble him to take this ethical problem to his mother. In the weeks following his return, Peggy had pressed him to break the engagement. If their love was to be rekindled, it could only happen if both retained unfettered freedom, she said.

The nobility of her spirit only made Wingate more wretched. His mother saw the matter in even loftier terms: if he was so much as uncertain about marriage to Peggy, he was duty- as well as honor-bound to break off the engagement.

That was done. When he saw the small announcement in the *Times*, he felt the anesthetized extraction of something that had been part of him. It was gone: the adhesion of their connected lives peeled apart.

They met but once more shortly after the engagement was broken. That summer while Peggy was parking near St. James Palace she heard someone call to her. It was Wingate; he had recognized her car as it pulled in. Coincidentally each had appointments near Picadilly and had allowed a few extra minutes for a walk around the long pond in front of the palace.

It was a difficult conversation, haltingly begun. After years of conversing at soul depth, polite inquiries about friends and relatives were uncomfortably shallow.

"I fear I've wasted much of your life."

"I don't think of it that way, Orde."

"How do you think of it? Here I am again presuming...asking you to do my thinking for me. I'm so indebted to you—and so unworthy."

"I shall never regret a moment we were together. That's not a judgment—only the simple truth."

"Why then do I feel so miserable?"

"That is your doing."

"At least now my doings will no longer be your responsibility."

"Please....You're reviving things that..."

He squeezed her hand but felt in return the pressure preceding release. In leaving Peggy he knew he was giving up a complementary personality who would have softened his presentation to the world. Now the sharp angles would remain; Lorna was more like himself, more willing to accentuate his eccentricities, adding more heat than temper to his ideas. Yet Lorna would owe much to Peggy, for now he was obliged to be the responsible partner. Variations of these thoughts were in his mind as he and Peggy concluded their walk.

"Are you going around the Circus?" he asked as they approached Picadilly.

"No. The other way."

They turned in separate directions, a couple for the last time.

Wingate's courtship of Lorna, begun like Mediterranean music, had to adjust to the rhythms of British life. He did not contact her again until the engagement was broken, a matter of anguished weeks for Lorna. Then he called her with what seemed more planning than passion.

First, he asked to meet with her parents. Why should they be brought in *prematurely,* she asked, for indeed Wingate had not yet asked Lorna for her hand. He had bungled the sequence, Wingate admitted, and pondered how Peggy would have corrected it. But he no longer had Peggy to rely on, and he told himself it was time he demonstrated what he had learned from her.

He set himself to wooing Lorna all over again, and the magic was quickly revived. In due course her parents were advised of their intentions and they wed in 1935, nearly two years after they met. Two years in England were followed by two in Palestine before he was assigned to an antiaircraft battalion near London.

6

Within months his battalion was firing at German raiders as World War II had begun. Then came the blitz and Wingate was about to fight for the survival of his country on its very soil. But he was forced aside in a disagreement over tactics.

Air defense policy for the isles was to engage German aircraft at maximum range and attempt to prevent them from reaching their targets. This was idealistic, Wingate protested: the bombers should be engaged when they were most vulnerable, which was during their bomb runs as they flew a straight course and fixed altitude. It was then, he argued, antiaircraft fire should be massed and converged on them, not dribbled into the sky as soon as the Germans crossed the coast. Damage to British cities might be greater at first but would diminish as more raiders were brought down. The generals disagreed; Wingate was sacked.

Lorna grabbed her purse and followed him down the stairs of their flat. "Why must we see Weizmann in the middle of an air raid?" she shouted over the rumble of bombs.

"For the simple reason that the Jews may be ready to fight the Nazis," he answered over his shoulder. "Our army is not."

They were the only people on the street. Tenements stood silhouetted by pulses of distant flame. Wingate pushed the floor starter impatiently. The engine knocked; then they lurched down the street.

"Watch that pole!"

He swerved. Headlights were banned in the blackout. Fires glowed in an artificial sunset but in the shadow of buildings the streets were dark—dark and silent except for sirens wailing like abandoned dogs.

*   *   *

Chaim Weizmann flinched at the heavy rap on his door. It was a reflex for Jews from Germany, all the more so for one of the founding fathers of Zion. His voice quavered.

"Who?"

"Orde and Lorna." They heard multiple bolts unlocking.

"*Hayedid.* Dear Lorna. Please come in. But why?..."

"It's time we stopped quaking in shelters. I'm here to lead us out into the war."

"I was about to call you with some news. Come downstairs. These raids grow worse." They descended to the sandbagged cellar, where a single light bulb dangled from a wire. Lorna blinked but Wingate stared at his host, hands on hips.

"What sort of news?"

"Depends on how badly things are going with you. Are you out of favor again?"

"Out of the army."

"You can't be!"

"I am. Resigning my commission is only a formality."

"Sit down. Lorna, may I bring you some tea?" She shook her head. "Brandy? Orde? No? Then let me fortify myself as I hear what folly..."

"The folly is out there. Only one side is fighting this war, fighting to win, and that's the Germans. I'd hoped I wouldn't find the same sniveling..."

"Orde, don't snarl at him."

"People can't *see* so they must be made to *hear!*"

"We hear you. Now tell Chaim what happened." The house shook as crowds of bombs stalked the neighborhood.

"Hear that? I could have saved this city. It's lost now, and so is the war."

"Don't say that," said Weizmann, "even in anger. Do not crush me with such an opinion, even if you believe it, for in matters of war you are too often accurate."

"Chaim, I'm here to offer my sword to Zion."

"Zion is already indebted to you."

"I've earned your trust."

"As no other Englishman has."

"Then entrust me with a new and greater mission."

"New?"

"We've talked of it before."

"I cannot withstand your arguments. But neither can I support them."

"My commitment to you is now final, Chaim. I'll not go back to the British army."

The bulb danced on its wire as a shock wave buffeted the walls. Weizmann sank wearily into a chair. "I told you I had news," he said. "News not to your liking but perhaps encouraging enough to keep you in uniform where you can..."

"I can do nothing in this army which defeats its own purpose."

"At least listen to him, Orde."

Wingate clapped his hands to his thighs. "Only if he'll listen to *me!*" He pointed his finger at Weizmann. "Or are you going to sit there stooped and cowed..."

"You needn't abuse your friends," said Lorna.

A picture had been knocked aslant on the shaken wall, a picture of the Negev Desert. Wingate pointed to it. "The Jews are a desert people. So we will fight the Germans first in North Africa."

"Each time you tell me I agree with your logic."

"Till now you've had no leader with experience in modern warfare. But now you have. I offer myself to command the first Jewish division."

Weizmann rose slowly, as if the burdens of his imperiled race had become a physical weight. "For reasons I can't explain—because I don't understand the reasons behind them—the Jews are not yet ready to fight in this war."

"Of course they're not ready. They need a great deal of training. The deserts in America are just the place. From training comes confidence; from confidence comes readiness for combat."

"The Jews, I'm afraid, are in a state of shock."

"What will get you out of it except *action!*"

Weizmann and Lorna glanced at each other. "I've asked Wavell," he said.

"Yes?"

"He is of course preoccupied in North Africa."

"Send him a hard fighting division and you'll get his attention."

"I asked him about you. We've exchanged letters. He can use you."

Wingate leaped from his chair. "To train Jews?"

"No. That's the hard news. If you are posted to the Middle East, you are not to make contact with the Jews. You would be barred from Zion—from Palestine. That is what I was going to tell you."

Wingate slumped back on the chair. "Sir Archie said that?"

"Yes."

"Sir Archie..."

"He thought so highly of Orde."

"He still does. But he regards you as too political to once again associate with us. Orde, I beg you to accept his offer. I think he would employ you in Ethiopia."

"Ethiopia?"

"Even your army agrees that in Palestine you had success leading small forces. Wavell feels you might be effective in raising such forces for Selassie. This is supremely secret, but apparently Selassie is to be sent to the Sudan to rally the refugees there. The rest is opportunity."

"Opportunity in Ethiopia?"

"Rout the Italians there and the Germans may have to intervene as they did in Albania. That might bleed their forces from North Africa. I must say I scoffed at the possibility."

"So do I. A sign of our government's desperation. Am I so slight a friend that you recommend I spend the war in such a frivolous side show?"

"You would prove your worth I'm sure. Victory is acknowledged wherever it is won. It may seem a false challenge for you, Orde, but take it. Show your stature. You will be a better spokesman for us if you do."

"Selassie's cause is a worthy one, Orde."

"My wife and dearest friend urge me into exile."

"Selassie is turning his exile into opportunity. Are you a lesser man?"

7

Four years earlier, in 1936, Haile Selassie had been transformed from a medieval despot to one of the twentieth century's most colorful and appealing figures. His day in the sun coincided with the twilight of the League of Nations. When Mussolini grasped for an African empire by invading Ethiopia, Selassie beseeched the League to condemn the Italians and provide him with modern arms to defend his realm.

The League did nothing, demonstrating to the world its final ineffectiveness. Ethiopia was completely overrun, and a harsh military government was imposed by the Italians while Selassie fled to exile in Switzerland under the patronage of Britain, a king without a kingdom.

But as king, Selassie had subjects by the thousands, many of them refugees who had fled into neighboring Sudan. Informal lines of communication were opened between the emperor in exile and leaders of the refugees. Communication ripened into a plan whereby Selassie would rally an army among them, lead it back into Ethiopia where the population would rise to greet their emperor, and overthrow the Italians.

That was Selassie's plan in all its detail.

Wingate knew nothing of the plan except that he must get to Cairo before the emperor. Only two men knew of the liaison to be formed between Wingate and Selassie: Wavell and Finley.

The overloaded transport spun slowly on its landing gear. A listless ground crew released the hatch to the cargo bay. A man dropped out like a bomb, a small man, as wispy as the Egyptians who hooked a ladder for the other passengers to descend.

"Orde!"

"Malcolm."

"How long have you been in that crate?"

"Four, five days. Lost track."

"And you haven't much time to get oriented either. Come on, let's talk in my car. How are you feeling? You look a little wan."

"We refueled in St. Helena."

"Oh?"

"I may have contracted Napoleon's malaise."

"You feel like an exile, do you?" They walked to a staff car, its patched tires and coat of dust an image of Britain's ragged forces in Africa.

"Yes I do," Wingate snapped. "One can be exiled from a country other than one's own. Why?" Finley turned the handle but the car door was jammed. "It's hotter in there, Malcolm."

"I'd rather not talk out here. Climb in on the driver's side, won't you? There. Sir Archie's sorry he can't see you. But he thought this might come up. He just can't take any risks in Palestine right now. The Germans in Libya are quite enough on his mind."

"How am I any sort of risk? Didn't I bring security to Pales..."

"This is the Second World War, Orde. Sir Archie feels—and I'll tell you frankly I agree with him—that the best way to get your mind on this war is to keep you away from Palestine."

"What if I raised forces for him there?" Wingate's words poured out: "Desert fighters, battalions of my Special Night Squads. Raiders behind the Germans' lines, raising hell with their airfields. I'll have them for you in two months."

"No. Finally and absolutely no."

"The Jews will fight the Germans like no other people on earth!"

"The last word is *no*. Now you understood this as a condition for coming out here. Sir Archie anticipated your recalcitrance. He told me to put you right back on that airplane if you balk. Your theater is Ethiopia now, not Palestine. Agreed?"

He nodded slowly, like a man hearing his doctor confirm a serious disease. "But without the Jews Sir Archie is throwing away..."

"He's willing to take that chance."

"Fumbling, indecisive as ever."

Finley gripped the steering wheel. "He has just saved your career—and not for the first time. I've got a lot to tell you and not much time to do it. If you can just preserve your belligerence for the Italians..."

"Sorry." His piercing eyes suddenly softened. He flashed Finley

the smile of a mischievous choir boy. "Here. These are from Agnes."
He placed a bundle on the seat beside them.

"How on earth did you get to Inverness?"

"Drove all night."

"Then back to London?"

"There was time enough to sleep on that flying snail."

"What does Lorna think of this new adventure?"

"She much admires Selassie."

"I'm not surprised. She identifies with improbable, solitary struggles, wouldn't you say?"

"You needn't be indirect, Malcolm. Can we get down to business?"

"It's business you should do well. Basically you are to start a war."

"Splendid."

"But it won't be easy. Though two armies face each other on the
Sudanese border, neither wants to fight. General Platt has only the
odds and sods left over from Libya. He sees his mission to be the defense of Sudan, not the invasion of Abyssinia."

"Ethiopia."

"Yes. Sorry. Glad you're accustomed to the modern name. Wouldn't
want to offend Selassie. Now for their part the Italians are content to
consolidate their occupation. They thought they had conquered King
Solomon's kingdom but instead have camped upon an aggregation of
impoverished tribes. It is these tribes which we hope will rally to
Selassie if he can gain a foothold in western Ethiopia. You have perhaps two days to set that in motion."

"I like starting from zero."

"Less than zero actually. Sir Archie is not sending you to Khartoum
to do what I've described. Platt would be offended—and quite rightly. To be correct, if Sir Archie wants an attack into Ethiopia he should
give Platt that order. But Platt is a consummate politician. He would
state his requirements for troops, aircraft, etc., none of which are available of course. Sir Archie would look like an ass. Nothing would result except recriminations."

"Malcolm, the great paradox of this great war is that hardly anyone wants to fight it. Not air defense, not the Jews, not the Italians,
not Platt..."

"Selassie wants to fight. You're to help him."

"I love the man already."

"How you proceed is up to you. Sir Archie cannot...You understand."

"I'll need arms."

"Somehow you must get them from Platt. I imagine you're thinking of ten thousand rifles."

"You disappoint me, Malcolm. Don't you remember all those talks we had? I'm not Lawrence—I'm his cousin. He was all wrong giving away guns to every Arab who asked. Firearms are a reward for proven warriors. I'll need no more than a couple of thousand."

"Well, your strategy fits our shortages anyway."

"But I must have a British cadre to train and lead Selassie's men."

"They'd have to be volunteers."

"Certainly."

"When the time comes send me the message and I'll put out the call. No guarantees you understand."

"That's enough for now. When does the emperor arrive?"

"Tomorrow night if things go right."

"Send him down the next evening."

"You want to get down to Khartoum before him?"

Wingate nodded.

"Here are some orders—cover, you might say. Transportation might not be so easy. The Khartoum flight is canceled more often than it flies."

"Nothing else flying anywhere?"

"Some bombers refit in Aden. I've known them to divert if the price is right."

"What's the price of scotch?"

"A fifth would probably get you a medium bomber."

"Malcolm, I must ask you to open Agnes's bundle."

With a wry smile Finley put it in his lap. It gurgled slightly.

8

Colonel Appleby first noticed him from a window. Wingate had dropped his kit bag and was inspecting the sentries' rifles as if he were sergeant of the guard.

General Platt happened into Appleby's office at that moment. They both watched with startled fascination, and were soon joined by the administrative officer, Major Hawthorne.

"Who could *that* be?" Platt enquired.

"Looks like Lawrence returning from World War I." Appleby's reference was to Wingate's unique pith helmet, a hard canvas headgear, wide-brimmed at the back to protect the neck from sun. Such a helmet had been out of the British army inventory since the 1920s but was still familiar to movie watchers of films like *Gunga Din*. "Hawthorne, do we have a new major scheduled in?"

"We're waiting for a quartermaster or procurement officer, sir. But of course we've been waiting since the war began."

Waiting was the principal activity at Platt's headquarters. Sudan was the ultimate backwater of the war; the sentries' rifles had been obsolete for twenty years.

This did not excuse the rust Wingate found on them, a fact he pointed out to the commander of the guard, along with the absence of screens before the sentry boxes. With a rock, Wingate demonstrated how anyone on the street could toss a hand grenade into the boxes and rush the headquarters. With that he walked toward the building while the officers inside glanced at each other with apprehension.

"General, would you like to meet this apparition if he turns out to be ours?"

"Yes. I'll ask him to donate that pith helmet to the Imperial War Museum."

*   *   *

Wingate swung the kit bag from his shoulder and placed his orders on Hawthorne's desk. "I'm down from Cairo," he said, skipping the formalities.

"Good day, Major," said Hawthorne courteously, and studied the routine format of the orders. "O. C. Wingate. Very good. And you are to be our new procurement officer, I gather." Hawthorne turned the HQ sign-in book and offered Wingate a pen. "How did you arrive? The Tuesday flight has been diverted for the last two weeks."

"Unscheduled flight," said Wingate, not looking up.

Unscheduled aircraft were a rarity in Khartoum. This and the peculiar air about Wingate's arrival caused Hawthorne to hand him off:

"Let me introduce you to Colonel Appleby, the chief of staff. And General Platt will no doubt want to meet you as well. Just leave four copies of your orders with me. Thank you."

As they walked toward Appleby's office, Wingate asked, "Who runs operations here?"

"How do you mean?"

"Tactical operations."

"There's no *war* here, you know."

"You have an operations section, don't you?"

Hawthorne took offense but concealed it with a sniff. "Of course. Lieutenant Colonel Birdwood's department." He gestured to an overweight, blustery officer at the end of the room. "Are you interested in that sort of thing?"

Wingate said nothing. Hawthorne knocked on Appleby's door.

"Major Orde C. Wingate, sir: procurement officer with an interest in ground operations." With a slight smile, Hawthorne withdrew as Wingate and Appleby exchanged salutes.

"Do sit down," said Appleby. "I must tell you that your headpiece aroused some interest even before you arrived. You had some difficulty with the sentries?"

"Nothing wrong with them, Colonel. It's the security that's wretched."

"How so?"

"No grenade screen or barricade to stop cars. Half a dozen men could rush the gate and wipe out this headquarters in minutes."

"Most unlikely. The only enemy are homesick Italians 500 miles

away in Ethiopia. And they pretty much keep to themselves. Live and
let live, you might say. You...ah...have some interest in more war-
like activities than procurement?" Wingate's eyes burned in confirmation. "Well I hope you're not in the wrong place. I see you're a
gunner. Antiaircraft? How did you get your DSO?" Appleby referred
to the single ribbon Wingate wore on his tunic, designating one of
Great Britain's highest decorations for heroism.

"In Palestine. With infantry."

"Right-oh. Now then, what's your background in procurement?"

"None."

"None?"

"I'll procure what I need for my operations."

"May I ask what sort of 'operations' you contemplate?"

Wingate looked at him steadily. "The liberation of Ethiopia," he
replied, and smiled to himself, for he had imagined the long silence
which followed.

Appleby was not to be bamboozled by a man who obviously did
things for effect. "The liberation of Ethiopia," he said, and gazed at
the ceiling for a moment. "I hope you brought a private army along
for that purpose."

"I will produce one."

"I see. Well....I'm not sure if I'm the person you should be telling this to. You seem privy to war plans that I am not. Let me see if
General Platt can be disturbed. Excuse me."

"May I have a glass of water?"

"Certainly," said Appleby, gesturing to his desk decanter.

General Platt's office adjoined Appleby's. With two soft knocks,
Appleby admitted himself. As he did, Wingate locked the outer door,
moved his chair to Platt's door, and pressed the drinking glass against
it to act as a microphone for the conversation within.

"General, that fellow with the pith helmet—name's Wingate."

"Yes?"

"I suspect he's a bit daft."

Wingate smiled as he heard the general chuckle.

"Don't be surprised," said Platt. "After all, aren't we the dump-
ing bog for the rejects from the important theaters of this war? Present
company excluded, of course."

"Thank you, sir. Yes, that would be my initial appraisal of this
fellow. However, he has a DSO. You don't get one of those without

some sharp combat somewhere. He acts a bit shell-shocked. Cracked while performing his act of heroism perhaps."

"Well, tell me: what's he here for?"

"Ostensibly he's our new procurement officer."

"Ostensibly?"

"He has no background in that sort of work. Instead he says he's here to liberate Ethiopia."

"Just like Wavell to send me one of his psychotics. Do you think he's dangerous?"

"I think you should form you own opinion, sir. Would you care to see him?"

"Must I? Can't we send him straight to the hospital?"

"It would be simpler to have him committed if two officers could testify to his rantings, sir. Perhaps he was only amusing himself with me."

"I've no time to get involved with medical proceedings. You and Hawthorne have a talk with him."

"Very well, General. However there *is* something about this man..."

"What?"

"I have the impression he knows something about Ethiopian politics. Something we're not aware of. You know he may be here to work under cover. That could explain why he knows nothing about procurement."

"Sir Archie didn't indicate some secret agent was coming down here."

"Sir Archie didn't say anything about Brocklehurst either."

"You're right there."

"And looking at the matter from a security viewpoint, it makes sense for Theater Intelligence to send down such a man unannounced, knowing that in a headquarters this small he would meet you in the normal course of introductions. And to make sure he did, they instructed this Wingate—if that's his real name—to behave so as to attract your personal notice."

"He succeeded in that. Well then—I suppose I should meet him. But keep a close ear at the door won't you, Tony? I don't wish to be trapped in here with a madman."

Wingate and the glass were back in place when Appleby reentered his office.

"Yes, the general is anxious to meet you, Wingate."

Appleby returned to his office, then drew his chair near Platt's door.

"Do sit down, Major," he heard Platt say, but then the voices became muffled. "Well now, what brings you to this part of Africa?"

"The emperor."

"The emperor. From what I've heard so far you refer to the emperor of Ethiopia, Haile Selassie."

"Lion of Judah, etc."

"Quite. Quite. And am I to gather you are some sort of emissary to prepare for...Just what am I to prepare for, if you please?"

"His arrival, sir."

"I can tell you that I would be put off by such a development, Wingate. I should be the first to be informed of any plans to bring Selassie back into this region. It does Sir Archie no good to present me with a *fait accompli*."

"The decision came from above Sir Archie, sir."

"No doubt. But am I not to be advised of the emperor's status? Is he to be a cobelligerent with us, a sovereign ally, a subordinate? These are questions in which I have a vital interest. And as usual I am not consulted. He's surely not coming soon, is he?"

"Perhaps tonight."

"Bloody Jesus! I can't accept that! There are ten thousand Ethiopians in southern Sudan. Do you know that? The relations between them and the Sudanese are delicate to say the least. If those refugees learn that Selassie is in Khartoum, they will likely riot." General Platt rose and paced restlessly. His voice now carried to Appleby. "Gigantic riots, I tell you. They will try to enthrone the emperor right here in Sudan. The governor general will demand the lot of them expelled. And I could scarcely blame him. There are two nationalities here in one nation. Doesn't Wavell realize that? Did he give you any instructions as to how I am to handle this debacle?"

"The emperor will lead his people out of Sudan. Back to their homeland."

Platt was a clever man. Within the British officers' corps he was better known for his political astuteness than his military abilities. His character, on this occasion, projected him even beyond the plot in which Wingate hoped to involve him. Platt regarded Wingate for a long moment—regarded him as a master might look at a chessman which would open a move of strategic importance; then he laughed as if he had seen through his opponent's strategy.

"So that's it!" He laughed with some satisfaction. "Very subtle—if also very Machiavellian. Ha! Very good! We let the Italians dispose of both the emperor and the refugees. My, that's cold-blooded though. Some fellow in M16 must have thought it up." Platt walked to the window and spoke with his back to Wingate.

"To tell you the truth, I'm glad now I've had no part in this scheme: I wouldn't want that much blood on my hands. My God, it'll be like the Children's Crusade. Think of it: to launch a thousand or so irregulars, armed only with rifles—perhaps a pair of machine guns per company—launch them against a European army well entrenched. The Italians have complete air superiority, you know. I couldn't spare a single Spitfire for Ethiopia." Then Platt sighed as if the cynicism of the plot was too much for him. "I can't believe Selassie won't realize that he's vastly outnumbered, dreadfully outgunned. It will reflect very badly on us when he and his followers perish."

"The emperor will prevail."

"Yes, of course," Platt snickered, becoming himself once more. "It's your job to believe that, isn't it? I suppose he's relying on help from the local chieftains in Ethiopia. Expects uprisings against the Italians."

"That would be useful but not necessary."

"Really? You obviously know nothing about the terrain on the border. You should see the escarpment. Selassie will march around it like the walls of Jericho. Now let me ask you something, Major: how does Sir Archie expect to arm this doomed rabble? And who is to lead it? There are no British here with suicidal tendencies. I don't even have a man who could help."

"You have now, sir."

"Very well—you are my sole commitment to this evil escapade. Now as to arms: where are they to come from?"

"Local procurement, sir."

"And what is *that* supposed to mean? Did you bring a sack of gold with you? And training: are you the extent of Wavell's commitment to make soldiers out of illiterate tribesmen?"

"British volunteers, General."

Platt struck his desk. "Not in *my* command."

"Then elsewhere in the theater, sir."

"Wavell expects to get British volunteers to train savages? That presumption fits well with the rest of this lunacy."

They were interrupted by a rapid knock from Appleby's door. He entered before Platt could invite him, for he brought news of Selassie's takeoff from Cairo. Platt clapped his hands to his hips.

"He is *not* flying to Khartoum, Appleby. Divert the plane the moment it crosses the border. I *do* control airspace within the Sudan, do I not?"

"Yes, General."

"Then divert him to the nearest strip."

"That would be Wadi Halfa."

"Fine. Now get Wingate on a plane up there. When you arrive, my good major, apprise the emperor—with all due deference—that he is not to enter Khartoum until I invite him. Appleby, we have a fiasco of the first water on our hands. It seems a children's crusade is to be mounted from here to 'liberate Ethiopia' if you will.... What is it, Wingate?"

He had thrust a piece of notepaper in front of the general. On it he had scribbled Platt's instructions: "Selassie not to enter K. till invited."

"As an informal minute of our first discussion, I suppose that will suffice," said Platt impatiently, and scrawled his initials on the paper.

"Thank you, sir. Now if the general will excuse me, I'm off to the airfield."

"Yes, be on your way."

9

Inbound to Wadi Halfa, Wingate knew he had succeeded with only half of his plan to command the forces which would rally to Selassie. Less than half actually. He had temporarily convinced Platt he was a special emissary from London sent to Khartoum as part of the Selassie affair. Indeed Wingate's colossal impersonation could be exposed by some random visitor from London.

This risk was relatively minor compared with the outcome if Selassie were not taken in by Wingate's bluff. He mulled over his possible approaches as the plane bumped through the thermal waves rising from the desert. He could not be coy with Selassie, he realized, for the bond between them must become too strong for Platt to separate. With that at stake, Wingate would probably have to startle the emperor into accepting him.

A shack served as the control tower at Wadi Halfa airstrip. It was manned by a lone British corporal who had lost an eye fighting Rommel. What visitors had landed recently? Wingate asked him. The corporal had never heard of Selassie but remembered a transport with two black men. A civilian car, one he believed belonged to the British consulate, had picked them up.

The corporal was fairly certain the passengers were in a Quonset hut two miles from the field, a place used for crew rest by the few flyers forced to lay over between Cairo and Khartoum.

Shouldering his kit bag, Wingate set out in the direction recommended to him. Rock-strewn desert, broiling to furnace temperatures, extended to the horizon. The heat shimmer contracted his view to less than a mile, so he trudged without a landmark to guide him. Presently the outline of a date tree appeared on the horizon and beside it the curved roof of a Quonset hut.

His knock brought no response; Wingate stood with sweat dripping into his eyes. A second knock and the metal door opened a crack. It was completely dark within, but Wingate could feel himself being examined.

"What is it?" asked a black man's voice in a tone between asleep and alert.

"I'm Major Wingate, special emissary from General Platt."

"Hand me your pistol and turn around." The voice belonged to a powerful Ethiopian bodyguard and factotum, as he was called. He stepped out of the hut, let his eyes adjust to the dazzle of the sunlight, and professionally frisked Wingate from behind. "Excellency, a man from General Platt," he announced, "Major Wingate."

"Bring him in," said a smaller voice.

Inside, three cots, a bare table, a lamp, and a few scruffy bags huddled in the shadows. The emperor wore only boxer shorts as he slowly fanned himself on the cot. Barely five foot two and 125 pounds, his bearing remained as impressive as his famous beard. His title, "Lion of Judah," struck Wingate when he first saw him, though at the moment the lion was languishing.

"Your Highness," said Wingate softly, and doffed his pith helmet.

"Why has Platt sent you?" Selassie inquired with the voice of a man who had asked and received many questions.

"I must ask one thing of Your Highness: that you give me your complete confidence, now and in the future, until you sit once more on your throne in Addis Ababa."

"This is the message you bring me?"

"That message is my own. From this moment I am your servant."

Selassie had dealt with many schemers, pretenders, and assorted pleaders during his reign. He was known as quick to judge, quick and intuitively accurate. "Give this man his pistol," he said. Factotum slowly obeyed. "I accept you as my servant. But as my servant now you stand to be discharged if you prove false in any way."

"I will tell you only truth—and everything I know."

"Tell me why General Platt has prevented me from continuing to Khartoum."

"He fears the reaction of your people there. And then the reaction of the Sudanese."

"My people are impatient to return me to the throne."

Wingate reversed a chair and sat down, his arms folded over the chair back, his eyes level with Selassie's. "You realize, sir," he said, "that I will be a servant different from any of your others."

"I've employed many soldiers of fortune. That's the role you've come to play, is it not?"

"I am a soldier of causes. Yours is as noble as any in the world today."

"Including Churchill's?"

"Churchill has not yet suffered invasion. He is struggling to repel a foreign army, not to expel it from British soil."

"Wouldn't you rather help him protect your homeland than help me recover mine?"

"The higher cause is the same, and for the sort of war at which I'm best I wish to attach my fate with yours."

"I doubt I would accept you under other circumstances."

"I understand."

"What do you understand?"

"How I may appear to you. You might well suspect me of being a British agent. My government is experienced in such perfidy."

"That is the obvious suspicion. The deeper one is about yourself. A man who discards his nationality, who steps outside the loyalties of his uniform—such a man should be watched."

"As I'm sure you will."

Selassie glanced at Factotum, who was staring to attract his attention.

"Perhaps we have a mutual dream," said the emperor cryptically. "Factotum—the sacramental wine."

Factotum fumbled among the valises, pulling out religious objects and vestments which caused Wingate to recall that the emperor was also primate of the Coptic Christian Church.

"We must share the goblet," Selassie said with a smile. Factotum poured a dark wine.

Wingate accepted the first sip. "Are there different symbols in the Coptic eucharist?" he asked.

"The same blood and body." Selassie drained the goblet and had it refilled. Wingate drank deeply from the second offering.

"Strange, I never gave a thought to how Christ tastes. Buoyant, fragrant, I would say."

"Did you expect a bitter aftertaste? Something woody perhaps?"

Wingate laughed. "Your majesty's humor is unique."

"The sense of humor can respond to as many stimulants as the palate."

"It's an ironic humor that drains the blood of Christ."

"Irony is my most common wine—a mild intoxicant at times. It makes many irritants acceptable. Do you use it?"

"Not as much as I should from the way you describe it."

"Here," said Selassie as he poured. "Drink deeply of this irony."

"You're very gracious." He quaffed the wine. "I'd not expected such hospitality."

"As much interrogation as hospitality."

"You need only judge my plans. My loyalty and worth will be demonstrated by them."

"I would first judge your dream."

"As you said, mine and yours are joined and mutual."

"Liberation?"

"Liberation."

"From all foreign influences in my kingdom?"

"All including the British."

"How would we go about it?"

"Imagine it first. Feel how liberation will feel. Your throne, your palace, your capital—how all will appear when they are once more yours. How you will receive news of Ethiopian victories."

"And when there are defeats?"

Wingate finished the goblet. "I don't know. I only know victories are more likely if you visualize them."

"And the defeats more acute when the visions fail."

"Perhaps. We must put our dream to its test."

"Start by telling me how I will arm my people."

10

Wingate spent the night in the Quonset hut plotting with his new sovereign. They were interrupted only by a servant sent from the British consulate with a dinner pail in the evening. The emperor was to take all his meals "in." By such signals it was clear the British authorities would not provide Selassie with even local transportation. Nevertheless, when the servant returned the next evening the Quonset hut was empty.

Factotum, with a portion of the Ethiopian treasury, had procured an ancient touring car; in it the royal party, now expanded by Wingate to three, began an eight-hundred-mile trek through the desert to Khartoum.

News of their progress preceded them. On the second day of the journey, after covering nearly two hundred miles with only minor breakdowns and overheating, the party saw a dozen figures standing far ahead at an isolated location where only robbers would have business.

Wingate had six rounds in his pistol, while Factotum carried several magazines for his Sten gun. There was no turning back, as they were low on gasoline; so Selassie ordered the car slowly ahead.

Wingate noticed that the band of men approaching were not employing good tactics for highwaymen: they did not fan out to take the car from all sides but came straight down the road where a burst from the Sten gun could cut down the entire first rank. He advised Factotum to shoot for the knees, but Selassie's servant said something which caused the emperor to sit up and smile. Wingate gathered they were talking about the robbers' garb, particularly their headdress.

"My countrymen!" Selassie exclaimed.

Recognizing their sovereign, they threw handfuls of desert flowers on the car while shouting liturgies of praise. Through the midday heat they thronged about the car as it proceeded to the next village, where sullen Sudanese opened creaky shutters to see what was disturbing their afternoon rest.

There was no gas at this first village, but the car continued on. Along the miles ahead more Ethiopians joined the procession; when the car ran out of gas, a hundred men pulled it with a hemp rope as thick as a man's wrist.

This moving welcome occurred on the northern fringe of the area where the Ethiopians had been squatting. As the car continued south, it was surrounded by a mile of joyous marchers who vied with each other for the honor of holding parasols over the passengers.

Rest then became the major problem for the emperor's party. They were given the best hut the local squatters could provide, but each night was loud with singing and prayers of thanksgiving. Wingate, even more than Selassie, found it hard to sleep as Ethiopians swarmed around their emperor like bees in service to their queen. They were lean and laughed off hardship. They looked bright, seemed teachable, and showed a fascination for weapons. Their hatred of the Italians matched that of Europeans for the Nazis. From his experience in Palestine, Wingate knew that no army fought like one seeking vengeance.

In time the refugee parade approached Khartoum. After much persuasion accompanied by threats from the Sudanese militia, Selassie halted on the outskirts.

So far, so good for Wingate. He sent a messenger to the British headquarters stating correctly that he had stopped Selassie according to Platt's instructions. By this time Finley's messages had crossed Platt's desk: short paragraphs in army bulletins asking for British volunteers throughout the Middle East command to train certain natives for missions which could not presently be disclosed.

Wingate now had his recruits—the Ethiopians swarmed around him by the thousands. He would soon have his training cadre—no matter if it would be an odd parcel of British soldiers; presently he'd have weapons if he could increase Platt's discomfiture to the point where he would be forced to provide them in order to see Selassie gone.

As Sudan flickered from boredom to bedlam, Wingate pondered his missing ingredient: a name for his force. When he found it in the Bible, he revealed the name first to Lorna.

Christmas, 1940
Outside Khartoum

Darling

I fled from those around me when I read your letter, trudging into the hills to find solitude to match my grief. Not he nor anyone should have been allowed to go. Ya'akov was far too important to us, but the bravest are always the most willing and always the first to die.

Men like him should be training Israelite units in America. Instead they have no outlet for their fury except individual missions with no promise but hideous death. How Weizmann could have allowed it is beyond my comprehension. At times he is incredibly naive—it means nothing that the RAF agreed to drop Ya'akov into Poland. Perhaps I should have stayed to inject some professional judgment in these decisions so obviously born of frustration. Do you think Ya'akov's mission was contemplated before I left? I suspect it was, and no one dared submit the plan for my opinion.

This blow has jarred my loneliness to insignificance. Our first Christmas apart, but how trivial a regret compared with the ordeals being endured by others. I miss you greatly nonetheless. Others suffer your absence as well, for your influence on me, the virtues you bring forth in me, the faults you mitigate. I feel myself hardening to brittleness, see my energy focusing into raw heat. It's dehumanizing, as war inevitably must be, or, rather, defeminizing is more accurate, as the feminine virtues of temperance and sympathy are discarded for ruthlessly masculine traits.

That's how I must appear to the men around me, Brits and E's alike. I open myself to no one. I have only you to reach for through these letters. I'm sure you'll save them. My enterprises in this corner of Africa will have no record except what I put down in my thoughts to you.

So let me go back a month or so. Malcolm did me good service. Selassie is what I've been looking for—a man with thirst for the blood of the enemy. With some innocent deceit I've insinuated myself between him and Platt. The situation is complicated but one must be sly in doing the Lord's work.

The affair began when Malcolm met me at the airport. We had an hour's talk. He spoke for Wavell, saying Sir Archie was too busy to see me. The truth is I don't believe he wished to be seen with me, for if my mission to Ethiopia comes to disaster (as everyone here predicts) Sir Archie's skirts remain clean.

The mission is to guide the emperor's passion against the Italians. Platt has misinterpreted Wavell's purpose to be an opportunity to rid the Sudan of refugees while at the same time removing Selassie as a prickle to the conscience of our Foreign Office. That's putting a cynical complexion on the matter but this is what Platt is like.

Whatever the motives involved, my purposes are being served. Platt is giving me arms so that Selassie and his men will depart for the frontier without delay. Wavell has slipped me some funds with which to buy camels and let me call for volunteers through Malcolm. My British cadre, Platt's guns, and Wavell's camels are still arriving, but I've begun training the E's without them.

At this point they are somewhere between refugees and recruits. There are five thousand of them milling around our shanty camp (we live in Platt's discarded tentage). I've formed provisional companies of two hundred men. Their numbers keep shifting as men are attracted by contesting leaders or alliances between families. The organization is beyond my control. I'm like the director of a play whose cast keeps changing roles during rehearsal! All the more confusing because my instructions must be translated.

There are only about two rifles for every five men, so I have the E's compete for the privilege of bearing arms. This I've done on a bayonet course which would daunt the armies of Hades. The first platoon I sent through hacked the targets to ribbons; the second reduced them to stumps—that put me in a fury but I must admire such spirit.

Thankfully this spirit in the E's is also infecting my British cadre. They're beginning to see this rabble as gifted but deprived children—guileless, teachable, endearing. They'll be a match for the Italians, I'm sure of that. I've settled on a name for them, this force *which Platt has compared with the Children's Crusade. I found it in Leviticus (which Cousin Lawrence would have been wise to read): "Many came to serve the Lord but Gideon chose only the few."*

My heart remains with you,

Gideon

PART II

The Colonel:
Gideon Force

11

Late at night, when leisurely diners were still celebrating the departure of another sweltering day, a jeep screeched to a halt in front of the Grand Hotel, where Wingate had requisitioned a room that served as both his quarters and his nighttime office in Khartoum. Two sweaty lieutenants carried bulging briefcases into the lobby. They wore soiled khakis in contrast to the dress tunics of some of the diners, which included Colonel Appleby.

Some tables were occupied by prosperous Sudanese businessmen. With Appleby was a dusky Nubian woman whom he knew as Fatima. She noticed him cover a chuckle with his linen napkin.

"Those lieutenants," he said in answer to her quizzical smile, "they're two of Wingate's men."

"That crazy man you told me about?"

"The same." Appleby took a sip of wine as he reflected, "It seems the lads are learning a primary lesson of the army—never volunteer."

Taking the stairs two at a time, the lieutenants reached Wingate's room and knocked.

"Who is it?'"

"Truesdale and Atkins, sir."

"Door's open."

Wingate was naked at his desk. He was training for the desert by brushing himself instead of bathing, a practice he developed in Palestine. He commended daily brushing—with the stiffest bristles endurable—to all his British cadre and had given a demonstration to his officers, so Truesdale and Atkins were somewhat prepared to report to a naked major.

"The administrative annexes, Major Wingate," said Atkins.

Inspecting Gideon Force. (*Courtesy Imperial War Museum.*)

"All the march tables except for the camel trains, sir," said Truesdale. Nutshells and fruit pits bounced to the floor as Wingate struck the table. "I'm deaf to excuses," he thundered. He pushed aside some cold tea, tore open the first of the bloated manila envelopes, and began to read as he wandered about the room, muttering epithets like "bloody idiots" and worse.

"What did your camels *do* for three days, Truesdale?"

"They refused, sir....In spite of all our efforts."

"Were you able to *load* them?"

"Yes, sir."

"Then you have but one small step to accomplish, and that is to move them." The lieutenants looked at him blankly. "Camels do not refuse, gentlemen, they resist. But their resistance to fire is brief. Get out there tonight, Truesdale, with several cans of petrol. Load the beasts and lead them for one measured mile across the desert." Wingate went to the window to show him where. "Lead them right along that ridge from there to there. I'd better see some fires before dawn. Now get out."

At the door, Truesdale looked back as if he and Atkins were brothers about to be sold separately into slavery.

"*Out* I say!"

"I—I'll wait for you, Cliff," Truesdale murmured.

"You'll wait for nothing." Wingate pushed Truesdale into the hall, reviling him till they reached the top of the stairs. The elevator door opened; a woman shrieked and recoiled.

"I'd better see fires on the ridge before I see the dawn!" Wingate bellowed down the stairwell.

He returned to his room, closed the door as if nothing had happened, took up Atkins's report and paced relentlessly. At intervals he stopped to scratch out passages, scratch his scrotum, and scribble notes. Apparently Atkins's work was almost adequate.

"What the hell is this about 'medical aid stations'?"

"D—details to be published, sir."

"There's nothing to be published. Gideon had no medicine. *We* have none. Gideon needed none. Do you understand? I'm raising the emperor's army, Atkins. I am calling it Gideon Force."

"Yes, sir."

"Many Israelites came forward to serve the Lord God Jehovah. Do you know your scripture, young man?"

"Not well, sir."

"Verily, many came forward. *But Jehovah knew what his army must be!* It's there in Leviticus for all to read. The Lord God Jehovah has given us our orders; set them out in clear terms. I must do as Gideon did, my man. I must cull out the weak and uncertain. Many have stepped forward to serve Emperor Selassie but only the *chosen* shall march with him to Ethiopia. And I shall choose. I shall choose. Are you ready, Atkins? Are you ready to serve the emperor—and to serve the Lord of Hosts?"

"I'll try....I believe so, sire. I mean, sir."

"The Lord chooses only the strong. You must be strong. And you must follow without wavering."

Atkins departed. Downstairs the lady had reported her shocking experience to the hotel manager, who appeared alarmed and gave some vague orders to his staff, but all the while he knew who the "exhibitionist" was and dared not disturb him. By then the diners had left, the kitchen had been mopped, and the hotel was dark except for Wingate's room, where he worked on toward morning.

He turned from his desk toward the window; despite blackout regulations he opened the drape. Sometime before dawn a small light appeared on the ridge, then another followed by a third.

At dawn Truesdale was in Platt's empty headquarters. He slumped on a desk, his head on his crossed arms, a briefcase beside him. The sound of the car he had been expecting awakened him. Bracing himself, Truesdale came to attention as Appleby entered wearing his uniform tunic and pyjama bottoms.

"You're Truesdale?" he demanded.

"Yes, sir."

"What's this emergency you called me about?"

"Approval for the iron rations requisition, sir. For Gideon Force."

"Gideon Force! I say, weren't you at the Grand last night?"

"Yes, sir."

"And now at 5:00 A.M. you roust me out of bed for Wingate's iron rations?"

"The requisition needs your signature, sir."

In spite of Appleby's snarl, Truesdale offered him a sheaf of papers. Appleby hurled them to the floor. Hands behind his back, he circled Truesdale, who came to a more rigid position of attention.

"Truesdale."

"Yes, sir."

"What are these?" Appleby touched his epaulets.

"Colonel's insignia, sir."

"Quite right. And what rank is your commander, Wingate?"

"Major, sir."

"Right again. And in the British army it is customary for..." He could not continue as Truesdale convulsed with sobs. He was breaking down while trying to remain at attention.

"Stand easy, my boy. No, do sit down. Now tell me what all this is about."

"Major Wingate is... is no longer my commander."

"He sacked you?" Truesdale nodded, holding his head. Appleby put his hand on the lieutenant's shoulder. "You're better off. Believe me, Truesdale, there's nothing, absolutely nothing, that a position in Wingate's expedition will do for your career except perhaps end it. Lads like yourself become attracted, quite naturally, to the lure of romantic operations. Don't hold that against yourself. Quite understandable. Where did you serve before?"

"Quartermaster, sir. In Cairo. My brother's in the RAF. He's always in combat...."

"Go back with quartermaster. It's decent duty. Combat's only a part of war, a smaller part than most people imagine. That is to say, you're expected to acquire a certain perspective in the army, Truesdale. Perhaps this experience with Wingate will give you some. Adventure is a siren for the military man. It's the steady, dependable officer who succeeds in the army, not the adventurer. That I'm sure of. Now why were you sacked?"

"Last night... I had to make the camels move.... I'm sorry, sir. I just can't discuss it now...."

"No need. No need to. And don't see yourself as a failure. It's that lunatic expedition which will fail. Most of those who march with Wingate shall never return. I'm sad to say it, but mark my words. Now, chin up, my boy. You're a lucky fellow actually. I'll speak to the quartermaster—put in a word with Colonel McDermott for you."

With a pat on the back Appleby started for his office. Truesdale dried his eyes.

"Colonel Appleby—would you, please?" The lieutenant assembled his papers from the floor. Appleby sighed as he turned to watch him.

"His spell is still on you, is it? Very well; the sooner Wingate gets

his iron rations, the sooner we'll be rid of him. And if he can devastate
the Italians the way he seems to devastate his staff, perhaps we'll have
the ideal outcome—mutual extermination. How many copies must I
sign?"

12

The Ethiopian encampment outside Khartoum resembled a shantytown
during a rummage sale. In a large tent ventilated by rips and dry rot,
crudely painted signs identified desks for the training, supply, personnel, and intelligence officers. These principal posts were manned
by British lieutenants and a few young captains. All their assistants
were excitable Ethiopians who knew little about what they were doing
and whose translations of English instructions sometimes led to strange
results. Frustration multiplied, since even corrections were subject to
more translational errors.

Selassie was rarely seen; Wingate had convinced him that for now
his role should be inspirational rather than operational. Accordingly,
Wingate set up the emperor's tent on a hill overlooking the camp so
that his new soldiers could look up from their toil and see the tent
shimmering in the thermal vapors like a castle in the sky.

The Patriots, as they were called, who originally assembled for their
king numbered about twenty-five hundred. Before they became Gideon
Force, Wingate expected an attrition of over 40 percent. This meant
only about two out of the original five Ethiopians would ultimately
need rifles. So Wingate had them compete for rifles on a bayonet course.

The course was in a sun-blasted lava bed, jagged with spikes of
cinder, where Wingate laid out nets of rusted barb wire under which
the Ethiopians crawled on their way to vaults, ditches, and rope traverses. Interspersed among these obstacles were dummies resembling
scarecrows. These were the bayonet targets.

Wingate first tested the course and came out bloody and tattered. The blood would replace itself but field uniforms were a premium item for the hard campaigning ahead. Since even Wingate was not prepared to run the course naked (though this was later used as a punishment for drunken soldiers), bibs of scrap tentage were reused by each group of recruits. Those without rifles were allowed to charge through with their native weapons, which for most were long, sinister knives or curved swords.

The most technically gifted of the Ethiopians (tested by their ability to light a hurricane lamp and tune a radio) were selected for the "artillery," which in Gideon Force meant small-caliber mortars. There would be one mortar for every hundred men. Only a third of the requisite mortars had arrived, and so stovepipes were used for training. Within a week Wingate felt that one crew was good enough to put on a demonstration for the emperor.

A great roar greeted the arrival of Selassie in his sedan chair. The fledgling mortar crew froze into bent-back attention as a British sergeant stepped before the throng and saluted the king.

"Elevation, two-niner. Deflection, double ought eight," the sergeant barked to his crew.

The tube swung around to that azimuth pointing directly at the emperor. Four bodyguards rushed forward drawing their swords.

Selassie rose in his chair, his arms outstretched, and in a biblical voice began to shout. The only word Wingate caught was "Italians." There was an appreciative murmur from the crowd; the bodyguards withdrew, and the mortar drill continued. The sergeant proceeded as if nothing had soaked his shirt except the early morning sun.

Wingate walked beside the sedan chair as it proceeded to the next demonstration. "That was excellent, Orde," the emperor confided to him. "Italian mortars were a terror weapon against us during the invasion. My men thought the shells came from birds the enemy had trained. You have done much for their confidence."

Wingate nodded. "What did you tell them when the mortar was pointed at you?"

"I said I was blessing the projectile as it passed over me to fall on the Italians."

13

The Ethiopian encampment at first seemed like an excellent quarantine area. Platt no longer had to deal with an hysterical mayor of Khartoum, though the governor general remained uneasy, and a week did not pass without an inquiry from him concerning details of the Ethiopians' departure. This pressure was enough to keep a trickle of supplies flowing to Wingate, who swore that all that was keeping Gideon Force in Sudan was the lack of a few radios, a hundred thousand cartridges, first-aid kits, canteens—whatever he believed could be extracted from Platt.

Then as Gideon Force progressed from squad to platoon to company tactics, more area was needed for maneuvering these larger formations. Though the desert seemed empty all around them, it was in fact thoroughly subdivided for grazing and other land rights by local Sudanese. In a country where several acres of desert were required to support a single camel, land was not abundant, and Gideon Force increasingly encroached upon it. Wingate was glad to report that he would soon be leaving the problem:

Khartoum
New Years Day
1941

Lorna Dearest,
 The new year is here, appropriately, as everything we do is new for everyone. I could give you a hundred examples; let one suffice. No, haven't even time for that as a delegation of Sudanese is about to visit me. It seems our firing is drying up their goats' milk....
 I resume this after several hours with the local chief. Not only are we sterilizing his goats, we've inflated the cost of camels. He hasn't

much longer to suffer, as I must get the expedition started in order to use the full moon at the escarpment. Anyway there are too many Sudanese around here spying for the Italians.

Another interruption. In fact it's January 2, late afternoon. The E's are whooping about the camp now that they've learned the crusade is soon to begin. Poor devils. So many will never see Addis Ababa. Authorities here say I'll never see the far side of the escarpment. No caravan in anyone's memory has crossed where I propose. That possibility doesn't trouble me, as this means there will surely be no Italian outposts to detect us.

My ethical standing has slipped another notch. I accepted a bribe from the local chief, simply pocketed the 500 quid for leaving his domain— something I was about to do anyway. No doubt I shall have to use the bribe for some bribing of my own as we approach the frontier. There would probably be fewer wars if they were not so profitable for the jackals.

Platt has not had the courtesy to so much as call on Selassie. You misinterpret the relationship between the two. They have nothing in common, even in regard to the Italians, who Platt fears may be provoked into a counterattack if our "foray," as he disdainfully calls it, comes to anything. I have nothing to do with Platt, an isolation I appreciate. I'm told he considers me an expendable fanatic and is now rather pleased by developments which are taking Selassie away from his doorstep. What is it about me that I find so little in common with my countrymen, that I prefer the company and causes of slighted peoples? Have I been so slighted myself? You always side with me, so objectivity is the one resource you cannot provide in answering such a question.

A small, insignificant deficiency from the abundance you lavish upon me. Half of my wholeness remains with you.

I must speak with my cadre now as their enlistment with me is over. To them as well as the E's, I must apply the standard of Gideon. If I could pay them all for continued service I'd empty Selassie's treasury to do so, but what I must have from them money can't buy. They must take a perilous fate without misgivings or inducements, accept my commands and what may be harder, myself. Exile has hardened me to the point where I can only observe rather than accept myself. I cannot ask others to do more; that ability is yours alone.

Orde

*   *   *

Wingate worked on at his desk, occasionally barking into the phone or looking up to question the arrivals on the state of their men. Presently Captain Adams informed him the cadre was assembled. Wingate got up to stretch, but Adams took this as his signal to call the group to attention.

"Atten-shun!"

"Tim, forget that command till we form up for parade in Addis Ababa." Wingate sat down on his desk. The volunteers, well accustomed to his informality, made themselves comfortable, lounging like athletes in a locker room.

"All right, for those of you who don't know it, today is an anniversary. It's been three months since you signed on. You volunteered for ninety days and those ninety days are up.

"I'll be brief: when you leave this tent, either you'll be a member of Gideon Force—ready to fight indefinitely in Ethiopia—or you'll go back where you came from. You'll go back with my thanks—nothing more. I've no time to write efficiency ratings or commendations. I don't want to keep any of you, so if you've already made up your minds to leave, please do so."

A few promptly got up and left, some brusquely, some reluctantly. Wingate nodded to them, thanking several by name. The first departures seemed to stimulate more. As small groups conferred, some left in twos and threes.

"Anyone else? Don't feel that your manhood is at stake. This won't be a big war down here, just a dirty one."

Two officers suddenly made up their minds. They looked at each other, got up quickly, and left.

"Could we talk about our prospects a bit, sir?" a captain asked.

"They're in the hands of God."

A noticeable pause followed. The remaining men looked off into space, avoiding one another's eyes. Another man withdrew. Then there was a pause which everyone interpreted as the last of the last chances.

"Very good, gentlemen. You know the departure arrangements for tomorrow night. We must use the moon and we've got to have it when we reach the escarpment. That's why we're leaving. Now let's get back to work." Wingate picked up the phone. Before he cranked it, a sergeant asked,

"Could you give us some idea of what to expect, sir?"

"You'll be fully briefed on the campaign plan once we get down to the border. Too many Sudanese around here."

"I mean is there something inspirational you could leave us with, sir. Perhaps a quotation from Moses?"

This brought a guffaw and dissolution of tension throughout the tent. Wingate held up the Old Testament, convulsing the cadre with laughter.

"Moses is beyond you—I can see that," he said. "Well, Mr. Churchill came up with a pretty good phrase recently. I believe he promised the people at home nothing but blood, sweat, toil, and tears." Wingate cranked the phone. "All I would add is that you'll probably sweat more down here in the desert."

14

Wingate had no illusions about keeping the departure of Gideon Force secret; everyone in Khartoum would know it the moment the camp emptied. The Sudanese would hold a feast of thanksgiving, and Platt a private celebration with the governor general. Thus Wingate could seek security for his force only in the secrecy of its targets and the scorched wilderness where it could hide even from Italian aircraft.

Three hundred miles away the border wound through desert badlands in front of the Ethiopian escarpment, a great geological demarcation between low desert and high plateau which, from Sudan, looked like the wall of a one-sided canyon. Using routes of ancient caravans between uninhabited oases, Gideon Force traveled by night in a long, thin column. A hundred miles were covered in the first six days, but when they came within range of the Italian air force, Wingate broke up the force into three detachments of approximately four hundred men.

Only the central force, the one led by Wingate escorting the royal party, would take the three-thousand-foot escarpment head on. Two of Wingate's best captains, Simonds and Harris, commanded respectively "Mountain" Force and "Capital" Force.

Wingate's campaign strategy was roughly this: Mountain Force was to slip across the frontier and ascend north into the mountains around Lake Tana, source of the Blue Nile. There the only British agent in Ethiopia had established liaison with supporters of Selassie, potential guerrillas who with supplies flown in from Khartoum would cut the Italians' communications between their seaport and the capital of Addis Ababa.

Capital Force under Harris was to push down the main road from Khartoum to Addis Ababa on the only asphalt road in the region, bypassing the Italian garrisons. As Wingate put it: Harris was to harass. He was to prickle the supply lines of the Italians on the frontier; convince them that an entire British division—some nine thousand men—was invading.

First Harris was to lay siege to the main garrison of the Italian frontier force in the town of Danghila on the Addis Ababa Road—a siege in the feudal tradition with one route of escape left open to the defenders.

It was audacious enough for Wingate to expect that the two thousand Italians in Danghila with their tanks and artillery could be convinced they were being besieged by Harris's four hundred guerrillas. However, Wingate was confident the Italians would stay behind the walls of the town and never patrol in sufficient strength to determine the size and weight of the force surrounding them.

Instead he expected the Italians to evacuate the town when they found their escape route lightly held. They would "break out" onto the road and fall back toward the capital. Waiting for them in ambush on that road would be Wingate with four hundred men, the group which retained the name of Gideon Force.

Strung out on the road, the Italians' artillery was ineffective. Forced by terrain into narrow defiles, their tanks could be blocked by mines. Burdened by equipment and broiled by the sun, the Italian infantry would shatter, then scatter from the ambush—especially if the route to Addis Ababa remained open—and leave their trucks and equipment to the Ethiopians.

Indeed the Italians were to be Selassie's main source of resupply. Platt could not be relied upon to make even half-hearted efforts to provision them by air, though Wingate joked that if Selassie radioed

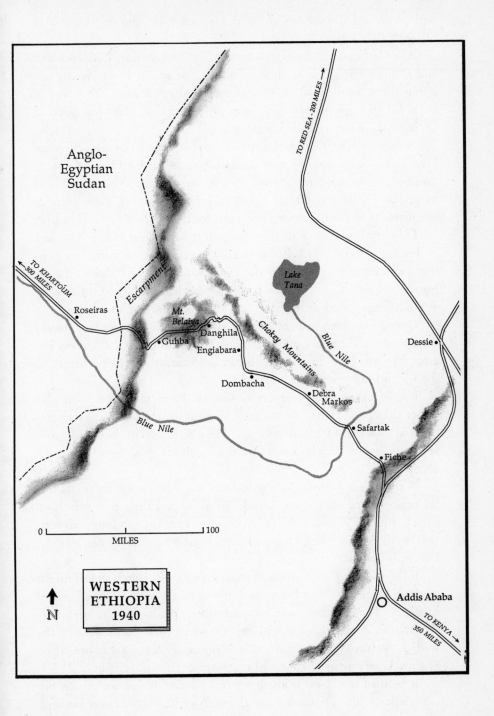

Anglo-Egyptian Sudan

TO RED SEA – 200 MILES

TO KHARTOUM 300 MILES

Escarpment

Roseiras

Lake Tana

Mt. Belaiya

Danghila

Guhba

Engiabara

Chokey Mountains

Blue Nile

Dessie

Dombacha

Debra Markos

Blue Nile

Safartak

Fiche

0   100
MILES

WESTERN
ETHIOPIA
1940

N

Addis Ababa

TO KENYA
350 MILES

Khartoum and said he was bringing his men back, the air would soon fill with parachutes.

After Wingate's "resupply ambush," as he called it, Gideon Force and Capital Force would link up again. Mountain Force would not rejoin them until the Blue Nile was crossed at Safartak. This was as far as his strategy projected. Armies can make final plans but guerrillas rarely can, he reminded Selassie.

No one in Khartoum had any notion of Wingate's plans; otherwise Platt would have marked it as confirmation of his Children's Crusade prophecy. Captains Simonds and Harris, the only professional soldiers to review it, balanced their grave misgivings against their faith in Wingate. It was faith rather than trust, for trust is based in rationality.

Every rational factor in the plan pointed to defeat at the least and to disaster as the most likely outcome. The odds, the disparity in equipment and experience between the Ethiopians and the Italians, the logistics, the terrain, even nature itself, all weighed singly and collectively as cold facts, added up to little less than inevitable catastrophe.

Only a man who had clutched at straws for the last five years could contemplate Wingate's plan with any enthusiasm. This man was the emperor, who saw, if nothing else in the venture, the opportunity to die like a king worthy of his ancestry.

For Wingate, the prospects of Gideon Force rested on principles rather than facts. Before he outlined his plan to Selassie, Wingate paraphrased an ancient Chinese general: "He who knows himself will probably win, while he who knows both himself and his enemy is certain of victory."

Wingate's knowledge of the Italians was based upon their lackluster performance against the Greeks in 1940 and their easy expulsion from Libya by Wavell. His only other insight was through conversation with Atkins, who spoke a little Italian because of his love for Puccini's operas.

If the Italians performed as Wingate predicted, Harris's bluff might work at Danghila—but even the Italians could not be bluffed out of Ethiopia. They might use an escape route to Addis Ababa, but what, as Simonds often asked, would happen when their backs were to the wall? A problem for the future, said Wingate. Directly ahead of Gideon Force was an enemy that would not retreat: the escarpment.

It loomed into view from thirty miles away. It dominated the horizon when Gideon Force reached the frontier. It watched over the double ceremony when the emperor reentered his kingdom and his little army split into thirds.

On that morning Selassie ordered a general assembly in one of the deep wadis, the rain-carved gullies crisscrossing the desert with deep shadows that could hide an army. Within the cool palisade Gideon Force rested as Wingate reviewed his strategy with Simonds and Harris. Three handshakes; then they took their leave.

Earlier Selassie had addressed the men of his departing forces. There was no English translation but war cries resounded through the wadi. Now it had refilled with silence as Wingate and the emperor sprawled on carpets in the sand.

"You're looking at me like Lorna does after the last guest leaves."

"Yes. I feel rather alone. Reassure me now that two-thirds of my men are gone."

Wingate began to strip for a brushing. "Beyond the Blue Nile there shall be a great reunion."

"If we fail on the escarpment, can we catch up with Simonds?"

"We shall cross it. I saw the route myself."

"From an airplane. What is seen from a height is not always present on earth."

"Is that a metaphor?"

"Orde, I have men who were raised in this region. They tell me there is no route here."

"Come, sire." Wingate pulled on his shorts. Slowly they clambered to the rim of the wadi. "The summit saddle, Your Majesty." He pointed to the bowed peak of the huge extinct volcano called Mount Belaiya. "The azimuth is 280 degrees. That puts the notch right here." He pointed to a red "X" on his map.

A dot appeared in the farthest sky, and grew with the faint hum of an engine. "There they are again, Orde."

Wingate shaded his eyes; his cracked lips parted in a smile. "In an hour he will see nothing but a grazing herd of wild camels." Selassie frowned in puzzlement. "I'm sorry. I hadn't had time to tell you. We're not moving out in column; we're turning the camels loose. They'll move toward the escarpment. They associate such mountains with water, smart beasts. We follow on foot a half mile back, making the most of the terrain for concealment."

"We will lose the camels!"

"No, they'll be stopped by the escarpment, you see. We catch up with them at our leisure. From the air they'll just look like some wild herd."

"You ask a great deal of your luck."

"I do. We must go now where luck can help us the most."

The Ethiopian Frontier
January 24, 1941

Dearest Lorna,

This will probably be my last letter till God knows when. It goes back with the courier to Khartoum, now hundreds of miles behind us as we have finally crossed the frontier.

My plan is in motion, the expedition under way. If I die out here it will be on the trail I set for myself. That is a quiet satisfaction which few besides you will understand.

But death is not on my mind. I dread failure much more. So let me close, for it's time to face the enemy. I hope my feelings come through these words—you know that my abruptness is not from lack of love.

It's simply that I must turn from you now in order to open the sluice of war which is the pressure behind my life.

Thus farewell for now, and if only for now, we shall reread this together in exciting communion. But if forever, then forever know that you have been loved to the utmost limits of the word.

Orde

15

In February 1941, the four hundred men of Gideon Force began their advance toward Addis Ababa four hundred miles away. Opposing them was a veteran force of sixteen thousand well-armed Italians, one of the most modern armies in the world. Immediately before Gideon Force was the three-thousand-foot rampart of the escarpment. Wingate approached it with the same stealth he would employ against the Italians.

Early on the morning after Simonds and Harris had taken their detachments off into the night, Wingate's camels began to emerge from the wadi. They slowly circled into a ragged herd and ambled toward the escarpment. Hours later, Gideon Force left the wadi, following the camels like beaters on a hunt.

The men's eyes darted between the herd and the sky. Twice during the day Italian aircraft passed overhead and the men turned into rocks. One plane circled, then flew on.

By midafternoon the camels plodded into the long shadow of the escarpment. The men arrived some six hours later exhausted and dehydrated. Wingate remained behind them on a high promontory that gave him a good look at the sheer face of rock. With him was an Ethiopian named Tafod, a native of the escarpment region. He knew of no pass where Wingate believed there to be one.

Wingate searched for it with his binoculars. Beside him was the map with the markings he had made on his reconnaissance flight months before.

"It's *got* to be there, Tafod. I must not be looking. It's got to be there."

"Sometimes when a man look too much he see nothing. You let me, please."

"I was in an airplane when I shot the azimuth," he answered in a rasping voice, "but I'll swear it was right."

Wingate slumped against a rock. Hot wind swirled the sand. Tafod squatted down beside him, propped his elbows on his knees to steady the binoculars, and studied the escarpment very slowly. He began to croon in a low voice, a song about how the sand and the wind were lovers who went everywhere and nowhere together.

He continued to hum as Wingate looked blankly ahead, the breeze starching his uniform with sweat. He sipped from a canteen while the sand and wind whispered to each other.

After a long silence, Tafod spoke: "You call on your God now."

"I have."

"No. Once I heard you speak from your Koran. Great words. Use them now."

"I am a wretched, crawling creature, Tafod," Wingate replied as the wind started to drift toward the escarpment.

"No, not now, Major, or you make your God like yourself. Now
is the time for Him to be all powers. A god of all power made the
escarpment."

Though his throat was too dry to recite the Psalms, Wingate moved
his lips. Tafod raised the binoculars again as the stirrings of the breeze
pulled sand away from the cliff like a gossamer veil.

He could see Gideon Force huddled where the rock leaped vertically from the desert. Tafod watched them and wondered how high, if
they all could stand upon each other's shoulders, they would reach on
the sheer face looming over them.

A sheer face but one that began to wrinkle as the wind slid sand
from some ledges and onto others. Tafod swept the binoculars across
new contours. A shadowy ravine seemed to form; he peered deeper as
a ledge revealed itself, rising, switching back, climbing several hundred feet.

"You do good azimuth, sir."

For a moment nothing registered. "What do you mean?"

"There are places..."

"Let me see!"

"Men can climb there. Maybe donkeys too. Camels cannot go."

"The Lord provides only a path, Tafod. It is for us to follow!"

Three of the best camel handlers began the ascent by moonlight. They
returned after dawn with a discouraging report. Camels were out of
the question. For most of the grade the climbers pulled themselves up
with their hands, teetering on ledges where their backs scraped the
escarpment while their toes hung in space. Only dynamite could widen
the path enough for camels.

There were no Italians within a hundred miles to hear the blasting, and the risk of attracting their air force was nothing compared
with the climb which would be attempted with but one favorable condition—a full moon. It had always been Wingate's first priority—the
consideration which determined his departure date from Khartoum—
the moon phase at the escarpment. Chalk-white above the plunging
shadows, the moon illuminated a night in which boulders thundered
down as men gripped and groped to clamp themselves against the cliff,
waiting for those above to progress.

The moon rose faster than the climbers. It poised vertically above them, then shadows filled the ravine like water flooding a shaft. Caught in the darkness, men and animals began to fall.

Morning found a third of the force still clinging to the escarpment, and a hundred camels abandoned at the foot of the cliff. Through binoculars Atkins searched for signs of life and death. As the day wore on the camels drifted away from a litter of broken carcasses. At first he could not distinguish the corpses because the sand blurred their size; then vultures spiraled down to begin their selection. They first mounted the thin-skinned humans before attacking the camel hides.

At the top of the escarpment the land changed in both climate and topography. Three thousand feet of elevation provided cool relief from the scorch of the desert below. Gideon Force had reached the level of the vast Ethiopian plateau, a tableland dotted with copses and cut by shallow brooks. But sand was thin on the plateau; the camels would go lame as they were driven deeper into Ethiopia. The nights were too cool for these lowland camels and many would sicken.

Wingate's plan was to slaughter them before they fell. Camel meat would be the staple on the plateau until the Italians resupplied him on the road to Addis Ababa. This road, still a hard march of eighty miles away, now replaced the escarpment as the next goal toward which he drove his forces of Gideon.

But even Wingate did not try to rouse his men as they lay exhausted in their first camp beyond the escarpment. Behind them rose the dust haze above the horizon in Sudan.

Men were drinking facedown in the pools of a streambed. Factotum found a spring under the dappling shade of some trees; there Wingate lay on his back in a foot of gurgling water. If this wasn't paradise, he told Factotum, at least it was the promised land.

Selassie approached as Wingate continued to soak, his eyes transfixed as if he were experiencing a grim bliss.

"Orde, who was lost?"

"Two British. Five patriots. Seventeen camels."

"Our first accounting."

"Yes."

"I heard them as they fell. Did you?"

Wingate's eyes closed; he stirred slightly in the water. "I am not so hardened as to be deaf, Your Majesty."

"I suppose you foresaw such horrors. When we first talked in the Quonset hut, you urged me to imagine the events ahead—victories."

"This may be our most important victory. We have scaled the wall. We've broken into Graziani's garden."

"You lifted us over—with the strength of your confidence. We will remember."

"Remembering is for later."

"Yes. For now let us share a sacrament." He called for Factotum to bring the wine. He told him to have Ishmael serve it, for Selassie wished his soothsayer to observe Wingate as the future formed on the rim of the escarpment.

16

To Italian aircraft, Gideon Force appeared like shepherds moving to upland pastures. With as many pains as Wingate took to disguise his force, Harris made similar efforts to display his. After splitting off from Wingate in the wadi, Capital Force moved by night for forty miles until they were astride the Addis Ababa Road. Harris then revealed his men to the Italian air force as he marched in long, dust-stirring columns, almost inviting air attacks.

None materialized. Harris then commandeered several civilian trucks which he forced to move abreast of him in convoy. He mounted machine guns and fired on Italian reconnaissance planes. Still the Italians could not be provoked to attack, even from the air.

Each night Harris countermarched both the trucks and hundreds of men, then started them forward again the next day over the same route. He thus produced the impression of thousands of men and vast quantities of material lumbering forward to crack the frontier defense by frontal assault.

His bluff was nearly too successful. A strong Italian outpost at the first Italian town of Guhba was expected to offer considerable resistance, so much that Harris was concerned whether he could bypass it.

Instead the garrison withdrew before even exchanging fire with the guerrillas.

The Italians next abandoned an extremely defensible pass along the slopes of Mount Belaiya. With his radio signals blocked by the mountain, Harris could not warn Wingate that the Italians might retreat straight through Danghila before Capital Force could encircle the town.

If that happened Wingate would be set in ambush on an abandoned road with the Italians and their precious supplies gone over the eastern horizon. If it came to that he and Harris would link up with no one to fight and little to eat. So in a situation that only the Italian army could create, the Danghila garrison might achieve victory by headlong retreat.

Gideon Force made good time toward the road. Each landmark raised the spirit of the pathfinders. Four days after they left the escarpment, Tofad rushed ahead to a promontory, paused for a look in both directions, then waved for Wingate to join him.

"The road to Addis Ababa," said Tofad as if he had built it himself.

"Yes, I've seen it in my dreams." He stood on a high, banked curve in the road perfect for ambush. "Atkins," he called over his shoulder, "get your sappers up here. Security out a mile, both sides."

Selassie and Wingate exchanged congratulations as they watched the men planting mines beside the road.

"Lot of soldier litter by the road, Major Wingate," Atkins called to them and held up some broken boxes.

"Any canteens?"

"I'll let you know."

"Yes, we need more canteens," Selassie observed.

"That's not why I asked."

"Why?"

"A soldier only drops his canteen when he's under fire."

"You don't imagine Harris..."

"We haven't heard from him, Your Majesty."

"Perhaps he is like you."

"What do you mean?"

"You don't communicate with Platt. Harris does not communicate with you."

"All the difference in the world. Platt wishes me ill, whereas Harris and I succeed only if we both succeed. I imagine his signals just can't get through Mount Belaiya."

"Let us hope so."

"Success always brings uncertainties, Your Majesty."

A whistle from Atkins. He held up three canteens by their shoulder straps.

"*That* is not a good omen," Wingate muttered.

"Do you believe in omens?"

"Perhaps that's the wrong word."

"No, not for us. We believe in omens, and that the future can be seen in some measure."

"My future is the present."

"Perhaps. But as a favor would you permit my soothsayer to examine you?"

"If you wish."

"When there's time."

"I hope I can wait. Would you tell me something first?" Selassie nodded. "Any particular reason for this scrutiny? Some incident that prompted your interest?"

"No incident but an accumulation of interest. You are very important to me obviously."

"I must tell you I hardly subscribe to preordination. I shall resent any prophecy that limits my future, so I'd rather not hear your soothsayer's report."

"My soothsayer reports only to me."

"Yet I've sometimes looked with favor at the disease of cancer. Once it is diagnosed, a man knows the span of time that shall be the rest of his life. His days are numbered but he knows the sum."

"You have a strange relation with death."

Wingate stiffened. Selassie wondered if Wingate's reaction was to the flash of a mirror from the ambush outpost.

"We got traffic!" Atkins called as his men scurried off the road. The mirror signal indicated one truck.

"You'll blow it up?" Selassie asked.

"Oh no. We're waiting for a convoy. Pray God that Harris let this truck through. The news of his siege must reach Dombacha."

Wingate focused his binoculars on the turn of the road. Shortly the sound of a motor grew louder. It was a medium-sized general cargo truck, its tarpaulin flapping loudly. Beside the driver hunched over the wheel was a single passenger who, in the instant Wingate could see him, appeared to be an officer. With a downshift of gears, the truck climbed the curving grade through the ambush and was gone.

"Well," said Wingate ambiguously.

"Well what?"

"There were some bullet holes in her tarp."

"Harris?"

"Could be."

"But has he done it . . . or just begun it?"

"If you ask me, that looked more like the first truck out of Danghila than the last."

Atkins waved his miners back onto the road, then climbed to where Wingate and Selassie were talking.

"What's the minimum number of trucks, sir?"

"I'd probably settle for three that size—and just hope they're carrying what we need."

"It's food we need, and it won't be on any ruddy truck coming out of Danghila," Atkins protested. "Let's chop a convoy from Dombacha. There's where the supplies are coming from."

"We'll see. But, Atkins, you must learn to get your mind on the war and off your stomach. Here. I saved an onion for you."

"I want to fill my stomach, Major, but not with gas."

"Maybe some Italian wine, aye, Atkins?" Selassie quipped.

"Now you're talking, Your Majesty."

"Seek ye first the Kingdom of Heaven, and all these things shall be added unto you," said Wingate.

"He even knows some of the New Testament," said Selassie.

"We need Jesus Christ himself," Atkins replied. "But I'd tell him we don't have enough water for a bottle of wine."

"But," said Selassie, "there are plenty of stones here to turn into bread."

"May ye both eat camel steaks throughout eternity," said Wingate.

"Cromarty says you can go forty days without even an iron ration, sir," said Atkins with a wink at Selassie.

"True," Wingate replied.

"Further proof," said Selassie, "that you are our messiah."

"Only a prophet. Like John the Baptist I precede the true messiah, spreading news of your coming."

"Major Wingate's a bit romantic, Your Highness."

"And you?"

"I'm here because I read about the Queen of Sheba and all the girls in your court."

"In my palace, Cliff—maidens you've seen only in fantasy. Nubians. Women of the pharaohs."

"Go on, sir. I need inspiration."

"Dancers. Supple as a slipper, skin of satin and silk. Orde, aren't you interested?"

"Atkins doesn't need such distractions. I'm immune to them."

"But aren't they small-breasted, Your Majesty?"

"Who told you so? You must climb them like the escarpment."

"You'll weaken him, sire. He'll stay awake tonight telling the others."

"You can't expect Cliff to live by your iron discipline."

"Out here I can. He's yours once we reach the palace."

"There's the road, Orde; there's the road that leads to my palace."

17

Gideon Force strained their ears as twilight cooled the air and increased the range of sound. Wingate listened for the thump of mortars from the direction of Danghila some thirty miles away. The night filled with splendid darkness and a panoply of brilliant stars but no sounds.

Atkins was optimistic. When the Italian truck reached Dombacha and radioed back to Danghila that the way was clear, the garrison would come down the road in a beautiful convoy. With that prediction, Atkins turned in. The watch over the ambush was split into halves, and he commanded the second shift.

Bidding him good night, Wingate and Selassie conversed in the darkness as they had on many previous evenings. The Englishman had done little but listen, for Selassie's life during the last five years had been a fascinating cavalcade through the capitols and private offices of the world's great statesmen. From close by he had watched the disin-

tegration of the League of Nations, the resurgence of Italy, the collapse of France, and the stubborn stand of Britain. There was scarcely
a major political personality in Africa, America, or Europe about whom
Selassie could not produce a personal anecdote. Wingate pulled them
out of him as if by interrogation.

"...but never Hitler?"

"Where would I have met him? I don't believe he has ever left
Germany."

"Hmmm," was Wingate's typical comment.

"Orde, sometimes I grow tired of my voice."

"How do you mean? It's a splendid voice. I've watched it work
magic with your subjects."

"There, you do it again: take my meaning, which you fully understand, and turn it in another direction."

"Apologies, Your Highness."

"I would prefer to hear more of you and less of my own ramblings."

"All that has been interesting in my life would not match the routine happenings during a week of yours."

"I believe the Americans say 'shit of a bull.' I've had to find out
things about you since you are so unrevealing. You were awarded a
high decoration in Palestine but you also got into trouble there."

"Everyone who enters Palestine gets into trouble of one kind or
another. First the Turks, now the British."

"Do not try to lead us back into geopolitics," Selassie scolded.
"When were you last in Palestine?"

"It has been eight months...and sixteen days."

"You speak of Palestine as a lover."

"When I hear 'Palestine,' I dream of Zion."

"Yes, I was told you were a Zionist."

"I still am."

"But you are a Christian, not a Jew."

"You are not the first to find that a paradox."

"I think Jehovah is your god, not the Trinity."

"Yes, I listen more to Jehovah because He is so much more specific.
As a soldier I appreciate clear orders. Compare the Commandments to the
Beatitudes, for example; the first are direct and unambiguous, the other
rather theoretical and..."

"No theories tonight, Orde. Before this war starts I insist that you
be personal. Why is religion such a passion for you?"

"Not religion. It is the passion of the search. The search within the obvious. The devil is obvious, my lord. This war is his work and delight. His eyes flash from every weapon. But above him is the creator, the hand that broke the escarpment from the desert and sprinkles the stars tonight. God is there. I am here. I see Him yet I search for Him—a passionate frustration."

"Did your family start you on this search?"

"Not in a direct way. They were deeply but conventionally religious. Their awe of God's mystery affected me, I'm sure."

"Your father, you said, was a colonel in India."

"He influenced me as yours did. Your father set you in your lineage. Mine set me in the tradition of god-fearing. God, the father."

"God is also mother."

"And as such I idealized mine. Sometimes Lorna too—now that I'm so far from her."

"But no children."

"Not yet."

"In how many years of marriage?"

"Five."

"You want sons I think."

"Gideon Force are my boys right now, sir. But, yes, I want a son very much. Lorna shall have my child, I have no fear of that."

"Factotum, summon Ishmael." There was a stirring beside them; Factotum began to descend the hill.

"We shouldn't allow any movement now. Why do you want your bloody soothsayer?"

"He will tell you about your children. He is very accurate. Do not doubt him. There is much you westerners do not believe that is still high knowledge."

"The stars have moved considerably, Your Majesty. I don't think we will see the Italians tonight. The most likely hour now is near dawn, so we should sleep."

"You don't often ask to sleep. I'll not have Ishmael disturb you."

The two were silent as they made themselves comfortable on their ground sheets. Selassie remained on his back contemplating the vast procession of stars as they crept toward morning. He felt portents that this night would be the last for many men, in Ethiopia and all across the world at war. The dark and the brilliance of the night seemed to be a fitting tribute for all who would never see another.

"What weapon should I use, Orde?"

"Huh?" came a sleepy reply.

"When we go against the Italians. I must show my men I can do battle."

"Lead from the rear, Your Highness. No one expects you in the trenches."

"I am not a military man, you know." He could sense Wingate smile in the darkness. "But I will share the fate of my patriots."

"Inevitably, my lord."

"You've led them here, not I."

"But it is you they followed."

"Their loyalty is my courage."

"Which is plentiful. You climbed the escarpment yourself. There was no royal way."

"The Italians are about to meet a mighty vengeance, Orde. For a time I will discard the robes of primate of the Coptic Christian Church. It was never my most comfortable role."

"Understood."

"I'm sure there are better Christians. But then the crusaders were not so Christlike either."

18

Wingate and Selassie were asleep when a signal candle bobbed far in the distance on the road from Danghila. Atkins gave a loud whistle. It brought both men upright in their bedrolls.

"The light moves up-down," said Selassie.

"That means no vehicles. Unless the wops are walking out, we've probably got some donkeys. Atkins!"

"Yes, sir!"

"I want all the animals. I'll shoot the man who shoots a donkey."

"Got it."

"Sharpshooters only."

"Got it."

The road was darker than the countryside, concealing eleven Italians as they slouched along on their donkeys. Through his binoculars Wingate saw their cloth hats shaped like half footballs and rifles slung across their backs as if they were coming home from a peacetime maneuver.

"No officers," Wingate murmured.

"No supplies?"

"No."

"When will we shoot?"

"Very soon."

A score of shots rang out almost simultaneously. None missed. With barely a cry the Italians lurched and teetered on their mounts, then toppled to the ground as the donkeys bolted up the road. The guerrillas sprang for them; the prized beasts were led away through the roadside minefield into the gullies to join the camel train in the hills.

"Nice shooting!" Wingate called into the fading darkness.

As neat as the ambush appeared, the killing was not complete. Drawing their long knives, a detachment of select guerrillas snaked through the mine field. These men were to be rewarded for their feats during the trek from Sudan. Their reward was the five Italians who watched death approach.

One tried to drag himself into a ditch where he detonated a small mine with his elbow. The approaching Ethiopians laughed as they ducked the splatter of bone and flesh, then twirled their knives. Atkins found himself trembling, for he understood the brief sobs for mercy.

Blood still gurgled through severed windpipes while he examined the bodies for papers. Atkins leaped back with a cry. He had reached in the pocket of a man who had been disemboweled; his hand felt the crucifix on the Italian's chest. The dead man's eyes opened and his hand gripped Atkins's.

Atkins' cry went unnoticed as mirror signals glinted off the first rays of the sun.

This time it was trucks. Two wires were touched to a battery on the hill. The road splintered and an engine block soared lazily over a cloud of oily smoke. More explosions erupted under the following trucks as they bounced into the smaller mines on the embankment. The convoy disintegrated like a severed string of beads.

Four machine guns thundered from the hills. The first vehicle shuddered under their concentrated fire, its tarp shredding, the chassis vibrating till the gas tank burst into flame, ejecting five Italians. They were caught, spun like drunken dancers till the machine guns dropped them and turned their spray on the second truck.

"Spread it! Spread it!" Wingate shouted, but the guerrillas ignored their training. Rather than raking the convoy with fire they focused it on successive trucks as if each in turn was to be individually executed. At the rear of the convoy Italians began to crawl away.

Their dark uniforms contrasted with the light sand. Sharpshooters plucked targets till they shrank into the rocks. Guerrillas left their posts to slip across the wasteland and search them out.

The signal mirrors flashed again. Above the hammering machine guns Wingate heard the growl of numerous engines approaching the bend. He wrenched Selassie by the shoulder.

"They've got to *obey!* Get your men back!"

The emperor was about to reply when an armored car rounded the bend. It braked; behind it were a dozen trucks. It stopped well short of the mines. Troops dropped to the ground and deployed with skill. The armored car's turret swung from side to side like a cobra seeking a target. The first burst furrowed the dirt below Selassie's dugout.

"Well, Your Majesty, we've got a fight on our hands."

"My men will redeem themselves."

The Italians were armed with submachine guns, excellent weapons for controlling civilians but without the range of the Ethiopians' rifles. The British managed to back the guerrillas off and begin sniping; then the machine guns on both sides subsided into sporadic conversation while the rifles began to dominate.

Windshields crumbled; ricochets whined off rock and metal. The armored car could neither advance through the wreckage of the first convoy nor back through the immobilized trucks of the second. Finally a mortar projectile landed squarely on the hood. The front axle fractured, the wheels smoldered in a bowlegged slant. A white flag rose from the turret.

The surrender brought a wave of cheers from the Ethiopians and set them off in a charge, a foolish charge, for when they closed within range of the Italians' submachine guns it was the guerrillas' turn to be outgunned.

Once more the British were able to pull the guerrillas back while the Italians used the lull to retreat toward Danghila. They could only be cut off by mortars. Wingate ordered rapid fire but what was to have been a curtain of steel across the road became an ineffective dribble.

He scrambled down into the gully where the mortars were coughing out their last shells. Sergeant Rawlings held up his palms.

"Down to four rounds per tube, sir."

Wingate pulled off his pith helmet. "Save 'em," he said wearily, "God knows where we'll get any more."

From the gully Rawlings had seen nothing of the battle. "Who's winning?" he asked.

"We're not winning but we're learning."

A patter of mortars turned their heads. It came from down the road. "Who's that?" Rawlings asked, but Wingate was already sprinting up the hill.

February 13, 1941
East of Danghila

Lorna my lovely,

I may be months writing this; we may have to capture Addis Ababa before I can post it. No matter—yesterday opened the first battle and the Lord blessed our arms dramatically! We battered an Italian convoy but they were able to break back to Danghila when Capital Force appeared.

My mortars went silent for lack of shells, yet I could see a bombardment falling on the trucks. Then a cheer went up from our outguards as the wops took flight into the hills. I stood bewildered till a dozen camels charged around the bend. Harris was leading, shooting his pistol around like a drunken cowboy! He saw the emperor, reined his camel, lifted his helmet, and led a cheer answered by every man in Gideon Force—myself included, as I was stirred as never in my life.

Selassie threw his arms around me. Security was forgotten, stray mines ignored. Only by improbable luck were none stepped upon by the rejoicing patriots.

Savage butchery accompanied our victory. I condoned it. Revenge is a most natural and satisfying emotion. We westerners for some reason look upon revenge as uncivilized, but this attitude insults much of the conduct described in the Old Testament. The Lord's vengeance must be expressed so that men can see its reality.

I must now temper Selassie's optimism. He feels this skirmish has won him the western province. Actually we have gained little except a few badly damaged trucks and supplies which will last no more than a week. But Selassie can almost see his throne down the road. It doesn't seem to matter there are still four hundred miles of that road.

Much renewed,

Orde

19

Owing to their dilapidated radios, there had been no communications between the guerrilla forces; it was not until a relay station was sent up the slopes of Mount Belaiya that Simonds could be reached. That meant a delay of two days for Gideon Force (now double in strength after its reunion with Capital Force), and this grated hard on Wingate.

The news from Mountain Force was also grating. The aerial resupply promised by Colonel Appleby had never appeared. Simonds was unable to learn why because his radio frequencies were incompatible with those of the British in Sudan. A deliberate mismatch, Wingate suspected. In any event, the hospitality of the local chieftains in the Lake Tana region was showing limits, and Simonds had been unable to employ them against the Italian garrisons, which were much stronger than those opposing Gideon Force.

Wingate loaded his wounded and an impressive amount of booty, along with the highest-ranking Italian prisoner (a major), onto two trucks and sent them back two hundred miles to Roseiras, the first British garrison in Sudan. He hated to lose the trucks, but the gas he had captured was not enough to keep them running long.

Through this display he expected his victory to have the maximum impact on the British. It would show by physical evidence that the guerrillas had penetrated deep into the Italian defenses and were driving on. With that appearance Wingate calculated that if the British wanted an influence in postliberation Ethiopia, they would get behind Selassie and start treating him like an ally rather than a nuisance.

The arrival of the Roseiras convoy did have such an effect but far beyond what Wingate had anticipated.

It had been a month since Gideon Force disappeared in the direction of the escarpment. Though out of communication, Selassie was never for long out of Platt's mind because of inquiries from Wavell to which Platt could only respond that the emperor had departed for his homeland in the hope of starting a guerrilla uprising. Cairo would be kept informed, but they should remember that communications were dubious in the wilds.

Was there a prearranged date and time for Gideon Force to report? Wavell's headquarters next wanted to know. Yes, Platt replied, but Wingate had missed it and all others subsequent. Had an aerial relay been sent up to try and locate the guerrillas? asked Cairo. No aircraft could be spared, Khartoum replied.

"And why all this sudden interest in Ethiopia anyway," Appleby huffed as he reread the messages. For Platt that question was even more puzzling. The Machiavellian scheme, as he had perceived it, was for the refugees to follow their king into the wilderness and probably never be seen again. Either all these inquiries from Cairo were cynical efforts to establish a record of concern or Platt had misread the basic scenario.

He had; so the chain of events that followed Selassie's departure mystified him for a time. News of Selassie's crusade had spread not only into Ethiopia but also into Kenya, a British colony where refugees had fled from the southern Ethiopian provinces just as those from the northern provinces had fled into Sudan. Major General Cunningham was the British commander in Kenya, and he wanted to get into the war. With a Kenyan force of fifteen thousand and a few thousand Ethiopians, he obtained permission from Wavell to attack the Italians from the south.

To improve Cunningham's chances of forcing the Italians to fight on two fronts (Wingate's sector was never expected to become a "front"),

Wavell urged Platt to begin an offensive into Eritrea, the northernmost Ethiopian province, which formed the country's coast on the Red Sea.

This instruction from Cairo followed close on the inquiries about Gideon Force. Thus Colonel Appleby learned with mixed emotions what "all the sudden interest in Ethiopia" was about. Soon he found himself nearly as busy as Wingate had been except now it was a British attack that would be mounted from Sudan.

Platt and his staff were struggling with the logistics of awakening their slumbering command when the news of the Roseiras convoy reached them. "Let me see his message again," said Platt. Around them in the general's office the fixtures that would go into Platt's field HQ were being dismantled. Through the window the blazing sun suggested the heat awaiting them until they were under a roof once more.

The Roseiras message read:

Danghila captured at small cost. Operations in Lake Tana region stalled for lack of promised aerial resupply. Please raise Simonds on one of *his* frequencies and accommodate him. His wants are few and visible support by British aircraft will do much to rally local tribes. Balance of GF will continue to attack on the Dombacha–Addis Ababa Road. Captured stores are expected to suffice for another week but I anticipate need for resupply in the vicinity of Debra Markos. The radios with which we began are useless. Could an operable set be dropped in on the SW slope of Mount B? A bonfire cross will mark the spot for the next week (18–25 Feb.). Regards, Wingate

"What cheek," Platt sneered. "Tell him I've got my own war to tend to now. Couldn't spare him a radio battery. Second thought, don't even respond to his message. He never replied to ours."

"This fellow, Simonds, might be of use to us if the going gets sticky in Eritrea," Hawthorne ventured.

"Yes, and our agent up there... What's his name?"

"Sandford."

"He's to take charge of Wingate's force around Lake Tana. They are to support *us* from this day forward. Set up the necessary command relationship. Promote Sandford if necessary. Make Simonds his XO."

"Very good, sir. However, the Ethiopians: we can do what we will

with the British cadre, but if Selassie calls for support I suspect the
Ethiopians will do his bidding rather than ours."

"They can only learn his bidding over our radios, am I right?"

"Selassie could use messengers. Who knows how quickly they can
move about. The Italian lines seem porous."

"Then the other way is to control the E's through Wingate. He
still works for me in the British army. He must simply advise Selassie
that Simonds and all his force...How many do you suppose he has?"

"No more than five hundred from the sounds of his resupply requests."

"You mean we heard his transmissions?"

"Didn't acknowledge them since we didn't have the aircraft."

"We do now."

"Yes, sir."

"Anyway, Wingate is to convince the emperor that the overall campaign—that is, my offensive and Cunningham's—is best served by at-
tachment of Simonds's force to me."

"With due respect, sir, I rather doubt Wingate will be convinced,
much less that he will help us convince Selassie. I'm not at all sure he
welcomes the introduction of major British formations into what he
regards as his theater."

"It *was* his theater but it is no longer. And I think Wingate is
perceptive enough to see the game he so rashly began has attracted
some big players. Cunningham and I both expect laurels."

"The advance Wingate proposes for his force helps Cunningham
more than us."

"Quite so. Instruct him to reinforce Simonds by a third. The balance of...what does he call them?"

"Gideon Force. 'Many step forward, few are chosen, etc.'"

"Yes. The balance of Gideon Force is not to advance beyond Debra
Markos until I further advise."

"I just hope we can get through to him, General. We have yet to
hear his voice on the air."

"Well, he needs radios. Apparently we didn't give him very good
ones. Drop one to him on Mount Belaiya as he requested. And stay on
good terms with him, Tony. I want Wingate to view me now as his
patron. My campaign could do much to advance his career. In fact, on
the basis of his startling success to date, have him promoted to acting
lieutenant colonel. And Tony, if he can help me get to Addis Ababa

ahead of Cunningham, I'll see that he comes out of Ethiopia a colonel. Do you think you could get down to see him—explain to him what the stakes are?"

"I hope I'm wrong, but I am uneasy about his propensity to cooperate. War seems to be a somewhat different involvement for Wingate than it is for us."

"I sense what you mean but I think you're wrong. He's in the army; he knows the values of the institution. If he does not, I'll guarantee you he will learn them as this campaign progresses."

20

The sound of an aircraft at twilight sent the Ethiopians ducking behind rocks, but Wingate looked to the sky expectantly. His hunch was right, for an RAF medium bomber circled Mount Belaiya. A white parachute puffed in the sky; a heavy bundle descended toward the slopes.

For the jubilant Ethiopians, the visit of the first friendly aircraft was another occasion for cheers and thanksgiving. It was also what Wingate hoped to be the final persuader in his effort to detach Selassie from Gideon Force.

A spacious cave at the base of Mount Belaiya, its mouth opening into a pleasant grove of trees, was the interim headquarters Wingate proposed for the emperor, arguing that it was necessary for him to show his court with all the appearances of stability, to hang out the royal standard, so to speak, where the chiefs of the western province could come to pledge their allegiance. "Your Majesty, your throne will not fit on the back of a donkey," was how Wingate put it.

Now this new, powerful radio had descended from the sky. With it, Wingate promised, he would be in daily contact with the emperor, advising him of every important engagement or counseling him whenever there was a significant development with the British.

The handsome radio came with a generator and even a can of fuel to get it started. The generator was first used to light what Wingate hoped would be acceptable new quarters for the emperor. "Very much like our ancient Scottish fortresses," Wingate remarked as he examined the interior of the cave. From here Selassie would be in direct communication with Platt, thereby eliminating Wingate as the intermediary between the two and leaving him free to wage his war.

"Cold and gray," was Selassie's opinion of his keep. "Better suited for Macbeth than for me."

"As I counseled at the ambush, Your Highness, you have a unique ability to lead from the rear."

"Don't try to maneuver me. Some famous statesmen have tried."

"My lord."

"My sword has not drawn blood yet. My subjects respect a warlord."

"With all respect, your best weapon is a scepter."

"In time. For now I should be seen more with drawn sword."

"We can summon a photographer. I will distribute pictures of you as we advance."

"Mine is an ancient kingdom. My people believe in a king on horseback, not on film. I would only send my most trusted lieutenant to be my presence where I cannot go. I'm not sure you are that man."

"What more would you know of me?"

"Things perhaps I could learn as we continue together."

Selassie's retinue set about to improve his opinion of the cave. They, if not the emperor, were ready to stop and hold court.

The new radio was studied with pride by the brightest of the Ethiopians picked to operate "the station of the king." Several incoming messages had already collected—technical transmission data, call signs—all the preparations and requirements that could be expected by Platt's headquarters. Wingate regarded the flashing, clattering radio as something of a time bomb. He had to be well out of its range when Appleby's calls started coming in asking for various reports and limiting Wingate's independence.

Selassie could hold off Platt—Wingate had no doubt of that—indeed the emperor could make counterdemands, alternative proposals, and in general act the part of a sovereign ally rather than a guerrilla subordinate. In short, Selassie knew Platt needed him more than Selassie now needed Platt.

"I believe I should continue with you riding behind the vanguard," was Selassie's conclusion as they dined with wine. His courtiers looked glum and glanced at Wingate as if he were their last hope. "I have not discharged my duty," the emperor added, "to lead my army simply by defeating one Italian garrison."

"Your leadership is needed here," Wingate replied respectfully. "Your greatest service to your cause and to your subjects is to remain temporarily in this stronghold and rally your chieftains."

"They will rally to me as I accompany you to further victories."

"If they had your courage I might agree. But they will hesitate to pay you homage under skies controlled by Italian aircraft. Your vassals will join you more quickly in the security of this stronghold."

"Their courage should be tested."

"They can avoid it. Abu Sharul, for example. When our forces approach the Chokey Mountains, he will invite you to his camp."

"Your personal safety, Royal Majesty," Factotum added.

"Indeed," said Wingate. "Summon your barons as is proper for their lord. Bid them to come here unarmed. Who knows what intrigues have occurred in your absence. And Gideon Force could not afford to send a large number of men to protect you."

"From what?"

"From possible treason, Your Majesty. From men who would collect the Italians' reward for your capture."

"All chiefs will meet me on the road to Addis Ababa and prostrate themselves before me!" Selassie mused as expectant silence hovered over the table. "For how many days will you rest here?"

"We depart in the morning."

"While the Lion of Judah remains in his lair."

"You reign once more, Your Majesty. Your royal responsibility is to your entire realm now that you sit once more within it. As sovereign, your army is but one of your agencies."

"I must receive reports from you daily."

"As you wish."

"All here bear witness that I command Colonel Wingate to render daily reports and await my acknowledgements." All at the table nodded; a few smiled at Wingate.

"Much of the fighting will be by night," he said, "but every evening when the situation permits I will send a report by radio."

"I shall remind your radio operator to do so even if you forget. Now, how do you expect the campaign to progress?"

"Though we are still far fewer than the Italians, we must appear to be more. If they discover how few we are, they could rally at Dombacha or beyond. I may need to call for Simonds to take them on the flank. In any case, we will fight by night in order to make our numbers appear larger."

"I have great confidence you will conquer the Italians. How will you beat the British?"

Wingate glanced around to see if any of his British cadre were still in the cave, then answered under his voice. "We're way ahead of Platt. He's just beginning and he's cautious. Cunningham is the man I'm worried about. The Kenyan border is closer to Addis Ababa than we are. He has six times our force."

"We must beat him."

"I shall."

"How?"

"We must push the Italians before us, cause them to think that security is to be found only in Addis Ababa. As they fall back on the capital they will thicken the defenses in front of Cunningham. Then you must try to negotiate with the Italians so they will surrender to us."

"I hope our chances do not depend on that."

"That is part of the long odds against us."

"The Italians know our memories. They will surrender to the British."

"That is something you should bargain for with Platt."

"Yes. Factotum, another bottle of wine."

"I hope you will excuse me, Your Majesty; I have many details to check before the morning."

"I have another appointment for you so don't disappear." Selassie spoke a few words to Factotum, who left the table.

"You're not letting me go easily, are you?" said Wingate as he saw the soothsayer accompany Factotum into the cave. "But all the better. I'm about to post Lorna a letter. Now I can tell her exactly how many children to plan for."

"Do not treat him lightly," Selassie murmured.

"The greatest in all Africa," Factotum added.

The table was vacated as Ishmael took his seat opposite the Englishman. Except for a white damask turban which he somehow kept remarkably clean in the grime of guerrilla life, Ishmael appeared in no way different from his comrades. After studying Wingate a few moments, he asked to exchange places with him so his subject could be viewed against the dark gray rock.

"A reader of auras, is he?" Wingate asked, but no one answered.

Ishmael uttered a few syllables. "He would like you to lie down. Lie down on the table, please," said Factotum.

"Whatever for?"

"He must feel areas of your body. It is necessary to determine what children will come from you."

Wingate knew better than to refuse. If this was the emperor's price for independence, it had to be paid.

"Tell him to stay away from my privates." Wingate stretched out on the Italian flag, which was now a tablecloth.

The soothsayer pressed his fingertips on Wingate's temples. Ishmael's eyes were closed but Wingate's watched him antagonistically. Wingate's heart was felt, then his pelvic bone. Finally, Ishmael reached into a small pouch dangling from his waist and produced what appeared to be freshly picked tufts of ordinary grass in no way remarkable except there were no green grasses within a hundred miles.

Ishmael placed them on the forehead and told Wingate to close his eyes. Thus he did not witness a peculiar phenomenon: though there was no breeze within the cave, the tufts drifted up into Wingate's hair as if wafted there. Ishmael reported his findings to Selassie in Ethiopian, then stepped up to Wingate's head and brushed the tufts to the floor.

"He thanks you for your cooperation," said Selassie. Wingate sat up and began to speak, but Selassie asked, "Was your father a soldier?"

"Yes. Didn't I tell you?"

"That was my recollection. But I didn't tell *him*."

"Is that all he has to report? What a disappointment. What about my kids?"

A quick Ethiopian dialogue, then Selassie announced, "You shall have a son, born of war."

"Well that's fine for a start. Didn't mention any girls did he? I'd be fond of a lass too." Wingate's hollow laugh covered his shock: until the last question, none of Ishmael's investigations had anything to do with Wingate's offspring.

21

March 20, 1941

Dearest Lorna,

By now you must have received my first letter, all fourteen pages. Nothing from you yet, but your letters are probably stacking up in Khartoum. What did you think of the prophecy? A son for a start. I suggest Jonathan.

An eerie session that was with the soothsayer. He pondered over me for many minutes. That sly Selassie was using him to mystically interrogate me! Can you imagine? Wonder what he learned. I doubt if he'll tell me.

I'm very glad for having dropped Selassie off in his royal cave. He'll be my buffer with Platt, and besides his retinue would get in my way. I've moved faster without him. We have come up on Dombacha. Villagers have slipped out to us with detailed information about the garrison. We number five hundred. They number six thousand. I'll be belly-crawling up some gully to get a better look at them.

March 23

Dombacha is ours! My men are amazing: they can inch across the most rugged and open country like lizards. For hours they lay immobile in the afternoon sun. Fifty of them got within hand grenade range of the Italians before attacking at twilight, spreading utter terror with long knives.

In support I fired all the tracer ammunition we captured at Danghila. Our machine gunners can't hit a pasture from the fence but it was a spectacular show evidently appreciated by the I's. I encircled the

town slowly for as many I's as stole away were that fewer to fight
today. Or ever for that matter. A man who flees once will flee again.

I want the contagion of fear to spread down the Addis Ababa Road.
Many of my men are cutthroats; I know that and I want the Italians to
know it even better. I respect any E's wish to conduct his private war out-
side my view just as I wish to wage my war unobserved by Platt or Selassie.

Not that I've grown bloodthirsty. In fact I hope to take the next
town by ruse. Atkins knows a little Italian so I've been preparing him
to do an impersonation. Be sure to read the next episode!

Love & more love,

Orde

"There's been a morbid turn in his thoughts," Mrs. Paterson remarked
as she handed the letter back to Lorna.

"Morbid? A prediction of childbirth?"

"And cutting throats. The Italians aren't fighters—he's proving that.
I wish he were attacking the Nazis. They deserves to be slaughtered."

"The Italians were equally cruel to the Ethiopians. I quite condone
any vengeance they take. This is not the first time you've suggested a
morbid streak in Orde."

"Beg pardon?"

"Our first home—do you recall your reaction?"

Her mother laughed though Lorna did not.

"A natural reaction to my daughter setting up house in a morgue."

"Which we converted into the finest quarters at Bulford. You never
saw it before our renovation—dumps of plaster, dead wires, and in-
sulation writhing from the walls."

"What I remember is how you could never rid it of the scent of
formaldehyde. And that embalming table you used for a dish drain—
on those rare occasions when you washed dishes."

"We washed them when we needed to."

"I never saw the bottom of your sink."

"Washing dishes as they are used is nothing more than a convention.
We simply found it more efficient to do them all at once. We would
drink wine and have a rite of cleansing. A *fest*, as the Germans say."

"Bizarre. I still say so."

"Perhaps to a mind set in unthinking routines."

"One of my routines is not to use serving platters for dinner plates."

"Once. And why not? Silver grows more lustrous with use. You gave us the platters after all. Didn't you want us to use them frequently?"

"Yes, they were for you and Orde..."

"So weren't you pleased that we enjoyed them so much? More, even, than you may have intended."

"I don't begrudge you that enjoyment at all. But the silver wasn't for the orangutan."

"Baboon."

"Whatever it was that slept in the vault, and banged my platter like a tin pan. What was his name?"

"She. Bathsheba."

"Ah yes, it was the goat that was male, wasn't it?"

"We had the trimmest lawn in the army."

"What an odd couple you must have appeared to the army. But how well suited you are for each other. That has been my happiness, Lorna. Don't mistake me."

Gideon Force surged through the abandoned barricades of Dombacha to be embraced by the liberated villagers. The guerrillas looted the Italian camp with glee, but they followed Wingate's instructions to leave the telephone line uncut.

Atkins was prepared to call ahead to the next garrison but his impersonation came sooner than expected when the phone jangled.

"You ready, Cliff?"

"Hope so, sir,"

"Sound more excited, frightened."

"Right-oh...*Salute!*" He shouted Italian into the phone.

There was a short question from the other end. In Italian Atkins identified himself as a doctor who had stayed behind with the wounded. He could hear the guerrillas battering down doors elsewhere in the building. He prayed the British would control them as their propaganda had promised.

How many were there? Ten thousand at least, with aircraft. He could see them strafing the road to the rear—and artillery—could the caller hear its thunder? Atkins also saw tanks from his window. He was asked for advice.

"Retreat!" he exclaimed. "Surrender!" He pulled out the phone cord. "Where was the call from?"

"The commander at Safartak."

"I hope he believed you. He holds the Nile."

Wingate referred to the Blue Nile. It rose in Lake Tana some fifty miles beyond the Chokey Mountains, the same region in which Simonds was operating with all the difficulties involved in serving two masters: Platt, who gave him orders as a British general, and Selassie, to whom the men of Mountain Force owed unquestioned allegiance. Platt's interdiction with Simonds was not yet known to Wingate but revealed itself like treachery as Gideon Force made ready to approach the great gorge of the Nile.

What he needed to drive the Italians from the far bank was a threat to their rear by Mountain Force. He had already alerted Simonds for such a maneuver when Gideon Force left Mount Belaiya. Wingate allowed ten days to reduce Dombacha; it fell in three. He was now ahead of schedule; he radioed Selassie to have Simonds hurry up. Selassie replied that Mountain Force was ready to move behind Safartak but the British could not. Wingate took this message as some garble or another translational misunderstanding.

"I'm not interested in the damn Brits getting here from Eritrea," he fumed to the radio operator. "It's Simonds I want down here on the double."

That sentiment went out in the "Venus" report, the call sign Wingate used in communicating with Selassie: Venus because as the evening star rose each night Wingate was to call back to the cave, a promise he kept so rarely that Selassie changed the call sign to "Halley's Comet."

The reply to Venus came back with the same sense as before: Mountain Force would attempt to comply with Wingate's request but would have to do so without their British cadre. Some explanation came by way of a postscript from the emperor scathing Platt and vowing no assistance to his campaign even if the Ethiopians never received another British bullet.

Wingate was a man with a knife in his back. He went into a sputtering rage that some of his British staff took to be nearly treasonable—and may have been if only the nationality of his uniform was considered.

"They did it to me in Palestine, Atkins. Now they're doing it again. It's criminal careerism! Military malpractice!"

"Sir..."

"Do you know the greatest enemies of the Ethiopian people? The two most evil figures in the kingdom? Do you?" Wingate drew his face up to Atkins's.

"Graziani, sir."

"He's the easy one. Who's the other?"

"The Duke of Aosta."

"No, the other is Major General Sir William Platt, OBE, DCM and S-H-I-T! And of the two, Atkins, if I had to spend eternity in hell with one of them, I'd choose Graziani. He's openly evil. He appears as he is—a loathsome beast.

"Platt and his toads are that greater evil which masquerades as good. What they're after is a new colonial dominion, Atkins. There's no other way to explain their conduct, robbing me of *my own troops* at the hour of greatest need. He did everything in his power to prevent me from even raising this little army and now he steals them, literally steals them, to support his petty diversion in Eritrea."

"I think we should try to see these events in another light, sir."

"You're young. You are still capable of looking through the shades of naïveté. My eyes have been opened—it's a sordid sight."

In such moods Wingate spent more time with his Bible. In such moods he spoke less and communicated more with his menacing eyes. He consulted only himself, and none ventured to engage him in the casual conversations enjoyed by men on campaign.

He needed the time to plan as well as to brood because as he approached the Nile gorge he realized he was coming upon a challenge that would have daunted any commander in history.

22

Unassisted, Gideon Force was left with the task of breaching the last and by far the strongest barrier between the escarpment and Addis

Ababa. Even before they reached the great gorge at Safartak there were lesser strongholds to reduce if the Italians chose to fight a delaying action as they moved up more strength to defend the Nile.

Italian confusion and demoralization were now his only allies; Wingate knew he had to exploit them if the Nile were to be forced. To thwart him, the only competence required of the Italians was the demolition of the bridge at Safartak. Once that span dropped into the abyss, a single machine gun could hold off Gideon Force until the end of the war. And Safartak was still a hundred miles away.

Discouragement soon followed the disappointment of losing Mountain Force. The Italians had become skilled in the art of retreat. At Dombacha they left no serviceable vehicles with which Gideon Force could pursue them. The Ethiopians were still principally on foot with a small "cavalry" mounted on donkeys and the few remaining camels. These soon lost sight of the motorized Italians, but the Italians kept watch on Gideon Force through their omnipresent air force. Strafed and bombed regularly by day, the guerrillas could make good distance only at night.

From the reports of his air force, Colonel Torelli, the commander for western Ethiopia, began to realize he possessed superior forces. "The cat is pursuing the tiger!" he raged to his subordinates; he ordered them to turn and fight both for the honor of Italy and protection of the many Italian civilians in Addis Ababa. "If we are to hand over our swords," Torelli berated them, "it shall be to a European army who will observe the conventions of civilization."

Torelli's rear guard made its stand at Debra Markos where a tributary of the Blue Nile rushed through a gorge nearly as formidable as the one at Safartak. Using local guides, Wingate marched far upstream, where Harris with a hundred men crossed hand over hand on ropes. With only the lightest arms, Harris's force set itself in ambush behind Debra Markos as Gideon Force had done outside Danghila.

Because of the gorge, Wingate could not flush the Italians out of Debra Markos, but the same effect was attained by patriotic villagers who set fire to their homes upon a signal from Wingate. As usual, his decisive stroke came at night. The defenders of the gorge, bombarded by mortars from the front and seeing the flames nearing them from the rear, lost heart and began to pull out.

This time Wingate offered them no escape. His men were allowed to slaughter without quarter, instilling the maximum panic among the fleeing Italians. Only vehicles were spared. The other Italian commodity Wingate ordered preserved at all costs was dynamite. Miraculously, nearly a quarter ton of the explosive was found just as the flames of the burning town were close to igniting it.

The Italian engineers had planned to use the dynamite to crater the road to Safartak, for hand detonators and some firing wire were also found. These and some blasting caps were clear signals to Wingate that providence still supported Gideon Force even if the British army did not. In the flames of Debra Markos Wingate made ready to fulfill the divine design. First he demanded to know the number of captured trucks.

"Five trucks—assorted sizes," an exhausted Atkins answered.

"Five! *Exactly* the number!"

"There may be another in there." Atkins thumbed back at the conflagration. "But I'm not sending anyone in to look."

"No! Look no more. Five smooth stones, Atkins. The Lord of Hosts needed only that many. We shall require no more than He!"

"Oh, Christ."

"No, he came later. David."

"I know," said Atkins, slumping down on a case of dynamite. "David and Goliath. Five stones for the slingshot. Kill for the Lord. Burn for the Lord!" Atkins flung his hat to the ground and looked at it between his feet. "We lost good men here, Orde. This town burned itself for you. For five lorries and a hundred sticks of this fucking dynamite."

"You're very tired, aren't you?"

"I am. And you are too. Your mind burned out back on the road."

"I'd hoped to send you on tonight but I see that you should have some rest. Or maybe I should send Harris."

"He burned his hand, you know. Or do you?"

"David needed but one hand."

"What in hell's the job?"

"The only job that matters—the bridge at Safartak."

"How?"

"It shall be revealed to you. For now, collect the lorries and divide this heaven-sent explosive among them. Have Comarty come talk with me. Then gather the wopalikes."

As Wingate consulted with the demolition specialist, Atkins gathered the "wopalikes" (a name Wingate gave them in the Sudan), who were scattered around Debra Markos in the aftermath of the fighting. These were the Ethiopians whose appearance or fluency in Italian allowed them to impersonate the enemy. For this purpose, the bodies of fallen foes had been stripped of their uniforms until the wopalikes were fully outfitted.

In Khartoum Wingate had explained that impersonators would be treated as spies, not as prisoners of war. The volunteers shrugged at this possibility. None of them contemplated capture, and if that were to happen they expected to be hanged or shot anyway.

Wingate's eyes imparted his plan as intensely as his words. "Last thing before you bed down, Cliff: pick twenty-five wopalikes. Volunteers only. Tell them they'll probably all be killed. You might think about that too.

"Make sure they're all in convincing uniform—they tend to overdress, you know. And the last thing—find yourself a dead lieutenant. There should be several lying around. A captain would be better, of course, but it will really be the fit of the uniform that matters. Are you with me?"

"We're going to mix into the retreat?"

"Quite right. Should be jolly fun. I much envy you the adventure; however, I must take my satisfaction from the plan."

"You're not worried?"

"I think you can do it."

"I mean worried about us—me and the wopalikes."

"You're confused; or I am. What is it that I'm to worry about: your competence or your safety?" Atkins looked at him steadily but could not compose a reply. "Cliff, dear fellow, we should have a good long talk on the joys of warfare, and we shall, we shall, on the east bank of the Nile while we drink Torelli's wine. But for now let me tell you from my experience—and nearly a lifetime of study—that war can be no more exciting than it is now."

"I haven't been looking for more excitement."

"Enjoy it while you can, Cliff. Army life has precious little excitement. Savor what there is and remember the taste."

At Debra Markos there were twenty-six surviving wopalikes. Atkins briefly quizzed them in Italian. By and large theirs was atrocious, but little more than basic speech was expected of Italian privates anyway.

Naturally the wopalikes were either black or dusky, but then there were many Somalis to be found in the Italian army of Africa.

Moreover, the wopalikes would be under the tarps of the trucks. The most convincing were chosen as drivers or the front passengers, while the most convincing of all—Atkins—would sit beside the driver of the leading vehicle. Providence had provided once again: this time the uniform of an Italian major of engineers. That branch of the army was ideal for the mission, though the rank was a bit suspicious for a man of Atkins's youth. One other detail was less than ideal: a jagged tear just above the belt in the back of the tunic where the late major had been run through with an Ethiopian sword.

"Try to keep your back in the seat, won't you, Cliff? Now before you go, I must tell you this little story about a villain named Zobi, and how death came to him under punctured tires."

23

In the weeks after Wingate's departure, Selassie devoted himself to restoring his royal identity. A fifty-foot structure was erected at the mouth of the cave and draped with hides, converting the subterranean space into the emperor's living quarters. Outside, the wattle structure was divided into the major compartments of the royal household. The dining area was removed to a pleasant glade where a camouflage parachute formed a pavilion.

Soon administrative appendages grew around the little community: a hitching area for the animals of visitors to the king; a display of captured weapons and a proper map room; a cluster of tents for the British cadre whose blueprints created western latrines (two for the British, two for the Ethiopians, and one for the royal throne).

Selassie received his guests in the dining glade. By the end of the first week three local chiefs with dominions covering a thousand square miles rode in on horses to pay homage. In the following weeks more important barons, a few in splendid cars, traveled hundreds of dusty miles to acknowledge suzerainty. The cars were immediately offered as gifts to the king; he graciously accepted a captured Bugatti.

The stream of important royal subjects pretty much coincided with the advance of Gideon Force. As Wingate pushed south and east, the chiefs who helped him—some with guides, some with platoons of fighters—hastened to Mount Belaiya to relate the extent of their support. Several chieftains whose provinces were still occupied by the Italians sent messengers through the lines with similar pledges of loyalty.

Thus all boded well for Selassie. Ever since the Danghila ambush his fortunes had been ascendant just as his soothsayer had predicted. Selassie even received a telegram from Roosevelt saying that while the world cheers a winner, it cheers loudest for a comeback.

There was no similar sentiment expressed by the British government. Churchill was pleased, of course, by the possibility of ousting the Italians. There was precious other cheer for him during the Battle of the Atlantic, the loss of Libya, and the retreat in Greece. But his Foreign Office could not decide with what voice they should speak to Selassie.

For security reasons they did not make public his exact whereabouts. "In liberated territory in the Province of Gomuz" was the location given in the brief Foreign Office press dispatch. Whitehall alerted Sir Anthony Eden to pay a call on Selassie as soon as Platt mopped things up and invited the diplomats to take responsibility.

So everyone, including Selassie, was looking past the defeat of the Italians, projecting plans that would have been fantasy six months before. Kings, generals, and diplomats were preparing to disember the corpse of Goliath while David was still waiting to hurl the decisive stone at Safartak.

Selassie ignored the possibility of defeat at the Blue Nile. Military miracles had become the expected result from the guerrilla army. Wingate's reports told of enormous problems, but the locations from where he transmitted marked an unbroken trail of victory. Matakal, Engiabara, Burye, Mankusa, Debra Markos: a string of villages, each twenty miles closer to the capital.

Somehow Wingate would break through at Safartak; of this Selassie was sure. He had justified Selassie's every trust, something no white man had ever done.

Selassie was thus prepared to offer him command of the national army, which, with modern munitions and equipment from America, could fight shoulder to shoulder with the Allies until fascism was expelled from Africa. In this role, Wingate would become a major world figure. Selassie would permit him to establish a foreign policy toward Israel, even explore the feasibility of an alliance between the infant nation in Asia and the ancient kingdom of Africa. In the service of Selassie, Wingate's influence would be boundless.

Yet Ishmael had not found Wingate in the future of the kingdom. The soothsayer's other findings were that Wingate was a man who took God's will as his own and his own as God's; a man who might set his mortal days by the clock he wears; a man on whom the moon would smile but not always the sun. Apart from such Delphic observations, the only propitious finding was that he would have a son born of war.

That was how Wingate's own life, said Ishmael, had begun. He was a twin, a merged twin, a supernatural heritage unusual but not unknown in Abyssinian arcana. Which meant that for a while during his mother's pregnancy Wingate had been two embryos. The twins had fought, for they had arrived simultaneously from separate stars to claim the same body.

The Wingate who now walked on earth had won his first war before birth, but his rival, whose substance was reabsorbed into his mother's womb, had nearly prevailed and lived as a hermit in the recesses of his memories.

There could be no exorcism. It was not necessary: the vanquished twin retained only the power to make judgments on him. Thus Wingate lashed others when he himself was lashed. But when his twin concurred in his conduct he acted with the strength of two men, or even more than two, for each brought his own birth spirits into temporary alliance. Selassie could only watch to see when his lieutenant was in union or rebellion with himself. Beyond that precaution there was only one other indicator of the position of his soul: how he spoke with his mate. The war, however, had left Lorna far away.

So too were the families of the six British left to tend administration in Selassie's court of the cave. Captain Adams was in charge. He dealt with the chamberlain and rarely had more than a glimpse of Selassie since the emperor settled into his royal trappings. Adams regarded this development with a sigh. The chamberlain, who had nearly saved Adam's life on a ledge of the escarpment, now dealt with him

rather formally, but not unreasonably, which was how Adams regarded
a new court policy concerning private mail:

"Censorship is common in the battle areas of your army?" the chamberlain asked rhetorically. Adams innocently acknowledged this to be
so. "And mail is reviewed to ensure that no secrets are revealed?"

"Outgoing mail. Yes."

"That is now the royal policy as well."

"How do you mean?"

"Please bring letters to me henceforth."

"Do you really think that's necessary?"

"Security is necessary. We no longer move about. The Italians could
bomb us."

"So we, ah, shouldn't seal our letters."

"If done, they will be opened and resealed."

"Does that apply to mail coming in from Gideon Force?"

"Most certainly."

"Colonel Wingate's personal letters?"

"There are no exceptions."

"There would be if *he* were here."

"The contents of all letters will be respected."

"As you wish."

"Thank you, Captain Adams."

24

The Italians' stand at Debra Markos was the first indication Torelli
was going to fight. His next delay position was some thirty miles closer
to the bridges, down the winding road where a nervous lieutenant hailed
the wopalike convoy.

"Make way, lieutenant."

He was taken aback to see Atkins's rank. "Sir . . . My orders are . . ."

"Your orders are to clear the way for me at once. Have you a radio?"

"No, *Majora.*"

"How will you know when to withdraw?" A machine gun crew drew nearer when they heard the question. The answer was very much on their minds. "God save you from the Abyssinians," Atkins said gravely, and nodded to his driver, "for no one else will." The trucks spewed gravel as they tore away.

"Have you room?" the Italians shouted into the dust cloud.

Twenty miles closer to Safartak Atkins stopped for a formidable roadblock. Piles of rock across the road were well guarded by machine guns on the adjoining hills. The captain in command wore a patriotic air and saluted crisply.

"I was advised there would be no more vehicles, *Majora.*"

"As you can see, there are. Make us a path through those rocks. Caputti, assist these infantry dullards."

Sooner or later the wopalikes would have to pass muster. Upon a shout from "Caputti" they sprang from the trucks with such vigor that the Italians stared.

"Somali engineers, *Majora?*"

"There are none better. Why do you think Torelli chose us to do the bridge?"

"The *bridge,* sir?"

Atkins appeared embarrassed at having revealed an obvious fact, yet one best not stated.

"*Majora,* you are going to destroy the bridge at Safartak?"

"Lower your voice." Atkins looked impatiently at his Ethiopians, who were rolling away the last rocks. "How many men do you have here?"

"Perhaps a hundred, sir."

"Torelli's sacrifice." Atkins looked away. "The gods of war are cruel who demand such offerings of youth."

"*Majora,* is there anything...?" Atkins shook his head. "I beg you, if you can help me now.... My father is well connected."

"What is your town?"

"Taranto."

Atkins sniffed contemptuously. "I can see where your connections got you."

"I implore! My family has vast wealth. Take me with you!"

Atkins made a move toward his holster. "If I took you in this truck..."

"Yes, yes!" The captain's hand darted into his tunic and withdrew a massive roll of bills. "Here are two million lire."

"Occupation currency. Worthless."

"My father has gold!"

"You cannot desert your men."

"They are conscripts."

"They will see you leave, then flee themselves. I need time to prepare the bridge. Someone must hold back the Abyssinians for another day."

"Lieutenant Incampo," he pointed to the hill, "is an excellent leader. Strong. Brave. Please, *Majora*. I am only recently married. I will name a child for you."

"Be a *soldier*, Captain!" Atkins was genuinely furious; his hand tightened on the pistol. "Don't make me shoot you as an example to Lieutenant Incampo." The captain began to cry. "If you have any letter, I'll be glad..." Atkins said in consolation.

"Can you wait, *Majora?* Only a minute?"

Atkins shook his head. "The guerrillas are commanded by a British officer. He treats prisoners well."

"Here is my address. Please tell my family that I am a prisoner."

"Gladly."

The next Italian position was well suited for defense and manned by five hundred infantrymen commanded by Lieutenant Colonel Molina, whose professionalism Atkins did not dare to test, so he feigned extreme fatigue from what he described in mumbles as a two-day flight from the massacre at Debra Markos. Only the urgency of the mission at the bridge had enabled his incomparable Somalis to fight their way back. The bullet holes in the tarps bore testimony to their bravery.

Molina was thus convinced. He knew the Safartak bridge was to be blown, but he was in radio contact with Colonel Torelli, who would advise him in plenty of time to pull back. Should Torelli be notified of the safe arrival of his Somali demolition team? Perhaps not, Atkins suggested: the Ethiopians could overhear the message and set an ambush between Molina's position and Safartak. Besides, he would have the convoy at the bridge in a matter of hours. With expressions of patriotic resolve, the two officers took leave of each other and Atkins began the last leg of his race to the bridge.

But speed was no longer of the essence. Gideon Force would have a stiff fight when they came up on Molina's position. Atkins estimated it could take Wingate a day and a night to capture it. Therefore, the wopalikes would have to wait because the final assault on the bridge required Wingate to be in a position to support them within minutes. If Atkins arrived at the bridge too soon, Torelli might order the convoy across.

Atkins sent his best man cross country to warn Wingate what to expect from Molina; then he pulled his five trucks into a gully where he could hear the battle when it began.

Wingate meanwhile was struggling. Since the breakthrough at Debra Markos, he had averaged about three hours of sleep in twenty-four. Atkins's assistance was badly missed, Italian prisoners were a problem, and Torelli's air force continued to hound him.

The road climbed easily through another saddle nubby with rocks. The scouts took cover, awaiting his orders. By chance it was from Tafod's vantage point that Wingate chose to study the Italians' position if there was one. They'd had ample time to disguise it if they chose to fight. Unbeknownst to Wingate, the saddle ahead of him was where Atkins had first bluffed his way into the retreat. Between Gideon Force and the bridge there were a dozen such potential defenses. Wingate's tactics were reduced to guesswork as he came upon each place.

Tafod smiled as he recognized the binoculars as Wingate inched his vision along the opposing ridge. Held or abandoned? Would there be machine guns or silence if the scouts darted forward? For a moment Wingate contemplated how Tafod's life would swing on his decision. He could feel the trust of the tiny Ethiopian along with his own uncertainty.

Time—time was the precious currency Wingate must save or expend, and there was none to spare if Gideon Force was to reach the bridge in time to support Atkins, for the surprise he achieved there would be as fleeting as a string of firecrackers.

A shadow next to a rock, streaks of dirt lighter colored than the surface soil—natural or evidence of an ambush? An ambiguously shaped object—a ration can or a stone? Impressions accumulated, but his instinct was overworked, fatigued, and he could not organize them into an opinion, an opinion that would become a decision to press on or fan out and attack.

"Tafod…" Wingate's order caught in his mouth. "Tafod, take your squad up there."

"Column, sir?"

"No, skirmishers. Take care. I can't make up my mind about that saddle."

The squad darted from boulder to boulder. Behind them Gideon Force roused themselves once again to advance. A metronome began to tick over the plateau, a silent marking of the exchange of time for distance as Tafod's men entered the range of Italian weapons if any were sighted on them. Wingate's binoculars were not on his men but focused on the suspicious positions where guns would flash before their vollies reached his ears.

The landscape kept its silent watch. A vulture heaved itself into the air when Tafod crossed the saddle and waved back to Wingate.

Rifles were slung, the advance pushed on. Now Wingate squinted into the sky, watching for the dot that would grow into a plane and hum and drone before it circled and attacked. No ammunition to fire back, only rocks for protection. Somewhere ahead a saddle would be defended. If the aircraft strafed while the Ethiopians charged, the vultures would feast.

When Wingate set about to flank the first roadblock, his instructions were misunderstood; the maneuver went off badly and cost Gideon Force a dozen men painfully wounded. They could only be left to be picked up by the animal trains where there was little more than first aid. All the while, Wingate continued to fume fruitlessly about the loss of Mountain Force.

He scribbled his broodings on paper that was beginning to tear from frequent foldings and unfoldings.

31 March

Italian bombers again. Knocked out one of my precious trucks. Would have sent back the wounded but now must wait to capture another one. Some fever. Looking forward to proper treatment in AA.

1 April

Morning again, my dearest. "Dawn in russet mantle clad..." I always think of you at dawn when even the war catches its breath.

A dawn is its own reward. I've seen every dawn since we left Khartoum. Would you like that name for our first daughter?

2 April

Shaking last night. I've got a proper case. Things going awry. E's never learn anything permanently. Must be retaught with their own blood.

3 April

Moving again after a sloppy skirmish. One of Atkins's men came back to tell us we've got a fight up ahead. Very tired, but a fight's what I need—gets all my resources up. Like a ride to the hounds. Bashi said I called to you last night as if we were riding together. Have I always been delirious about you?

4 April

Took what should be the last Italian strongpoint before Safartak. You're much younger than I. Dead Italians lying about. They're your age. Felt like I'd been killing your peers. Handsome devils, some of them, but how soon the body decays. Morbid day, I suppose. Death seems to be announcing a festival ahead.

6 April

Atkins off for the bridge. I shall soon see Safartak. My fever's up but so are my expectations! We are on the eve of our greatest battle.

For now,

Orde

25

A great battle was far from Torelli's thoughts. He expected little difficulty in withdrawing his five thousand men behind the Nile. Once the bridge disappeared (an entire engineers' company had been working on this task for a week), he could walk away and watch the guerrillas shake their fists at him.

The war was already lost on the other fronts. Platt's divisions, assisted decisively by detachments of Mountain Force, had lumbered down from Eritrea, around Lake Tana, and routed the listless Italians from Dessie, the last important road junction northeast of Addis Ababa. Platt's Spitfires now ruled the air over all Ethiopia, so Torelli had lost track of Gideon Force. This unintended favor was Platt's single contribution to the attack on Safartak, an attack about which he knew no more than Torelli.

Cunningham's divisions were virtually at the gates of Addis Ababa, with only the British reluctance to destroy the capital keeping them from marching in. The Italian commander in chief, the duke of Aosta, proved a far more able negotiator than he was a general. He kept Cunningham busy bargaining over terms of capitulation while concealing the collapse of Italian resistance.

On Torelli the duke bestowed the most important mission of the crumbling Italian empire—to ensure that surrender would be only to the British. At all cost the Ethiopians were to be prevented from regaining control of the government. Therefore, Torelli's force would have to hold the Blue Nile while the British fanned out into the rest of the country to receive the Italian surrender. In this, the duke, Platt, and Cunningham were in an unstated accord: Ethiopia was to be a campaign in World War II, not the first defeat of colonialism.

It was disquieting for Torelli to hear Molina sign off the radio as he began his withdrawal in front of Gideon Force. Molina had fought mightily, he told Torelli, but the guerrillas seemed to have intimate knowledge of his defenses and were about to envelope his flanks. Torelli ordered the retreat be orderly; in no event should Molina allow himself to be cut off, for at the first sign of the Ethiopians the bridge would be destroyed.

Molina's force needed no such reminders; at dawn they were in headlong flight for the bridge. Wingate's mortars urged them on while his mule cavalry slipped through the gullies parallel to the road.

Horns blowing, Atkins's five trucks wove through the stragglers, powdering them in a plume of dust. He drove through the confused retreat until he rounded a curve and came upon the bridge.

Its defenses seemed to cancel Wingate's plan. On a bluff above the far bank were antiaircraft guns and two tanks held back like watchdogs by the plunging shadow of the gorge. On the near bank, twelve machine gun pits looped around the bridge.

Day and night, mules, vehicles, and Italian soldiery had been streaming across the Nile. The steel girder span was the sturdiest structure Atkins had seen since Khartoum. A glance at its abutments showed them to be packed and wired for demolition.

A Sicilian captain hailed Atkins's truck. Traffic backed up as he inspected it. In the back were four soldiers who did not awake. Since they were engineers, the captain gave no thought to the dynamite or why it was covered with a pyramid of sandbags. Traffic was honking, Atkins was rude, and the captain was harried.

"Where's Borsolino?" Atkins demanded.

"Who?"

"The engineer commander!"

The captain pointed to a staff car on the far bank, and Atkins roared ahead. His other four trucks stopped at the near side of the bridge, the occupants apparently asleep; the drivers got out and crawled under the axles as if to inspect them.

Atkins searched for an oil truck and found one in a gully across the Nile. The driver was asleep.

"I have four trucks that need oil. Follow me!"

The driver roused himself lazily. "I cannot recross without orders from Lieutenant Riera."

"He's at the trucks. Get moving!"

Atkins's sergeant climbed in with the driver. Both vehicles started back across the bridge, boring through the fleeing traffic. Shouts and horns blared in angry cacophony as a staff car pulled Atkins over. A military police officer began to upbraid him. From among the wopalike trucks a knife cartwheeled through the air and buried in the officer's spine.

He twitched and fell in an instant of silence, then whistles and alarms pierced the air like wind filling a vacuum. Jittery officers drew their pistols though their men trudged on in desperate numbness. In their retreat it seemed murder was understandable if it unblocked the bottleneck.

A detachment descended from the hills with orders from Torelli to summarily execute the murderer. Mutiny seemed to rise from the gorge like a draft as the tanks lowered their sights on the chaos at the west abutment. Suddenly a flare spurted high into the air from Atkins's trucks, its green-colored streamers visible for miles.

The oil truck lurched forward, its driver dead from a pistol shot to the temple. The wopalike trucks roared onto the bridge, pulling up side by side at the middle. The Ethiopians shot out their tires, then raced for both ends of the span.

"The enemy!" Torelli screamed. His tanks swiveled their turrets in confusion—they could not tell friend from foe in the melee.

On deflating tires the undercarriages settled toward the roadbed, long detonators suspended below them. In quick sequence the five trucks exploded, the blasts directed downward by the sandbag pyramids piled on the dynamite.

The explosions scattered Torelli's infantry like popcorn. The bridge shuddered, its roadbed gouged and impassable to vehicles.

The craters still smoked as the wopalikes scrambled for the demolition wires. Atkins ignited the oil truck. Its smoke swirled over the bridge, masking the abutment where he crouched. Only a dozen of his men were still alive, but hidden in the wreckage they could fight on unless the Italians organized an attack.

In the machine gun pits the Italians started organizing. Sergeants passed down orders for the attack that would take them to safety across the bridge. Atkins glanced at his watch—Wingate was late. In minutes he would be too late. Then a sprinkle of mortar fire sprouted dust around the machine gun pits.

It was a salvo from the advance platoons of Gideon Force set in motion by Atkins's green flare. The Italian machine guns swiveled to meet the new threat while Torelli's engineers hastily planted mines on the road leading away from the east bank. He called for artillery fire from miles away where the gunners had no view of the deadly confusion. Overhead came a sound like tearing paper, ending in bursts killing Ethiopians and Italians alike.

Torelli's barrage, the smudgy column of smoke, and the faint staccato of small arms urged Gideon Force toward the bridge, where they fanned out around the machine guns surrounding Atkins.

These Italians, like Atkins, found themselves fighting in two directions. They were not up to it. White undershirts waved above the machine gun pits. Atkins turned his attention on Torelli's men as they formed for a belated attack from the east.

They were stopped by British bullets cracking over Atkins's head, spurting dust on the east bank. He looked back down the road. Somewhere among the riddled trucks, dead donkeys, and contorted corpses the guerrillas were invisibly advancing.

It had been less than an hour since a knife opened the battle for the bridge. It was about to end as Harris blew a whistle launching a hundred whooping, sword-waving warriors in the sort of charge they loved. Harris had promised that if they followed British tactics until they reached the bridge they could charge across like Ethiopians. Harris's jaw dropped when they did. He told Wingate, "It was like the nineteenth century fought the twentieth—and won!"

Atkins waved Harris's first squad forward onto the bridge; they were decimated before they reached the craters. The survivors took up fire to cover the second squad, which reached the far abutments.

A scout car screeched to a stop. Wingate rolled to the ground. "Cliff—knew I'd find you here!"

26

The fury of Torelli's artillery was his grumbling exit. His army slunk away from Gideon Force never again to turn and give battle. When the heights had been swept of Italian spotters, even the artillery stopped.

"Sorry I couldn't save the roadbed," said Atkins as his hand was bandaged.

"Small matter. We'll pick up some vehicles on the far side. Come on. Let's see what Torelli left us."

They strolled across as their troops in single file sped down the edges of the bridge that was their prize. Harris grabbed Atkins in a bear hug as his troops began to praise God in falsetto.

At the smoldering craters Wingate and Atkins paused to crouch by the bodies of the two wopalikes who had held back Torelli's counterattack.

"Know their names?"

"He was called Louie. Drove the second truck. You should have seen them go for the abutments, Orde. Twelve of 'em. Only these two got back."

"No braver troops in the world."

"If these blokes didn't get the wires, we didn't get the bridge."

"Twelve you say? We must get their names. When Selassie sees what they did, he'll raise them a monument."

"I'll want to be here when he does." They continued across the bridge past a leg dangling in the superstructure and other litter of death. "My head's still swirling."

"And so shall Platt's when we beat him to Addis Ababa."

"Think we can, sir?"

"Did I think we could capture this bridge?"

"I just hope the Lord provides some lorries. Now there's a nice one." They had reached the end of the bridge. "Let me see if I can get it running." Atkins began to jog toward the truck.

"Probably needs petrol, Cliff."

Wingate looked away as a messenger arrived from Harris up the road. Atkins was halfway to the truck when the dirt erupted under his foot. The explosion was small and efficient: a German "shoe" mine designed to maim rather than kill. Atkins's foot was gone and the stump shattered through mid shin. He fell to the ground staring at the new end of his leg.

"Stay where you are!" Wingate shouted.

"Oh God..."

"Press the artery!" Wingate removed his belt as he carefully fol-

lowed Atkins's footprints. Where there was one mine there were surely
more.

Wingate looped his belt below Atkins's knee to form a tourniquet.

"I...I lost ma' leg."

"Stretcher!"

There was none to be found. Wingate and two Ethiopians carried
him to safety, slowly walking backward in their footprints. On the
road Atkins began to babble.

"I blew off a man's leg at Debra Markos, aye?"

"You'll walk again."

"Now I got me own blown off. God's work," he gasped.

"God provides for his servants."

"I lost it. I lost it..."

Atkins turned ashen as he lapsed into shock. He would not let go
of his tattered trouser. Wingate treated his lesser wounds as Gideon
Force continued to swing by on the road. Medics were scarce but eventually one appeared from the column.

Atkins was carried to the shade of an abutment. The truck he was
about to examine was readied to take him and the other seriously
wounded to the rear and out of the war. As he revived with blood
plasma, Atkins grew fascinated by the legs of the men marching by.

"A leg for a bridge," he said dopily. "Is that a bargain, Colonel?"

Wingate was slow to answer. "It all depends on one's point of view,
doesn't it?"

"What's yours?"

"It must be different from yours at the moment."

"Aye. I think I'm bein' punished for enjoyin' the war."

"Did you ever think about the price?"

"Sure, I knew there was a price." In spite of Wingate's gesture
Atkins rose on his elbows. "But I never expected to pay it. Aye?"

"Don't, Cliff."

"You think I'd swapped me leg for a bridge?"

"You were ready to give your life."

"That's different."

"It's..."

"If I'd been killed I wouldn't have to live with the trade...."

"You wouldn't have made the trade?"

"God no!" Atkins subsided once more. His truck slowly moved
out onto the road; Wingate walked beside it.

"I'm putting you in for the Victoria Cross."

"Bugger the Victoria," said Atkins hoarsely. "You got your bridge. I lost my leg. You win. I lose. Winners go on to the next round."

"Cliff, somewhere we must talk about this. You'll have a whiskey instead of plasma." Wingate stopped as his scout car roared up. "We'll see how we're thinking then."

Wingate saluted him; Atkins was too weak to return the farewell. They were never to see each other again.

In 1946 Atkins returned once more to the bridge as the guest of honor when Selassie unveiled a bronze tablet at the east abutment and re-named the span "The Bridge of Twenty-six Heroes," among which Atkins and five of his wopalikes were the only survivors.

27

In a new dress uniform Selassie paced and smoked nervously as the chirp of the radio went on with the longest message ever received from Gideon Force.

The battle and the casualties were briefly reported, then followed the closing passage which caused Selassie to drop his cigarette on the floor:

> I shortly expect to break all remaining Italian resistance in central Ethiopia. Nothing stands between Gideon Force and AA except British duplicity. Platt has ordered me to halt so that Cunningham's Kenyans can liberate your capital. Therefore I urge you to bring the largest following of warriors you can assemble. Bring them to Fiche. Summon all your chiefs there so your entry into AA surpasses any ceremony the British generals can contrive. Orde.

Selassie's progress to Safartak was hardly more rapid than Wingate's had been. Dombacha, Debra Markos—all the villages where battles had been fought delayed the royal progress with proud tours of sites where Ethiopians had conquered and Italians had fallen.

At Engiabara the emperor's convoy met the trucks returning from Safartak. For the wounded who could not rise in greeting, the tarps of their trucks were rolled back to view the king. Selassie bestowed medals on each and gave a blessing for one who had died en route.

Atkins was carried to the former headquarters of the Italian commandant, to dine with the emperor and drink Tuscan wine, and narrate how the battle plan had developed.

"Orde told me to send half my boys to the far bank, and that's exactly how many it took," said Atkins. "He told us what wires to look for and those were the ones that mattered. He told me where to find an oil truck, and there it was. He told us what to expect from Torelli and that's just the way they reacted. Like he'd seen a movie of the battle before it happened."

"Are you as impressed by his political foresight?"

Atkins quaffed his wine. "Glad you asked, Your Highness. Orde's going to start his second war if you don't watch him."

"He said he's received orders from Platt to halt outside the capital."

"Orders never bother him. He's not acknowledged one from Platt."

"Yet I believe he's loyal to me."

"Absolutely."

"That puzzles me. He could be gaining great favor with Platt. Why should he side so fervently with me unless he wishes to remain in my service?"

Atkins looked away. "I probably shouldn't say it but I think he'll only stay with you till final victory here."

"Thank you for being frank with me. I've seen other things that show you are right."

Two hundred miles ahead, Wingate was savoring victory at the last mountain village before the road from the escarpment descended to the capital. This village was Fiche, where he had requested his rendezvous with the emperor. Fiche fell without a fight. Indeed, the only problem the Italians presented were the numbers in which they surrendered. Gideon Force had no provisions for them so they were simply disarmed and sent on toward Addis Ababa where Wingate hoped they would impede the progress of the British.

He began collecting the swords of Italian officers; the pile grew on the rear seat of his scout car. His prize was from the household staff of the duke of Aosta, whose personal sword, a gift from Mussolini, now awaited presentation to Selassie.

The emperor's now splendid retinue approached Fiche. First came the outriders representing every major tribe in the realm; then, as flank guards, came miles of fierce horsemen with ancient arms. On the road itself was a legion of captured Italian officers shuffling sullenly like slaves of a Roman conqueror. These unlucky captives had appealed to Wingate to spare them the humiliation but he ignored them.

Following the prisoners of war was the Ethiopian infantry which had recently rallied to their emperor. Gideon Force watched their approach with some contempt, for the newcomers had seen no fighting. This column halted before entering Fiche and drew to the side of the road in two ranks that stretched to the horizon. Through these ranks the emperor would pass before reaching the outskirts of the village where Gideon Force formed his guard of honor.

All these arrangements Wingate and Selassie worked out by couriers. Selassie agreed to the final episode as well, a procession of sixty miles to his palace, where his agents were preparing the city for his arrival. Addis Ababa was now in British hands, occupied by both Platt's and Cunningham's troops, but before they could install a provisional government, Selassie would make his presence felt.

The emperor added one additional touch without Wingate's knowledge. Rather than drive into Addis Ababa in an Italian touring car, he would ride like previous emperors—on a white Arabian stallion.

As he changed to his new mount, he gave an unexpected order summoning his soothsayer. Ishmael was far back in the parade; by the time he reached his lord, Selassie was impatient to continue.

"What have you learned of Wingate?"

"He does not reveal himself to his mate."

"Nothing in his letters?"

"There has been only one. It shows only his sickness, Your Highness, though translation may cloud what has been told me by the chamberlain."

"Sickness?"

"Fever."

"Nothing else?"

"He does not understand himself so he can reveal little to others."

"Will he serve me?"

"He has."

"His fortunes?"

"Separate from yours."

"Mine are to prosper."

"His will not. His death will be in the land of his birth."

"Do you know where he was born?" asked Selassie, astonished.

"No, sire."

Selassie mounted his steed amid new cheers; soon he reached a rise in the road above Fiche where, his chieftains arrayed behind him, the emperor approached his reunion with Gideon Force.

Artillery salutes began to boom. Drawn up in disciplined ranks, Gideon Force could not restrain themselves when Selassie raised his hat to them. Rifles old and new discharged in a wild display over the wreckage of the Italian army.

Wingate stood in front of his newly polished scout car. When Selassie acknowledged him, he made a sweeping salute with Aosta's sword, then held it up, pommel at his chin, till the emperor drew rein in front of him.

"Your Majesty!" Wingate thundered for all Ethiopia to hear—and the small arms stopped. "Gideon Force awaits your orders."

Selassie's small figure drew up in the saddle as he shouted his reply:

"As Gideon Force has led the attack for five hundred miles, *we* now command you to lead us to our palace in *Addis Ababa*."

The moment the Ethiopians heard the name they understood, a stupendous roar of approval and gunplay rolled down the valley. Some citizens of the capital claimed to have heard it. It rolled away quickly like a thunderclap, for Wingate's answer was awaited.

"We shall obey our emperor!" More wild cheering broke out but stilled for his next words. "We present Your Majesty with the sword of the duke of Aosta."

Wingate snapped the pommel to his hip and marched up to Selassie's horse to hand him the sword, but the emperor gestured to throw it up to him instead. It soared; Selassie caught it by the pommel, then stood erect in his stirrups to brandish the sword over his head.

It waved high in the air; he rotated it in all directions for the multitudes to see—then all the emotion of liberation broke free as he snapped the blade on the crown of his saddle.

Once more he held the sword aloft, a broken half in each hand, then flung them to the ground.

The cheering, now mixed with tears, continued as Selassie dismounted to embrace Wingate. As they trooped the lines of Gideon Force, Selassie whispered:

"Orde, dear fellow, you must ride this beast the rest of the way."

"Sire, as you can see..." Wingate gestured to his shorts.

"Sacrifice once more for me, please. Tonight in my palace I shall make amends."

28

The procession, with Wingate now leading it on the white horse, wound down the final hill into the outskirts of Addis Ababa. Gideon Force marched three abreast before their king. On the flanks the outriders fired into the air like heralds sounding trumpets of arrival.

This spectacle approached a British outpost. The lieutenant in command studied the parade through his binoculars, then ran to his radio. He had difficulty making his transmission clear as the citizens of Addis Ababa began pouring onto the road.

Colonel Appleby was Platt's liaison officer to General Cunningham's headquarters. For most of the morning the phones had been silent but now they began to jangle simultaneously.

"Appleby here. Oh dear. Yes. Yes. Yes. Pay him all honors. We can't risk an incident. No, protocol will be down shortly. And then of course the general will call. Quite. Carry on."

Taking a deep breath, Appleby knocked on Cunningham's door. "Well, sir, those small arms were just what we suspected. The Lion of Judah has returned."

With the emperor.

The procession to Addis Ababa. (*Courtesy Imperial War Museum.*)

"Get me a copy of that signal we sent Wingate," said Cunningham. Appleby already had it in his hand. "Thank you." Cunningham reread it like a judge reexamining critical evidence. "Advise General Platt—flash precedence. Make sure there's no trouble clearing his plane into the airfield."

Platt's plane, a converted Lancaster bomber, was en route to Nairobi for a courtesy call on the governor general of Kenya. Upon receiving Cunningham's message the plane turned back to Addis Ababa.

Because Platt was the overall British commander in Ethiopia, Cunningham was waiting for him as the bomber taxied to a stop. An exchange of salutes and the generals were off to Cunningham's headquarters where they consulted in front of a huge street map on which the principal thoroughfare to the royal palace had been labeled "Probable Route." Platt held forth with venom:

"You were right to recall me. If you had seen the havoc in Khartoum when he arrived *there*. . . ." He glanced over to Hawthorne, who looked up as if to heaven. "And that wasn't in his capital. It was in *mine!*"

"Frankly I'm not quite as concerned," said Cunningham. His officers blanched and Platt's men drew themselves up. "A little spectacle seems quite in order," Cunningham continued, unruffled. "After all, they've just beaten a modern European army, liberated their country, and reinstalled their exiled king. Seems a little merrymaking is..."

"Alan, I circled the city twice before I landed."

"I noticed."

"Those were not merrymakers spilling out into the streets."

"My troops were also received most warmly when we took the city last week."

"Every Ethiopian now has two guns: the one he was hiding from the Italians and the one he nicked from the Italians when they surrendered. The population of Addis Ababa is an *armed mob*. They outnumber our troops about twenty to one, and they nearly outgun us man for man."

"General, we are *allies* of the Ethiopians. In the campaign they operated under your command."

"Did they now! Hawthorne, how many orders did we send—that is, how many 'requests for cooperation' did we tender to the emperor?"

"Fourteen, sir."

"And how many were obeyed?"

"Nil."

"Hadn't realized," said Cunningham.

"You were coming up from the other direction."

"But didn't you have a direct channel to Wingate?"

Platt laughed drily. "Yes, dear Wingate. I believe you've tried to communicate with him yourself. What success?"

Platt was interrupted by a burst of rapid fire. "I say, isn't that a machine gun?" The others listened intently but Cunningham seemed unperturbed. "Alan, is that not *machine gun* fire we're hearing?"

"Mmm. Sounds like it. Seems to be from the northwest side of town."

"I did empower you to preserve law and order in Addis Ababa."

"General Platt, I do not feel that either life or property is endangered by this outpouring of joy and freedom. All the wild gunfire we're hearing is going out into the air. If I have a concern, it is for some random passing aircraft."

"Your optimism served you well in battle, Alan. However, in the circumstances of *civil insurrection* it should have a new factual basis."

"Insurrection?"

"Tony." Platt walked to the window as Hawthorne explained:

"Our last instruction to Wingate was for him to keep the emperor out of Addis Ababa till you consolidated military government here."

"Why do you hold Wingate responsible?"

"From agent reports we know that Gideon Force received the emperor's entourage at Fiche this morning."

Platt turned back to the discussion. "Alan, you told Wingate the same thing, didn't you—keep Selassie out?"

"Yes I did. That was my only message to him."

"You may as well have asked the Pope to stay out of the Vatican. And speaking of Italians, how do you propose to protect them?"

"From what?"

"From the rage of revenge that will probably sweep this city in the wake of the emperor's arrival."

"We've had no instances of atrocities against the Italians."

"You've not had to share your authority with the emperor in this matter."

"You expect him to decree death to the Italians?"

"He need issue no decrees. He can do everything behind our back. He simply lets it be known he would not be displeased to see Italian blood running in the streets. It would be a popular political move for him and could be accomplished by a nod of his head."

"We shouldn't be surprised if Gideon Force is rather anxious for some bloodletting," Hawthorne added.

Platt nodded and continued, "Consider the consequences of a massacre here. Our whole war effort against Hitler and Mussolini is based on the moral sterling of our cause. It is the fascists who slaughter the helpless, not we.

"Think of the reaction in America with its large Italian minority if there were a massacre here. *We* are responsible, Alan. What I'm saying is that I will back you 100 percent if you rearm certain reliable cadres of the Italian army. Their military police would be a good place to start."

"What!"

"It would not be unprecedented, General Cunningham," Hawthorne interjected. "In the Middle East during the last war—when safety against retaliatory massacre was threatened...."

"Our professional fate is as much at stake as the Italians' lives," Platt said as if in conclusion.

"Gentlemen, I can't believe what I'm hearing."

"Hear those machine guns, Alan. Think of the alternatives. Do you want your troops to defend the Italians? Or shall they defend themselves? Would you like a shootout with Gideon Force?"

"Wouldn't mind seeing that," Hawthorne muttered.

Cunningham rose from his seat. "It is to Gideon Force that I look for the control you have despaired of. I have never met Colonel Wingate...."

"Acting colonel," Platt corrected him.

"Perhaps acting major, sir," Hawthorne added.

"It wouldn't matter if he were a lieutenant. He is an officer in His Majesty's army."

"To which monarch are you referring?" Platt sneered.

"I refer to George the Sixth, King of England, your sovereign, mine, and Wingate's. He wears a British uniform."

"We're not even sure of that," said Platt.

"Will you grant that he holds a commission in the same army as you and I? No doubt he has been a great trial for you."

"Soon it will be my turn to try him."

"Unless he turns coat completely," said Hawthorne.

"In which case, Alan, you may have to capture him."

"This is simply incredible. I hadn't any idea."

"You were immersed in your campaign."

"I knew of Wingate's doings. He drew off great numbers of Italian troops who otherwise would have opposed both you and me."

"True."

"He was far more successful than anyone ever expected."

"Granted."

"One of my pilots reconnoitered the Italians' position at Safartak. Thought it would be impossible for a force ten times as strong as Wingate's to break through."

"I don't doubt it."

"Why we used to give a cheer whenever we got news of his victories—maybe the greatest of which was scaling the escarpment in the first place. General Platt, I'm not one to judge a man on the say-so of others. Deeds speak louder than pillory, and Wingate's deeds have been extraordinary."

Hawthorne smiled. Platt sat down before he spoke.

"I've been very severe talking about him today. I started with an opinion quite similar to yours. He hadn't proved his military abilities at the time but one could sense the almost mystical forces that animated him. Though he deceived me from the start, I tried to sympathize with his single-minded demands. His requests for support were preposterous, believe me.

"Well, I'm not going to detail the change of mind I experienced concerning the person of Orde Wingate. At present he is a threat to us—to you and to me and, more importantly, to the best interests of Great Britain's war effort. . . . Yes?"

"Nonetheless," said Cunningham, "I propose to make every effort to gain, and if need be, command his cooperation to preserve law and order here."

"That's what I *want* you to do."

"Good. I will extend to him the laurels of victory and the olive branch of peace."

"Forget the laurels. If I know Wingate—and I think I do now—he will trumpet his victories himself."

"Then I will echo them. What I would like to do now is go out and meet the emperor's procession."

"I suppose that would be good manners. Make an excuse for me, would you please? I really must get on to Nairobi. And, Alan, take a strong bodyguard with you."

"Shall I alert a tank platoon, General Cunningham?" Appleby asked.

"Thank you, no. Alert my driver."

"I won't have your blood on my hands," said Platt. The two generals' eyes met. They were conscious of the presence of their staff and how unseemly it would be for one general to overrule the other in such a personal matter.

"I ensure my own safety," said Cunningham. "I trust that is a prerogative of my command."

"In this case alone it is not," said Platt, lowering his eyes. "My apologies, Alan."

Cunningham flushed. "How big a 'bodyguard' then?"

"Take that tank platoon. And at least a company of mounted infantry in armored cars."

"Christ, it'll look like I'm going out to meet Rommel."

"Rommel and Wingate have much in common."

"And if I bring him to heel?"

"Get him out of Ethiopia. Use any aircraft including mine. Ship him off to Cairo. I've requested a board of inquiry there."

"General Platt, I ask your permission to retain Wingate temporarily as a liaison to Selassie's court. He would be an immense help in so many ways, not the least of which would be the situation with the Italians. Gideon Force will follow his orders. They could be a very stabilizing influence."

"You're overruled, Alan. Wingate is to be dispatched to Cairo as fast as an aircraft can fly. Once you capture him his days in Ethiopia are over."

29

Wingate was experiencing an intoxication known to few men. At the very head of the triumphal procession he was the focus for the tumultuous emotion of the crowd. The rest of the world would have its ecstasy of victory four years later, but that day in the early spring of 1941, while the Axis powers prevailed everywhere else, Wingate had conquered.

Each time he raised his battered pith helmet, the multitude roared. Praise and rejoicing sounded with every hoofbeat.

To such adulation Wingate slowly succumbed. Lawrence had never been so treated by Arabs, nor had Clive by the Indians. Save Wellington, no British historical figure whom Wingate could recall had been so embraced by the people of another nation, and none by another race. His belligerent expression, which everyone seemed to remember from the time he reached Khartoum, gradually melted in the warmth of universal admiration.

In such a glow he approached the palace, remembering how Selassie had described it. He was almost upon the honor guard before the sight of British uniforms broke his reverie. The British regulars had done their share, Wingate would admit, and had a perfect right to be part of the celebration, yet Wingate felt little emotion at seeing his countrymen and fellow soldiers again.

An unfamiliar general stepped forward with courtly grace. Wingate rendered him a sweeping saber salute; he returned it perfectly and stepped to the door of Selassie's car.

"Your Majesty, on behalf of George VI and General Sir William Platt, I welcome and restore you to the royal palace of your realm."

Selassie returned the salute quickly and stepped from the car. "Thanks. You are General Cunningham?"

"At your service, sir."

"Please accompany us. Orde, how are your bare legs?"

Wingate dismounted painfully. "I wish you'd told me we'd be exchanging mounts. General Cunningham, sir."

"Wingate." The British officers shook hands.

To applause from the crowd, the three ascended marble stairs to an immense vestibule. Selassie turned for a parting wave.

"Our loyal subjects: from this hour we declare three days of thanksgiving, prayer, festival, and holiday."

The cheering swelled in waves as his words were repeated back through the crowded blocks of the city. Platt at the airfield thought mayhem had broken out.

Inside the splendid palace, Ethiopian officials, retainers, and British staff in ranks of protocol awaited Selassie's entry with a dignified surprise party. Polite applause greeted him; Selassie glanced around, then spoke a hard word to his chamberlain, who shrugged his rejection of responsibility. The emperor was in no mood for a formal reception, and so the greeters mingled amid canapés and champagne.

"Liberated champagne, Your Majesty," said Cunningham as he offered the first glass. "Compliments of Sir William."

"Thoughtful."

"May I propose a toast?"

"All in good time. Let joy precede protocol in our palace."

"Indeed. May I know your wishes as to a reinvestiture ceremony?"

"There shall be none. We have never ceased to be king."

"Quite so. Sir William would be grateful to know if there will be other festivities."

"Look around you for festivities. Platt can come to any of them."

Cunningham glanced at what was becoming a noisy party. "Sir William was inquiring so that he could arrange a state dinner at an early occasion."

"Where is he?"

"Called away by the governor general of Kenya. He sends apologies with his congratulations and his promise to return as soon as possible."

"He need not hurry."

"Your arrival was somewhat unexpected. Nevertheless, Sir William is most eager to renew acquaintances with you."

"We see. Orde!" he called out over a growing hubbub. "You will

stay here tonight and I . . . we'll have a doctor examine you in the morning."

"Your gracious Majesty," Wingate replied, moving closer so Selassie
would not have to raise his voice.

"And we've reserved quarters for you at my headquarters," said
Cunningham pleasantly.

"Anywhere with sheets."

"You are our guest tonight," said Selassie. "Plan to stay at least a
week before we talk about returning you to your countrymen."

"Your servant."

"Let me introduce you to my operations officer, Wingate. He'll
need a prompt debriefing from you. Oh, Cooper . . ."

A smartly turned out colonel stepped forward. "Yes, sir." He knew
what his job was; he turned to it at once. "Wingate," he said, "how
are you?"

"Hello."

Selassie was drawn away by dignitaries bringing tribute. As he inspected a casket of jewels, Italian musicians struck up a Strauss waltz.
With relief the conductor noted that no offense was taken at the music
of an Axis country. Meanwhile Cunningham and Cooper flanked Wingate, who seemed to float above the cocktail conversation around him.

Cunningham smiled as he noticed Wingate's chafed legs. "Cooper
can see that you get a proper uniform in exchange for a history of your
campaign." Wingate smiled distractedly. "My God, I'd heard you were
a horseman. How could you have ridden from Fiche in your shorts?"

"A royal decision, sir."

"We'll fix him up," said Cooper briskly. "Pop in around 0700
please."

"I'll hardly be sober then."

"No matter. Come as you are. . . ."

They were interrupted by the emperor. "Orde. Orde!" he called.
"Come meet Sultan Einadine. And look who's here!"

"Simonds!"

The commanders of Gideon Force and Mountain Force embraced
among a throng of well-wishers. Cunningham and Cooper stood back.

"They've been through a lot," said Cunningham quietly.

"They've put Platt through a lot. Do you think he sees me as being from Platt's camp, sir?"

Cunningham ignored the question. "I hate to part him so abruptly from his wartime comrades. He has a soldier's bond with them."

"Hawthorne said we may have to kidnap him."

"That you may. I'm moved by this man, Cooper."

"With all respect, sir, I must move *him*. I'll bet my rations there's a signal from Platt on my desk asking when Wingate's plane departed for Cairo."

Cunningham watched approvingly as the guests lionized Wingate. "The taste of total victory, Cooper, is a nectar few of us will sip. And at this moment he can rightfully quaff a full measure."

"Speaking of full measures, sir..."

Cooper alluded to the entrance of a flight of dancing girls as the violinists gave way to drummers and native reed players. What began as a celebration progressed to a revel. Outside, Addis Ababa throbbed to a joyous cacophony.

Wingate too was learning abandon. The chamberlain sent a dusky, superbly proportioned dancer to ambush him. Like the Italian commander at Debra Markos, he found no avenue of retreat.

"I've asked her to show you the palace," Selassie winked as she swept him away. "She'll introduce you to my special night squad."

Champagne spilling from his glass, Wingate reeled down a vast marble hall as the dancer gyrated around him. A servant opened a door. Wingate peeked in.

"Hello. What's this?"

The dancer drew him into a chamber of hedonism conceived by Italian imagination to display the wealth of a looted kingdom. The room's sumptuous appointments were lost on Wingate as the dancer slipped behind a gossamer screen where he could see her strip in silhouette. Thus distracted, he barely noticed the entrance of four other nymphs selected for the variety of their beauty.

He never heard the door close behind him. Outside the servant remained in attendance. It was unlikely that more champagne would be needed, for Wingate's chamber was well stocked, but if he ever hungered for more of the banquet or if hashish could heighten his senses, the servant was there to fetch it.

30

Wingate awoke as he always did—at the first light of dawn. He groaned to realize his body's habit had not changed with his transformed circumstances. He would have relapsed into sleep, but one of his recent acquaintances was also awake and eyed him coyly. He checked his body for a response.

"It's no use, my dear. I'd need a splint."

She understood no English but smiled, swirled a cloak around her, and stole away. One of her colleagues began snoring. Wingate clapped his hands.

"Thank you, gentle maidens. Thank you very much." They awakened quickly and looked to perceive his desire.. "Thank you one and all."

Exchanging giggles, the dancers scampered out into the hall and departed to another quarter of the palace. When they opened the door, Wingate saw a breezy colonnade facing east, where the tints of dawn were seeping through the mountains. Sleep could wait for a few moments as he took in another Ethiopian sunrise from his new setting.

Beside him was a marvelous goblet heavy with jewels. A samovar stood next to the cushions on which he had slept. It was hot with a mint tea that both settled the stomach and cleansed the head. A richly embroidered caftan and supple sandals had been laid out for him. A scent of frankincense rose from his skin; sometime during the night he had been annointed with exotic oils.

Wingate eased himself out onto the long porch. Below him in the courtyard a fountain murmured. He leaned against the marble rail, listening to early birdsong; then, yawning with contentment, he left the goblet on the rail as he returned to his chamber and its cushions.

*   *   *

The reception area of the palace was strewn with debris of celebration.
A few servants slowly cleaned up. They found one reveler sleeping behind a tapestry. This caused no surprise, but the arrival of a sharply
uniformed British officer carrying a suitcase did. He announced himself as Major Miller and asked to see Wingate. He waited patiently for
the half hour it took to rouse the chamberlain.

"Yes, Major. What could possibly bring you at this hour?"

"A thousand pardons, but a military headquarters continues to operate through all circumstances. I'm Major Miller. I've come to see
Colonel Wingate in a most important matter."

"Poof! Only a German invasion would be important now." The
chamberlain yawned insultingly and ambled away to his rest.

"Could you direct me to his quarters?"

The chamberlain did not bother to look back. "Go away, please.
Don't return till late afternoon."

"My orders are to wait until I see him."

"You may be waiting a week. We will be celebrating at least that
long."

"Could I deliver a message to Wingate?"

"If you can find him. But please—I must insist—do not wake anyone else." The chamberlain drowsily waved off further questions. "Good
night," he said, leaving Miller with a perilous task.

Discreetly nudging open a succession of doors, even more discreetly
closing them, Miller made his way around the ground-level rooms. It
took him an hour before he ascended to the colonnade where a bejew-
eled goblet sat on the railing. In spite of his urgency, he had to stop
and admire it.

Wingate's door was ajar. Miller straightened his tie and entered;
he cleared his throat to no response.

"Sir. . . . Colonel Wingate, sir." Miller set down the suitcase loudly. "*Ahem. Colonel Wingate, Sir.*" Maintaining as military a posture as
possible, he leaned over to grasp Wingate's shoulder. A moment of
confusion; then he rolled over and regarded Miller blankly. "Colonel
Wingate: good morning, sir. Major Miller. Colonel Cooper sent me
over to fetch you."

Wingate seemed to be coming out of anesthesia. "You what? . . ."

"I'm from GHQ."

"Platt?"

"No, sir. General Cunningham."

"And what do you want?"

"In a word, sir—you."

"You want me?"

"At Colonel Cooper's office if you please."

"I don't please. Kindly go away."

"This was arranged between you and Colonel Cooper."

"Cooper?"

"Yes. The operations officer."

"Have I met him?"

"Apparently so."

"And he wants to see me now? In the middle of the night? Operations? They're finished. The war's over."

"I believe it is midmorning, sir."

Wingate felt the untanned strip of skin at his wrist. "Did I wear my watch last night?"

"Your attire was a matter of interest to General Cunningham. He has taken the liberty to present you with an issue of service dress." Miller opened the suitcase. "Best estimates were that you wore a medium small. A reliable tailor is waiting to provide rapid service. He also has a selection of hat sizes and uniform shoes. Can we go, sir?"

"How kind of the general. However, I'm indisposed. Do close the door as you leave, won't you, Miller?"

"What I've said is to be presented to you as an order if necessary."

"Now you've done that so you can run along."

"Perhaps you aren't aware of some changes in your chain of command."

"Maybe not. Platt assigned me to the emperor back in Khartoum."

"Gideon Force is now attached to General Cunningham."

"Hope he supports us better than Platt did. Couldn't be any worse."

"It is concerning Gideon Force that Colonel Cooper wishes to consult with you. Matters of pay, their eligibility for British decorations, I believe."

"Hardly the sort of thing your operations officer should worry about—especially so early on a holiday."

"Quite so. Perhaps I mispoke him. Though I know those are concerns of General Cunningham."

"You seem to beating around some bush. You'd better get to your point before I go back to sleep."

"Well to be perfectly frank, sir, Colonel Cooper looks very much to you for control of the emperor's followers—particularly in regard to the Italians."

"I see." Wingate contemplated for a moment. "Sooner rather than later I suppose. I'll be with you as soon as I shave. What's the matter?"

"From all appearances, you seem well shaven, sir."

Wingate ran his hand over his face. He strode to one of the ornate mirrors on the wall (there was also one on the ceiling). "You're right! And someone cut my hair."

"Yes, you're nicely barbered. Full service accommodations, I'd say."

"You don't know half of it."

"Shall we go?"

"So that's Wingate..." was the whispered remark throughout GHQ. Officers who had no business in Cooper's office drifted through anyway to catch a glimpse of "the Lawrence of Abyssinia," as the visiting press were calling him. They became a distraction, so Cooper escorted him to Cunningham's waiting room. Up to that time their conversation had been about ordinary administrative matters, nothing of the urgency Miller had suggested.

Wingate slouched into an overstuffed chair. The comfort, the well-appointed room, seemed to bring back his earlier fatigue.

"Coffee?" Cooper suggested. "Afraid the Italians didn't leave us any tea."

"Thank you, no. I'd gathered there was to be some new mission for Gideon Force," he said in an effort to hold back sleep.

"A new alignment, yes. Where's your kit, Wingate?"

He shrugged. "Back at Fiche for all I know. What do you mean by 'alignment'?"

"Mmm. Haven't been keeping track of things, have you? Well, it will be forwarded to Cairo."

"What will?"

"Your kit."

"Cairo?"

"Yes."

"Why?"

"The reason, I believe, is that General Wavell wants an immediate report from you on your operations."

"Does he." The Wingate of Safartak seemed to return to his voice. "I thought *you* were debriefing me."

"Change of plans. Your expertise in unconventional operations has relevance for North Africa now. Maybe you can do to Rommel what you did to Torelli. A debriefing here would be of only historical interest."

"Change of plans, aye? Or perhaps the plan all along."

"I don't follow you, Wingate. But I follow orders. General Platt's Lancaster is ready to depart. You'll be on it."

"General Platt!" He slapped his forehead. "I'm blind: no report here, no report to Platt. It's straight to Cairo for me. I suppose orders are already prepared." Cooper nodded and handed them over. Wingate scanned the few lines with disgust. "So I'm shanghaied. Do you think there is another Brit in this kingdom who has Selassie's trust?"

"Simonds is quite capable of . . ."

Wingate grabbed the phone. "Get me Gideon Force." He received a short answer from the operator. "Why is the extension closed?"

Cooper swallowed hard and answered. "Gideon Force has been disbanded." Wingate dropped the phone. "The troops have been returned to Ethiopian control. The British cadre are reassigned throughout the theater."

Cooper clasped his hands behind his back. Cunningham had told him this aspect of the Wingate matter would be difficult; Cooper hadn't thought so but now he did.

"Platt," said Wingate blankly. "Only Platt could do this." He walked to the window and stared out. "He destroyed Gideon Force overnight."

"Cunningham wants to see you before you leave. I'm afraid that's shortly." He went to the general's door and knocked softly. Cooper departed, leaving Wingate staring out the window. Cunningham crossed the room to share his view of the road back to Fiche.

"You won those hills—if it's any consolation."

"Gideon Force. I once called them savages."

"I call them the toughest fighting men in this campaign."

"I never bade them farewell."

"Believe me, I would have gladly given you that opportunity." Cunningham put his hand on his shoulder. "My troops would have passed in review for Gideon Force, a tribute both you and your men deserved." He removed his hand. "But I was overruled."

"Some of my men are to be buried tomorrow."

"I'm afraid I cannot even grant you that....Be assured there will be a British guard of honor. Sir William bears no grudges against the dead."

"The wounded. Could I visit the hospital briefly?"

Cunningham shook his head. "I've been allowed no discretion whatsoever."

Wingate looked up as if he were once more at the foot of the escarpment. "Then I shall take my cause—and theirs—to Cairo."

Wingate was driven in a cargo truck seated among a squad of well-armed British soldiers. They were eager to converse, but Wingate's stunned expression and an onset of chills kept them respectfully silent.

The airfield was nearly empty; the truck pulled right up to the door of Platt's converted bomber. There was no one to see him off, but Wingate looked back anyway and saw one Ethiopian behind the wire fence. Wingate's eyes widened. He took a step toward him, for the man looked familiar.

"Sorry, sir. No time for farewells." The officer expediting the flight glanced at Wingate impatiently.

It was the gleam of the white turban Wingate recognized. From under his cloak a knife flashed to Ishmael's throat. He grabbed his knife hand at the wrist. With the blade still at the skin, he stood like a mannequin while the bomber rolled away.

31

But for the crew of two, Wingate was alone in the plane. The bomb bay had been converted into a flying lounge complete with a movie projector. Where the waist guns were usually mounted, a wet bar had been installed across the entire width of the fuselage. The cost of converting the bomber to the general's flying office could have kept Gideon Force in bullets for a month.

The bar was fully stocked, but with his hangover Wingate had only mineral water. He realized a clear head was needed to cope with whatever Platt had concocted for him in Cairo. His anger predominated over his apprehension, however, for he knew Cairo was Wavell's city, not Platt's. The wheels of injustice would be far more difficult for Platt to crank than if the destination were Khartoum.

Shortly after takeoff Wingate went forward to the flight deck. When he introduced himself the aviators became curious. Imagining him to be a special sort of VIP (the copilot thought he was to be awarded a Victoria Cross by Wavell at the airport), they readily agreed to alter the flight plan and retrace Gideon Force's route of advance.

Sitting back in Platt's swivel chair, Wingate watched Fiche, Safartak, Debra Markos, Danghila, and the escarpment slip under the wing. He began jotting notes for his defense but became lost in the passage of the terrain and its memories.

By the time the bomber descended over the pyramids, Wingate felt confident that his accomplishments would be recognized. If there was one admirable value in the army, it was that success commands forgiveness. Failing to follow established recipes could be overlooked if the chef produced a platter of victories. That Wingate had done. The number of his peccadillos was large, but they added up to little more than individualism and small breaches of military manners. Such was Wingate's misappraisal of his situation.

He had failed to learn why his enemy was nicknamed "Implacable Platt"—obviously no reference to doggedness in warfare but rather a reputation for letting no score go unsettled. The general knew the internal battlefield of the army better than Wingate knew guerrilla tactics. In bureaucratic warfare, Wingate was Torelli and Platt was Wingate, a mismatch made all the more uneven by the disparity between their ranks.

The bomber taxied into the VIP area and cut its engines well away from the terminal. Two trucks met the plane. In an arrangement that struck the aviators as very odd, they were driven away before Wingate debarked.

Two majors, faultlessly correct, awaited him at the foot of the ladder, one a military police officer, the other from legal branch. Major Ferris, the lawyer, spoke first:

"Major Orde C. Wingate?"

"So I'm back to major, am I? What other good news do you have for me?"

"Major Wingate, I am charged to deliver to you two sets of orders, the second of which must be read to you in the presence of a witnessing officer who in this case is Major Shackleford representing the provost marshal."

Ferris handed Wingate the orders returning him to his permanent rank of major. As his promotion to lieutenant colonel had been authorized by Platt's headquarters, so too was this demotion. On the date of the orders Wingate had departed from Fiche; he was impressed by the planning behind this retribution. "Thanks very much," he said.

"The second general order reads as follows: 'Paragraph One: A Board of Inquiry is directed to convene no later than 1 July 1941 for the purpose of investigating the conduct of Maj. O. C. Wingate during operations in Sudan and Ethiopia during the period....'"

Wingate had anticipated the loss of his brevet. The possibility of a board of inquiry had also occurred to him, and at first he looked forward to explaining how he was opposed more effectively by Platt than by the Italians. But as Ferris read the bill of indictments, Wingate perceived that they did not involve his campaign so much as his violation of procedure and standing orders. He was charged with failing to do this and failing to do that. He was put in the logical dilemma of explaining a negative: why *didn't* he do certain things rather than why he *did* do others.

Major Shackleford advised that his freedom was restricted to GHQ and his billet at the Continental Hotel.

"How about the hospital, Shackleford? I've got a dose of malaria."

"Your request must be directed to the president of the board."

They dropped him off at the Continental. In his grimy room the ceiling fan flapped ineffectively. Though the worst heat of the day had passed, Wingate was sweating profusely. He stripped and began to flip through the phone book for GHQ. He found the number for Wavell's office but felt too dispirited to call and so lay down on the squeaky bed with its concave mattress.

His troubled mind would not allow him to nap. Though slightly nauseous, he roused himself to call Finley. From him he could learn the lay of the land; learn when Wavell could dissolve this ridiculous board in exchange for a written reprimand perhaps, one he would later have expunged from his record. He would offer to apologize to Platt—

whatever it took to thaw the situation so he could get some rest, some home leave, then back to Africa to make a Torelli out of Rommel. Optimism alternated with disheartenment as he dialed Finley's number.

Female soldiers in the British army were part of the Auxiliary Territorial Service, or, ATS. An ATS answered.

"Sir Archibald's office."

"Colonel...make that Major O. C. Wingate here. May I speak with Finley?"

"GHQ number, please."

"Beg pardon?"

"Are you a visitor, Major?"

"Is Finley there?"

"I'm sorry, he's in Malta."

"Damn. How about Sir Archie?"

"Have you an appointment, sir?"

"No. That's what I want."

"Concerning what matter?"

"Ethiopia."

"Isn't that over? I think I should connect you with Brigadier Enright. One moment please."

A chill shivered through him; yet Wingate's forehead remained beaded with sweat. He felt so faint he did not respond when Enright answered.

"Hello. Hello."

"Yes, sir. Major O. C. Wingate here."

"The secretary told me that much. What do you want? I'm damn busy."

"I was advised in Addis Ababa that Sir Archie wanted my report on the Ethiopian campaign—wanted it immediately."

"Write it down then."

"Inasmuch as I was flown up alone in General Platt's plane, I inferred there was some urgency in Sir Archie's request. I assumed he wanted a face-to-face debriefing before I began a written report."

"You do a bit of assuming for a major. Do you think there's anything urgent about Ethiopia? We're facing another Dunkirk in Greece and you think Sir Archie has time to hear stories about Ethiopia?"

"I have an urgent matter for his attention. I bring a personal message from Emperor Selassie."

"Wait a bit." Wingate could not hear Enright's short consultation with Wavell's secretary. "You can drop the message off here at my office."

"It was oral."

"If it's not important enough to write down, it's not important enough to interrupt the commander in chief. I'll leave Sir Archie a message that you're in town. What was the name?"

"O. C. Wingate."

"Has he met you before?"

"Yes. In Palestine."

"Where are you staying?"

"The Continental."

"Temporary duty here?"

"No, sir. Permanent orders."

"Were you assigned to Ethiopia from here or out of U.K.?"

"Here, sir."

"How long were you in Ethiopia?"

"Counting my time in Sudan, nearly a year."

"Then that would make you a new arrival in Cairo. Follow procedure, please, and report to New Arrival Section before you begin any other business."

Wearily Wingate put down the phone. He'd had no food all day but nothing interested him except sleep. His head swimming, he went to the window and let the shade roll up. His view was of the fire escape on a crumbling building. He poured a finger of rum into the smudgy sink glass, raised it in a toast to the unseen sun, and remembered the dawn at Selassie's palace.

32

He awoke late and put off his hospital visit in order to scout out GHQ.

It reminded him of the small mining towns near Sheffield: single industry, self-contained, everyone moving and talking as if synchronized to an institutional clock. At GHQ, the three elemental substances—gas, liquid, and solid—were smoke, tea, and paper.

By comparison. Platt's headquarters in Khartoum was a model of austere efficiency. A previous commanding general had likened GHQ to a warship, but for Wingate it was a ship of fools. Soul-destroying, enervating, unhealthy: these broodings ran through Wingate's mind as he slouched down the hall to New Arrivals.

He drank so much water from the cooler that others in the room took notice. As he watched another officer being processed, he remembered the vultures picking over the Italian dead at Danghila.

"You're next, major."

Wingate did not get up. "I'm Wingate of Ethiopia."

"I'm Cole of Hampshire. Come on now, let's see your orders." Wingate walked over and handed them to him. "You're here for a board, are you? That may take some time. Two of these officers were posted to Libya."

"I'm here to report to Sir Archibald Wavell on the operations of Gideon Force in the Ethiopian campaign."

"Gideon Force?" Several enlisted persons turned their heads. "You don't look like a chaplain to me!" Major Cole laughed in spite of Wingate's burning stare. "Of course. Now you have several things to do." He consulted a sheet thumbtacked under acetate on the counter which divided the room.

"First off, get rid of that beard. The barber's in Room 1412, bomb shelter level. Policy in GHQ is mustaches only. Second, get some polish on those shoes: they look like you marched from Khartoum.

"Speaking of walking, you'll need a swagger stick. They're not regulation but are strongly encouraged for staff officers. Hmmm. Trouble is, pending the board, you're disqualified for staff, aren't you?" Cole became bemused by this administrative oddity.

"All right, forget the swagger stick for the moment. You can start processing while I find out what the precedent is." He dropped a packet of forms in front of Wingate. "The office number of each station is marked in the right-hand corner. You'll need initials from each.

"And let's see, your background is in procurement. By chance do you have any experience in salvage? There's an IOC requirement for the wrecks out in the desert." He glanced at the orders. "Oh, blast. You're restricted to Cairo, aren't you?" Cole shook his head. "As I said, these boards take a great deal of time. I'm afraid you might be in casual status for some months. Well, off you go. I might know more when you get back."

Cole looked up, puzzled, for Wingate did not pick up the packet of forms.

"What if I don't process?"

"Now why wouldn't you do that?"

Another new arrival entered, a clerical, bespectacled officer fresh from England. He pretended not to hear the colloquy.

"I am not a link of sausage," Wingate answered, "or is 'processing' a term we've picked up from American industry?"

"Look, Wingate, this is a big headquarters. It requires some uniformity just to keep people from falling through the cracks. Processing is efficiency."

"Processing is buggery." Wingate took up his hat to leave.

"Wait a bit. For your own good wait a moment. Since you seem to be a man of action, you'll probably contact people all over this headquarters."

"Most probably."

"Till you're processed, you won't have a GHQ number. Have you thought of that? Without a GHQ number you're a nonperson, as the Russians say."

"People become nonpeople by being processed."

"That's a matter of opinion. Have you had occasion to call on anyone of importance?"

"Yes."

"What was the first thing his secretary asked you?"

"My GHQ number."

"You see?"

"Then I'll just jolly make up my own number. Could you recommend any? Are high numbers better than low ones?"

Cole was quite amused. "Yes, life should be so simple. First off, uttering a false GHQ number is a Class II(a) violation of the Articles of War. Second, the GHQ number presents your whole processing profile to the person you call. The secretary simply reaches over to that number in the file, pulls it, and out comes all the data you've provided during processing. It's the latest efficiency, Wingate. Some day the whole world will be like this."

"An instrument of the devil."

"No, an excellent prescreen for all calls. Now won't you oblige me by filling out these forms?"

Wingate turned them over page by page as if looking for a scorpion. He read a sampling of questions and answered them for Cole.

"I was born in India. Does a secretary want to know that? Or what about my children, 'if any'? My primary school, my source of commission, my hobbies, whether I wear glasses?"

"Yes, I sometimes wonder who reads all those items. And you're right: it's all found elsewhere in your records. But don't you see...." A second in-processing officer entered and looked impatient. He was a colonel. "I'll be with you gentlemen in a moment." Cole lowered his voice and tried another tack. "Don't you see that disclosing such details is, well, 'ceremonial'? The act of telling us all these inconsequential things is a way of pledging your loyalty to the headquarters. And when we give you a GHQ number, that indicates your acceptance into our extended family."

"A sort of bar mitzvah."

"Exactly! Now be a good fellow..."

"No."

"Why not?"

"I am an orphan."

"There's a place to tell us that—item 43: 'parentage.'"

"A military orphan. I'll have no part of your extended family."

"Think of it...well, like the Officers Club."

"I'll not join that either."

"All right." Cole consulted a regulation. "All right then, you'll be paying full rates for your room. Full rates for your meals. No credit at the hotel bars. No swimming pool privileges. And..." He examined some fine print. "I can't believe this is still in effect. But according to this, you'll have to make your reasons for not joining known to the CG himself."

A third officer entered for processing. He with the earlier arrivals began to inch toward the discussion.

"There, you see?" said Wingate. "This seems to be the fastest way to see Sir Archie."

"You must realize that this is superseded. Sir Archie can't be bothered with such trivia."

"Nor can I."

"I'll make you a bargain, Wingate. Fill in all the other stupid little forms and the requirement to join the Officers Club will be waived. And you'll get a GHQ number."

"Who will waive it?" said Wingate in mock outrage. "You can't do that. It's against the rules."

The colonel had had enough. "I say, could we get started? It's getting on to lunchtime you know."

"Here are your packets, gentlemen," said Cole. "I think you'll find them self-explanatory." The three officers took seats and began filling out the forms. "Here, Wingate, be a good fellow and do the same. Come back when you've been around the stations; we can talk some more."

"Agreed, *if* I get my GHQ number in advance."

"Can't do it."

"Yes you can."

"No I can't."

"Yes you can. You know you can. If I had all these papers filled out right now, you would give me a GHQ number."

"But you haven't."

"But I will."

"You will?"

"I said I would."

Cole sighed and crossed off the last number on his master list. "Your number will be 8692. Before it's official, it must go on a card with your picture. You get card and picture when you finish processing."

"I'll be on my way."

"Start with the medical station, won't you Wingate? You're not looking any too well."

With a nod to the waiting officers, Wingate left.

"What a cheeky fellow," said the colonel loudly. "Did I get his name right—Wingate?"

"Right, sir," Cole answered. "O. C. Wingate."

"I believe he's that guerrilla chap from Ethiopia," said the third arrival. "Had no right to hold us up that way."

The colonel agreed. "You'd think the army was designed for his personal convenience."

"Wouldn't want him in my officers club."

"Nor on my flank in battle. He might take a mind to withdraw while I was attacking. Where is he assigned, Cole?"

"'Need to know' information, sir."

"Rubbish. It'll be in the phone book. Sticking up for him, are you?"

"Colonel, I don't believe he'll have many friends in this head-quarters."

33

Except for the physical examination, Wingate did not process. He thought it no more deceitful to lie to Cole than to build redundant campfires to deceive the Italians. The enemy was not entitled to integrity, and the bureaucracy was as much an enemy of freedom as fascism. More dangerous because more insidious.

In London, these would have been interesting propositions to debate with the Jewish scholars as they sat before a fireplace with brandy. In the sweltering heat of Cairo they were unexamined truths as seen through Wingate's now jaundiced eyes. Fever seemed to have cleared his mind the way thin air clears—and distorts—the mind of a Himalayan climber: outlines and spatial relationships are sharper, and because of that all the more deceptive.

He felt he had come upon a great truth: that reciprocal responsibility between an individual and an organization is a one-sided hoax. That was because though both individual and the organization have names (e.g., Wingate and GHQ), they are not ethically equivalent because one has a sense of personal responsibility while the other has only a collective purpose. Any mutual promise between the two is therefore illusory and meretricious. As a corollary, no bureaucrat qualified for treatment as a person except in a setting outside his job.

Wingate did take the physical examination in order to save himself a visit to the hospital. He also suspected that if his condition were diagnosed as serious—and he had no doubt that it was—he would be immediately hospitalized and denied the opportunity to pursue what justice he could extract from the system.

That almost happened anyway. Wingate's temperature hovered between 102 and 103. The doctor was about to call an ambulance when he looked around to find Wingate gone.

He found his way to a small office in the department handling logistics and payrolls. "Combat Allowances" was the title on the door. An ATS was the receptionist.

"Yes, Major," she said.

"Wingate: 8692. I've corresponded with Colonel Marleybone while I was in Ethiopia."

She searched her file. "8692 you said? I have no listing for you, sir. Ethiopia. Winthrop? No, Wingate...*Lieutenant Colonel* Wingate, O. C.?"

"Formerly lieutenant colonel."

"Yes, I remember now. You wrote about the hard-lying allowances for your men. Well, sir, Colonel Marleybone replied on 23 June."

"Never received it. May I see your copy?"

"I'll reproduce it." She started typing.

"I'll just read over your shoulder." He did. "That festering arsehole."

"I beg your pardon!"

Wingate stormed into Marleybone's inner office and locked the door. The colonel rose in alarm.

"You're the swine."

"Get...get out....Polly!"

Marleybone lifted the phone but Wingate yanked it from its jack.

"Hard-lying allowances is the subject, Colonel Marleybone, and you're about to reverse yourself and approve them for Gideon Force, which has been recently and shamefully abandoned."

"Who in God's name are you?"

"In God's name, I am their former commander. Wingate: 8692 to you."

"Ethiopia?"

"Damn right."

"I must check the file. It's with my clerk."

"Your miserable reason for disapproving the extra pay was that my troops were operating *behind* enemy lines rather than on a 'front.'"

"Yes, I recall that. The regulations are very clear. There is no mention of hard-lying allowances for troops behind enemy lines unless they are prisoners of war."

"I see. I should have let my command be captured!"

"What's more, if I remember correctly, you did not submit the necessary vouchers within the required time. Administrative directive 6–164 clearly states..."

Marleybone's face began to run as if Wingate was watching him through a clear pane onto which oil was seeping. The colonel's voice took on a buzzing vibration which followed Wingate as he stumbled out the door. "This incident will be reported..." was the last thing he heard.

He found himself slouched in a chair in the GHQ dispensary. A thermometer stuck from his mouth while blood drawn from his finger was squeezed between two small plates.

He had been talking to a doctor for some time but didn't know his name. Wingate stared dully ahead and listened.

"You've got malaria, Orde. You've had it for some time. Is this your first attack?" Wingate shrugged wearily. "You should be hospitalized at once." Wingate took out the thermometer, looked at it, and started to get up. "Wait."

"I have too many enemies to wait. Small men. Platt's agents. They want me in a hospital. Thank you, doctor...."

"You need complete rest."

"Have to see Wavell. Then I'll rest."

"Sir Archie makes the rounds at the hospital once a week. I'll be sure to mention your case to him... if you'll just let me get an ambulance."

"Are you telling the truth?"

"My psychiatric colleagues would probably describe you as paranoid."

"Yes, I'm sick. I'm sick of this bureaucratic oppression, of this army that fights its own purpose. It's drained me."

"I'll give you medications, five gallons of quinine water, and a sack of ice. Promise me you'll use them. And rest. For the next twenty-four hours at least you must have complete rest."

"I must write my report."

"Not for twenty-four hours."

"I must prepare my defense."

"Not yet."

"I must respond to Marleybone."

"Let me intervene with him."

"I must fight. I must keep on fighting."

"You are a formidable enemy to your own health."

The doctor drove him back to the Continental; on the way Wingate fell asleep. When the elevator began its slow ascent, he felt as though his head had remained in the lobby.

Woozy and amnesic, he found himself talking on the phone with someone he couldn't remember calling.

"You agree then that I am to render a report..."

"There is no directive from GR that you submit one," said the voice.

"Then Platt was lying."

"You may submit one if you wish. I'm simply saying, Major, that we can provide you with no clerical services. We have no listing of your GHQ number. Our only data show you are in casual status and facing a board."

"No clerical help."

"No."

The report was an outpouring of bitterness and incomplete memories. It was written laboriously with a fountain pen while Wingate shivered under wet sheets. The maid was so alarmed that she called the floor boy. He could procure native and otherwise suspect remedies for a range of diseases.

Wingate's was clearly malaria. Had he tried Atabrine? Wingate shook his head. What would it do for him? A sure cure, he was assured. And some hashish perhaps? Excellent quality, hard as granite, reasonable price.

Within an hour the floor boy returned with Atabrine but no directions for its use. Wingate took it in aspirin-size doses but to no effect. He increased the dosage until he felt his head clearing, then proceeded with the report, which, when finished, seemed quite lucid. It was nearly two hundred pages in length, including its annexes.

The descent in the elevator blacked him out for a moment, but when he stepped into the lobby the world seemed nearly right. He couldn't remember when he had last eaten or that a night and two days had passed since the doctor delivered him to his room. The only thing unusual now was how loud everyone's voice seemed and the frequent glances he received when he reached GHQ. There he addressed the report to Wavell, then staggered back to the Continental to sleep for twelve hours.

34

No one saw Wavell without going through his chief of staff, Brigadier Enright. His ATS pushed a button under her desk when Wingate appeared like an apparition in front of her desk.

"Yes?"

"I'm Wingate of Ethiopia."

"Your GHQ number?"

"Bugger my GHQ number. Has Wavell got my report?"

The silent buzzer brought a sergeant from an outer office. He regarded Wingate like a bouncer sizing up a dangerous drunk.

"I'm sorry, sir," said the ATS, "I can't trace your report without a GHQ number."

"I brought it over...can't remember when. Hand carry. Eyes only for Wavell."

"Was it receipted?" Wingate shook his head; he couldn't remember. "You're from Ethiopia? When you reported to New Arrivals did they give you a visitors' pass?" The sergeant went over to a small cabinet, pulled a file, and handed it to the ATS. "Oh," she said, her eyes widening, "one moment, please."

She knocked on Enright's door and entered while the sergeant stood with his arms folded like a prison guard. The clerk returned and exchanged glances with the sergeant.

"Brigadier Enright will see you, Major." Wingate only looked at her. "He will see you in his office, sir."

Enright's ribbons fit the image of the combat soldier he had been.

He was well prepared for Wingate: the chairs where visitors would normally sit had been moved so that Wingate was obliged to stand. He advanced to the edge of the desk and stared at Enright.

"It is customary to offer a salute when reporting to one's superior," said the brigadier. "But then you have no respect for custom or courtesy, do you? Indeed, I have left the door open in case you resort to the sort of violence you inflicted on Colonel Marleybone."

"Who's Marleybone?" said Wingate vacantly.

"If my judgment were to be followed, Wingate, you would now be in one of three places: in irons, in the hospital, or en route to Great Britain.

"To my thinking your conduct here best qualifies you for a court-martial. However, you have two benefactors who have interceded and had their way. Doctor Nutting has persuaded me that while you were in the throes of malaria you should, for legal purposes, be considered *non compos mentes*. I can countenance that though I would put you down as inherently unbalanced rather than the victim of disease.

"General Wavell's coddling of you is less understandable. He has dissolved the board of inquiry recommended by General Platt. You now face no charges arising from your conduct in Ethiopia.

"Apparently adopting Sir Archie's indulgent attitude, Colonel Marleybone has advised me he will not prefer charges against you for that assault in his office. That leaves you scot-free. Except that I have decided not to pamper you.

"You are on report for four violations of regulations, all of which I have entered in your records. In reverse order of importance, they are: One—appearance unbecoming an officer as evidenced by the frowsy mop on your face. Two—Disrespect and lack of military courtesy. Self-explanatory. Three—Obtaining a GHQ number by false pretenses. That is, failure to process. Four—Submitting an official report containing libelous, inaccurate material known to be not in the best interest of His Majesty's armed forces and prejudicial to good order and discipline. It is about this report that I gather you are here today."

"Did Sir Archie read it?"

"He did."

"Can you prove it?"

Enright rose, flushed with anger. On a wooden leg he thumped across the room and slammed the door.

"I can prove anything I say! I am not a liar like you!" He lowered his voice but not its intensity. "But you are not one to put me to any proof, *Major*. Come to attention when I speak to you!"

"This is the best I can do."

"Playing the sick man. What a disgrace. Look at you. Shabby... part of your role as a martyr, I suppose. I even doubt if you're sick—except in your warped mind. Here!" He flung the last page of Wingate's report in front of him. "There is Sir Archibald's signature."

"I have the right to speak to him about it."

"Your report is a closed matter—except as evidence of the fourth charge I have declared against you. A copy has been forwarded to Stonegate and you can expect to see it when you are cashiered."

"I wrote it longhand."

"So I noticed."

"I...I have no copy. I had no clerk."

"Too bad."

"May I have back the original?"

Enright tore it up and let the pieces flutter down into his waste basket.

"There goes you Ethiopian dream world. Trash. It's a tale of brigandage—a gang of robbers pillaging a retreating army. Political intrigue. Insubordination. General Platt's forbearance was astonishing. A renegade like you should have been relieved in the first week. Yet you fancy yourself as some Lawrence of Ethiopia, don't you?"

"Did Sir Archie approve hard-lying allowance for my men?"

"Yes he did. All your Zulus will get bonuses to add to the booty they stripped from corpses." Wingate was no longer paying attention.

Enright folded his hands. "I've seen many officers in this war who were nothing more than civilians in uniform. They made tremendous blunders. I would have thrown them out with the shaving water if our manpower needs were not so desperate. But every one of them was trying to be an adequate soldier, Wingate. The very worst of them were trying to do their duty. You, in contrast, defile the concept of duty. You're a Judas to the officers corps. You are a termite gnawing at the foundation of our code, a vermin spoiling the stores of discipline..." The interoffice phone rang. "Enright."

It was Wavell to advise him that his voice was carrying.

"Sorry sir."

"Who's in there with you?"

"Wingate."

"Let me see him."

"Yes, sir. Report to the commanding general."

To do so, Wingate went through the clerk's office. She averted her eyes.

He had not heard Wavell's voice for over a year, and it seemed to mirror his own fatigue. Papers were adrift on his desk as if he were moving—which he was.

"Orde. I hope you're recovering." They shook hands. "Sit down. I'm saving you from a dressing-down you deserve. You know that, don't you?"

"You read my report."

"Hurriedly. I've had to do everything hurriedly. You see, I'm being sacked. We're in something of the same boat. The difference is that you're being packed off because of your victory while I'm losing my command because of defeat. Defeat in Libya. Defeat in Greece. Defeat in Crete. Defeat everywhere. My fate is more deserved than yours."

"My recommendations?"

"I endorsed several of the important ones. You have convinced me there is a place for large-scale operations by regular forces in the enemy rear. Your ideas for the future are as bold as your operations in the past.

"You started us in motion toward the single victory which the British army has achieved in this war. Do you know that? Of course you do. It must be bitter for you to come back to such a reward."

"Where will my report go?"

"Nowhere I'm afraid."

"Are you going to London?"

"Initially. I don't know what shelf they'll find for me after that. Maybe the Far East."

"Can you advance my paper in London?"

"Would you want me to? My recommendation is a kiss of death."

"My report, for all its criticisms, is a history of victory. It would be welcome reading for the prime minister."

"Yes, Winston reads enough of defeat these days."

"You know him?"

"For many years."

"Will you bring it to his attention? It has applications for any theater."

For a moment Wavell was silent with troubled reflections.

"I should try, I suppose. But I won't. It would be futile. I must be honest with you, Orde. Your ideas strike the shield forged by the military for its own protection. You've flouted every safeguard and shibolleth the army relies upon for its mental security. You've disregarded rules, bypassed procedures, ignored channels, refused instructions—in short you have devised your own ways to wage war and left many traditions broken in your wake. What's worse, you have succeeded. You've made many people wrong—publicly wrong. They've seized upon your obvious disrespect for them. They will use that to discredit everything you did. Did Enright have anything to say about your military conclusions or recommendations?"

"No."

"He's typical of the opposition you face. He has as much bravery and fortitude as you. He lost his leg at Tobruk saving his driver from a burning tank. Dragged his stump across the desert for two days.

"However, he has none of your imagination. In the army, imagination always jars security.

"If there had been a different, a more imaginative way to fight Rommel, Enright's leg might not have been lost. But it was, you see. He needs to believe that this sacrifice was inevitable under the circumstances—that the orders he followed were the best that could be devised. Do you follow?"

"Bugger Enright."

"There are too many Enrights to bugger. They all wear much more rank on their shoulders. I would be one voice speaking against a chorus. A tired voice. A voice sounding in defeat."

"You will not help me then."

"I am powerless. Ineffective."

"And I am alone."

"A rebel is hard put for companions. Nor do you make friends easily."

"I have no voice."

"The army does not want to hear it."

"So it is with the prophets."

"Prophets are respected only after they die."

"Yes. That's very true, isn't it?"

"Orde, I wish you well."

Dazed and oozing sweat, Wingate passed Enright's open door.

"One moment," the brigadier commanded. "I'm giving you a direct order to cut off that beard."

"It shall be done."

35

Doors and corridors went by in endless progression. He seemed to trudge a treadmill, leaving him stationary as activity went by him. Esoteric acronyms on the doors. Officers immersed in incomprehensible routines, their faces like mannequins. Uniforms like his own but an army as alien to him as the *Wermacht*. It had not been so long ago that he had related to them, in important ways had been one of them: a bright lieutenant, an ambitious captain. Now he was in disgrace, among them but not of them. He felt no loss, only a numbing disillusionment.

Then into the street, eyes throbbing, head aching—into the wider stream of humanity. He felt more in common with the Egyptians. Their struggle was understandable: a complex economy routed them through the teeming streets while a durable culture sustained them. They pushed carts not paper, a hard but simple life more like the one he knew from Ethiopia, a life he suddenly missed with bitter yearning.

Yet not a life to which he could return, not now, not after being ostracized from his profession. He could rejoin Selassie but not as a pariah. He could rejoin the Zionists but not as a renegade. He could rejoin Lorna but not as an outcast. He could only do what he had the power to do. He would return with honor as his sense of honor now defined it.

Which meant he could not return alive. The Egyptians scurried by him but all, it seemed, in the opposite direction. Life was going one way while he was going the other.

It was a long weaving walk through the back streets to the Continental, long enough for Wingate to feel a sense of regained control. What does a man control in his life, he pondered: not its beginning and too little of its time—only its end. That came as a revelation to him, and meant that the unendurable need not be endured. The final option always remained open.

Better to burn out like a meteor than expire like an ember.

His last remark to Enright bothered Wingate. It sounded as if he were submitting at last to arbitrary authority. The remark had confused him; it wasn't what he had wanted to say. In afterthought he produced excellent repartee—something about an officer's worth depending upon what was in his head rather than what was on his face. And if a beard were a bar to military greatness, Enright should reacquaint himself with the portraits in the War Museum.

"It shall be done," Wingate had replied to the order to cut off his beard. Then it occurred to him how this was the best of all answers because it was prescient. It was his soul speaking without the intervention of his mind. Yes, he would cut his beard and his throat with it. Let Enright remember his order.

Wingate reached the hotel when it was filling with off-duty officers. The bar was growing crowded. Looking at them, Wingate felt for a moment as he had when his rugby team was about to depart for another school to play a match. Hours before, the young Wingate had learned he had not made the team.

There was only one other passenger in the elevator with him— Colonel Thornhill, who was billeted in an adjoining room. As they ascended, Wingate experienced the nervousness of precombat. Death was approaching as it had at Tiberias and Safartak, this time as a certainty not a possibility. Nothing could go wrong, however. No luck was involved: no artillery would misfire, no lieutenants would be out of place, no man would flinch—unless it were Wingate.

That possibility, rather than the hereafter, was the great unknown. He reviewed what would be involved for him.

His hand was steady as he shaved with slow, methodical strokes. He finished and felt his skin for smoothness. The malarial attacks had familiarized him with a hard, irregular pulse so he noticed little unusual in the way he felt.

Then a wave of guilt and anguish left him heaped upon his bed. He searched for paper and pen. This would be a message to Lorna, but it never came. He could only wonder what she was doing at that moment and whether his spirit would touch her as it left the world. He flung the pen against the wall.

The walls were so thin Thornhill heard it.

Too much to explain and too few answers. He would not spend his last moments in futility—his life had been too full of that. Life was futility: that's why he was leaving it.

Deserted and left behind: those would be her sentiments regardless of any rationalizations he could put down on paper.

The shame of abandoning her would be the last torture inflicted by his puritan conscience, that selective conscience which could walk over carnage head in the air and eyes on the horizon yet devastate him when his performance fell short of his standards.

This time he knew his conscience to be right: suicide was inexcusable in the present, unforgivable in the hereafter. Here during the bloodiest war in history, while lives were snatched away by the millions, Wingate was tossing his to the winds of eternity.

But his conscience did not suffer; his conscience could not be humiliated, nor would it have to live with the terms the world pressed down on him. Let his conscience go unsullied into afterlife; meanwhile Wingate had some messy details to finish up on earth.

He noted the date: July 4, 1941. Orde Charles Wingate, 1903–1941. He stropped his hunting knife, the blade which had skewered mutton in the wilderness of two continents. He would sacrifice himself as he had seen the nomads do, by opening the jugular.

He looked into the mirror, then turned away.

His right hand holding the knife reached around to the left side of his neck. The skin was tough, his hand weak. The blade went no deeper than the windpipe. He stopped—he could not remember if he had locked his door; that seemed an important detail.

The knife stuck from his neck as he stumbled across the room. When he bumped against the door the knife clattered to the floor. Picking it up nearly caused him to pass out but he managed to reach the sink and take up the knife again, this time in his left hand.

With all his strength he rammed it into his neck, opening a new gash from the other side. He swayed for a moment in front of the mirror, his blood sounding in the basin like a slightly turned faucet. He fell with the darkness that descended on him.

Colonel Thornhill heard the thud and roused himself to investigate. Peeking under the door he could see the growing stain of blood.

"God in heaven..."

A pass key was rushed to the floor; however, Wingate had left his key in the hole. Thornhill and the hotel manager put their shoulders to the flimsy door and burst in.

Wingate had already lost much blood; in a matter of minutes he would have lost too much. Thornhill applied direct pressure to the wounds as an ambulance wound its way through the crowded city streets. It was a close thing but the army medics arrived in time.

He was traumatically unconscious for over an hour, then anesthetized for the operation, which began at once. It was initially unsuccessful, as an attack of vomiting undid the surgeon's efforts. His delirium was such that his hands were constrained so he could not reopen his wounds. His nurses reported that he cried loudly to God, supplicating for mercy. There was a rasp in his voice that would lessen but would remain with him for the rest of his life.

Rumors and theories about his suicide began circulating even before he regained consciousness. It was said that his recommendation for a guerrilla brigade in the Tibesti Mountains had been laughed down by Wavell. Others called his attempt a sham designed only to bring him recognition through infamy because he was undeserving of genuine fame. Strange hallucinogens from Ethiopia were also ascribed to him. His wife had been faithless or vice versa. Whatever the conjecture, he was now the best-known major in GHQ.

He was of course a ruined man as well; consequently, even the scorn of men like Enright seemed canceled. For the high command in Cairo it was as if his attempt had succeeded; that is, Wingate was dead so far as the army was concerned. The only thing left to do was the decent thing—to send home his remains to be received by the unconditional love of those to whom he was dear.

This was accomplished without delay. He was booked on a hospital ship, *Llandovery Castle,* which would call first at Durban, South Africa, where patients deemed able to continue would transfer to a transport bound for Glasgow.

Manfred Parnell, psychiatrist and chief medical officer aboard, was invited to dinner in Cairo by Colonel Bates, Enright's adjutant, and given Wingate's entire file, both medical and military, from Britain,

Palestine, and Ethiopia. Was psychotherapy normally provided at sea? Bates asked. Most certainly, Parnell replied: often cases of battle fatigue and neuropsychiatric disorders responded to the extended treatment that only such a long voyage allowed.

"Doctor, you realize he's rather a special case, I'm sure."

"All my patients are special."

"Of course. As you know, a medical board in London will rule on his fitness for future service. I don't suppose you've formed a preliminary opinion...."

"If I had it would remain confidential—between Wingate and myself."

"Quite so. The board will determine, among other things, whether he should ever command troops again. That will assuredly be his desire if he is permitted to remain in uniform."

"Whether he's fit to fight, so to speak?"

"Yes, that's the way we soldiers would put it."

"I'm not a soldier so forgive me if I find that question rather odd in Wingate's case."

"Why so?"

"Well, is there any question that he's fit to fight? From what you gave me to read he's apparently the foremost guerrilla fighter in the British army. Perhaps in the world, Major Finley tells me."

"Wingate's record is extremely controversial. If he remains in the army, there is no guarantee he will be placed with guerrilla forces. With a clean bill of health he would be eligible to command British troops. You're aware of that possibility?"

"Yes."

"The board will give great weight to your opinion, for you will have observed him for several weeks. Do you feel that's long enough?"

"Probably."

"I needn't tell you about the excellent convalescent facility at Durban."

"Somehow I perceive GHQ would not be displeased if he were to remain there for a time."

"Please don't misinterpret me. GHQ would only be displeased if he were forwarded to U.K. with a premature judgment of his fitness."

"Be assured. I'm aware that men's lives are at stake."

"Indeed they are. Very grateful to hear you say so."

"Colonel Bates, I have a boy in the army myself."

36

With a melancholy moan from its foghorn, the converted ocean liner slipped its moorings at Ismalia. *Llandovery Castle* was not all white as later hospital ships would be, but it bore a huge red cross on a white field amidship. She ran with all lights burning and sent out periodic signals on an international frequency advising submarines of her location.

Most of her passengers were casualties of the desert fighting in Libya, but there were also survivors from the evacuations of Salonika and Crete. Wingate was the only man aboard who had seen action in Ethiopia.

The sea was now red with patches of algae from which it acquired its name. On deck, Wingate slowly opened Lorna's letters beginning with the earliest postmark. This process of moving from the past to the present made it seem it was she who would die at the close of the last letter, for so great was the demarcation caused by the suicide that he felt both their previous lives had ended. Seeing her again would be like a meeting in the hereafter.

Dr. Parnell was too busy with his administrative duties to examine Wingate, but he heard of him from other patients. He learned that at dawn and dusk Wingate spoke scripture, sometimes reading but often reciting from memory in a rasping voice that contrasted oddly with the inspirational words he spoke. He always began his "sunrise service" with a verse from Psalms: "If I take the wings of the morning, and dwell in the uttermost parts of the sea, even there thou art with me."

With medical matters settled into ship's routine, Parnell reread Wingate's history, then made the first appointment.

*   *   *

"Your readings are much appreciated, Orde. I hope you shall continue them." Wingate nodded. "You've always read I gather." Another nod, this one slower. "Publicly? Sometimes publicly?"

"Never I think."

"That's the great benefit of a ship like this: enforced idleness, time to do things never done before. Do you like it so far?" After hesitation, Wingate nodded.

"How?"

"If it will help me."

"Help you how?"

"Recover."

"From what?"

"You know."

"Your suicidal impulses?"

"Is that what you call it?"

"What do you call it?"

"That's good enough."

"How far back do they go?"

"July 4, 1941."

"How about June 1939?"

"I was in Palestine, doctor."

"I know you were. Fighting around Nazareth. Nearly killed yourself then, didn't you?"

"Wounded."

"Do you get the connection?"

"Yes. But it's wrong," he said dispiritedly.

"You see a great difference in exposing yourself to extreme danger and creating that danger yourself?"

"Don't you?"

"I see similarities."

"That's your job, I suppose."

"Yes it is. Do you have a job too—regarding yourself?"

"Yes."

"Good. Let's work together. Let's go back to the first high risks you took. You were a considerable horseman I've learned. Always cutting out from the field and blazing your own trail." Parnell waited for affirmation.

"Need I answer? There seems little I can tell you about myself... that you don't know already."

"Why did the hunt club call you 'the otter'?"

"I could always find a crossing. Where others couldn't."

"Why?"

"They didn't look. They didn't listen."

"You did."

"Yes."

"What told you?"

"The way the water moved. The way it sounded."

"So did you feel very different from the other hunters?"

"Never gave it a thought. It wasn't so much that I was different, just better."

"What makes you better?"

"At riding to the hounds?"

"More broadly. What makes you a better guerrilla leader?"

"The Spanish have an expression, 'in the land of the blind the one-eyed man is king.' I have no competition in the British army."

"You had some worthy foes in Palestine—like that fellow you killed under the truck."

"Guerrilla warfare, more than anything else, is an exercise in imagination. It's serious speculation on 'what would happen if?' What would happen if they mined that trail? What would happen if we did? How would a certain action affect the settlers? How would it affect the Arabs?"

"You enjoy your imagination."

"Yes."

"Warfare, I gather, is your passion." Wingate nodded tentatively. "Have you others? Other passions?"

"My wife," he said after some deliberation.

"Is passion the right word?"

"I don't know."

"What word would you use?"

"This is within your medical business, Dr. Parnell? I've never had . . . 'treatment' before."

"Do you think it should not be my business?"

"I'm a very private person."

"Even your privacy is my business. *You* are my business. You, me, all of us, are clusters of opinion. I'll be asking for yours constantly." Wingate nodded. "Now what word would best describe your relationship with Lorna?"

Wingate pondered. "Close."

"You told her you tried to take your life?" Wingate shook his head. "How will you tell her?" He shook it again. "Will you still be close when you do?"

"Your questions are torments."

"I've no wish to torment you, Orde. Just know from the start that we'll be dealing with hard questions, ultimate questions; questions for which there may be no answers, but answers we will pursue nonetheless."

"I hope you start with easy ones."

"Don't expect tender treatment from me. My job is first to evaluate, then perhaps help if I can."

"I understand. Basically you work for Enright, don't you?"

"I do not. I work for your welfare and those who may serve under you. Now let me start with the obvious question: why did you slit your throat?"

"A horrible combination of evils."

"What were they?"

"I was taking some crazy chemical—self-treating my malaria."

"Why didn't you let Dr. Nutting treat you?"

"I saw conspiracy everywhere."

"Do you still?" Wingate nodded. "Who is aligned against you?"

"Most of the army."

"Why is that?"

Wingate sighed. "Probably started with Palestine. You know about that from my dossier."

"Why did you side with the Jews?"

"I have a bond with underdogs."

"Go on."

"When I was a schoolboy, when I was a cadet, whenever I seemed odd to others..." Wingate fell into silence.

"Go on."

"I know how it feels to be disliked, to be shunned. In Palestine I found a colony of such people. I was drawn to them."

"And to their cause?"

"Later."

"And what about the cause of the evicted Arabs?"

"They touched me too. But there was little I could do for them. They were victims of their class."

"Yes."

"I had no means to protect them from their Arab landlords. But I could get back at...at those vultures...through Hagana."

"Hagana let you protect the Jews while at the same time thwart the greedy Arab landlords."

"Exactly."

"How did you make contact with Hagana?"

"Through David Hacohen."

Parnell shuffled through Wingate's voluminous file. "There's probably something here about him, but why don't you tell me?"

"Hagana was very feeble from a military point of view. More a debating society than a guerrilla organization. They distributed some small arms around the settlements but little more."

"Who was in it besides Hacohen?"

"Moshe Dayan, Menachem Begin—just well-meaning civilians except for Hacohen."

"Ben-Gurion? Weizmann? Wilensky?"

"Basically pacifists. Only Hacohen had any military abilities."

Parnell read for a moment. "Would you like to hear what he wrote of you?" Wingate nodded; the first trace of a smile returned to his face. "Well, he says you had the look of an ascetic—he should see you now. A somber face, eyes deepset and penetrating...untidy hair... and conversation that was direct, uncluttered, and devoid of formal politeness. On the mark I'd say. You didn't win him over right away, did you?"

"They suspected me of being a British agent."

"In time you seem to have persuaded Hacohen anyway, that your devotion to Zion was genuine."

"Jews are inherently suspicious. It took Hacohen and Wilensky to convince the others."

"Wilensky: what do I have from him? But of course, he gave you the name, the code name, by which you were known to the Jews. *Hayedid Shelka*—did I pronounce it right?" Wingate nodded. "And it means?"

"Your friend. That meant Wilensky's friend. It was shortened to *Hayedid*."

"So you became known simply as 'the friend.' I don't suppose they had many others among the British officers."

"No."

"Was it in Palestine that you took up the practice of dry scrubbing rather than bathing?"

Wingate smiled. "No, I learned that on my Libyan expedition. Did Hacohen say something about me scrubbing down?"

"He notes that you came to the attention of his wife."

"I used to massage my toes with a pencil after dinner. The feet are very important in the desert you know. We used to call them our 'personnel carriers.'" Parnell smiled, but Wingate's remark only seemed to have reminded him of his feet. "Could we resume later, doctor? I like to walk while the decks are uncrowded."

"Of course. See you after breakfast."

37

Parnell arranged these early morning sessions even though they were outside his routine (Wingate's was still to rise with the sun). Once more Ethiopian dawn would be his when *Llandovery Castle* passed by the coast of Eritrea. He was unusually sullen that morning and Parnell noticed.

"Didn't it give you satisfaction to see the shore of the country you liberated?"

"No."

"The last memory is the one you remember?"

"Yes, and it's bitter. Selassie is king once more but Platt rules."

Parnell pointed to a thick stack of affidavits. "There's not an officer on his staff who had a charitable word for you. Did you have a single friend in Sudan?"

"I've never tried to make friends."

"Why not?"

"It's not worth the effort, the hypocrisy."

"Hypocrisy?"

"To be liked I must pretend to like other people."

"And you don't."

"If I do... there's difficulty letting them know it."

"Difficulty or reluctance?"

"Yes, more like reluctance."

"Do you like yourself?"

"Rarely."

"When?"

"When I'm planning. When plans succeed."

"As when?"

Wingate clasped his hands behind his head and stared at the rug. "Safartak."

"A brilliant victory." Wingate started to reply but became puzzled by his thoughts. "A spectacular triumph as your severest critics agree."

"Yes. So why shouldn't I be different from them? They can't do what I can. Why search me for the usual patterns of popularity?"

"We observe the normal to understand the abnormal."

"I synonymize normality with mediocrity."

"Normality has its virtues; it provides firm ground on which to face vicissitudes. Normality is security."

"I trade security for more heady rewards."

"And when you don't receive them you slit your throat." Parnell had been watching the eyes, preparing for the moment when they swung onto his with full, piercing force. Wingate focused on him as if Parnell were Zobi in the shadow of the truck with their duel still in doubt.

"Yes," he hissed, "I'm an all-or-nothing person."

"Have you ever stopped to wonder why? Most of us make compromises at one time or another. Very little of that in your record."

"Or in the Bible."

"The Bible seems to speak to you in quite personal terms."

"It was drummed into me. My family was very churchy. Plymouth Brethren. Bible thumpers."

"Did you have a favorite biblical story?"

"Joshua." Wingate answered quickly. "My Ethiopian campaign was modeled on the way Joshua deceived the enemy, how he used guile to conquer strength. So too did David and Gideon—both underdogs who came out on top."

"Is the Bible more for you than a military textbook?"

"It is the story of the Jews."

"Whom you greatly admire."

"Because of their defiance of history's odds. I was drawn to them because they were embattled, oppressed."

"Yet you argued with them constantly."

"Because their leaders were forever working on accommodations with the pasha or the mufti or some duplicitous sheiks. Compromise, you were saying. That was their weakness." Wingate gestured at the thick file on the desk. "Did Hacohen mention our last argument on the subject of compromise?"

"Tell me about it."

"I reminded him of the compromise he was negotiating when he had to flee Germany."

"With whom?"

"The Nazis."

Parnell audibly exhaled. "Yes, you were never afraid to shame the Jews. Quite remarkable. Yet in what I've read each had something fond to say. What do you supposed endeared you to them? I realize you suffered wounds in their behalf."

"I reconnected them with their great military traditions—with Joshua and Maccabee—how through the ages the Jews survived like pines on a crag. I joined a thousand-year tradition of defiance. I wanted more than anything else in my life to shake my fist with the Jews and shout with them, 'We won!'"

Parnell closed his notebook with an inner smile, for he took Wingate's arousal as a healthy sign. "Orde, think a bit about defiance."

"Get to the bottom of it you mean?" Parnell nodded. "How?"

"I would like to regress you."

"Hypnosis?"

"Yes, with the aid of hypnosis. It's entirely up to you, and your cooperation must be genuine."

"I'll let no one control my mind."

"No one but you. We'll simply watch some of your life like a movie; make comments when it's over."

"I've never done this before."

"You never tried suicide before."

"Agreed."

"Are you comfortable?"

Wingate closed his eyes. Parnell had him imagine his chair slowly descending on an elevator, descending ten floors; he had him see each number as it slipped by and count them down aloud. When he reached 'one,' Parnell said the door was opening on the most pleasant place in his life.

"What do you see, Orde?"

"The garden," he answered slowly as he examined his mental surroundings.

"How old are you?"

"Five. Six."

"Where?"

"I'm in Lodolf. Such beautiful colors."

"See how vivid they are. Is it warm in the garden? Is there a breeze?"

"Very pleasant."

"You feel the breeze, don't you?"

"Yes."

"Where is Lodolf?"

"In the garden. Everywhere. It is my kingdom."

"Who are your subjects?"

"Lady Drusela. Baroness Elfrida."

"Who are you?"

"King Harold."

"What are you doing?"

"Playing. It's all make-believe."

Wingate smiled faintly, submerged in deeper silence as Parnell watched his eyelids flutter.

38

Llandovery Castle passed through Bab al-Mandab, the strait between Asia and Africa, then took an easterly course before swinging around the horn of Somalia. The quiet lapping of the Red Sea changed to the rolling surges of the Indian Ocean. The endless procession of gray-green waves seemed to draw the passengers into themselves. The decks were less crowded; men became solitary wave watchers.

"...three,...two,...one," Parnell intoned as Wingate emerged once more. He reluctantly opened his eyes, his breathing still slow and peaceful.

"We're getting somewhere, aren't we, doctor?"

"No hurry. You enjoy these sessions?"

"I do."

"But?"

"Are they helping, do you think?"

"You help yourself. As you did in make-believe."

"Today I was Prince William, the Abandoned."

"The three of you played many roles. Was there never anyone in Lodolf except your two sisters?"

"Many...very many. While I'm silent I imagine an elaborate universe of characters. Today we joined the Northern League."

"Involving whom?"

"Characters from Defoe, Scott—many from Mallory—Tennyson."

"You interact with them?"

"We share their adventures and perils. Whatever we were reading in those days became part of Lodolf. All nonsense, of course, but great fun."

"But today you were William, the Abandoned. Who abandoned you?"

"My sisters."

"Why?"

"Well, I didn't read well. Surprising isn't it, since reading is now one of my great pleasures. I was started off on the Bible but quickly fell behind my younger sisters. Rachel and Sybil used to tease me with their reading ability." Wingate smiled. "They would read out of Grimm's and ooh and ah, and say things to each other like 'Isn't that marvelous!' Taunt me, you see, about what I was missing."

"They teased you into literacy?"

"Exactly. I was a dull little fellow but I could be provoked into learning."

"That was when your father had retired and returned from India?" Wingate nodded. "Do you remember much of India?"

"Not a thing. Sometimes a smell will be reminiscent; curry especially. I was only born there. Odd isn't it?"

"What's odd?"

"That I remember nothing about my earliest childhood."

"Not even a playmate?"

"My sisters only."

"During the Lodolf period?"

"Only my sisters. My family was very protective. I think they feared the world would corrupt us. I know this sounds extreme but we had no playmates outside the family. I doubt I met a dozen other children from the time I was six till I was twelve."

"Birthday parties?"

"Restricted to the family."

"Dances?"

"Certainly not."

"Cricket, football?"

"No. I've never cared much for ball games."

"Or other team games?"

"A bit of rugby."

"Well, Lodolf must have become tiresome by the time you were twelve."

"There was always church," Wingate remarked with a sigh. "We were a most religious family."

"Plymouth Brethren, I believe you told me."

"Yes. Fundamentalist, evangelical. One of my sisters is a missionary in Turkistan."

"Now you were the first of how many children?"

"Seven."

"Often a child coming from a large, closed family has trouble adjusting to the larger world. Was that your experience?"

"Yes. I was a dayboy. I carried all sorts of religious prohibitions into Charterhouse. I used to think it scandalous when my schoolmates attended concerts on Sunday. My parents, I'm afraid, reinforced my intolerance."

"Were you popular in school?"

"Lord no. For some reason the kids called me 'Stinker.'"

"Sounds as though you were combative even then."

"Not at all. I think I had fewer fights than anyone. You see, when they were kicking about on free afternoons, I'd go to the chapel and catch up on my prayers."

"You were that devout?"

"By family standards, no. By kids' standards, very much so. I thought I was backsliding from God while I was in school. To everyone else I must have seemed quite churchy."

"How were your academics?"

"Indifferent."

"Athletics?"

"Nothing. I've always had coordination and stamina but not to apply to organized games. There were no individual sports I was drawn to in school. I took up riding later."

"What about military training?"

"It was just drill and parade at that level. I was nothing more than a lance corporal."

39

For several days Wingate was laid low by malarial attacks. These were waning in severity but not in frequency.

"Getting them out of my system," Wingate assured Parnell. "The bug is losing its strength while I am gaining mine. I'm always pleased to have an enemy attack me. When he uses up his strength, his threat to my plans diminishes."

"I should like to hear a bit about your plans."

"In London I may receive a more sympathetic hearing for Tibesti." This was a plan he had urged upon Wavell before Selassie came into the picture. In southern Libya are the Tibesti Mountains, an ideal site from where Wingate could raid Rommel's supply lines. He had proposed the formation of a brigade of West Africans, led by himself, to move into the region and strike across the desert supported by a small detachment of the Royal Air Force.

"Straight off you will advance Tibesti with the high command?" Wingate nodded. "So continued service in a British uniform is your first preference?"

"Had you thought otherwise?"

"I wasn't sure whether Great Britain or Zion had first call."

"If Zion called for me I would fly to their colors. I have your absolute word that you will never repeat this sentiment, don't I?"

"Absolutely."

"There will be no call while the goodwill of Whitehall is more important to Zion than my services. However, if I'm sacked, I would surely seek my fortune in Palestine."

"You would revive the Special Night Squads?"

"Hardly. They were an expedient of that prewar time. SNS was the work of a captain. Israel will need a general after this war."

"What if you are not that general?"

"Then Lorna and I will live in a cottage, study our art books, and buy a gramophone like yours." He had borrowed Parnell's phonograph and collection of classics each morning after his session and returned them after lunch.

"Now let me guess which of my records are your favorites. The Beethoven."

"Yes."

"Then the Mozart?"

"Fortieth only."

"I should have guessed. You go in the romantic direction from Beethoven. Tchaikovsky was second?"

"Piano only. *Romeo and Juliet* is fine. The rest, maudlin."

"You don't care for his string pieces?"

"Not his nor anyone else's. Why listen to a small ensemble when you can hear a full symphony?"

"All right then, which of Beethoven's? *Eroica?*"

"Sometimes I worry that you're typecasting me. Ninth. Then Seventh, then Fourth."

"And he is your favorite of all composers?"

"No. Shall I tell you?"

"Let me come at that indirectly. Could you describe your musical aesthetic? How you perceive the art form, that is."

Wingate tented his fingers and looked up at the ceiling as it slowly inclined with the sea. "Now that's the sort of question I enjoy. The kind Lorna and I delighted in discussing. It goes to the product of the mind rather than the method of production. Seems to me you psychiatrists should examine that orientation. But the critic creates his own standards, doesn't he?"

"Less abstraction please."

"Well you said you were going to be indirect so let me be. How is this for an abstract answer?...No, I shall get to *it* indirectly. Let us start with the senses and God's hand in them. Smell and taste are trivial; no art form attaches to them."

"You've been eating army rations too long."

"Point taken, doctor, point taken. Now the third sense, that of touch, is also bereft of artistic content. Indeed, touch is entirely utilitarian except in sex. That's where you find the highest tactile gratification—in sex."

"What does God have to do with all this?"

"In a moment. Just let me round out the five by mentioning the two high senses, sight and sound. Through our eyes and through our ears we perceive beauty and appreciate art. Painters and sculptors will argue with this, but God rules the visual arts though nature. Consider how a sunset preempts in impact any artwork of man.

"But with sound, the situation is reversed. God has left the medium to man. No sound in nature can compare in impact with a passage from Wagner. Music is man's own art, an expression he shares not even with God."

"That's quite profound, Orde," said Parnell. "I understand why you would wish for your thoughts to be examined by themselves."

"Maybe in the next century they will be."

"Was your suicide a statement for posterity?"

"A presumptuous statement."

"Never to be repeated?"

"God no. Never."

"Even with all the Platts and Enrights in the world?"

"All the more because of them. I'll not let my death be their victory."

"There's a great deal more I need to know about you, Orde, but I'm beginning to believe you no longer a threat to cut your throat again. But that way, you would only imperil your own life. More important is my obligation to those who may serve under you. I see a clear possibility of you taking men with you in some joint sacrifice."

The rasp returned to Wingate's voice. "If that's insanity, I share it with every soldier who has ever held command."

"Yes, this is a much closer question than that of your solo destruction. I don't mind if you argue with me about it, Orde. You are certainly your own best spokesman."

40

Wingate's malaria subsided, but his fever suddenly rose dangerously. Noticing his difficulty in speaking, Parnell had him examined. Septic tonsilitis was discovered, not surprisingly, as the knife blade had punctured the voice box. The psychiatric sessions were suspended over Wingate's protests.

When they resumed, Wingate was uneasy that Parnell seemed to have lost particular interest in Wingate's formative years and led him back into Palestine. At one point Wingate snapped that there was more biography than therapy in these sessions. Parnell replied his charge was to judge, not to cure. A cure, if there were one, required more time plus permanent facilities such as those which awaited the ship at Durban. This casual comment almost revived the Wingate of Cairo.

"This is a most unfair double standard you apply to me, doctor. You are now asking whether I should ever again be allowed to risk my life. Quite a different question than before."

"Risk yours and others."

"My commission allows me to do that already. As it does every other officer. The king has authorized us to take prudent risks with life. To withdraw it is a royal rather than a medical decision."

"I am a crown physician."

"And would you, in good professional conscience, single me out as too reckless to be entrusted with command?"

"Possibly."

"Without recognizing that the real butchers of the army hold the higher commands? Look at the casualties. I saved lives by guile and maneuver."

"If you don't rest your voice, I must break off this session."

"You are goading me! That's the plan, isn't it? Put me in a fury so I'll be distraught for the doctors in Durban!" Wingate coughed painfully.

"I've warned you. Here, drink this before you explode. Now I want you to focus your intellect on this hypothesis: everyone who does not agree with you at all times is not in a conspiracy."

"You are..."

"You cannot argue with a hypothesis—you can only test it." Wingate glowered. "Now tell me how prudent you were with the SNS."

"How do you mean?"

"You were just telling me how proud you were of the low casualties in Gideon Force. What about the Special Night Squads? There you took civilians with no military experience and sent them out into the night to clash with the Arabs. With what result?"

"With the result that the Jewish settlements were saved! They were pitifully defenseless before I organized them."

"I asked you about casualties."

"Casualties can only be considered in comparisons. Those of the SNS were light compared with the civilian dead if the raiders continued their depredations."

"That's fine. But tell me, is there less fighting now than before the Special Night Squads? Less loss of life?"

"I think so. The Arabs no longer attack at will. They respect the arms of the Jews."

"I hope so. But as an ignorant civilian I see you creating a third army in Palestine where there had been only two. Fewer armies, it seems to me, lead to less bloodshed."

"Yes, that's a very ignorant observation, even for a civilian. There's only one army in France now—Hitler's—where before there had been three. Can you wonder if I suspect you of trying to infuriate me?"

"Have you noticed how easily you are infuriated? On the one hand I'm encouraged by the arousal of your spirits—when we started these sessions you were nearly catatonic—on the other hand, you're stoking up the furnace of resentment again. Do you remember how high the heat was in Cairo?"

"I've told you: I have a thermostat now. Or do you expect me to become a contemplative? God has restored my *life*, not just my existence."

"You think God could not do without the old Wingate?"

"That furnace you spoke of tempered me. There's not a new Wingate—I'll not promise you that even if it means my commission—but there's a tempered Wingate. So I may be even harder than before."

"Yes. Harder on yourself. Harder on your men. Harder to live with. Harder on the conventions which support the army. That's exactly my concern."

Wingate began pacing, something he had not done in previous sessions. "You cannot put conditions on me, doctor. There's no place for me on limited duty or in some noncombatant role."

"That would be foolish. Your value to the army is in combat, nowhere else."

"Agreed. You must give me a clean bill of mental health or have me either committed or cashiered. Freedom is unconditional."

"Yes, it's a stark choice I must make. Your cause is not helped by your adamancy; yet you are completely forthright, and that is a quality I must respect."

"I'm not being deliberately difficult with you, Manfred."

"You aren't difficult at all. You're probably the easiest patient I've ever had. Everything is on the surface; you hold nothing back. What you don't know about yourself is perfectly evident."

"Not to me."

"Then you must not have been listening to yourself during all these sessions."

"Please review what I should have heard." Wingate walked faster, and looked everywhere except at Parnell.

"You defiance for a start. Whenever there's an opportunity for defiance, you seize it and multiply its consequences."

"Specifics, please."

"The hazing at Woolwich. All cadets were run through the gauntlet. What did you do? You walked through. Defied them to strike you. Even your tactics seemed based on defiance of expectations."

"Doctor, that's an excellent definition of surprise," Wingate said with genuine admiration. "You're right. I seek it in every engagement."

"Your suicide—the ultimate defiance. Could there be a more defiant act than to cut one's beard by cutting one's throat?" Wingate lowered his eyes. "Authority in any form is your enemy. Victories came to you when authority and an armed foe were enemies to be defeated in tandem. You seem doubly inspired under those special circumstances. In Palestine it was the Arabs and the British. In Ethiopia, the Italians and the British. In London, the Germans and the British."

"I was defeated in London."

"Indeed you were. You need allies like the Jews or Ethiopians to serve your purposes. There may be no foreign allies next time, Orde. That is why your fitness for command is so problematic." Wingate glared. "You know the perfect place for you in the army?"

"No."

"You should be parachuted into Germany. As a prisoner of war you could defy both the enemy and authority together."

"No doubt that will be your recommendation. I congratulate you on a thorough analysis. Is there more?"

"Quite a bit. I like to organize patients' attitudes under three relationships: man to mate, man to man, and man to God. We've hardly touched on your marriage. Your position with God is much more important to you than it is with most men, and we're going to explore that before we land. It's your relationship with other men which has been our principal subject because it is my job to try to sort it out and advise the army what's to be done.

"So what do we know of your relations with other men? In a self-contained society like the army all relations are professionally tinted. That is, you've never struck up a friendship with the milkman or some casual civilian acquaintance."

"I had friends from the hunt."

"Yes. Glad you remembered them. They're an exception. But do you allow that all your important relationships, outside your kin, were in or around the military?"

"That's my profession."

"Indeed. I meant that as no criticism."

"Thank you."

"Oddly enough for a maverick, you are very much committed to certain values of the military. Your sense of mission is exemplary. In fact it is overriding. You will never subordinate it to other military values such as discipline, deportment, respect for rank, and so forth. Yes?"

"Those, as you say, are values, not missions."

"Any military practice you see as creating its own purpose rather than that of supporting the mission is the arch sin of hypocrisy."

"Hear, hear."

"So for you, once a mission is stated—liberate Ethiopia; protect the Jews—all else is valueless except that which serves the mission..."

Wingate interrupted: "Regrettably missions are not stated so unambiguously."

"Ah yes, but you see them to be. Since the mission is clear to you, you assume others will see it with the same clarity. With great effort and patience you will explain to anyone that your means are the correct ones. You welcome the suggestions of others—Harris, for example—and adopt them without any egotistical impedence. When the mission seems to call for it, you will be devious, ruthless, and perhaps worse. Tiberias, for example, where you let the townspeople perish so that you could ambush the raiders."

"Bad example. I couldn't have saved them with my squad."

"Since all who disagree with your way of attaining the mission are per se wrong, they incur your disrespect. Your way of showing this is defiance. As we discussed, your suicide was an act of ultimate defiance. I'm persuaded that you've outgrown that behavior."

"Again I promise."

"Along with defiance is a burgeoning suspicion that those who oppose you, or even disagree with you, are in a conspiracy. This very much colors your relationships. It ill becomes you since suspicion of conspiracy is sloppy, lazy thinking. It's the easy answer which excuses you from searching for other reasons—reasons which could show your faults.

"People like you fall into this habit because of their lack of empathy. You judge people wrongly because you cannot take their point of view or put yourself in their place. Probably the brilliance of the mission does not let you see the nuances of personality."

"May it always be that way. If the mission does not outshine all else, there is no reason for soldiers."

"That would make a fine epitaph for you. However, consider for a moment Colonel Marleybone." Wingate halted, placed his hands on his hips, and glared at the doctor. "His mission was to see that the army paid premiums only to those authorized by regulations..."

"You've used two words that are anathema: 'authorized' and 'regulations.' We are not authorized to breathe; yet it is necessary that we do. War is not regulated; it is fought. If..."

Parnell raised his hand. "You needn't go on. I'd just like for you to consider there are many missions within the largest ones."

"True enough, so long as they are recognized as secondary."

"As is all else secondary while you are captive of some exalted mission. In your eyes it excuses all your behavior. It subordinates values of a larger context. In short, the end justifies whatever means you see fit."

"You go very far."

"Actually I've only taken your relationships in one direction—up among your superiors. It's the other direction which concerns me even more: how your crusading affects your men. I've had no record from those below you, only from above."

"I told you about Harris, Simonds, Atkins. The Jews I trained were in a sense subordinates."

"And I gather they for the most part urged moderation upon you."

"Harris, those fellows?"

"No, people like Sadeh and Shertock."

"I did not command them. The SNS followed me of their own free will."

"With the Jews that is more understandable. You indeed were adopting their mission rather than they serving yours. Let's leave the Jews aside as a special circumstance. In the future you may be commanding British subjects. I must search your character to see if your zeal would unduly endanger them."

"My Brits in Ethiopia were all volunteers. They volunteered to be commanded by me. And I didn't promise them any maypole dance either."

"How many would volunteer again I wonder? You told me about Atkins. At the end he seemed to have perceived a dark drive within you."

"Cliff? What did he ever say about a 'dark drive'? I put pressure on him; I put pressure on all of Gideon Force. That's war, doctor: pressure, sleeplessness, and grime."

"What did he say to you at the end?"

"Good-bye."

"This is serious, Orde."

"You mean about losing his foot?"

"Yes."

"I don't remember his words."

"You spoke them."

"That must have been while you had me under hypnosis. What did I say?"

"'Losers go home; winners go on to the next round.' Remember that?"

"That's what he said? Come to think of it . . . that's pretty much what he did say."

"It had a major impact on you."

"I didn't even recall it till you reminded me."

"You turned quite emotional when I regressed you to that incident."

"Anything can happen under hypnosis."

Parnell shook his head. "Atkins's statement was the major incident you brought up from the entire campaign. The only memory to bring tears."

"So? The man had just lost his foot. I actually have feelings, believe it or not."

"The feeling of cost to others—the price which must be exacted for victory—is a feeling which you very successfully suppress or sublimate, I don't know which. This is a very un-British characteristic, you know. I've had occasion to examine a number of high-ranking officers after Rommel kicked them across Libya. Their problem was the obverse of yours: they were *too* concerned for the preservation of the lives entrusted to them."

Wingate snorted. "You can bet Rommel was not. We're going over old ground again. In the end, quick victory is always the best way to save lives."

"An excellent rationalization, especially when victory is quickest when pursued your way. But you're right; this is old ground. We can leave it, but would you just tell me the first thoughts you have concerning Atkins's statement?"

"First thought?"

"Yes. Don't stop to use your intellect."

"It just seemed to sum up something. The losers drop out; the winners move on. Like some great elimination contest. It was as if I had been plucking on a number of single strings; then suddenly there was this chord which used them all."

"That's fine, Orde. Let's leave it at that."

41

As *Llandovery Castle* swung to the east of Madagascar, rumors began that a Japanese submarine was tailing the ship. This was October 1941. England and Japan were not at war, but the British Empire in the Far East was naked of defenses except for the fortress at Singapore. A stab in the back, such as Mussolini had inflicted on France, seemed imminent.

Durban was but twenty-four hours away. Parnell had yet to tell his patient what the recommendation would be. Wingate still suspected treachery but had bridled himself with noticeable restraint.

"Have you been praying, Orde?"

"Yes, damn you."

"I promised you a session on God. This will be it, and this will be our last one."

"Praise God."

"Nearly everyone has remarked on your Bible toting; yet you described yourself as the least religious member of your family. Moreover, you fell away from the Plymouth Brethren and you're not a churchgoer. Judaism seems to interest you only with its blood and thunder. There's some paradox here I'd like you to talk about."

"My God is a personal god. I need no intermediaries."

"Does He love you?"

"He has a place for me in His design. This is demonstration of His love."

"Do you please Him?"

"When I do His work. Now I know what you'll ask: how do I distinguish His work from my own? I don't know because I've never found any tension between the two."

"The killing we spoke of previously: how do you think He views it? Does He grieve for fallen Italians and Nazis?"

183

"I've never asked Him."

"This will take much longer if you're going to be flip."

"God only bestows such understanding upon me as I need to do His work. I am not perplexed by the death found in war. Therefore, I have not troubled my maker with philosophical questions."

"Do you pray for the fallen?"

"I only pray that God's will be done."

"Do you pray for the safety of others?"

"Yes."

"What if it were God's will that you cease from waging war?"

"He would have to make that very plain to me."

"Suppose it had been you rather than Atkins who had lost his foot?"

"Then it would have been plain to me."

"What did He think of your attempted suicide?"

"It was an unpardonable sin that only He could pardon. He did. By that He clearly marked me to serve Him with greater responsibilities."

"Like Clive and Frederick the Great?"

"I'd forgotten about Clive!"

"He should be your patron saint. He tried three times."

"I'm grateful to learn that."

"Well, we may as well conclude on that happy note."

"We're done?"

"With God."

"What else is there?"

"Only my recommendation."

"Which is?"

"I have no medical grounds for declaring you unfit."

"No grounds whatsoever?"

"No grounds on which a military board could rule against you."

"Am I to be congratulated? Are you?"

"I'm not congratulating myself. You see, I have a boy in the Royal Ulster Rifles. A lieutenant about Atkins's age. Serving in Assam at the moment. Hoping the Japanese start something in Burma. He would have been your first volunteer for Gideon Force."

Parnell heard the rasp in Wingate's throat as he breathed deeply. "Should your son ever serve under me in war, I can make you one guarantee: he shall not die needlessly."

Parnell looked away. "I suppose that is all a father could ask of you. Though there seems to be more. Much more. It continues to amaze me how society can take my boy away and make me feel truly guilty for wanting him back at any price."

"Manfred, I make a suggestion to you with all the strength of which I'm capable: look at some films—of Spain, of Poland, of France, of Greece, of Ethiopia. Such films are plentiful at GHQ. See if there is any alternative more loathsome than the boot and face of fascism. I think you will wish you could shoulder arms. I think you'll be glad your son can."

"Perhaps. Perhaps. Now convince his mother."

"I convinced mine."

Parnell sighed. "How different we all are. Orde, I've very much profited from these sessions. I apologize for the stress they no doubt caused you. In your health, you should not have been subjected to it. It was almost malpractice on my part."

"Nonsense. I demanded these sessions. You have done me a great service which I shall never forget. I feel prepared," said Wingate with a twinkle "for the final judgment, for I doubt it it could be more rigorous than your examination."

"You face an earlier judgment, and one probably more painful."

"Yes..."

"I wish I could see the two of you together. Would you like a name in London?"

Wingate fidgeted. "Yes. Please. I...I will tell her myself, but later a counselor might be helpful."

Parnell consulted an address book, scrawled a note, and sealed it. "Hawthorne Terrace," said Parnell, handing him the envelope.

"St. John's Wood?" Parnell nodded. "They looked to my regiment for air defense at one time. Shall I say good-bye?"

"I shall come ashore. You may depart the same day if *Empress of Australia* is at quayside. But let us say good-bye. We shall both be very busy later."

"You do God's work, doctor," said Wingate, taking his hand. "I pray that I shall too. Till we meet again."

"Good-bye, Orde. Pray that God shall grant us peace."

Durban was a dingy whaling town but a welcome sight for the patients so long at sea. They were helped down the gangplank, some walking, some in wheelchairs, some on stretchers. The townspeople gathered in silent curiosity as the reality of the faraway war visited them. Heads lifted momentarily as a native military band struck up some patriotic airs. The commander of the convalescent camp took over matters briskly. His first act was to segregate those remaining from those who would ship out at once for the British Isles.

There were two lists for this purpose: one compiled by Parnell's staff aboard ship and the other that of an advisory cabled from Cairo. The two were identical except for a half dozen names, Wingate's being one of them. Customarily the ship's list superseded the advance list without question; it was expected that treatment at sea might cause some unexpected recoveries. However, the camp commander asked specifically about Wingate; so Parnell was obliged to authorize his forwarding in writing.

This he did without hesitation and without asking the reason for the exceptional procedure. He tried to find Wingate but was caught up in the administrative bustle. He remembered his oversight when the horn of the *Empress* announced its departure. It caused him little regret; Wingate's recovery was too fragile to bear the weight of a continued conspiracy.

For one of the few times in his life, conspiracy was not among Wingate's concerns. He was at sea for weeks and bedridden until his new hospital ship rounded the Cape of Good Hope. Then, as if the name of the headland echoed in his spirits, he rid himself for the last time of his throat infection.

The spring of the southern hemisphere seemed to advance upon the *Empress* as she steamed north. Once again all ship lights were ablaze—an island of peace floating toward war-torn Europe.

There was a comic festival for Poseidon when the equator was crossed. Wingate watched his fellow patients as they watched the merrymaking. In formless pyjamas and rough-cut bathrobes, they were relearning how to laugh. For most, their contribution to the war was over. Like spent athletes they would remain on the sidelines as their substitutes continued the contest.

The losers go home, the winners go on to the next round. Wingate pondered Atkins's insight as a summary of war. But no chain of thought developed; the insight seemed too fleeting to incorporate into wisdom. Analysis emptied Atkins's words of their significance.

Wingate was going home a loser but only a temporary one he was sure. He would advance to the next round without looking back. There was only one reference to his past that lay ahead: Lorna must be told how he nearly forfeited his future. Telling her would be like cliff diving: the plunge and the cold darkness would be deep but return to the surface was sure.

42

The November skies of the Atlantic were mottled white and blue as *Empress of Australia* continued north, until the overcast of the British Isles reached out to them like the ghosts of ancestors. Soon the skies were as somber as the sea.

Nervousness seeped into the ship as it approached the first fog bank. U-boats controlled the approaches to Britain, where in the mist the white gleam of the hospital ship was indistinct. Regular blasts of the foghorn were melancholy fanfare for the returning wounded.

"The boys are always edgy at this point in the voyage," the first officer advised, "but just watch the morale when we reach Kintyre. Hope your passage was pleasant, Major."

"An interlude if not an idyll. There's much I like about hospitals both afloat and ashore."

"I don't hear such compliments often."

"Well my honeymoon was in a hospital, you see, in Bulford."

"Overextended yourself, sir?"

"That wasn't the problem," Wingate laughed. "No, we lived in the annex of a hospital. Successors to the terminal patients you might say."

"She's waiting for you, I imagine."

"At dockside."

Lorna's letters, often reread on *Empress of Australia*, convinced him
he could draw life from her once again. Their philosophical enjoyments
were not like prewar luxuries which could only return with peace. More
so than other couples, their relationship was suited for wartime. It
was not focused on home and children but on feelings and thought
which together amounted to understanding.

She would understand when he told her what he had done. She
would not at first because he did not understand himself what had
possessed him, but in the process of describing the development of
suicide he would be explaining it to himself.

The headlands of Kintyre were lost in the fog. The banks of the Clyde
were almost as obscured; so the returning veterans heard the sounds of
their homeland before they saw it. Each parochial air by the military
band drew a cheer from the patients bundled on deck. "Scotland the
Brave" accompanied the lowering of the gangplank, for this was Glasgow.

Stretchers and wheelchairs went ashore first. Wingate would be
among the last to debark for he was among the healthiest. He thought
back to when he was trundled on board *Llandovery Castle:* the months
at sea had been like "taking the cure" at a sanatorium. Consequently,
Wingate was anxious for the meeting he had once dreaded.

As he leaned on the rail of the top deck, he tried to identify her,
but all below were indistinguishable in heavy winter clothing. Lorna
knew he would be standing apart somewhere. She saw a figure alone
and thought of waving, but he was so motionless she knew he was
absorbed by the scene on the quay.

And so was she. To view the debarkation, the crowd drew together. The greeters quieted as stretchers came down the plank; paths were
made for their kin. Some on the stretchers were so heavily bandaged
they had to be studied for identification. Names were called.

"Paul, Paul?" Lorna heard a woman murmur as each of the terribly
wounded went by.

Sometimes a hand rose from a stretcher in feeble recognition as
bouquets clutched in gloves withered in the cold. A hush remained on
the crowd until the last ambulance rolled away.

Then the walking wounded flowed down the plank. They had been watching too, and each seemed imbued by their relative good fortune. Many had spotted loved ones; on canes and crutches they found the waiting arms as the band broke into waltzes.

Wingate left his vantage point and slipped into the stream of debarking patients. Only as he approached the last few steps did he closely examine the faces below.

They held each other silently. Little warmth flowed through her sweaters and overcoat. Closing his eyes, he sensed her as support.

"Orde, are you all right?"

"I think so."

They looked at each other carefully before they began a long kiss.

"You're ruddy cold," he said.

"Hadn't noticed. You're ruddy thin."

The night before on the outskirts of Glasgow she had found a pub famous for its hot toddies. The waiter smiled as he approached with the steaming mugs.

"Compliments of the management, Major," he said, and some longshoremen nearby raised their cups to the couple.

"Thank you very much," said Wingate, returning the toast with one hand and taking Lorna's with the other.

"Ya' gaive it ta' the Jerries, I'm sure," said the waiter.

"The Italians," said Lorna.

"Just as good."

"Down the hatch," Wingate added. The steaming liquid nearly scalded his mouth.

"*Laheim*," said Lorna softly as they turned to each other.

"Your letters were everything for me, Lorna. I don't suppose I wrote as often." She moved some hair away from her face, a gesture that told him she understood. "But there wasn't an hour I didn't think of you."

"There wasn't a minute for me."

"I remembered your charm but not how charming you are."

"Your lovable abstractions." They kissed over the table.

"I hope you find in me what you did before." He stirred his drink.

"And why shouldn't I? You've never changed except for the better."

"Don't let the occasion slant your judgment."

"All right: I exaggerate, but only a bit. You change very little and that is my pleasure."

"Have I ever shocked you?" he asked with a seriousness she missed.

"How could you shock me? Others often. Not me. Unless I count the time you put Bathsheba in uniform for the regimental ball."

"You helped."

She smiled in recollection of dressing the baboon. "Yes, but the idea was yours, and it startled me."

They joined hands to laugh together.

"Do I seem to be beating around a bush?" he asked.

"Not that I'm aware of. Now that's a rather leading question, Orde."

"Yes. I hope I'm leading myself correctly."

"Should I assist or let you muse?"

Wingate raised his head and turned it to her in profile. "Did you notice?"

"The scar..."

"It's by my hand."

"Orde!"

"And there's one to match on the other side."

"Your voice..."

"Much better than it used to be."

The steam from the toddies rose between their faces.

"I was told you had malaria."

"I did. I do."

"When?"

"In Cairo. I don't want to tell you about it now, but I will, I promise you."

"It happened in Cairo?"

"In July."

"I don't know what to say. I don't know what to think."

"I've asked God's forgiveness. I ask as much for yours."

"You would be gone now. We wouldn't be here talking. I'm dumbfounded. You would have... *left!*"

"God drew me back." Wingate loosened his collar as he was beginning to sweat.

"Your fever?"

"No, my confession." She took out a handkerchief. "I'm purging myself, Lorna. I'll be better for it."

"I want to walk."

"We must finish these." She couldn't. While he sipped his toddy, she looked away, ignoring a tear that clung to her cheek. "Can't you look at me?"

"I want to leave. Now."

Stonily she stared out the window while he thanked his well-wishers. Outside the couple took an ascending path into deepening mist. Lorna's arms were straight, her hands thrust deep in the coat pockets.

"Orde, did you once think of me?"

"I tried to write something for you. But I sank in rage and despair." They strode on in a silence he broke by kicking a rock. "You're going awfully fast."

"Can't keep up? Am I faster than the Italians?" It was his turn for silence. "What determination, Orde, what single-mindedness! Jab yourself on one side, then make sure on the other. There must have been a *moment* in between. What did you think of?"

"I don't remember."

"What *do* you remember?"

"An overpowering anguish and betrayal, Lorna—insufferable guilt with only one escape. I know this sounds incredibly selfish but I just couldn't suffer anymore."

"Yes, quite incredible. Your suffering had nothing to do with me, did it?" she asked as a statement. "Didn't it seem possible to lessen your guilt by stopping the knife?"

The uneven path caused him to stumble. "You're trying to separate ingredients in a caldron. Every insane evil was combined like a witch's brew."

"Just where was I in the brew?"

He struck his hands on his thighs. "I don't know. An element of the total guilt and failure. I'd failed on the most important side of my life. The failure infected the rest...the rest of my being."

"The most important side: the guerrillas, Selassie, battles, and arguments. The most important involvements of your life." His chin began to quiver. "Thank you for what must be difficult candor." She halted. "Would you weep with me?"

His face filled with contrition and his eyes with tears. In the mist they were silhouettes, vividly motionless like opposing pillars at Stonehenge. Finally she shivered. He gestured that they should retreat from the penetrating chill of the hill but she wished to climb farther.

"Orde, what a wretched homecoming."

"I deserve no better. You do."

"The wounded from the ship. The maimed. Pitifully grateful for even an ember of life."

"I know. I thought I'd found a place for my remorse . . . till I watched them carried off."

"Then what did you think?"

"How I had spurned what was most precious to them."

"And to their wives."

"Yes."

"I don't suppose I can ever understand."

"Nor can I, fully. But I've come to grips with the worst of it."

"How?"

"A heaven-sent doctor on the ship. Pulled a great deal out of me. Put some things in place."

"Then I must go to him too."

"Not possible, I'm afraid. He treats only war casualties."

"Don't I qualify?"

"I'm sorry for your hurt. Deeply, eternally sorry."

She slowed the climb until it halted as if the hilltop were unattainable. She slowly dried her eyes, then took his hand as they began the descent.

"Orde, what did the doctor say, what did he do?"

"Therapy was incidental. His job was to gauge me."

"And prevent recurrence?"

"There will be no recurrence."

"Did he say so?"

"No, I do."

"How can you know—what if the stresses build up again? You'll always have malaria, won't you, and enemies who provoke and frustrate? How can you know?"

"How can I know I love you?" he asked rhetorically.

"You didn't love me in Cairo! What an answer!"

"I'm afraid Cairo contradicted the poet's axiom. Love does not conquer all."

She exhaled audibly. "The battle isn't over."

"In what way?"

"In two ways. You've not conquered this, no matter what the doctor said."

"He guaranteed nothing. What's the other way?"

"Love is still in the fight. *Never* abandon me as an ally."

PART III

The General:
Chindits

43

The winter of 1941 to 1942 was the most turbulent time of his life. It was spent in London, where he remained in convalescent status awaiting the decision of the medical board. He had to prepare himself for two eventualities: if the board recommended anything less than restoration to full duty, he would resign his commission and put himself at the service of Zion. With many of the Zionist leaders present in London, he was again able to conjure the vision of a Jewish division to fight the Nazis, this time invoking American sponsorship.

British resources were too skimpy to support the mobile division Wingate had in mind, whereas the United States, at war for less than a month, abounded with resources, industry, and ideal training areas in their southwestern deserts. Jewish influence was stronger in Washington than in London, so Wingate's expectations of American support were justifiably high.

However, if the medical board decided in his favor, he was eager to return to Africa and match his skill against Rommel with the "Tibesti Plan," long dear to his heart and suddenly topical in important circles. In London he was not a renegade major but an exotic warrior—and rarest of all in the British army, he was a victor, reason enough to give his ideas a hearing in the war cabinet.

The army high command was somewhat ambivalent about him. His Ethiopian report had been forwarded routinely by Wavell and then gathered dust at the War Office. But when Wavell came through London on his way to his new assignment in India, he urged the chief of the imperial general staff, Sir Alan Brooke, to read it. Wavell made the same recommendation to his longtime friend Winston Churchill. Wavell had transited London in September; so at the time Wingate reached Glasgow his report was still circulating.

But no one in the high command, no matter what he thought of

195

the Tibesti Plan, wanted to back Wingate pending the decision of the
medical board. Instead he was told to relax, take care of himself, and
try to be just one of the thousand majors in the army. There was war
almost everywhere in the world, and if fit for service, he was assured
there would be a place for him.

But Wingate was not for waiting. He could sense the British Isles
had become claustrophobic after two years under the Nazi siege. He
felt he must seize the hour while he was still a refreshing novelty, and
so he used the Ethiopia debriefings to reinvigorate the Tibesti Plan.
He was encouraged when more details were requested by Brooke's office. Favor from on high seemed to shine on him as he was awarded a
second DSO for his Ethiopian service.

But then, unknown to him, his glow began to dim. The Tibesti
Plan was forwarded to Cairo, where his detractors replied that opera-
tions along the lines Wingate contemplated were already under study.
Wavell's successor favored using British regulars rather than west Af-
ricans; the former would be about a quarter of the number of the force
Wingate's proposed and far more mobile in desert-worthy land rovers.
Their principal tactic would be hit-and-run raids on German airfields.

Thus Wingate's plan was largely preempted. Moreover, Cairo's reply highlighted the comments of General Cunningham, who added
this footnote:

> I am uncertain to what extent Wingate's attempted suicide has
> upset him, but if he is back to the man I used to know I would
> gladly accept him myself as a guerrilla leader. I would, however,
> be chary of allowing him too much rein politically. It is along
> political lines that he appeared to me most unbalanced.

Naturally Wingate never saw this note but those whose support he
was seeking did. It made them wary. It confirmed for them his pre-
dilection to go to outside channels. He was reestablishing himself as a
renegade though an admirable one. This left him in a sort of exalted
limbo. The army regarded his ideas with respect but not enthusiasm;
they would decorate him for his accomplishments but not promote
him for his potential. They would not, for their own political reasons,
challenge his access to the high civilian leadership, but they marked it
against him when he used such access.

That was Wingate's situation, but he did not perceive it. So far as he knew he was making progress with the Tibesti Plan, the medical board seemed favorably disposed toward him, command of a Jewish division could be in the offing, and all these possibilities made for an exciting convalescence. His health became as robust as his spirits.

For Lorna the sea change in her husband was less noticeable than it was to him. Though in Africa much in him had been jarred loose, it rearranged into patterns she could recognize.

They went over his letters together. He related Selassie's anecdotes; they discussed the soothsayer, his predictions, the strange doings in the cave, and his incredible appearance at the airfield.

"The knife flew to his throat," Wingate related.

Lorna shivered. She rose to heat some tea and change the mood. "If he's omniscient, I'll surely have a son."

"And before the war is over," he said, glad to lighten the subject.

"Eerie."

"Isn't it?"

"Was he—this Ishmael—connected in some way with what Lieutenant Atkins said about you?"

Wingate stirred his tea thoughtfully. "No connection that I can see."

"There seems to be."

"You can make connections I can't."

"I think there's something there. Had they ever met?"

"Maybe around the camp. Atkins thought he was nonsense, I suspect."

"What about Dr. Parnell?"

"Superstitious? Lord, no."

"What had he to say on this subject of...death?"

Wingate's eyes glazed in recollection. "He saw me as some... bearer of death. He allowed me high intentions. But he saw me as unwittingly dangerous, possibly a transmitter—maybe a magnet—of death for others. Multitudes of others. He wasn't altogether clear; his opinion wasn't sharp on this point. He seemed to see some foreshadowing of death about me. That may sound eerie too but it was not the way he expressed it."

"And how did you reply?"

"Well, with the obvious fact that commanders in war hold the power of life and death. Though that didn't seem to address his concern. He couldn't reformulate it so we left the subject. Yet this was the only time his personal emotions surfaced in our talks. Are you picking up another connection? There seems to be one hovering somewhere."

"I feel that too." She walked around the room but nothing more came to her. "It's something yet to be resolved for you, Orde. I feel that. It seems that you must be shown something about being alive."

"How could I have had a greater lesson?"

"Yes. And you live life so fully. That's why I don't have a grip on what these incidents are to tell you."

"God reveals in His own time."

"Yes," she said with a smile as warm as the teakettle, "that will have to be our answer for now. And let us not prove Ishmael wrong."

"We owe him as much. Come, lass, sit on my lap."

"Is that how the Ethiopians do it?"

"I must tell you about my night in their harem."

"Don't tell me; show me."

Shortly after New Year's, 1942, the medical board rendered their decision. Wingate was restored to Category A: fully fit for unrestricted service. That was the good news. The remaining news was less bad than startling. Wingate was posted to the headquarters of the new Far East command with prospective duty as liaison officer to "the Chinese, of all people!"

His disappointment was in the final sinking of his Tibesti Plan. He was offered to Cairo; they reacted indifferently. General Cunningham would use him if he were assigned, but if someone else wanted him that was fine. That someone was Archibald Wavell, who somehow seemed to appear like a fairy godfather at major junctures in Wingate's career.

Wavell's summons this time rang with ambivalence. The assignment perplexed Wingate. Here he was, Britain's foremost expert on Middle Eastern guerrilla warfare, intimately acquainted with the Libyan desert (the site of his expedition to the lost oasis) where Rommel was now being fought; here he was about to be posted to China.

"There is no spot on earth where the flag of the British army flies more remote from the Middle East. I'm a thousand miles closer to Rommel here in London than I will be in Chunking."

"Hadn't realized that," replied the colonel who administered majors' assignments. "Do send us a postcard, won't you?"

And that was pretty much the army's attitude. Last month Wingate had been pestering them to restore him to duty. Now they had. His next and last appeal was to a brigadier who sat close to Sir Alan Brooke.

"General, the Chinese may already be the most competent guerrillas in the world. I could sit at the knee of Mao Tse-Tung and learn a great deal, but that wouldn't advance our war effort."

"Mouse who?"

"Mah-oh Tsay-tongue, sir."

"Never heard of him. And since you have, that makes you one of our leading Sino experts. Good luck, Wingate. Best regards to Sir Archie."

44

This was a new war which Wingate would join. Britain had been locked in mortal combat with Germany and Italy for nearly two years. The big chips were on the European table; nothing of importance was gambled in the Far East except two capital ships which the Japanese promptly sank. Even the Americans, who had been attacked by Japan, not Germany, agreed the priority for men and matériel was for Hitler, not Tojo. That meant leftovers for the Far East, and in this respect Wingate had worthwhile experience: both Ethiopia and the Far East were subordinated to Hitler's war.

Before Pearl Harbor, Japan's activities had rarely made news in besieged Britain. When in the spring of 1940 Hitler overran France and Holland, the balance of power in the Pacific flipped wildly in Japan's favor. The former colonies of Indochina and the Dutch East Indies were virtually helpless and extremely inviting.

The first Japanese move was into Hanoi, from where China's supply line to the west—the Burma Road—could be bombed. Japan had been gnawing territory out of the Chinese mainland since 1933. They were opposed ineffectively by two armies, that of the warlords headed by Generalissimo Chiang Kai-shek (the Kuomintang party), and the guerrilla army of the communists under Mao Tse-tung.

Japanese espionage was by far the best in the Far East, reporting the general weakness of Anglo-American forces, especially in warplanes. The temptation grew too great, the opportunities too numerous, for Japan to resist. As Hitler was establishing a "new order" in Europe, Japan would install a "co-prosperity sphere" in her neighborhood.

The Japanese war plan was essentially to grab and hold. It started with the sneak attack on Pearl Harbor to neutralize the American fleet (the British had no significant naval presence in the Pacific at that time), shortly followed by invasions of the Dutch East Indies, the Philippines, Malaya, and Hong Kong. All except the Philippines fell in short order.

The performance of the British army was particularly inept. At Hong Kong, despite strong natural defenses, they succumbed in two weeks with combat losses twice those of the attackers. In Malaya the British commanders ignored the jungle which covered the peninsula. They considered it impenetrable, and so they didn't train their troops in it; they felt it was no place to be at night.

The Japanese did exactly the opposite. Lightly clad and equipped, they were able to infiltrate through the jungle time and again, bypassing British roadblocks, enveloping their defenses. About the time Wingate received his orders to join Wavell, the British army withdrew from Malaya onto the island of Singapore. They had lost nearly 50,000 troops in the jungle, but at last they were in a mighty stronghold invulnerable to infiltration by the wily "Japs."

Wingate heard the conversations around the War Ministry in early February. The situation was being compared to the summer of 1940, when, after France's sudden defeat, the British faced the Germans across a formidable strait. The same situation obtained in Singapore: the mainland was lost but the island fortress should easily be held by 80,000 Commonwealth troops.

With redoubtable shore batteries, Singapore could hold off the navies of the world, but there had been too little improvement of defenses on the strait during the previous month while the Japanese had been driving down from the north. During two nights in early February they put assault troops across the strait. Fighting savagely, they pushed a British force larger than their own into a tight perimeter around the city. Within a week they forced capitulation, the largest surrender and the worst disaster in the long history of the British army.

The next onslaught came through Thailand into Burma. That country, rich in oil and rice, was to form the western buttress of the new Japanese empire. To preserve Burma for the British empire Wavell had an odd lot of polyglot units without artillery, signal equipment, and antiaircraft guns, while the sky belonged to the Japanese air force. Like their comrades who had perished in Malaya, they were roadbound and untrained in jungle fighting.

Nevertheless the Japanese mission was a difficult one; they had to move fast because the spring monsoon would make military operations impossible. Virtually unexplored jungle carpeted the jagged mountain ranges which sealed Burma's borders from its neighbors. The Japanese penetrated this unknown wilderness with a fortitude and determination never seen in a modern army.

They also struck along the coast of Burma's southeastern panhandle and made rapid progress into the vast delta region of the Irrawaddy, a river as mighty as the Mississippi. Situated at its mouth is Rangoon, the port for practically all of Burma's commerce with the outside world. It fell a week before Wingate reached New Delhi.

It took him three weeks by air to get that far. The Singapore catastrophe had overloaded the supply lines while at the same time taking many of the transports out of the system for tactical resupply. The war was still a thousand miles away, but the GHQ at New Delhi already had the air of defeat.

His renunion with Wavell was short and unsentimental. On any other occasion it would have been cause for celebration because Sir Archie awarded him the acting rank of full colonel (a two-grade jump) and command of all guerrilla operations in Burma. Almost as an afterthought, Wingate inquired about his original orders in London assigning him as a liaison officer to the Chinese army.

"Well, you'll have a chance to see them though I don't know for how long. The generalissimo has released two armies to protect the terminus of the Burma Road at Bhamo."

"I'll surely visit with them. Do we have liaison with those armies, sir?"

Wavell laughed. "Worried about your Mandarin?" Wingate opened his hands. "Well, they have an English-speaking commander—name's Stilwell."

"Oh, yes. The American general. Thought he was Chiang's chief of staff."

"Titles mean little in this strange theater."

"Just why is Stilwell there?"

"Roosevelt's been bankrolling Chiang's army for months. Stilwell's to see what the Americans get for their investment. Glad he's there. We couldn't find out a thing about the Chinese in Burma otherwise."

"So I shouldn't even consider their potential as guerrillas."

"No. Don't consider the Chinese for anything. Just take a look and be glad you won't spend the war with them."

"Then where should I look for guerrillas?"

"Well, you know about the Bush Warfare School. From there you must take your guerrillas as you can find them. The lowland Burmese aren't proving to be very reliable as regular units. However, they're the only natives with sufficient education to understand modern weapons. The tribesmen in the hills are your best fighters. However, they're better with a blowgun than a Bren gun. They hate the lowlanders, so you'll need to be both a warrior and a diplomat."

"Fine, sir. Now all I need is your mission." Wavell looked at him blankly. "My initial objective, sir. Rangoon?"

"I like your spirit, Orde."

"I wasn't seeking a compliment, sir, but an objective for my operations."

Wavell leaned forward on his elbows. The eyes that had watched defeat on three continents focused on Wingate's. "In truth and in secrecy, your objective is to survive. It's bitter to say, but the Jap cannot be stopped in this campaign. We must withdraw again, probably all the way back to India. I want a veteran cadre to escape. 1942 will be a year of retreat and defeat. What I want is the makings for a counterattack in 1943."

For once Wingate was stunned.

"Do you remember how the survivors of Dunkirk looked?" Wavell continued, "the shock on their faces? That was the look of our men when they escaped across the Sittang. Lost all their heavy equipment. Psychologically we're in worse shape here than after Dunkirk or Tobruk.

There at least we understood the nature of the army that whipped us— we've known the Germans for a long time.

"The Japs are something altogether different. They have one foot in the twentieth century and the other in the twelfth. Medieval savagery combined with modern arms. They are a ferocious horde bent upon demonstrating the superiority of their race. And they're doing that daily in Burma. Along with daily atrocities. They take prisoners only for the pleasure of torturing them. I don't want to sound like a propaganda film, but all I've said is true."

"Well, I hope I can get a cram course at the Bush Warfare School," said Wingate with feigned jauntiness.

"Know your limitations, Orde. And get out alive."

"An overconfident army in pursuit creates many opportunities for ambush."

"Good. Think along those lines. Small operations. Pinpricks. Create confidence in some young, tough officers who can help us later. If you must take chances—and knowing you, you will—keep the stakes small. You can't think of Rangoon as you did of Addis Ababa."

"I'm beginning to miss Ethiopia already."

"What you're going to miss," Wavell replied, "are the Italians."

45

The headquarters of the Burma Corps, as the British forces were called, was near Mandalay; Wingate arrived there on March 22. The front was two hundred miles to the south, but Japanese bombers brought the war to Mandalay every day. Wingate's plane zoomed in and out again without cutting its engine. Almost before his feet hit the ground the plane taxied to take off. His kit bag in one hand, Bible in the other, he made his way toward the only person in uniform, a Sikh military policeman holding back refugees from the fence around the airfield.

"I'm looking for General Hutton's headquarters, Corporal."

"Gone I think, sir."

"Got to be around here somewhere."

"Very few military vehicles anymore, sir."

Dust raised by a thousand shuffling feet clogged his nostrils. The refugees poured by, clustered around creaking ox carts. Finally an army truck wound its way among them, its horn blowing continuously.

Wingate waved it down. The driver hesitated to stop until he saw Wingate's rank. There were several Indian soldiers in the truck but none spoke English. The driver was hell-bent on his destination, wherever that was.

They rumbled into wooded acres surrounding a ramshackle estate. Wingate could see uniformed figures at the windows. The truck lurched to a stop as an Indian medical orderly raced toward it.

"Pray God you are the surgeon!"

"Regretfully no. Is this a hospital?"

"This and the forest around us." As the dust settled Wingate saw what he meant. Men were lying in small groups under the trees. From their stillness he knew some were dead.

The orderly noticed the Bible. "Please come this way, Colonel." In the back of the building were a number of large tents, more ragged than those of Gideon Force. A staggering stench disclosed their contents, for ambulances regularly dumped off the wounded, returning to the front past Hutton's headquarters. While he waited Wingate read verses for the dead and dying.

Headquarters of Burma Corps buzzed with conversations about evacuation, Japanese paratroopers, fifth columnists, saboteurs, and insurrection. Wingate set aside his Bible and pith helmet to move about anonymously—like a reporter getting the feel for a story. No one asked him who he was; staffs from disbanded headquarters floated freely in the rear. No one knew Wingate and he knew no one.

Until he felt a clap on his back, "Orde, old chap!"

His greeter was Colonel Allen Johns, a classmate from Woolwich whom he had tutored in English. He was the inspector general for Burma Corps, and so he knew some of the worst details of the unfolding disaster.

"You're just the man we need here," said Johns enthusiastically.

"We've got to get off the roads and into the jungle. Let me show you around."

As they walked Johns told him how in Rangoon a thousand trucks and five thousand tires shipped from the United States, through great efforts and the U-boat peril, had been piled together and burned to prevent capture. Yet now Burma Corps was immobilized for lack of vehicles.

Milling through the halls were colonial officials and displaced bureaucrats of the disintegrating imperial civil service. There were few Burmese; the local populace was backing away from the British as they watched the success of the Japanese.

The depressing day grew long, but before Wingate could depart for the Bush Warfare School he was to advise General Hutton of his presence and intentions in Burma. He learned, however, that there had been major changes in command. If the British couldn't move fast against the Japanese, they could shuffle their generals with bewildering speed.

Hutton was out; Slim was in. Wavell was out but up; he was replaced by "the hero of Dunkirk," Sir Harold Alexander. The durable Wavell was Alexander's new boss as commander in Chief of the Far East. It was Slim to whom Wingate should be introduced, but as the new commander of Burma Corps, Slim was visiting the units at the front. Wingate would have to wait until late at night to meet him.

Slim was somewhat known to Wingate by reputation. He had enlisted as a private in World War I, had fought in Mesopotamia, and had commanded a crack division in the Middle East. If nothing else he was a fighter. His experience and sympathy with unconventional warfare was nil except that he had been an addressee for Wingate's Tibesti Plan.

It was 1:00 in the morning when Slim's aide woke Wingate to tell him the general had finally gone to his tent. There might be a few minutes to talk before he went to sleep.

Wingate found him dozing at his desk.

"Excuse me, sir." Slim's eyes opened.

"You must be Wingate," he said, extending his hand. "That's the most famous hat in the army. I hope it's bulletproof. What time is it?"

"One o'clock, sir."

"Then tomorrow's disasters will begin in a few hours. Sit down.

I'm sure you've gathered the situation here is at least desperate. I expect to be run out of Burma. Stilwell and the Chinese won't be far behind." He broke the point of his pencil on the desk. "It's damned humiliating. I realize you've had very little time to get on top of the situation, but do you think there's an opportunity for your kind of work after we leave?"

"Guerrillas?"

"What else?"

"I think you probably have people better suited to raise Burmese guerrillas than I—people who have been here a long time, who know the language and the tribes. I can't even pronounce Burmese names."

"You'd probably have about three years to learn. I don't expect we'll be back before then."

"It would probably take me that long. If you recall, sir, I trained Gideon Force under peacetime conditions. I was able to take the offensive when I chose to. That situation of course does not apply here."

Slim's jaw, shaped like the horn of Africa, thrust out at Wingate. "That's a sound analysis, but it surprises me coming from the Lawrence of Ethiopia."

"What good would Lawrence be here? I'm not without my ambitions in Burma, General Slim. Did you happen to read my Tibesti Plan?"

"I did—but don't expect me to remember anything about it." His head slumped forward from fatigue.

"The Tibesti Plan was a product of my guerrilla experience; its thesis is long-range penetration by *regular* troops trained and equipped for long-term operations behind enemy lines."

"Sounds interesting but I'm not thinking well enough to follow you. In any case I can't spare you a squad of riflemen."

"Give me five thousand when you get back to India."

"I may not have that many left from this whole corps."

46

The next day Wingate was directed to the Bush Warfare School, a collection of huts and bunkers concealed in a rubber plantation. He found the "school" abandoned because the "faculty" were out raiding the Japanese. Bush Warfare School was actually the cover name for an operational headquarters commanded by an accomplished Jap fighter Major Bruce Dalton.

As the new commandant of the school, Wingate had much to learn. He described his impressions in his first letter to Lorna:

> I've been several days now waiting the return of my new command. Seems Dalton with a couple of dozen men is in the Pegu Hills looking for a bridge to blow. We have a twenty-four-hour radio watch here, but wisely he has not chosen to transmit, and I don't expect him to except in some emergency.
>
> I divide my day between here and Slim's HQ ten miles away, a distance I march twice daily with a forty-pound pack. I must be fit for the inevitable retreat which no doubt will send us over some difficult mountains to India....
>
> The prospects for us now are dismal. The front will crack as soon as the Japs drive a wedge between the British and Chinese. I haven't been able to get down to either side of the front for lack of solid information about our own forces, much less the Japs. We probably won't locate them till they burst into Mandalay.
>
> The only ambition I have for now is to see more of Burma before we are kicked out—for I'll be back one way or another. When Dalton returns (pray God he does) I'm sure he can find me a vehicle. Meanwhile I must search for a plane to see the terrain firsthand from the air. The RAF is no help. They're gone—shot from the skies or withdrawn to India and China. They did a fine job, I'm told, but as with

*everything else in Burma they were undermanned and -equipped.
Whereas the Japs gave us another of their unpleasant surprises with
the "Zero" fighter, an aircraft which has won our admiration and
fear.*

While awaiting Dalton, Wingate interacted increasingly with Slim's
staff and set the tone of relations for the months to come. From the
start these were prickly.

When Wingate learned that an ammunition dump was about to
be destroyed before it fell into Japanese hands, he mentioned to Slim
that if the munitions could be evacuated and hidden, they would provide a valuable cache for friendly guerrillas. "Good idea," said Slim.
"Take whatever you can use."

That "out-of-channels" authorization was resented by some of Slim's
staff, who became increasingly offended by Wingate's direct access to
the commanding general. They cooperated to deny him the chance to
inventory the supply dump, which was summarily blown up.

This rebuff was nothing compared to the incident of the "Spotter's
Pagoda."

On the road between Mandalay and Kalewa, British supply trucks
were bombarded from the adjacent jungle by mortars of a Burmese
fifth column fighting for the Japanese. It was quickly suspected the
fire was directed by a spotter with a radio atop a nearby pagoda. Because these incidents involved guerrillas, albeit hostile ones, Wingate
was sent to investigate and "put a stop to the interdiction," in the
words of the chief of staff.

After camping alone in the vicinity of the ambush, Wingate as-
certained that the fire could only be directed from the pagoda; indeed
there was no fire at night when the spotter could not see the road. As
a religious shrine, the pagoda could not be stormed by infantry or otherwise damaged, and so Wingate decided to booby-trap it.

At night the spotter was absent; he probably entered the pagoda
early in the morning disguised as a worshipper. When the moon had
set, Wingate climbed the pagoda and carefully investigated the upper
terraces where the spotter probably had his post. On a terrace Wingate
found cigarette butts and what looked like wrappings from a radio
battery. Nearby Wingate concealed a hand grenade, replacing the handle with an electric firing cap which would detonate upon receiving
the sort of signal transmitted by the spotter's radio.

The next day when a small convoy went by, an explosion puffed from the terrace. The mortars fired no more and Wingate returned to Mandalay.

He reported the resolution of the incident to his friend Allen Johns, who congratulated him for his ingenuity. Wingate was hiking back to Bush Warfare School when a jeep swerved up beside him. The chief of staff, Brigadier Arden, wanted to see him at once.

"The Buddhists are up in arms," Arden said gravely. "You defiled their pagoda."

Wingate laughed. Surely Arden wasn't surprised by the Buddhists' reaction but they could easily be placated. No one had seen Wingate enter or leave the pagoda; so the grenade (which did nothing except pepper a few of the massive stones) could have belonged to anyone, including the spotter.

"This has become a serious matter, Wingate." Arden went on in a judicial tone, "I shall have to render a written report."

"To whom? Why? . . . What the hell's going on, General? My orders were to eliminate the ambush—that was the mission you gave me."

"Since civilian sensibilities are involved, I've put Mr. Quartermain in charge of the investigation—and assured him of your full cooperation."

Quartermain was one of the displaced bureaucrats from Rangoon, nominally responsible for civil administration in the region of the pagoda, though he had never visited the site. He with an Indian stenographer were waiting in the hall as Wingate, muttering in Hebrew, left Arden's office.

"Colonel Wingate, could we get into this matter? I've reserved the conference room."

"What did Arden tell you?"

"This is better discussed in privacy."

"Maybe so."

With the door closed, Quartermain began. "I must ask you to take an oath."

"I've plenty of them on the tip of my tongue."

"Without your cooperation," Quartermain cleared his throat, "this will be much more difficult."

"All right, I'll answer your questions." Quartermain nodded to the stenographer, who began writing. "If you'll answer just one of mine. Who told you I had anything to do with the pagoda?"

The civilian reddened. "By policy I am not authorized to reveal sources of any of my information. This policy is your safeguard as well, Colonel; your statement shall remain confidential."

"My statement is that bloody fifth columnists are liable to die. The one in the pagoda got exactly what he deserved. And whoever got him deserves a pat on the back." Wingate reached over his shoulder and patted himself. The stenographer looked at Quartermain questioningly. "End of statement."

"I'm afraid it's not acceptable. I'd hoped for a somewhat informal inquiry, but if that is not to be, it is incumbent upon me as the Crown representative in this case to advise you of your right to retain counsel. In the present unsettled situation, civilian attorneys may not be easily available. However, I hereby proffer a list of those in Mandalay approved by the governor general." Quartermain pushed a list across the table. "The stenographer is minuting my action."

"Suffering Jesus."

"Alternatively, in exercise of the broad authority granted to me by Brigadier Arden, I hereby offer you discretionary use of military counsel if you so request."

Quartermain raised his hands as the building shook from a stick of bombs exploding nearby.

Wingate grinned. "Thoughtless of the Japs to intrude on a matter of this gravity."

"Do you request counsel, Colonel Wingate?"

He mused for a moment. "*Any* officer?" he asked.

"Excepting generals. And the officer must be willing to serve."

"Johns. My old schoolmate."

Quartermain squirmed nervously. "Impossible."

"That swine!" Wingate stormed from the room.

He found Johns heating tea water in his office. Wingate glanced in as if he were just passing by. "Allen," he said in the best of humor, "I have some Greys here in my kit."

"Capital! I've been drinking so much Ceylonese my eyes are starting to slant."

"Be right with you."

As they stirred their cups, Wingate remarked, "You know this pagoda comedy is losing its humor. I may be in for a court-martial."

"You don't say," said Johns with concern. "Arden asked me what I knew about it."

"And you told him?"

"Well, what you told me."

"Nothing more?"

"Well...the priest's complaint. But that came to me through channels you see."

"You informed the priest that I set the grenade?"

"No! Actually...I—I feigned that I really didn't know you well. You were new here, that is, and had been given the job of clearing the road. Milk?" Wingate shook his head. "I thought you did a bang-up job, personally. Forgive the pun."

"Thanks, but your statement is part of my indictment, Allen."

Johns looked down and stirred furiously. "That's regrettable."

"*You* are regrettable."

Despite the front collapsing almost within earshot, Brigadier Arden would not let the pagoda matter go unresolved. He called in Wingate, said he was receiving an official "oral reprimand," and proceeded to deliver it. The reprimand concluded with the admonition that a headquarters must pull together—that "team players" were needed.

"You didn't send a team out to clear that road, General; you sent one man."

"I miss your point."

"My point is that not all competitions are for teams, sir. At the pagoda mine was an individual match."

"You may interpret it as you please. There was a lesson there if you choose to see it. If not, I consider the matter closed."

The lesson as Wingate saw it, left him more disheartened than furious. In a letter to Lorna he wrote:

I would have reacted differently in Ethiopia, but perhaps I have become the sadder but wiser man. It seems to be the inescapable infection of a headquarters—perhaps of any large organization—that men see their advancement in the downfall of others. How Allen has disillusioned me. Somehow he perceived me as a rival though I covet nothing he possesses. Jealousy? Perhaps; I cannot see into the hearts of men. I can only see the appalling reflex of bureaucrats and other climbers when

they imagine the smallest threat to their personal agendas. . . . How right
was Shakespeare in saying that he who "filches from me my good name
robs me of that which does not enrich him but makes me poor indeed."
This incident has left me sick to my soul, and tempted to remain with
whatever men Dalton brings back, no matter how few. Better to fight
the Japanese here than my craven countrymen when we regather in India.

47

An outcast once more, Wingate found solace on his conditioning hikes,
which he increased in speed and burden. Then one night as he reached
the outskirts of the school, he heard a sentry's quiet challenge from
the forest. It was the voice of one of Dalton's raiders.

A hurricane lamp glowed softly in the headquarters shack. Behind
it was Dalton, a young, handsome major with eyes as deep as his experience, seated at his desk fighting through a backlog of paperwork
with fatigued determination.

They took to each other at once. Dalton was a self-taught guerrilla
leader: steady, reliable, practical. They both believed the cardinal military virtue was to surprise the enemy, and shared an abiding distrust
of staff officers.

Dalton's twenty-five raiders had done little damage but they hadn't
expected to. He and Wingate agreed nothing decisive could be accomplished in the present campaign—that the military situation was
really beyond influence.

"What do you suppose is left for us in Burma?" Wingate asked
after long discussions led to longer ones.

"If we're not going to stay behind, we should use the time to scout
the areas where we'll be returning."

"You've read my mind. Can we get transport?"

"Vehicles? Sure. I've got some rovers stashed in the woods."

"Any aircraft?"

"I don't know if AVG has any two-seaters left."

"Who?"

"American Volunteer Group."

"The P40s with the shark's mouth?"

"Right. They call them Flying Tigers. Chennault owes me a favor. We pulled one of his boys out of the jungle. Which area are you interested in?"

"Up north. Between the Chindwin and the Irrawaddy."

"I was going to take the faculty up to Myitkyina. Someday we're going to hit..."

"The railroad," they said together and laughed.

"Now the Japs," Wingate asked, "what are their weaknesses? All I hear makes them out to be little yellow supermen."

"Can't encourage you. There's one tactic though which anyone should follow when fighting the Japs: make them attack on ground of your choosing. Attacking them is like grabbing a nettle; they fight to the last man and defend every tree. But sometimes they'll attack rashly if you give them an opportunity to be heroic."

As Wingate had expounded to Dr. Parnell, a strategic offensive leading to tactical defense was the combination for victory. Dalton seemed to be rephrasing his doctrine for Burma. It was one of Wingate's corollaries that a soldier well dug in on defense was the numerical equivalent of more than three soldiers attacking him. Thus, he reasoned, a British force of three thousand, when it appeared in the enemy rear, would require ten thousand Japanese soldiers to dislodge them.

As the American light bomber cruised over the terrain at five hundred feet, the jungle slopes revealed few obvious defensive strongholds. The hills dominated but did not overpower the landscape. Surging rivers wove through the wilderness, their watersheds veined by lesser streams invisible beneath overhanging trees. Wingate was distracted by the variform treetops: some like round bushes, some like towering spires, and every shape in between.

A wondrous arena for war, Wingate thought, as he watched the tapestry of greens blend with the shadings of gullies and glints from the canopied streams. In a month these would be foaming torrents. The monsoon was already gathering in the Bay of Bengal; when it rolled northeast it would stop the war.

The remnants of Burma Corps were to withdraw through this wilderness before the monsoon's onslaught. In the Indian hills they would have to regroup, replenish, and be reinforced before facing the Japanese again. There would be a period of about six months before campaigning could resume on either side. Wingate knew however, there would be no interlude for him: he would be fighting a crucial battle, his longest struggle, with Slim's staff. He would be fighting for the two most precious resources—men and aircraft—in the most undersupplied and understrength theater in the war.

He soon lost his first skirmish with Arden. Wingate requested that the faculty of Bush Warfare School be flown out to India to begin preparations for a counteroffensive in 1943. He did not prevail. Arden contended the faculty was the ideal rear guard to cover Burma Corps' retreat. Slim concurred.

Wingate minuted his objections but did not otherwise clash with Arden. The rear guard duties would further season his cadre, and they would be withdrawing over terrain which they might recross if Wingate could mount an expedition in 1943. So he played the role of the good subordinate, saving his strength for the wrestling match that would occupy the center ring when all the contestants reassembled in India.

Thanks to Dalton's recruiting, the faculty had grown to nearly a hundred. There remained the question of what Wingate would do with himself after the faculty was parceled out to the retreating units. Wingate was torn between two requirements. The first was personal: he needed to steep himself in the jungle, learn its lore as he had in the desert, and hear bullets crack once again. In 1943 he would be leading jungle fighters; so he very much needed to become one himself.

On the other hand, if he gave Arden and his crew too much lead time in New Delhi, they would plan him right out of the war. He must gain Wavell's ear quickly (Slim would be too busy fighting the battle of the withdrawal), sell his concepts before his enemies could muster their counterarguments, and present Slim with a *fait accompli*.

Given this choice, Wingate decided to fight the larger war. In late April, he turned over command of the faculty to Dalton. If all went reasonably well, they would be reunited in India in about a month.

For once Wingate found himself urging caution on his subordinates:

"Not too many heroics, Bruce," he counseled self-consciously. "The faculty is probably more valuable than the troops they're protecting."

"Don't worry. We know there's a bigger game coming."

"Yes, don't sacrifice yourself in the first inning."

"You'll need as much luck as we."

"True. I must be at my best. As ingratiating as a shoe salesman."

"What are you going to call it—the product, so to speak, the concept?"

"Well, I thought I'd adopt the name of the concept I used for the Tibesti Plan: 'long-range penetration.' How does that sound?"

"For army terminology, that's pretty sexy."

48

Wingate could have flown to New Delhi on the next plane. Instead a gruesome fascination kept him in Mandalay for a few more days. It may have been the final humiliation of the supine headquarters that he wanted to witness; then too he wished to see if any of the staff would show surprising fortitude as their professional jobs began to affect their personal safety.

Even before the rumble of their artillery reached Mandalay, the Japanese spread their terror. The survivors of Burma Corps were the messengers. Colonel Grimshaw, the intelligence officer, was the first to hear many hideous stories, but with these totally discounted he had corroborated eyewitness evidence of two routine Japanese practices.

The first concerned captured colonial troops. The Japanese offensive relied on speed; they made no provisions for prisoners, and so they were disposed of immediately. Moreover, the Japanese had learned the value of "field sanitation" from western army manuals and realized that

decomposing corpses were a health hazard for their own troops. Grimshaw described their solution as a combination of oriental inhumanity
and occidental logic—that is, General Kawabe's troops burned their
prisoners alive, sometimes heaping them in bamboo houses after breaking their legs, at other times dousing them with petroleum around
the oil fields. The victims were mostly Indians.

A different fate was reserved for British prisoners. To dispel traditions of western intimidation, Britishers were murdered individually, usually by Japanese replacements who had not yet killed an enemy
in combat. The British were stripped to exhibit their white skin, then
tied to trees for bayonet practice. Death was never the result of a single thrust.

Civilian atrocities were too routine to be even noted. These Wingate
could see for himself. Before colonial times Mandalay had been the
royal capital for the Burmese dynasties. A moated eighteenth-century
palace was the centerpiece of the city and a landmark for Japanese bombers. During one horrific air raid hundreds of civilians had taken shelter
along its massive stone walls. Many were blown into the moat to swell,
burst, and putrefy in the soup-thick algae. Wingate could not walk
within a mile of the palace because of the stupefying stench.

In the burned-out acres which had once been the neighborhoods of
Mandalay, the only life remaining was that of the scavengers. Dogs
and pigs rooted the entrails of bloated corpses while crows pecked out
the eyes. These were the choice viands: muscle and sinew were left for
the rats, who now owned the city completely. Gorged to the point of
immobility, their eyes glowed like sheets of red plankton when headlights came upon them.

It was enough to sicken even the Chinese, calloused by seven years
of war against the Japanese. "In all my life of long military experience," Chiang wrote to Churchill, "I have seen nothing to compare
with the appalling unprepared state, confusion, and degradation of the
war area in Burma."

Burma Corps, which had been holding the invaders out of Mandalay, disintegrated like a sack full of water. Wingate could wait no
longer. He drove the last of the school vehicles to the airport and
camped all night beside the plane which would take him to India.

*It seemed an abject thing to do [he wrote Lorna] to be so obsessed for
my personal deliverance, but such was the miasma of defeat during*

those last hours. I've never before been so swept up by a situation that was utterly beyond me.

My last view, before altitude removed the intimacy of the country-side, was of the road to Kalewa clogged with misery. The dust rose in the heat and carried with it a smell detectable even in the aircraft. What has God wrought? It seems Burma is expiation for our every colonial sin since the seventeenth century.

This letter was continued several days later from the Maiden Hotel in New Delhi, where Wingate billeted for the next two months. It would be his headquarters during his campaign for long-range pene-tration, or LRP, as his strategy came to be called.

How quickly that scene has vanished; yet I realize every day and night thousands of souls are struggling through the grasp of the jungle. It still bothers me at times—teatime especially, when I sit comfortably in fresh laundered clothes—that I am not sharing the hardships with those I will take back to war. I hope they understand; I think I do, and so far I haven't been letting them down.

Though I've been working slowly I think I'm building a steady foundation for my proposals. On my best behavior, I've been ingrati-ating myself with the joint planning staff (JPS), a group of officers Sir Archie farsightedly put together last month. Slim has only a sub-altern here at present, so I think I can make headway. Stilwell sent a Chinaman, and the American air force is also represented.

The AAF is a peculiar lot with exciting potential for my plans. Indeed I must employ their transports, which are now dangerously and unproductively supplying the Chinese with flights over the Himalayas. All the supplies in the world are valueless without the will to use them in combat. This clearly the Chinese will not do, not against the Japs anyway, only against each other to preserve feudal satrapies.

The American chap, Stratemeyer, realizes this but has no voice with Roosevelt, who harbors an unreasoned passion for turning the Chi-nese hordes upon the Japs. If I can win over Stratemeyer, convince him to allocate me a mere dozen of his transports, I have the beginnings of LRP.

I call the Yanks peculiar; their principal peculiarity is one from which I can very much benefit. This war for them is more a job than a cause or a struggle or whatever other term describes the reasons and motives for which we British are fighting. This war, as the Yanks seem to see it, is an irritating interruption of "the American way of life"—something to finish and get over with. With such an attitude they are supremely impressed by efficiency. What becomes of Burma or all of Southeast Asia after the war doesn't interest them in the slightest. But show them a plan that will work and work quickly and you have their support. Perhaps I should have been born an American, for it is exactly this attitude for which I have been searching among my countrymen.

The Doolittle raid on Tokyo (which did little according to the RAF) has heightened the attitude of the Americans that they "can do," to use their phrase. I have high hopes for gaining their cooperation, lower hopes for obtaining the forces I need from Wavell. It's men I need, and men we don't have. The following information is most secret: Burma Corps' strength three months ago was over twenty-five thousand. Since then the Japs have inflicted some 13,500 casualties upon us—we really don't know for sure till the last columns straggle into Assam. No more troops will be sent to Burma from elsewhere. We are at the end of the line for everything. So I will have to fight for every private. I need at least four thousand. Barely a hundred belong to me now, and how many will survive the retreat is known only to God.

Pray that He will entrust me with another Gideon Force, dear Lorna.

49

The troops he coveted began dribbling into India in early May 1942. Most were immediately hospitalized. Consequently, the six-month monsoon might not be long enough for the preparations necessary for even a small counteroffensive. This seemed to be an unspoken premise for many key members of Wavell's staff: 1943 would be another year for holding out, 1944 was the earliest date for offensive ambitions. The Americans began to suspect that Burma might remain dormant till Hitler was beaten and British forces released from Europe. At present, they were still perilously engaged in North Africa.

In this atmosphere, the Americans began to call long-range penetration "the only game in town." Most British saw it otherwise: "like fucking from different sides of the bed" was a popular description originated by Colonel Coburn, Wavell's operations officer.

Actually, LRP remained a nebulous notion; Wingate wished it so until he had developed all its details and presented them formally. In New Delhi it was known only as a vague plan for extended raids into upper Burma. Most assumed its success depended upon guerrilla support. To confuse his enemies, Wingate fostered that impression, which was exactly contrary to fact. He saw long-range penetration as an historic addition to the modalities of war. It did not rely upon guerrillas; instead, it could replace them as a threat to the enemy rear.

Before the advent of aerial supply and radio communication, armies had confronted each other pretty much intact. Though small formations might detach themselves temporarily from the main body of the army, the principal fighting elements (infantry, artillery, tanks) maneuvered together to gain or withhold important terrain from the opposing army. Consequently, moves which armies could make against each other were limited to penetrations along the front or swings around the flanks.

Operations against an enemy's rear, even in modern times, were limited to air strikes, guerrilla activities, or short raids. Never had it been contemplated that major formations could operate independently and indefinitely behind enemy lines. Gideon Force had not done so; they penetrated the enemy front, then drove the Italians before them. The paratroop divisions of World War II never did so; plans for their employment always provided for quick linkup with a ground attack by the main army.

In brief, Wingate proposed to do what only Hannibal had ever done before in warfare: insert major formations in the enemy rear where they would operate independently and indefinitely. This Wingate believed to be possible through aerial resupply and radio communications.

In LRP he would combine a strategic offensive with tactical defense. Inserting his forces behind the Japanese army was a strategic move; once there they would only attack where the enemy was weak and vulnerable. When attacked themselves, it would be on strong positions of their choosing. Success would be assured if Wingate constantly surprised the enemy but was never surprised himself.

Long-range penetration was not a strategem applicable to any theater. It required that the enemy's rear be a wilderness where the penetrators could hit and hide, and where enemy vehicles were neutralized by impassable terrain.

Because he could take no vehicles, Wingate would also be without artillery except for the lightest mortars. In place of vehicles Wingate would rely on mules. These were as plentiful in India as camels had been in Sudan. For big loads and jobs that called for bulldozers, Wingate considered elephants. To complete his military menagerie, he planned to use courier dogs and homing pigeons.

Which of these various expedients were practical he did not know; neither was their practicality as important as the planning they represented. When Wingate presented his formal proposal to Wavell, Slim, and their assembled staffs, the one possibility which could undo him was the appearance of unpreparedness for some contingency. Let Coburn laugh at his elephants and war dogs: what Wingate could not afford was to be caught without an answer.

The Americans tipped him off when they saw possible pitfalls for aerial resupply. When Wavell's supply officer called the AAF about parachutes, the Americans informed Wingate of the problem. As usual, it was shortages. Huddling with him, American aviators made some calculations: if there were no other requirements for parachutes throughout China and India, there were still only enough for two resupply drops to a force of four thousand men.

Wingate's jaw dropped. This was a ghastly projection, but far better to learn of it from the sympathetic aviators than the supercilious logisticians. Once more there was an expedient: "parajutes."

50

Colonel Philip Cochran, commander of the airlift to China, put Wingate onto the idea of parajutes. If there was not enough silk in the British empire to make parachutes, in India there was plenty of jute, the natural fiber from which burlap is made. Despite their shared "can do" attitude toward the war, the American found Wingate amusing and bemusing. As Cochran later told a journalist about their first meeting:

> You might ask Wingate a military question, like the average rainfall in Burma in March, and he would go off on a lecture about the effect of rainfall on Burmese monasteries and the Buddhist religion. In our first talk I said: "What do you intend to do?" And he went into one of his orations. . . . He kept talking about "long-range penetration," which meant nothing to me. He mixed everything up with scholarship and the history of war. I didn't know what he was talking about. A lot was about things that were over my head and that I didn't care about. . . . We finally ended it by saying that I'd come back the next day.

Thus Wingate initially came across as "another British bullshitter," the agent of an elaborate hoax to filch some transports from the Chinese. But at their next meeting, Cochran fell under his spell:

> I suddenly realized that, with his radio direction, Wingate used his columns in the same way that fighter-control headquarters direct planes out on a mission. I saw it as an adaption of air to jungle, an application of radio-controlled air-war tactics to a walking war in the trees and weeds. Wingate had hit upon the idea independently. He knew little about air. In his own tough element he

was thinking along the same radio lines that an airman would about tactics among the clouds.

I realized that there is something very deep about him. . . . He is the kind to convince men by saying, "We're going to do this or that, and we're going to win," in such a manner that there is no argument.

Cochran, of course, was speaking for himself. There would be major and lengthy arguments when Wingate put long-range penetration on the table for a decision. This event, anticipated like a championship prizefight by the military community in New Delhi, occurred on July 4, a coincidental date that aroused the enthusiasm of the Americans and the reflections of Wingate, who would have been dead for one year if his Cairo plan had succeeded.

If this was a prizefight, the heavyweight in the ring was Slim. With every survivor of Burma Corps back in India and a dribble of replacements from the Middle East (Rommel had finally been pushed back to Tunisia), there were no more than fifteen thousand healthy troops in the theater. The Japanese had triple that number. Slim's plan was to slowly season his army through limited probes along the Burmese coast. To form a reserve for this purpose, he had to further thin his gossamer defenses, which were stretched over seven hundred miles. This front rested on an extremely defensible range of hills, but with the Japanese's proven skill at infiltration, no one was feeling safe.

Slim's command was designated Fourteenth Army. It needed troops badly. Wingate wanted to take a third of them for himself. Slim was a three-star general, Wingate a newly promoted colonel. Slim, by one count, had forty-seven colonels working for him. Wingate had one major. Obviously the prizefight would have been no contest were it not for Wavell, the referee. As theater commander in chief, all the assets in India were his to allocate. He could give everything to Slim or any percentage of the troops he wished. He could give troops to Wingate, then put him under Slim's command, or retain command of Wingate's force himself.

Wingate, of course, wanted to work directly for Wavell. Though Slim was the antithesis of Platt, Wingate saw him as a potential threat to his independence. Thus, stakes on July 4, 1942, were high, almost as high for Wingate as they had been a year before.

The Commanders Conference, as this decisive meeting was called, was a formal affair in the viceregal mansion. It was stenographically transcribed for an official record. Arrangements were the responsibility of Major Adrian Fox-Boynton, secretary to the general staff in Wavell's headquarters. F-B, as he was known, had been on the joint planning staff during the previous months and had listened to Wingate a great deal as long-range penetration took form.

Recognizing a certain sympathy in Fox-Boynton while respecting the neutrality of his position as secretary to the conference, Wingate managed to win a round even before the prizefight began. It was on a question of attendance. Wavell could invite anyone he chose, but the fewer from Slim's camp the better for Wingate. He convinced Fox-Boynton that Slim and Brigadier Arden were quite enough.

Wingate expected Slim to raise general and doctrinal objections while Arden found fault with details. Additional opposition was anticipated from Wavell's principal staff; they worked for Major General Prentis, Wavell's chief of staff, whose views on LRP were not yet known.

The format of the conference was somewhat like a debate. Wingate went first, elaborating on a written synopsis of his Plan Mercury, so named because his force would "slip through the Japs' fingers like quicksilver" on an expedition across upper Burma. Moving undetected through the jungle, he would cut supply lines and harry the Japs' logistical troops, thereby drawing Kawabe's attention from the Burma coast, thus assisting both the Fourteenth Army's offensive and a Chinese thrust to reopen the Burma Road.

Why couldn't guerrillas do this job? Wavell's operations officer asked. They could, Wingate agreed, if there were time to train and supply them—perhaps three years. How many men would he need? Five thousand, he answered, bringing Slim out of his chair. Wavell would see his resignation before Slim turned over "a third of his army for a Hollywood escapade."

Wingate replied that the size of his force should be determined by the "weight of the punch we want to land in the Japs' gut." Wavell announced the question of numbers was premature at this point in the conference, and asked that the presentation continue.

The staff then quizzed Wingate in turn; the most telling of their arguments seemed to be that behind-the-lines operations as he was proposing had always been performed solely by volunteers, whereas Wingate was asking for whole battalions rather than individuals. Grave misgivings were also expressed concerning the British soldiers' capability in the jungle; to date they had been no match for the resourceful Japanese.

Wingate replied with three points: first, that the Americans were holding their own against the Japs in the jungles of the Solomon Islands; second, the Japanese had learned their jungle craft in a few months, for there were no jungles in Japan or northern China where they had previously been at war; and, third, he would take several months to train his force in the jungles of central India.

He acknowledged that the enemy air force must be neutralized in order for his aerial resupply plan to work. At present the Zeros and Spitfires were fighting for control of the skies though the Americans expected to gain superiority by the time Wingate was ready to launch Mercury.

The subject of the shortage of parachutes then arose. Wingate was prepared with a short filmstrip of the parajute successfully landing a 200-pound case of rations. Wavell was impressed. Slowly Wingate seemed to be meeting the important objections; Slim's staff eyed him warily when the conference broke for lunch. They ate hurriedly, then caucused in Prentis's office. The stenographic record showed the afternoon session opening abruptly:

GENERAL ARDEN: What about your wounded?

COLONEL WINGATE: That is my most difficult problem. When possible we will evacuate them to areas where small landing strips can be hacked out of the bush. Colonel Cochran is requesting some light, high-ground-clearance planes for that purpose.

GENERAL PRENTIS: Do you have any commitment from Arnold, Phil?

COLONEL COCHRAN: No, sir. Such a plane is still in development. We'd really need to capture an airstrip if we're going to get any number of casualties out.

GENERAL PRENTIS: Please proceed, Colonel Wingate.

COLONEL WINGATE: We will constantly be looking for reliable Burmese and hill people who could hide and attend our wounded. But I'll not mince words: in some circumstances the wounded will have to be abandoned. This harsh reality will be emphasized and reemphasized in training so that every man knows he must be his brother's keeper.

GENERAL ARDEN: Left to the Japs? Wingate, you haven't seen what they do to prisoners. They're nothing like the Germans or Italians. Far worse, far worse.

COLONEL WINGATE: For myself, I intend to carry poison. That option will also be offered to every rank.

GENERAL ARDEN: General, I think Mercury can be discarded on the basis of the morale factors alone.

GENERAL PRENTIS: Colonel Evans?

COLONEL EVANS: I agree with General Arden. Worldwide personnel policies provide no authorization for several aspects of this plan: no mail, no contact with anyone but the enemy for months on end. Life would be that of a fugitive, not a soldier. And then to announce as policy that the wounded will be turned over to the Japanese for bayonet practice.... We could certainly expect a visit from the inspector general. If Wingate's entire force were volunteers, things would be in a different light. But as presented here, I, as theater personnel officer, cannot support Plan Mercury.

COLONEL COBURN: Nor can I. If the Mercury forces are not all volunteers, then I demur on ethical grounds: we simply can't abandon our men to torture. On the other hand, if Mercury is to be all volunteer, then my objection is this: the call for jungle experts may be answered in great numbers. They will all end up with Wingate, thereby sifting out the leaven we need to raise the jungle proficiency of the rest of the army. Instead of spreading our most precious knowledge and experience throughout the army, we would be concentrating it in units which will never be part of the decisive campaign.

COLONEL WINGATE: The experience of these men should be used against the enemy as soon as possible—that's with me.

GENERAL SLIM: I'll get them into action on the Arakan. In fact, without an offensive by Fourteenth Army on the coast, Mercury will be left hanging out in the brush.

COLONEL WINGATE: I beg to differ, General. If the Fourteenth Army does not attack, it is all the more important for my force to do so. There can be no vacuum between opposing armies. One or the other, somewhere in the theater, must attack. Let us be the attackers, or otherwise the initiative, the momentum—and, yes, the psychological superiority—shall remain with the Japs.

GENERAL SLIM: I hope you're not questioning my offensive intentions, Colonel.

COLONEL WINGATE: In no way, sir. Everyone in His Majesty's army knows you to be a fighting general. I simply ask to fight with you and be the first to go into action.

GENERAL SLIM: What you propose delays my offensive. First you'd take a third of my forces, siphon off the best of my men, then monopolize all the aircraft. To put it in soldier's language, Wingate, first you'd strip me, then you'd [verb omitted] me.

GENERAL PRENTIS: Without Fourteenth Army attacking in the Arakan, the Japanese will have nothing to do but concentrate on Mercury. Thirty thousand of them, Wingate, hunting you down.

COLONEL WINGATE: In which case we can disappear as untraceably as we arrived. We will have achieved our purpose if we never exchange fire with the Japs, for we will have forced them to turn completely about to deal with us.

GENERAL ARDEN: My mind keeps returning to the wounded, gentlemen. I don't believe the British army ever in its history has pronounced a deliberate policy of abandoning their sick and wounded, volunteers or not. And to the Japanese...

GENERAL PRENTIS: Are you at all acquainted with the evidence we've accumulated on Japanese atrocities? Prisoners have even been crucified... and worse. The Shintos view prisoners as already dead. It is their practice to cremate them dead or alive.

COLONEL WINGATE: I have no illusions about Japanese treatment of prisoners. I will make a point of their barbarism in training my troops. I think they will fight better for knowing what to expect in the event of capture. Eighty thousand of our troops gave up in Singapore without a fight. There will be no surrenders in my command.

GENERAL WAVELL: I don't think this is a question of giving up. It's often your best and most aggressive soldiers who become wounded.

COLONEL WINGATE: They will quickly learn that they must rely on each other for evacuation.

COLONEL COBURN: So you would have two or more healthy men carry around each casualty. If one of your men is shot, that puts three out of action.

COLONEL WINGATE: Not for long. A desperately wounded man is hauled into the jungle. He will die there before the Japs are likely to find him. The lesser wounded man struggles on. He is a burden to his comrades but he does not incapacitate them.

GENERAL ARDEN: That is the most cold-blooded description of casualties I've ever heard. I hope we've not shocked our American allies.

GENERAL STRATEMEYER: After Bataan, nothing shocks us except the Japs.

COLONEL EVANS: I could name some other people who would be shocked. Look at the proposed troop list for Mercury: Composite Gurkha Battalion. Is the viceroy to tell the Prince of Nepal, our loyal colonial ally, that his sons are to be abandoned to death by torture at the hands of the Japanese? Or the Second Battalion of the Burma Rifles: you will probably say their casualties will be taken care of by the local population. But what of the Thirteenth Battalion of the King's Liverpool Regiment? They will hardly pass as Asiatics. Is the prime minister to write to their families: "Your loved one was severely wounded in North Burma and left behind in the care of the Japanese. This was done all according to plan..."

GENERAL PRENTIS: Quite so. General Wavell, if there is military justification for this operation, I feel it may well be overidden by political considerations.

GENERAL WAVELL: What do you say, Orde?'

COLONEL WINGATE: I say that images of the Burma retreat may be too fresh in some minds. Only green troops fell by the wayside in great numbers. Bush Warfare School lost only a handful. Mercury will be more like that. I will train these men like no other British have ever been trained before. I forecast that about a third of them won't survive the training.

COLONEL COBURN: Survive?

COLONEL WINGATE: Will wash out. The rest...

COLONEL COBURN: Will the survivors be so tough that bullets bounce off them like Superman? Will your training immunize them to wounds?

COLONEL WINGATE: No, Colonel Coburn. The training will simply prepare them to face war as the Japanese do. The Japs, to give them their due, are consistent. They give no quarter but neither do they ask for any. When they are captured they expect to be put to death. My men must be prepared for the same. I shall make certain they are. We will all know that the rules we play by in Burma are those of the Japs.

GENERAL ARDEN: So the wounded are to be comforted by the knowledge that they are permitted to kill Japanese prisoners.

GENERAL SLIM: Ethically untenable.

GENERAL PRENTIS: Puts us on the same level as the Japs.

COLONEL COBURN: That isn't training, that's decivilizing.

COLONEL EVANS: Devastating to both morale and discipline.

COLONEL HEMPHILL: That would play right into the hands of their propaganda.

COLONEL NOBLE: Morally repugnant, if I do say so.

COLONEL ARDEN: Unconscionable.

COLONEL WINGATE: Well. I assumed that the greatest initial obstacle for Mercury would be the Chindwin. I feel now it is morality. If that's the case, and if that's what is preventing your approval, let me promise you this: after completing the training and before we enter Burma, I will advise each man in writing as to what can be expected for the wounded. Each man will then be permitted to withdraw from my force if he so chooses. That option, I hope, will meet the objections regarding the voluntary nature of LRP. In the end each man who crosses the Chindwin with me will be a volunteer.

GENERAL PRENTIS: You may be crossing the Chindwin alone, Colonel Wingate, but on that understanding, duly recorded, I think my ethical reservations are suspended.

GENERAL WAVELL: I concur. Orde, your plan is approved in concept. As to numbers and equipment, I think we need only rough figures at this point. Bill, be honest: what can you spare?

GENERAL SLIM: Two thousand.

GENERAL WAVELL: Orde, what's your *minimum* requirement?

COLONEL WINGATE: Four thousand.

GENERAL WAVELL: I'm giving you three thousand. We'll leave the question of aircraft allocation for a later conference.

51

"Bruce," Wingate exclaimed over the phone, "meet me at the Imperial!"

"How did you fare?"

"I'm buying."

He hung up almost giddy. Three thousand men—a full brigade and inevitable promotion to brigadier. He could imagine Enright and Platt reading the announcement in the *Army Gazette.*

He sat at one of the clusters of wicker on the impeccable lawn while turbaned waiters moved like swans between the tables. He ordered gin and tonic while watching the huge orange sun depart with the heat of day. Giant crows lumbered across the lawn of the Imperial Hotel, the British Raj reigned supreme, and all seemed right in the world.

His new command consumed him like an illicit love but it also meant reconciliation with his horrid old mistress, the army. A reconciliation forced by the Japanese, Wingate realized, and his enemies at GHQ were legion; their number would probably increase with his new stature, but the army for the first time had acknowledged his abilities, not just his courage.

He had a sudden impulse to telegraph the news to Lorna but quickly realized what a breach of security that would be. The very existence of his force must remain very much a secret. The conference had concluded by giving Wingate's force the cover name Seventy-seventh Indian Brigade (though there would never be any Indian units in it). It would receive its components at Saugor, five hundred miles from Burma, and the call for volunteers would be solely by word of mouth.

"Colonel Wingate."

"Huh?"

"Major Fox-Boynton. I was at the conference." Fox-Boynton would have been hard to forget. He was tall, regimental, and wore a monocle.

"Why of course! Won't you join me? I've started a small celebration."

Fox-Boynton sat down, arranging his cap and swagger stick with aplomb. An imperceptible movement of his head summoned a waiter. A week ago Wingate would have prickled at the manners of such a man. However, he knew something of Fox-Boynton's reputation and it belied his appearances.

"Bruce Dalton is about to join me," said Wingate. "His reports of your doings during the retreat were complimentary."

"Bruce is generous."

"Not often. You must be good."

"I am."

"Like your job?"

"It has its advantages."

"Such as?"

"The ear and counsel of Sir Archie. In fact I took counsel with him today—after the conference."

"I owe him everything. What did he counsel?"

"I asked him if I should join fortunes with you—presuming that you'd have me of course."

"Yes?"

"He said if I were married that it would not be a good idea. But if not, I shouldn't hesitate. I'm not, so I'm not hesitating, and I'm here to ask you to take me as your first volunteer." He adjusted his monocle.

"On one condition: that you'll not allow yourself to be wounded!"

They shared a macabre laugh as Dalton arrived. The three drank considerably and talked louder than they should have about such a top-secret topic. Later Wingate thought about this indiscretion but rationalized that if LRP were so little understood by the British high command, it would be incomprehensible to a Japanese spy.

"Do you think we should be having dinner?" Dalton asked when he realized that their talk was becoming sloppy.

"The chicken Bengali here is excellent," said Fox-Boynton.

"Let's have it," said Wingate, and they ordered.

"You didn't tell me the command setup," Dalton remarked as if it were a small concern. Actually it was second in importance only to the creation of the brigade.

"By George, you're right," said Wingate. "What the hell is it anyway, Adrian?"

"Purposely ambiguous, I'm afraid. Sir Archie won't make two close calls in the same day. He went against the consensus, as you well know, in approving Mercury."

"Did he! Bruce, you should have heard the chorus against me. Like a morality play and I was the villain."

"Good casting."

"Sir Archie," Fox-Boynton continued, "is a conciliator more than a commander. By the way, four thousand was your negotiating figure, wasn't it?"

"Of course. I know Sir Archie too."

"So what's the command setup?" Dalton asked again.

"Organizationally I answer to GHQ. However, my operations are to be 'coordinated' through Slim. Vague enough for my purposes."

"And for Wavell to refer you to Slim if you press him too much," Fox-Boynton cautioned. "Sir Archie finds you somewhat intimidating. You will have to remain on good terms with Slim."

"Bill's all right. It's Arden and his toadies I can't stand. Prentis didn't seem to be much of an ally either."

"He goes where the wind blows. Today he was waiting for Wavell's cue."

"What was it?" asked Dalton.

"The wounded must waive their rights," Wingate pronounced, thumping his glass on the table.

"How's that?"

"Any man in the brigade can fall out if he doesn't approve of the wounded policy. A decision of the moment. All was lost if I didn't come up with something."

"That's what I thought," said Fox-Boynton. "You won me over at that point. I told Sir Archie if Wingate can make a snap decision like that with four generals breathing on his neck, I think he's the man to be with in the jungle."

"I won't let you be killed needlessly, Adrian," said Wingate, then looked around as if he'd heard an echo.

"Something wrong?" Dalton asked.

"Seems I made that promise to someone else. Can't remember who at the moment."

Running southwest to northeast across the center of India is the Vindhya Range, a jungle-carpeted expanse of hills similar to those of Nagaland, where Mercury Force would make their entrance into Burma. Far from GHQ, where nature looked its worst, Wingate established his training camp. The nearest town was Saugor; nearby Wingate set up his headquarters, content in isolation with his new command.

The nucleus of the force was the faculty from Bush Warfare School. They were to Mercury Force what the British cadre had been to Gideon Force. In the Sudan Wingate's manpower was much more primitive, but in India the mission for which he prepared was infinitely more difficult. Time pressure was greater on Gideon Force, whereas coordination with other forces was a much bigger problem for Mercury.

Most of his troops came from three disparate organizations. The first and the best were Burma Rifles, a battalion of native veterans of the British army. Wingate's second battalion were Gurkhas, colonial troops from Nepal. Experts in junglecraft, they differed with Wingate's theories of jungle warfare, a difference he compared with solo sailing and sailing with a crew. The Gurkhas took to the jungle as individuals, which made them superb scouts, but in coordinated maneuver of units they were overcautious and sometimes unresponsive. Like the Burma Rifles, the Gurkhas were commanded by British officers, many of whom could not adjust to Wingate and were sent packing. Whatever the frictions, Wingate was glad to have the Gurkhas, whose stoic bravery was legend throughout Asia.

The last third of his force was 100 percent British. This was the Thirteenth Battalion of the King's Liverpool Regiment created in a wartime levy after the cream of the army had been lost in France and Africa. "The Kings," as they were called, were overage and overweight from sitting around coastal defenses in England and garrisons in India. The Kings loomed as Wingate's greatest challenge and potentially his greatest reward. If he could train these substandard troops to where, as Wingate put it,

> the Japs can no longer barge through us, the Fourteenth Army will look at itself and see the seedlings of self-respect.
>
> To this end I have an ally which no one else perceives. It is the jungle. We look at it now like novice swimmers peering down into the abyss, seeing every shadow as a shark. I must transform this perception. The jungle is at worst a neutral barrier for both sides. It clogs vision and movement, but in this respect the jungle favors inferior troops like mine. For a single rifle firing down a jungle trail halts a superior

force. Every encounter is an ambush, every battle a surprise. I much prefer my role to that of the Japanese commander. I will be looking for opportunities to surprise while he will be looking for me. Soon it will be he who interprets shadows; then the jungle will no longer be neutral by my full ally.

I see this, dear Lorna, as nature's compensation. She exposed me in her desert; now she will enfold me in her jungle.

52

Fox-Boynton called daily from Delhi with a list of problems. One of them was an irony for Wingate: in Ethiopia mules had been as rare as unicorns, in India they were overrunning the animal markets but muleteers were scarce.

"We'll train them," Wingate replied, looking at his schedule, trying to find time where there was none. "What else?" he sighed, as the discussion had been long and the phone connection poor.

"Hemphill is upset about the term 'Mercury Force.' Mercury is the name of the plan, which is ultra-secret. We should have a name for the force that doesn't use Mercury."

"What?" Wingate nearly shouted as the line was broken by static. Fox-Boynton repeated.

"For once Hemphill may have a point. Wait a bit." Wingate turned to Au Thang, his liaison officer from the Burma Rifles. "Remember those griffins in front of the pagodas? Don't they represent lions?"

"Yes, sir."

"What do you call them?"

"Chinthé."

"Chin-thait? What's the plural?" Au Thang shook his head. Another officer sought his attention and Wingate resumed his discussion with Fox-Boynton, who, at its conclusion, mentioned Hemphill's criticism again. When he did, Au Thang had gone off to other business.

"OK. As a provisional code name," said Wingate, "we're going to be the lions or the griffins, I'm not sure which. That's 'chind-thit' in Burmese."

"Like 'bandit'?"

"*Chin*dit. Like we take it on the chin from Coburn."

"Roger. I'll advise all concerned that we are Chindit Force."

"No, just the Chindits. Like the Gurkhas or the Black Watch."

Rather than follow any conventional army organization, Wingate divided his three thousand Chindits into six "columns" of approximately five hundred men each, with a uniform mix of faculty, Burma Rifles, Gurkhas, and Kings. They were assembled in mid-July 1942. "You will live or die by ambush," were the first words they heard from Wingate, so squad by squad they trooped down trails where trip wires released dozens of tethered balloons to bob up in the foliage while the Chindits dove to the ground and blazed away. In the first weeks most balloons drifted mockingly in the gunsmoke. Marksmanship improved as the men learned to fire low in overlapping arcs.

Balloon popping was child's play compared with what followed. Jungle marches progressed from eight to fifteen to twenty miles per day and sometimes half as far by night. At one time or another every man had to lead his platoon as a pathfinder. If he went wrong, his platoon got lost with him. There was no rest till the correct destination was reached, and a late-night arrival meant less sleep before "stand to arms" the next morning a half hour before the first light of dawn. Every morning for five months there was "stand-to," for this was the favorite hour for the Japanese to attack.

Care of the injured was exactly what care of the wounded would be in Burma. A man who collapsed from the heat—as nearly a quarter of them did during the first month—received only the assistance of his fellow soldiers. No ambulances accompanied the field exercises and no aircraft were sent to the scene of accidents unless the injured men's comrades could carve out an airstrip from the jungle.

Individual loads were normally from fifty to sixty pounds and borne at all times in the field. In Burma Wingate expected to reduce the loads to forty pounds so the men would feel light of foot. Mules were reserved for radios, mortars, and extra ammunition.

When the monsoon broke, the field training only became more

intense. Boots and uniforms disintegrated, as did the health of the men. As Wingate had predicted, attrition curved gradually toward 33 percent; with the undertrained Kings it was higher. As he reported to Colonel Coburn,

> The first thing when setting out to train for LRP was to root out the prevailing hypochondria. . . . No man will be evacuated for diarrhea unless his platoon leader has examined his stool. . . . Our lieutenants are platoon physicians, with equal powers of life and death. If a man must be left on a tactical exercise, he must be left.

This happened several times. The first occurred when a Sergeant Foreman of the Kings plunged into a streambed, breaking his femur. His patrol was hacking its way through dense bamboo to set out marking lamps for a resupply drop for an entire column. Heavily burdened, Sergeant Foreman's squad could neither extricate him from the overgrown streambed nor carry him to the drop zone if they had. Calling up from the green darkness, he ordered them on with their mission and to mark the trail back to his location. The drop was received and Foreman later saved.

"He's a Chindit," said Wingate when he heard of the incident. The sergeant had suffered a permanently disabling compound fracture and was about to be evacuated.

Wingate squatted beside his stretcher. "I can't take you over the Chindwin, but we're going to need good men at the Assam CP. Want to stay with the Chindits?" He did, and became a permanent member of the rear headquarters.

Consequences of the other serious training accidents were not so satisfying. On a night patrol, a corporal of the Kings fell asleep and could not be found. With a mission to accomplish, the patrol went on. A woodcutter discovered the skeleton in 1947. The third abandonment occurred when a Gurkha lieutenant suffered a collapsed rib cage when crushed between two mules who then bolted into the jungle. By the time they were recovered, night and rain had fallen so darkly that the injured lieutenant was lost. The next day Dalton sent back a patrol to look for the man but continued the tactical exercise with the rest of the column. When the maneuver concluded, a full-scale search found the lieutenant dead of injury and exposure.

These and similar incidents, only less serious because they were not mortal, drew the attention of the IG—the inspector general—the ombudsman of soldiers who could not find redress within the chain of command. IGs could report their findings to London if necessary.

Allen Johns at Fourteenth Army was the first IG to receive complaints about the severity of Wingate's training. He rightfully concluded he would be thrown out of the Chindit HQ; so he passed his reports on to GHQ in New Delhi, leaving General Prentis with the task of bringing Wingate to heel. Citing the time pressures of his training, Wingate would not leave his camp, and Prentis could not get a grip on him at Saugor.

That had been tried and defied by Wingate's policy for visitors to share rather than observe the rigors of the training camp. Already officers from Delhi had been subject to unheard-of indignities.

Swagger sticks were forbidden. One careless major from GHQ forgot the ban and saw his Malacca broken over Wingate's knee. Office uniforms fared badly on such visits because of Wingate's policy of running everywhere. He believed it to be a pernicious tradition of the British army that officers must at all times appear cool and unruffled. On the parapets of World War I this tradition produced models of awesome courage (and thousands of dead lieutenants), but in the short visibility of the jungle the men could not see the proud carriage of their officers. In the jungle, to be both seen and heard by their men, leaders had to scurry to and fro between them. To nurture this habit, Wingate had them run when going about their business in camp. If you were an officer, you ran. Wingate saw no reason to exempt visitors from the policy.

The Chindits owned but eight vehicles, six of which were ambulances. This gave him the perfect excuse not to meet visitors, who then had to whistle up an Indian jitney for a grueling ride to the border of the camp. Here they were greeted by barbed wire and a sign announcing that trespassers would be shot.

A sentry sent a courier dog off with the message that a visitor had arrived. An hour might elapse before he was provided with a mule. "It's quite realistic," Colonel Kelly described his first and only visit. "You feel you're behind the lines from the moment you arrive. Except when you reach the cantonment you're not sure if you're in British headquarters or a Japanese prisoner-of-war camp."

53

Coburn arranged for a showdown. All of GHQ's principal staff officers, headed by General Prentis, flew down to Saugor's commercial airport in Wavell's converted bomber, which made an excellent conference room. Wingate's invitation was from Prentis; so no excuse was plausible for him not to attend. Since the conference would be on board the bomber, GHQ would not have to suffer from mules, sprints, or broken swagger sticks.

Moreover the simple, purposely vague agenda was sure to entice Wingate. Ostensibly this was a training conference with no mention of IG complaints. Wingate would be lured by the orders for Exercise Shakedown, a full-scale two-week maneuver for the Chindits against British paratroopers who would play the part of the Japanese while the Chindits tried to cut roads and a railway similar to their targets in Burma.

Wingate welcomed the test, which would begin with a long written order from GHQ detailing the Chindits' mission and support. He would receive the exercise order at the conference.

On a sweltering day in early October the bomber taxied to the Saugor terminal. On the door was Prentis's two-star medallion; inside he was seated in air-conditioned comfort with his staff, who had all placed their swagger sticks conspicuously in front of them. An orderly opened the door, admitting a draft of overheated air and the view of Wingate, Dalton, and Fox-Boynton in jungle dress astride mules. These they tethered to the gangway of the aircraft.

"At least they're not going to ride them up here," quipped Colonel Noble, leaving his colleagues laughing for the Chindits' entrance.

"I imagine Orde is the Lord of la Mancha," said Prentis, extending his hand, "but which of you is Sancho?"

"Depends on the windmill," said Fox-Boynton. He was the only man to have the regard of everyone on the plane.

"First off," Prentis announced cordially, "Congratulations. We couldn't see a thing from the air. You surely have the best camouflaged brigade in the Far East."

"Thank you, sir," said Wingate, "though there's not much competition. My, this is a large audience for a training conference," he said as he recognized the inspector general.

"Thought we'd all save time and gas with one trip."

"May I have the order?"

"Surely." Coburn handed Wingate a bundle of papers, maps, and transparencies. Dalton and Fox-Boynton began posting the maps; Wingate read the order as Prentis continued. "What Shakedown, as this exercise is called, hopes to accomplish is just that: shake down the stray bolts in your organization; test your tactics and procedures. Bob, why don't you take over?"

"We've put you up against the Sixth Parachute Brigade," said Coburn. "A tough lot. Ought to be a good show."

"What's this 'parenthesis simulated' mean next to the supply drops?"

"No aircraft."

"Then no Shakedown."

"Beg pardon?"

"I've been telling you for months the Chindits do two things the army doesn't. One: communicate entirely by wireless. Two: resupply entirely by air. They're the key and crux of our operations. If you're not going to give us aerial resupply, I'm not sending the Chindits out. We'll deploy the radio teams and have a communications exercise instead."

"There are simply no aircraft, Orde. Requirements for the Hump you know."

An RAF officer backed up Coburn: "The Doolittle raid sent the Japs into a panic over the safety of their cities. They've been pushing the front west at a rate of ten miles per day. The Chinese are fighting for their lives."

"If you say so," said Wingate. "I'm just telling you if the exercise doesn't include aerial resupply, my training time is better spent doing other things."

"Couldn't we drop your resupply out of trucks?"

"Not unless you also drive trucks to Burma when I need them. I've simulated nothing but Japs in my training, gentlemen. I won't compromise in what should be our dress rehearsal for combat."

"The shortage of aircraft is regrettable; however, you must make do with what you have just as you will against the Japanese."

"When the Chindits were created, Sir Archie made me responsible for their readiness. I'll not participate in an exercise which does not contribute to that purpose. Shakedown, as I read it, does not. You may as well have a naval maneuver without oilers. Or a farting contest without beer. Or a fu..."

"Colonel Wingate," Prentis interjected, "perhaps we should table Shakedown for the moment and let F-B and Coburn discuss it back there." He gestured to the sleeping compartments at the rear of the bomber. "Meanwhile, there are other matters we would bring to your attention."

"I have a query for Colonel Coburn: your order says the Sixth Para is our enemy. How are they getting into the exercise area?"

"By parachute, of course."

"By 'simulated' aircraft or out of the back of trucks?"

"Quite facetious."

"You've got transports to drop these palace guards and none for the Chindits? *We're* the ones going into combat in a few months while they're parading around Delhi."

"They only require a single mission, Wingate. The transports return nearly empty from China. Cochran drops them into your exercise en route back to Imphal. One drop."

"Very well, give me one drop."

Coburn and Noble made some rapid calculations. "According to your memoranda," said Noble, "you require four drops for each two weeks in the field."

"We'll live on one."

"Quarter rations?" Noble asked.

"Right. The rest we get from the jungle. Come on, Coburn, play fair. If Sixth Para gets a drop, we do too."

"What about it?" General Prentis asked of Coburn, obviously seeking compromise.

"Frankly, General, I feel we have delivered the order approved by Sir Archibald. If the Chindits do not see fit to..."

"Call the Sixth Para, Bob," Prentis said with the slightest arch of his brow. "Work something out with Browning. Now, while we're on training, Orde, the IG would like to mention some attendant incidents."

54

"You could have maneuvered around Coburn," said Fox-Boynton, as the mules carried them back into the jungle. "Instead you hit him head-on."

"Well," said Dalton loyally, "they're not likely to take on Orde again."

"No, they're much cleverer than that. From now on we'll have to be on guard against sabotage."

"Slim's a fighter. Perhaps he'll take my side now," said Wingate wistfully.

"On the contrary. Look for GHQ to gang up against you with Slim. They can undermine you in countless ways. I'm very apprehensive, Orde."

"I seem to have a way of undoing myself."

"You certainly aren't free of self-destructive tendencies."

Authorization for the resupply drop was Wingate's sole victory in Shakedown. It took place in a rain which diminished the airworthiness of the parajutes. The drop itself was near disaster. Most of the chutes missed the jungle clearings and became hopelessly tangled in high trees. Chindits had to scale them and cut down the supply bundles. This took a tortuously long time, setting back the march timetables by many hours, hours regained by longer marches and less sleep.

One column became completely lost, taking itself out of the exercise for days. The reason primarily was faulty maps. Wingate suspected GHQ had issued them deliberately. Other evidence of sabotage was in the radio batteries and crystals, which constantly malfunctioned.

The mules also proved to be agents of GHQ. Loads slipped from their rain-slicked hides. They seemed to be led only by the renegades among them: if one went astray the rest followed, but if one came back into column he was alone.

Of the three Chindit targets they scored on but one. It seemed impossible for the columns to coordinate for an attack. On one occasion Dalton secretly encircled a village so the only way into it was a trail on which another column was already marching. The plan was for an ambush of the relief force, which would be sent to rescue the village after Dalton began his attack—a manuever similar to the one that brought Gideon Force its first victory in Ethiopia. Somehow the ambush column did not get into position, though all this required was for them to pull off the side of the trail. Instead the relief force of paratroopers attacked right into the rear of the column. If blank ammunition had not been used, the column would have been destroyed.

The Sixth Parachute Brigade's prisoner-of-war cages filled with Chindits. By the end of the exercise, the umpires had assessed Wingate a third of his force. What could not be assessed was the ineffectiveness of the remainder. Boot-sucking mud, shelterless rest, leeches, natural hazards, and subsistence on quarter rations left the survivors stumbling zombies. All told, Shakedown was a rattling experience.

So much so that Wavell canceled a postexercise critique. This disappointed the gloating paratroopers and detracted from GHQ's revenge, but the feeling in New Delhi and Assam was that Wingate had received his comeuppance.

Wavell summoned Wingate to New Delhi for a private chat, where he had to endure the ignominy of walking through GHQ. He looked straight ahead, ignoring half-concealed snickers. Wingate closed the door and sank into a chair.

"I think Shakedown erred on the side of severity," Wavell remarked considerately.

"We just mucked it up."

"There was muck enough, but I think the Chindits performed remarkably. You gave Sixth Para all they could handle."

"Our force ratio with them was one to one. The Japs are just as good and double or triple in numbers. I'm disappointed, almost discouraged."

"You're understandably tired, Orde."

"There was something missing with us. We didn't know what to do when plans went wrong. Our instincts were wrong. Yet I'm no less convinced that the LRP concept is sound."

"Then don't worry. If it is humanly possible, I know you and the Chindits can do it."

"Too many errors. Too many missed signals. Too many people who didn't know what to do—who had to be told. Too many mistakes the Japs won't let us get away with. Maybe we just don't have the initiative needed for jungle warfare. Initiative may not be part of the British psyche. I don't know. I'm laden with doubts."

"You've got another month, Orde. Use it to recoup. I know you can make your points without putting the Chindits through another ordeal."

"Initiative can't be taught."

"It has to come from within, in my opinion. And when it is lacking a man does not see its value if he is nearly starved and completely exhausted. You've used the whip, Orde, and I haven't restrained you though there has been much pressure on me to do so. Now I ask you to apply some ointment to the lashes. Let the men rest so they may reflect. Long-distance runners taper off their training as the day of the race approaches. I urge you to take their example.

"And for yourself," Wavell continued, "please reflect on the original LRP concept, the premise that a force can operate indefinitely behind enemy lines. I've become convinced that 'indefinitely' is unrealistic. The unique strain was evident even in the two weeks of Shakedown. You must have seen how the men's performance decayed over time. There is some temporal limit for men in constant peril, a limit set by time alone and not the ferocity of combat."

"That's a well-considered point, Sir Archie. I don't know how I'll incorporate it but I shall try."

"My other observation on Shakedown regards the tension I felt between the Chindits on one side and GHQ and the Fourteenth Army on the other. I don't wish to trace its development; I simply demand that it cease."

"I've been told I'm my own worst enemy."

"I said as much in Cairo. Is there no way for you to wage war without declaring it on your own army?"

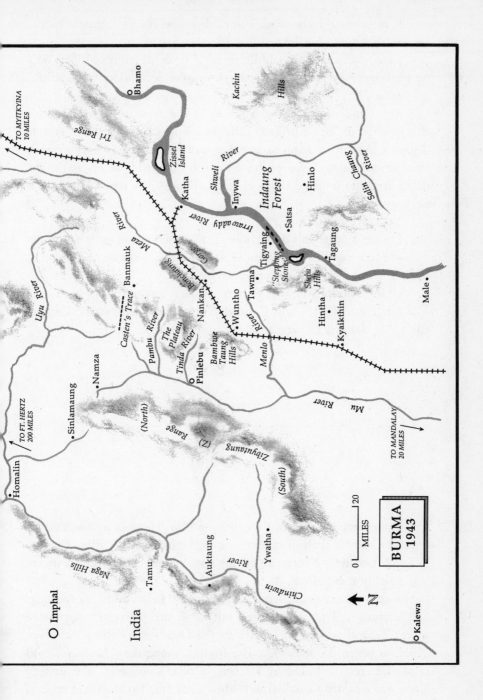

"It is because I am what I am, objectionable as I appear to my critics, that I win battles."

"Sometimes I wish I could keep you in a kennel, turn you loose only for the hunt. Nevertheless, I'm requesting your promotion to brigadier."

"Sir..."

"My confidence in you is as strong as the opposition I've faced for this promotion. But a brigade calls for a brigadier; that much no one disputes. Assuming acquiescence from London, you may start wearing these immediately." Wavell tossed two bright red epaulets across the desk. Wingate fingered them gingerly, then slowly replaced his colonel's insignia.

"You give me new heart."

"Do me a favor and don't hold it over the fellows out there."

Wingate looked straight ahead as he passed the desks. Stunned silence remained in GHQ after he left.

"I can't believe it," said Coburn in deep shock.

"Strangest of all," said Colonel Noble that night at the Officers Club, "he seemed to have an air of humility about him."

55

The gloom from Shakedown was behind him. He rang up the RAF to request a seat for their next bombing in the Irrawaddy Valley. Colonel Wingate would have been turned down with a sneer; Brigadier Wingate was quickly manifested.

From the bomber, a living map unfolded below him, its contours and features well set in his mind but he wished to retrace them once more. Takeoff was to the east into the clouds blanketing the Naga Hills, at seven thousand feet the highest range the Chindits would cross. Its crest was held by a string of Slim's outposts. The eastern slope was a no-man's wilderness where only small patrols had clashed since the British expulsion six months earlier. Running north to south parallel to the Naga Hills, the swift-flowing Chindwin marked the western edge of the Japanese conquests.

Two hundred miles to the north, India, Burma, and China came together where a series of parallel gorges funneled four of the world's mightiest rivers out of Tibet. Compressed by comb-sharp ridges, the Yangtze, Mekong, Irrawaddy, and Brahmaputra rushed side by side before fanning out thousands of miles through the ancient civilizations of Asia.

This great mountainous convergence marked the northern limit of the war. Beyond lay the perpetual snowcaps of the Himalayas, where not even Japanese ambitions extended. Just south of the parallel gorges at the foot of the peaks was Fort Hertz, the only outpost in Burma still held by the Allies. In September 1942, while the Chindits were still in early training, a hundred Australian paratroopers descended on the fort and found no one but a nearby camp of hill tribesmen. These they organized into guerrillas and went hunting for Japanese.

Though well north of where the Chindits would operate, Fort Hertz figured in their plans. An unknown number of Japanese units had been drawn up there to exterminate the guerrillas. Wingate would be striking the rear of this expedition.

Easing the pressure on Fort Hertz, however, was not his principal mission. That lay eighty miles east of the Chindwin, where the Mandalay-Myitkyina railroad supplied the Japanese Eighteenth Division. This veteran force held the western terminus of the Burma Road, which once provided overland access to the long embattled Chinese armies. Now supplies could reach the Chinese only by way of Cochran's transports flying over the roof of the world. His efforts were not enough; the Chinese armies were slowly starving for the necessities of war.

From guerrilla reports, it seemed the Eighteenth Division was deployed to defend against an unlikely attack by the Chinese from the east. Wingate's thrust from the west would thus take them in the rear as it would the Fort Hertz expedition.

Some fifty miles south of where the Chindits were to cross it, the Chindwin swings southeast to its confluence with the Irrawaddy. The bulk of the Japanese army, a hundred thousand strong under General Kawabe, were deployed in an arc between the lower Chindwin and the coast. Here from the Arakan Range they had been fencing with Slim,

whose thickest defenses protected the important Indian port of Chittagong.

Wingate's thrust would slip around the Japanese flank, which thinned
into outposts north of Kalewa. Operation Mercury was designed to support a concurrent attack by Slim along the coast. Thus coordinated, Slim
and Wingate would keep the Japanese busy, confused, and hopefully unable to concentrate against either of them. There were even some hopes
for a push by the Chinese down the Burma Road, but no one was expecting much.

This was the strategic picture at the end of 1942 when Wingate
looked out of the bomber for a final inspection of the wilderness which
would be his battlefield. It looked tidy from the air: first the watershed of the Chindwin, about thirty miles across, to the Zibyutaung
Range, which was more a plateau atop a steep escarpment. The Z
Range, as it was called, sloped eastward into the valley of the Mu, a
tributary of the awesome Irrawaddy, one of the world's great rivers,
with a carrying volume and width equal to the Mississippi.

The Irrawaddy, a hundred miles' distance from the Chindwin, made
a natural eastern boundary for the Chindits' operations; however, Mercury included contingencies for part of the force to move beyond the
river into the Kachin Hills, where the tribes remained loyal to the
British and which might serve as a base for linkup with the Chinese.

Wingate's aerial reconnaissance went no farther east than Katha,
the rail terminus on the Irrawaddy. Winding back through the jungle
to Mandalay, the single track was beckoningly exposed to attacks from
the jungle. Bombing raids with the few aircraft available were ineffective against it. However, well-set demolitions at bridges and gorges
might inflict lasting damage.

Darkness had settled into the valleys when Wingate's bomber turned
for home. There were no lights below, not a single village with more
than a few hundred Burmese. Neither were there any permanent Japanese garrisons except at Katha and Pinlebu. For the Japanese, these
would be two islands in thousands of square miles of jungle seas.

Wingate would not see this terrain again until he was on it in February 1943. After some consulations with his column commanders, he
decided to close down the Saugor camp before Christmas and take them
into the Naga Hills behind the Fourteenth Army front, the starting
line for his expedition.

We are marching to Imphal for Christmas {he wrote Lorna}. After a thousand miles by rail, the troops are ready to march. We will average only about fifteen miles per day, for we must move by night, not for security so much as for traffic control. By day convoys own the narrow road, which is too dangerous to drive in the darkness (due to washouts, fallen trees, etc.), so we shall sleep by day and walk by night.

22 December 1942

A splendid beginning for this day. A night of steep climbing brought us to the height of the Imphal Plateau. There, when I awoke, was a panorama which must be God's pride. Range upon range receded in paling shades divided by mists curling up from the valleys to meet the morning. "How beautiful upon the mountain...." The switchbacks of road were such that I could see all the columns arrayed in trail, each at a different elevation. The exertions of our training have been hard, hard indeed, but moments like this seem to be God's reward for our labor. I drank in this scene of Mars and Earth feeling that every man with me was glad to be a soldier at this hour, at this place.

Christmas Day

We are camped outside Imphal, having completed our last march on Christmas Eve. Yes, there was a star to guide us; it was Venus, I believe, that shone down from time to time as clouds parted in restless patterns. A single twinkling light, while here below the engineers worked on without respite, their giant lights flooding patches of the dripping hills, their gnashing gears and shrieking engines battling with the slithering earth. How blindly we struggle in our work with scarcely a glance to the heavens in their silent splendor.

Is it only this single day which gives us pause? Even the world war seems to catch its breath for a moment. I even wonder for the Japanese across the hills. It is a strange feeling, as if we were all caught in the same crime by a glance from the Godhead.

It is beyond my understanding, so I return to my personal evidence of God's presence on earth—your love for me. How very much alone I am without you, my own. I am too overcome to write more now but I shall after the new year. May God protect us both in 1943.

56

Like the groom before his wedding or the prizefighter before his bout, Wingate spent the first month of the new year receiving visitors and well-wishers. Wavell was first to call; taking his lead, General Prentis and his staff (including a very gracious Coburn) paid respects, offered support. The Chindits were working closely now with the front-line troops through which they would pass en route to the Chindwin. The Fourth Corps, commanded by General Scoones, would attempt to distract the Japanese as Wingate stole into their territory.

By late January the last guests had gone like the end of a farewell party. Wingate had been resentfully busy briefing them while Fox-Boynton and Dalton supervised some late-hour exercises with aerial resupply. Finally the Chindits seemed ready. Now there was time for eleventh-hour ruminations, forebodings, and expectations. Wingate shared them with Dalton and Fox-Boynton, who would command the flanks of the expedition while Wingate took the central column through to the Bonchaung Gorge, where he planned to bury the railroad under a landslide.

"Of course the drops went badly. This is the first time an aerial logistic system has ever been attempted—ever, in the history of warfare." This was Fox-Boynton's opinion after he and Dalton (both now colonels) had reviewed the practical deficiencies of the January exercise, the last before the Chindits went to war.

"There are many firsts for the Chindits," said Wingate placidly. They were sitting before his tent on a knoll that viewed some of the encampment. In twilight, the rum ration had been distributed; Wingate, Dalton, and Fox-Boynton were drinking theirs with mango juice from sections of bamboo.

"Yes there are," said Fox-Boynton. "Had you considered, Orde, that you are probably the first general to walk into battle since Roman times, maybe earlier?"

"And maybe the first to use elephants since Hannibal," Wingate smiled. "This expedition will be a unique combination of the most primitive and the most modern forms of warfare. I'm counting on the Japs not to fathom it. What do you think, Bruce?"

"The Japs are slow to react. I've told you that."

"Yes, but I need reassurance. I'm like a homely woman who constantly needs to be told she's attractive."

"Speaking of homeliness," said Fox-Boynton, "everyone is watching to see if you will grow your Ethiopian beard."

"I intend to. Once we cross the Chindwin."

"So the men may as well?" Dalton asked.

"That's up to the column commanders. The Japs denigrate us for being hairy, don't they?"

"So I'm told. You know, Orde, what I said about them reacting slowly doesn't mean they won't slash at us when we make contact."

"I know. I expect that. What I'm counting on is a considerable lag in their generalship from the time we collide till they develop a counterplan."

"What worries me is the pattern of our drops. If they were to plot them on their maps, they'd watch us moving east, then turning around and coming back. It's coming back that worries me most."

"Who says we will?"

"You mean go out through Hertz?" Fox-Boynton inquired.

"That's one possibility. But what about a base in the Kachin Hills? Sounds as though you fellows haven't considered that seriously."

Evening shadows prevented the three from seeing each other's expressions. Dalton and Fox-Boynton both sipped from their bamboo mugs before Dalton answered. "Six weeks, Orde; eight weeks is stretching it, and ten weeks is the very limit. We can't stay back there any longer."

Fox-Boynton nodded agreement. "We can't live out there indefinitely."

"You saw how everyone started deteriorating on Shakedown," said Dalton. "Frankly I don't think fighting the Japs will be that tough physically: the loads won't be as heavy, the rations as short, the marches as long—you know what I mean. But there's something about... what did you call it, Adrian?"

"The fugitive factor."

"Do you understand that, Orde? Apparently you didn't experience it in Ethiopia or Palestine."

"No I didn't. I know what you're describing, but I think it can be overcome with confident, competent leadership."

"Not entirely," said Fox-Boynton. "And not indefinitely. The leaders' competence is going to erode over time and through systemic exhaustion; the men will be the first to notice. I saw it on the retreat."

"There could be a creeping panic," said Dalton.

"I don't accept that," Wingate snapped. "When we inflict panic on the enemy, we recharge our batteries. A boxer does not spend himself with telling blows; it's cautious sparring and frustration which drain him."

"That attitude worries me," said Fox-Boynton from the darkness.

"Well, your worries are shared by Wavell. He made much the same points with me after Shakedown. It gave me pause, and so do your remarks, but I have my own equation that accounts for the fugitive factor, creeping panic, or what have you."

"You're welcome to the rest of my rum if your equation works," said Dalton.

"And I'll cut you a mango," Fox-Boynton added.

"All right then. Think of war in all its manifestations: on land, at sea, in the air. We expend some spiritual substance as we fight. Let's call that substance courage. Every man has a finite quantity of courage. When it's gone, he's ineffective and must be taken out of the war.

"Now one way of looking at the forms of warfare is by comparing their respective expenditures of courage. When there is safety, there is no expenditure: the courage tap is off. When there is certain danger, the tap is on full. Consider Fighter Command. During the blitz they sat around their comfortable crew lounges in perfect safety till the claxon sounded. Then they scrambled aloft and vectored onto a flight of enemy bombers. A fighter pilot knew quite precisely the nature of the danger and knew also that he would be in combat no longer than his fuel lasted. Maximum courage expenditure, adrenal supercharge and all of that. A sharp fight, then end of mission, back to the lounge, maybe off to the pub. Taps closed; safety restored.

"Take the other extreme: a sailor on convoy duty. Danger does not engulf him at predictable times but seeps into his life. He doesn't know what U-boats he will engage or if he will at all. His courage tap is set for a slow trickle as the convoy spends weeks at sea.

"Suppose we have twins then: one an airman and one a sailor with equal quantities of courage. One pours his out in rushes, the other in a trickle. Both will eventually be drained but not over the same time. No *more* courage will be required of one than of the other, for each has the same quantity.

"Let us move to the battlefield, specifically this one in Burma. Let us compare a Chindit with his twin who is a ranker in the Arakan. Slim's man is quite safe a few hundred yards behind the lines. Even when he's in his defensive position, he feels relatively safe, for he has provided for his safety with sandbags, earthworks, etc. His courage tap is barely open most of the time. Then down comes the attack order: jump off at 0400 to seize some hill. Adrenalin starts to mount; he's pooping scared; his tap is wide open for a period of hours. Then the attack is over. Successful or not, he digs in; the rations come up and the routine of the army is reestablished.

"Now the Chindit: we'll enter the great jungle sea as undetectable as a U-boat. We strike when and where we choose, not where the Jap does. We march a lot but we rest when we must. We control the tempo of our war; the ranker in Fourteenth Army cannot, for Slim has pieces of terrain he must defend or seize.

"I will be watching the gauge of the Chindit's tap. When I see the level dropping low, we'll go into harbor. Like the Kachin Hills: there the local tribesmen will provide outposts and security. There we can carve out permanent landing fields. There we can be safe so the taps are closed and the reservoir of courage preserved.

"In sum, we can fight our type of war indefinitely. In fact, we can husband our resources of courage longer than Slim for we have better control of the taps. Have I won your rum?"

"Not mine," said Dalton.

"Maybe a mango but no more," said Fox-Boynton. "All I've heard is that rankers are like airmen and Chindits like sailors. These are apt comparisons in some ways but not for explaining the unique strain of operating behind enemy lines."

"There is no Shangri-la back in Burma where we can swing in hammocks and let the Kachins look out for us," said Dalton. "I'm surprised you think so."

"Let me try to put your equation in mathematical terms," Fox-Boynton proposed. "Could we say, in all forms of warfare, courage is the function of danger and time of exposure? That is, C equals D times T?"

"Admirable. Sir Archie said you were a smart one. I'd not change your equation, just modify it to C *must* equal D times T"

"Well that destroys your thesis. T is very much an element of the equation. We can't expect to stay back there indefinitely."

"Just till the end of the war. Sailors will ply the seas till then."

"You're greatly underestimating the D in the Chindit equation," said Dalton earnestly.

"I certainly haven't to the troops."

"No," said Fox-Boynton, "and well that you haven't. Do you see how D can also be a perceived D? If a man *thinks* he's in danger, he must draw on his courage even if he is not."

"Yes, but we can wean him from that. He'll soon learn that all birdcalls are not Japanese signals, that shadows are not tigers."

"Orde, I realize that as the father of LRP you have to display more confidence than any of us. You've got to believe Mercury will work. I believe it, Bruce does, Wavell does, but from listening to you tonight I think your confidence is...exaggerated."

"I'll sleep better tonight," said Dalton, "if you were just trying us out a little."

Wingate rose, a motion in the shadows. "Well I'm going to have another tot, even if you won't give me yours."

Fox-Boynton studied his silhouette. "Let me tell you what disturbs me: your plan is so exciting you're possessed by it. It seems to drive you, rather than you driving the plan. Some things are going to go wrong, Orde. I don't know how you'll react."

Wingate drained his mug. "They said the same thing about Special Night Squads; the same about Gideon Force. In fact they didn't even like my plans much. Things did go astray. Victory seemed to abandon us at times but in the end it was there. It was there because I *saw* it! I see it now. I'm not looking at anything else. Good night, gentlemen. Bruce, you have no reason for insomnia."

57

4 February 1943

Dearest Lorna,

The monsoon which is dissolving in the skies has left its clouds upon our armies. Slim's Arakan offensive with its limited ambitions was showing some progress last month but has now bogged down. This was the offensive which I was to support much the way my attack supported Cunningham in the last months of Ethiopia. To draw the attention of the Japs to the south, Scoones was to advance southeast from Kalewa. Now this is not to be. In spite of the engineers' prodigious efforts, too few roads are ready to supply his thrust. How ponderously dependent is the conventional army; how light and mobile the Chindits.

As anyone could have expected, the Chinese have backed out of their role. This leaves only the Chindits with any offensive intentions and against odds much greater than expected.

As Wingate wrote, the Chindits were bustling in preparations. Faces were tinted with jungle camouflage, weapons zeroed, and radios put through operational checks. Veterinarians slit the vocal chords of mules so their brays could not betray a column in the jungle.

It seems that peril is my natural environment. I must crave it or otherwise I would not create it in all I do. The prospect of death is not so much exciting as addictive—remember, we spoke of this in Battersea. Like an alcoholic I must have peril in order to hear my inner music. That you should love me for this, rather than in spite of this, is the greater marvel. In loving you I embrace the part of me I force underneath with my fellow men. I was always different with my mother than with Father. Could this division have begun with them?

These last hours bring me to summarize myself as you can see. Across the Chindwin it will be different; I will be different. Retrospection will be over, giving away to immediacy and intuition. I may not be right when the bullets crack through the leaves. That I never know in advance for intuition comes by grace, the only quality not burnished by preparation and training. If I am not right it will be because I do not see how to reach the higher truth I have already seen. That truth is the concept of LRP! If I do not prove its worth, I will be like a sloppy mathematician who cannot apply the axioms.

That is my pitfall. In this I part from my comrades as they prepare for our mutual adventure. The lads cleaning their rifles tonight are anxious to prove themselves while I pace about pondering how to prove a concept. The ranker has but a vague idea of LRP. For most it means rations dangling from parachutes. For me my soldiers are rather vague entities, while LRP is as tangible as the peak of my tent. Only in the consequences will we unite.

So too will the rest of our army. If the Chindits stake out a claim in the jungle, the stature and confidence of every man in India will rise with ours. Such a consequence will also give the Japs new thoughts about the war they have so barbarously inflicted on Asia. This is an expedition fraught with consequences. As its creator I watch it begin, knowing that its history will grow beyond mine. That is my reward given in advance. To plan is to create, and creation is the sole activity we share with God.

Except for love. And love as I know from you is a gift not dependent on any worthiness.

Orde

Plan Mercury was for a three-pronged penetration of the frontier wilderness, each prong containing two columns, five hundred men, and two hundred mules per column. The three forces would cross the Chindwin evenly spaced across a hundred-mile front, then progress in parallel to the railroad about a hundred miles away. In this way, if one or even two of the forces were blocked by the Japanese, the remaining force had sufficient strength to punch through to the railroad.

Fox-Boynton commanded the northern force, Wingate the center, and Dalton the southern. Dalton's was the most difficult mission; initially he was to draw Japanese attention to him, and he could succeed too well.

Wingate reasoned that there was no hope keeping the expedition

secret once C47s began filling the skies with resupply drops (the Allies now had parity with the Japanese in the air). So Wingate intended
for Kawabe to think a reconnaissance in force was probing around his
flank at Kalewa: a short hook directed to the southeast.

North of Kalewa, Kawabe had only a thin screen of outposts incapable of watching the entire length of the Chindwin. Nevertheless,
the expedition could hardly move east undetected. Wingate therefore
wished to give the other two crossings the appearance of feints, covering Dalton's near Kalewa.

This ruse was further elaborated by impersonation: at the first village after his crossing, Dalton had an officer play the role of Wingate
complete with a brigadier's red epaulets and the unmistakable pith
helmet. With a "brigade headquarters" party he would procure huge
quantities of rice from the village chief, known to be a Japanese sym-
pathizer. To complete the deception, Dalton would take an early supply drop in broad daylight. North and Central forces meanwhile would
march as far east as possible before taking their resupply drops, and
then only at night. By these means Wingate hoped to deceive Kawabe
of the true orientation of the Chindits until they had a good head start.

The Chindits broke camp on February 11 and marched together
for two days to the trail fork at Tamu, the last Indian village on the
western slope of the Naga Hills. Here, as the three forces separated,
Wingate issued his last order of the day to the Chindits collectively:

Today we stand on the threshold of battle. The time of preparation is over, and we are moving on the enemy to prove ourselves
and our methods. At this moment we stand beside the soldiers of
the United Nations in the front trenches throughout the world.

A minority always occupies the front line. A still smaller minority accepts with good heart tasks like this that we have chosen to
carry out. We have all had the opportunity of withdrawing and
we are here because we have chosen to be; that is, we have chosen
to bear the burden and heat of the day. Men who make this choice
are above average in courage. We therefore have no fear for the
staunchness and guts of our comrades.

Our motive may be taken to be the desire to serve our day and
generation in the way that seems nearest to hand. The battle is
not always to the strong nor the race to the swift. Victory in war

cannot be counted upon, but what can be counted is that we shall
go forward determined to do what we can to bring this war to an
end.

Finally, knowing the vanity of man's effort and the confusion of
his purpose, let us pray that God may accept our service and direct our endeavors, so that when we shall have done all, we shall
see the fruit of our labors and be satisfied.

> O. C. Wingate
> Commander
> Seventy-seventh Indian Infantry Brigade

Every man was handed a copy as he went up one of the forks at
Tamu. Most dissolved in the sweat and rain, but many were preserved,
some as keepsakes, some as evidence, some for the curiosity of interpreters. As the action developed in the following weeks, a faction of
Slim's staff officers saw an uncharacteristic tentativeness and lack of
animation in Wingate's message. Others saw it expressing a perspective and maturity beyond the typical prebattle pep talk.

Lorna was struck by its unstudied expression and unfocused impact. "Doesn't sound at all like Orde," she said to her mother. "He
would probably write five drafts for an occasion like that."

The most interested interpreters of the order were the Japanese.
When found on a dead Chindit it was passed up to Kawabe's intelligence officer, Colonel Yamasakura, who circulated it without comment.
In the enemy's headquarters it was mildly admired for its last paragraph, which seemed to have a resonation with Shintoism.

Yamasakura then consulted his "order of battle"—the information
about the British units and their principal commanders. Seventy-seventh
Indian Infantry Brigade was listed as sort of a national guard in central
India with no prior combat experience. Wingate had been promoted so
recently that his name did not appear in the order of battle.

Yamasakura was a worldly man by the standards of the Japanese
army; he had even traveled in Europe while attending a German staff
college. He recognized the name Wingate from somewhere, and after
much research in the *London Times* he came upon some mention of Wingate in Ethiopia and a picture of him in pith helmet with Selassie and
a camel. This was enough for Yamasakura to suspect the message to

be disinformation: it was inconceivable for the British to send one of their proven desert experts into the jungle.

Thus when a report drifted back that a British brigadier in a bucket-like helmet had bought a ton of rice east of the Chindwin, Yamasakura scoffed at the foolishness of an obvious British ploy. Still he was left with a riddle: why did the British want it to appear that a bogus brig-adier (probably leading a bogus brigade) was maneuvering around the Japanese flank?

The descent to the Chindwin was so steep that only the thickness of the jungle prevented men and mules from plunging down the hill-side. Loaded to seventy pounds per man, the Chindits reeled from tree to tree. The elephants and bullocks had to be brought around by an-other route after the crossing site was scouted and secured. Men and beasts arrived on schedule an hour before dark. Through carefully parted foliage, a thousand eyes examined the rushing river; it looked impos-sible, far beyond the capabilities acquired in training.

But Wingate had his resources. The crossing party had investi-gated this and alternative sites on small patrols over the last month. The Chindwin was little more than a quarter mile across, not more than ten feet deep, but with the current of water flowing through a ruptured dam. Expert swimmers had tested it and allowed for a mile of drift.

Deflated rubber dinghies and outboard engines were passed hand to hand down the hill, assembled, and launched into the flood, tow-ing nylon ropes. The ropes provided the first major problem: they sank and snagged in the skeletons of trees on the bottom.

A section of rope was freed, only to sink and snag again. Even working from both banks, the swimmers lost much time; underwater they worked in utter darkness. One man was swept away, either un-conscious or too concerned for security to shout for help.

Under a full moon, dark figures trooped into the water, vanishing in the surface shadows to reappear as drifting dots on the dappled wa-ter. A ponderous splash marked the entry of an elephant, its handler perched behind its ears, as it pounded across with the burden of a float-ing island.

The mules lived up to their worst reputation, kicking, balking, voicelessly braying—bolting free to carry away valuable loads never to be seen again. Forcing one into the water was the work of a squad; even when towed by their handlers, many turned about at midstream, leading others back to the west bank in spite of a thousand Chindit curses. Messenger dogs became aquatic mule herders with inconsistent results. Some mules were tethered to bullocks who crossed docilely, but others seemed to conspire and tow the bullocks back.

All the while rafts ferried back and forth, but because of the mules, columns became confused, crossing priorities changed and countermanded, and Wingate slowly maddened. The crossing that was to have been completed by dawn was barely under way. Wingate had to make his first decision of the expedition: continue the crossing or suspend it until the next night, when more order could be expected from the previous night's experience.

The moon had dimmed, so clouds might be low enough to insulate the crossing in the morning. On the east bank all patrols reported no signs of the enemy. Wingate ordered the crossing to go on.

The sun rose on amphibious chaos: naked men spouting water as they clung to rafts or thrashing hand over hand along the guide ropes; tiny boats rocking precariously as shaven-headed Gurkhas righted teetering loads of mortars and projectiles.

Bamboo was lashed together to form animal chutes so that groups of mules could be tipped into the water, where the outboards frightened them forward. Finally, more by happenstance than design, the mules on the east bank began to amble about, peacefully grazing within sight of their recalcitrant brothers. Around noon, the mules seemed to decide among themselves that life on the opposite bank looked better than the abuse they were receiving. By twos and threes they swam over to Burma.

Ropes were recovered and the banks stripped of crossing apparatus as the sun burned off the cloud cover. Exhaustion and confusion greeted Wingate when he crossed with the last party. Reports came up from the companies: loads were scrambled; no platoon had what was needed to proceed.

Wingate took the rest of the day to sort out men and equipment. As darkness fell a signal light flashed from the west bank: Wingate's report was overdue. He signaled back; "All has gone wrong but undiscovered" and the light blinked for the last time. They were more than a day behind schedule, but the British were marching once more in Burma.

58

The Burma Rifles led. Trail breaking was not necessary: native woodcutters and foragers had laced the jungle with filament-wide trails; crisscrossing these were tunnels smashed through the trees by wild elephants.

The trees still dripped, but the great rains were over for the season. The heat was heavy but more sufferable than the leeches. At every halt they dropped from the leaves in a soft patter. Thin as needles, they advanced like inchworms, the heat sensor in their heads waving back and forth to find warm blood.

Leeches were thick around abandoned settlements where the natives had once tended cattle. The region was dotted with such ghost villages; their names moved with the villagers and their slash-and-burn agriculture. Thus it was possible to ask a native, "Does this trail go to Sinlamaung?" and receive a correct answer; yet the Sinlamaung on the map marked the location of the village ten years earlier, which at present might be miles in the opposite direction.

Such problems had yet to surface. For the first few days the marching was fast and easy through a flat teak forest; no difficulty with Central Force except incipient overconfidence. North Force was making excellent headway as well. It was Dalton in the south who occupied Wingate's thoughts.

South Force skirmished with the Japanese the day after their crossing. Dalton flushed a platoon out of a village and killed a score of them, an excellent beginning that went sour when the Japanese covered their retreat with a volley of mortars, panicking Dalton's mule train. He had just taken his first resupply drop, so the train was fully loaded. There was no alternative but to stop and sweep the jungle for the lost mules. This took two days, during which the Japanese picked up the scent.

Mindful of his mission, Dalton rallied and led the pursuers farther

south, then broke contact and force-marched thirty miles east in sixteen hours, a prodigious speed for jungle travel. This feat still put
him twenty miles west of Central Force and fifteen miles south of his
planned route. Soon he had to pause another day to take a full resupply
drop.

All this Wingate learned by nightly radio reports. All three forces
communicated in code with Cochran to schedule resupply drops. Scoones
relayed reports to Slim, who had moved his HQ down closer to the beleagured Arakan front. Wavell in New Delhi kept track of the Chindits
through Slim.

Wingate first reported when his three forces came abreast at the
foot of the Z Range. Around him the headquarters for the night took
shape as a small clearing was hacked out of the underbrush. From back
in the jungle the radio mule plodded forward. It snorted when relieved of its load, its handlers heaving the black metal cases together
while the mule nuzzled the ground for bamboo sprouts.

The wire antenna slithered up the vines to entwine in the foliage.
Meanwhile a Gurkha assembled what looked like a rowing machine.
He was the radio's power source, cranking a rotor with two long spokes.
He stripped to the waist, seated himself at the generator, grasped the
handles, and began a swimming motion with his arms.

The sun plunged into thickets of scrub and rattan, its light vanishing as if turned off by a switch. Men moved between half-light and
shadows from tiny blue flames heating tea and food tins. In spite of
mosquitos, sweat-soaked shirts came off, for though the sun had gone
its heat remained part of the deep silence.

Jeffers, the radio operator, threw a switch; a red light glowed. The
Gurkha's shoulders bulged as he cranked against increased resistance.
Jeffers nodded to major Kane, Wingate's executive officer.

"George," said Wingate.

"Yes, sir," Kane replied, shuffling through a deck of code cards.

"Feel anything at all historic?"

Kane smiled. "Not till Coburn replies."

"We're not a theory any more."

"Some people are going to be surprised."

"No doubt."

"Any personal message for the occasion, sir?"

"No. Our location speaks for itself."

Jeffers clamped on the earphones and tested the key. The red light

winked synchronously with the tap of his finger as the radio chirped a
thirty-second message from Burma to India.

The war correspondents in Imphal were well trusted. If Coburn asked them
to withhold a story for security reasons, they did. In return they were let
in on some weighty secrets. They were not let in on Mercury, however,
even though Wingate's promotion set the correspondents snooping for more
information about what this desert expert was doing in India and why,
with his checkered background, he had been made a brigadier.

The three correspondents slouched in their chairs listening to the
dismal news from the Arakan; they drew their pencils while the briefing
officer concluded his presentation to Slim:

"And finally, sir, in the north we received our first communication
from the Chindits. They have apparently slipped right by the Jap outposts and are receiving their second resupply drop tonight."

"You say, 'slipped...by'"

"Yes, sir. Wingate reports no enemy contact for four days, and
from monitoring the Japanese radio we have no indication that they
realize he is in Burma."

"Who are the Chindits?" a correspondent asked.

"Colonel...excuse me, Brigadier Wingate will be all too happy to
tell you when he gets back."

"When will that be?"

"Probably in a couple of months."

"Any background, sir?"

"Didn't he run some guerrilla bands for us in Ethiopia?"

"Selassie's right-hand man, wasn't he?"

Slim dismissed the briefer and turned in his chair to face the press.
"Gentlemen, this is Burma, not the Middle East. Wingate's whereabouts must remain utterly secret. We all hope his diversionary raid is
a success. Meanwhile the main campaign is on the Arakan front, where
we expect to conduct a successful defense."

"You're defending while Wingate is attacking. Is that the plan?"

"No, those are your words." Slim rose, jutting his jaw. "And without my explicit approval you are not to print them."

But the word was out, even if it wasn't printed, and the word was
"Chindit." In the following weeks Mercury became reams of unfiled
copy, a story all the more fascinating for its repression, which secrecy

required. "Wingate's Raiders," "Clive of Burma," and "the Phantom Army" were some of the romantic terms used for LRP. The expedition was compared with Shackleton's to the South Pole, with the "Lost Battalion" of World War I, and other epics. Upon his return Wingate would be like Lindbergh, who while in flight knew nothing of the reception awaiting him on earth.

His return was far from Wingate's mind. His concern was for the laxity of his troops as they now sauntered through the jungle dropping wrappers and cigarette butts in their wake. Wingate upbraided the officers and manhandled some of the offenders, but he realized what his columns needed was a scare or a fight or both.

The scare came first—at the third resupply drop. It was at night like all the others but included a glider landing as well as parachutes.

The drone of the C47 was early. The engines sounded overworked from towing the glider. It disengaged and began its silent swoop toward the ground. The wind freshened. Kane, watching, bit off a cry as the nose rose like a breaching whale. The glider poised for an instant between flying and falling; then the nose pitched forward into the jungle.

The thunder of the crash rolled across the night; its echo had not returned from the hills before parajute bundles filled the sky.

The Chindits were hushed. Death seemed to have arrived like the first sprinkle of a monsoon. Kane rubbed his eyes.

"American?" Wingate asked softly.

"Looked like it."

"Get a patrol out. We haven't much time. What was it carrying?"

"Fodder. Sergeant Major!"

In the moonlight Wingate gazed at the tangled ridges poking down from the misty Z Range. Progress would be slow in the coming days, and from the air the Japs could spot the crashed glider. The fate of the expedition might depend on how large a force they sent to investigate. Over the flat terrain to the west they could close quickly on Central Force as it struggled up the slopes ahead. Wingate walked away to contemplate his next move.

The bundles were collected, the mules loaded before the patrol returned. The three-man crew were American and they were dead. Gurkha scouts hurried ahead to find a route up the ridges.

"We need a diverson," Wingate announced as he joined Kane and the headquarters column. "Raise F-B at stand-to."

Kane nodded. At the first light of dawn, while the column continued to snake through the jungle, the radio mule was unloaded. Jeffers oriented the antenna to the north. He scribbled on the code pad as Wingate discussed the gist of the message with Kane.

"We must assume the Japs now know that someone is in their jungle. Since we have attracted their attention, we must spread it over as wide an area as possible. Tell F-B to look for an opportunity to attack."

59

An opportunity arose when Fox-Boynton bumped into a Japanese supply column on the trail outside Sinlamaung. Twenty Kachin porters, bound together at the neck like a chain gang, were collapsed under a banyan tree guarded by a scraggly squad of Japanese who were gunned down in a single burst. The Kachins were carrying a ton of rice to Homalin, apparently to support the Japanese expedition against Fort Hertz.

News of this encounter was transmitted to Wingate with Fox-Boynton's comment that the rice would be good mule feed and consequently he could skip his next resupply drop.

The porters had marched from Pinlebu by way of Namza over a "high-speed" trail by jungle standards. Questioning them further, Fox-Boynton learned they had seen trucks at Pinlebu, the only major garrison west of the railway. This was something of a surprise because British aerial reconnaissance had revealed no road in or out of the village. Apparently the Japanese had constructed a corduroy track from Wuntho on the railway to Pinlebu. The road was probably a link in a supply route: Wuntho-Pinlebu-Namza-Sinlamaung-Homalin and north to the Japanese advancing on Fort Hertz.

The Japanese would not miss the rice gang for several days. This

interval gave Fox-Boynton time to slip around Sinlamaung and prepare a proper assault on Namza, where a Japanese company could be
expected. Wingate meanwhile could cross the Z Range and pick a favorable ambush site on the trail that ran along the Mu River.

It would be a variation of Danghila all over again: when Namza
called for help from Pinlebu, reinforcements would charge up the trail
into Wingate's ambush. This was a sound, professionally conceived
plan which, if guerrilla tactics had been taught at Woolwich, would
have received the highest mark.

But it didn't satisfy Wingate, who saw the action drawing Japanese attention to Namza. Even with a successful ambush, both Wingate
and Fox-Boynton would need to hotfoot east with only a day's lead
over the Japanese infantry converging from Homalin and Pinlebu.

This eventuality would put Wingate in a worse situation than now;
presently only Dalton was sought by Japanese forces, and he had successfully broken away. Wingate and Fox-Boynton were marching unnoticed toward the railroad. The Japanese would get on their trail only
if they began spotting the resupply drops, such as the site where the
glider crashed.

Plans always seemed to come to Wingate as he slept. He woke
Kane and began talking as if the two had been discussing strategy for
hours.

"We don't want to ambush the Japs coming out of Pinlebu, George."

"Beg pardon, sir?" said the brigade major sleepily.

"They'd be more vulnerable on the trail, I'll grant you, but I want
them in garrison and to stay there."

Kane rolled over on his side. The shrouded campfire flickered over
Wingate's beard. Kane had been warned of the peculiarities of Wingate's creative process, how he sometimes put forth outrageous propositions to test the reaction, provoking counterargument to sharpen
his own thinking.

"Sorry, sir; I'm not following you."

"We must attack Pinlebu."

That was enough to bring him wide awake.

At Imphal Wingate had constructed a gargantuan sand table twenty-
five by fifteen yards to a side. Pinlebu was at the center of this terrain
model and the focus of the column commanders' concerns. The sand
table was meticulously proportioned to include most of northern Bur-

ma. Developed and scaled from aerial photographs, every significant hill and stream were depicted in such detail that rapids and gorges could be studied for their potential as fords.

With a long pointer Wingate had slowly moved with the column commanders along the edge of the table with comments like, "You should be here by the end of the first week," or "these fields would make good DZs." The column commanders found the table a great benefit in perceiving Wingate's plan as he discoursed upon it.

Always Wingate tapped the cluster of huts labeled "Pinlebu" to emphasize how it must be avoided or neutralized or in some way bypassed. He spoke in allusions such as how one must tiptoe by a hornet's nest or how the Hump pilots offset their courses to avoid the Himalyan peaks. Pinlebu was the dragon guarding the treasure (indeed its code name was "Dragon"), the cyclops watching the mouth of the cave, in both cases a monster not to be slain but to be slipped around while asleep or otherwise distracted.

"*Attack* Pinlebu, sir?"

"When they find the glider and all that hay, they'll know we're not here just to piss in their jungle. Now I want them to think we are more— much, much more." Wingate propped up his map. Kane took out his message pad and pencil. "Fox-Boynton doesn't need his next drop. Send it here, four...make that five nights hence." Wingate pointed to where the Pinlebu-Wuntho trail crossed the Bambwe Taung Hills. "Briggs's company is to receive it and make sure the Japs see it. He's to fight with them a bit, then rejoin us up here; or if the pressure is from the north, drop down and join Dalton."

"The drop is to fall into Jap hands?"

"Exactly. It's to be all 105 rounds. I want Kawabe to think we've brought a corps into Burma." The howitzer projectiles belonged to the heavy artillery of Fourteenth Army. Wingate had only small mortars. "Tell Cochran to sabotage some of the fuses. I hear the Japs are using our captured 105s."

"Yes, sir."

"On the next morning I want an air strike on Pinlebu to support our attack." Fighters were very scarce even to escort resupply drops. Rigging them to carry one bomb apiece was inefficient, but Wingate had been promised one air strike; this was to be it.

"We can get to Pinlebu in two nights. Scout the defenses for two more. We'll come at it from the southeast. Pin them against the water. Blaze away all night. Break off in the morning. Leave lots of trash behind—our boys are good at that."

"If we break off in the morning—they'll have all day to chase us, sir."

"We'll have plenty of ambushes ready for them. That's the other thing: I want them led south while we cross here and head north. In fact I want the mule train north of the Tinda the whole time."

Pinlebu was situated at the perpendicular confluence of the Mu and the Tinda, an excellent junction to mark the air strike and a corner into which the Japanese could be boxed. Other than that, Wingate knew nothing of how the village was situated or how many Japanese were in it.

To obtain essential intelligence, Wingate called upon his Burmese equivalent of the "wopalikes."

With the Japanese invasion, a fifth column of anticolonialists appeared, which soon took up captured British arms and was recognized by the Japanese under the name of the Burmese Independence Army (BIA). Since the British expulsion, the BIA had been used as a local security force to free the Japanese troops for the Arakan. Despite their services the Japs held the BIA in contempt.

To impersonate the BIA nothing was required of the Burma Rifles except that they don native garb.

Wingate had two Burmese from Wuntho. One he sent with Captain Briggs, his ace company commander, to receive the deception drop in the Bambwe Taung Hills. The other led a platoon of BIA impostors to the outskirts of Pinlebu while Central Force rested in the eastern Z Range. The Chindits were hungry, but a resupply drop so close to Pinlebu was out of the question. They as well as their mules began to eat bamboo sprouts.

Wingate, the two column commanders, the mortar commander, and the leader of the mule train accompanied the impostors—a venture which his critics later cited as an example of daring blurring into insanity. The reconnaissance was worth the risk, said Wingate, for the commanders must see their objectives before their troops were brought out of hiding to attack.

60

Kane was left in charge of Central Force. If Wingate did not return within forty-eight hours, he was to march north to join Fox-Boynton, who would assume command of the entire expedition. Wingate had scarcely departed; hardly had the jungle grown dark before the radio chirped out the first query from Fourteenth Army: it was simply, "Advise intentions."

Kane pushed back his hat. A reasonable request at this stage of the campaign but one most difficult to answer as the only intentions that mattered were in Wingate's head. Kane glanced over at his commander's pith helmet, left behind as too conspicuous for the perilous reconnaissance. It sat by the radio like the sphinx.

The request for the air strike no doubt had pushed Slim's curiosity to a demand for more information. What were the Chindits' intentions? Kane knew them only in broad outline. A forthright officer, Kane sent back what he knew:

"Northern Force: ambush LC near Namza, then proceed toward Banmauk. Central Force: attack Pinlebu, await developments. South Force: proceed toward Kyaikthin. Authenticated by Kane, Brigade Major."

Kane's answer was acknowledged but within a half hour Colonel Johns asked it be repeated. It was, confirming there had been no garble in the first transmission. Brigadier Arden came back next, requesting authentication by Wingate. Not available, said Kane: Wingate conducting preattack reconnaissance. Kane added the code word cautioning that more transmissions might compromise the Chindits' location. This was acknowledged. Kane could imagine the befuddlement at Fourteenth Army but not the attention the Chindits were attracting at the moment.

By now some of the esteemed members of the press, like Michael

O'Day of the *London Times,* were monitoring the Chindits' messages
nearly as quickly as they were decoded at Fourteenth Army. The intention to "attack Pinlebu" staggered the correspondents as much as
the officers.

Slim would not comment but cautioned once more that no operation in the Far East was more secret than the Chindit expedition; any
leaks by the press would be tantamount to murder. Slim would not
second-guess Wingate, who, he said, still possessed his full confidence.

Nevertheless, O'Day drew Colonel Johns aside. "Is Wingate crazy?" the correspondent asked.

"We don't think so."

"But Pinlebu—that's suicide."

"You didn't ask if he were suicidal."

"Is he?"

"I must leave that to your research."

"What military justification could there be for attacking Pinlebu?"

"Michael, let me tell you a little anecdote: I was Orde's bridge
partner at Woolwich. His play was erratic but his bidding was astonishing, sometimes leaving our opponents with disastrous contracts, but
other times leaving me to play impossible hands. I once asked him
why he so misinformed me. His answer was, 'Better to fool two opponents at the cost of misleading one partner.'"

"Yes?"

"That illustrates how his mind works."

"How?"

"Don't try to lead me."

"He's trying to fool the Japs?"

"Obviously. His style involves a great deal of ruse. And remember, too, Wingate is rather paranoic."

"Remember? I don't know the man at all."

"Well, take this from a 'nonattributable source': Wingate is deeply
suspicious, even irrationally so. This...I really musn't go on."

"You can't stop in midsentence like that. Is it true his suspicions
extend to the British army?"

"Since you bring it up, I can vouch for that."

"You're suggesting he's just *saying* he'll attack Pinlebu?"

"I'm suggesting nothing. I'm just saying that a man as intensely
secretive as Orde might inform us of a plan he has no intention to
carry out. Why? Well no one is absolutely confident of the security of

our codes. He may be testing them to see if the Japs react to his message. He probably has Pinlebu surveilled right now to see if a flurry of activity follows his message."

"He doesn't mind fooling you as long as he fools the Japs."

"From the bridge tables of Woolwich to the jungles of Burma perhaps. Is that a good line?"

"Maybe you should have been a journalist."

"Could you put in a word for me with the *Times?*"

"You know Wingate better than anyone here, don't you?"

"Possibly. He's not an easy man to know."

"Any more anecdotes?"

"I've probably talked too much already. You should try Arden."

O'Day took Johns's advice and found Slim's chief of staff alone in his office.

"Do you think Wingate will attack Pinlebu, General?"

Arden looked down at his desk. "Said he will, didn't he?"

"Why?"

"The expedition is largely experimental. Perhaps he is testing another of his theories."

"Such as?"

"Well, no one has tried to storm a strong Japanese position like Pinlebu. Wingate may think he knows a way to do it."

"You couldn't be serious."

"One is never quite sure with Wingate. He's a fascinating man to listen to when he discusses tactics. I recall his postulating that the element of surprise in an attack may outweigh all other factors. Do you follow?"

"I think so. Do you think that's possible?"

"No. But the element of surprise may have never been exploited to the degree Wingate envisions."

"But this isn't some peacetime maneuver."

"You're quite right."

"A thousand lives are at stake." Arden nodded agreement. "Are you sure Wingate will attack Pinlebu?"

"Can't say that I am."

"But he told you he was."

"Yes."

"Isn't that an official report—of the most serious kind?"

"It certainly is."

"If it's false?"

"That will be a matter for General Slim to mull upon."

"What would you do if you were Slim?"

"You know I'm forbidden from second-guessing."

"That only applies to Wingate."

"I would be prudent not to second-guess my commander either."

"What chances do you give the expedition at this point?"

"I'm afraid betting also comes under the category of second-guessing."

"What's his motive—his real motive in all this?"

"All right, if this is absolutely unattributable, I think Wingate wants to convert the entire Fourteenth Army into Chindits. To do so, he must succeed spectacularly. Now that's all I'm going to say. Don't try to draw me out."

"But suppose he fails spectacularly?"

"He is an 'all-or-nothing' sort of a person. Besides, if he fails, he will find scapegoats everywhere, mostly here in this headquarters if I know him at all. Now really, that's my last word on Wingate."

"Pinlebu: The Test of a Concept" was the fourth story on the Chindits that O'Day had ready for the day when censorship lifted. Rereading it, he realized Colonel Johns's hypothesis about Wingate trying to fool the Japanese could not account for Kane's message; for if the intention to attack Pinlebu was false, the remaining information concerning North and South forces was accurate. It was unimaginable that Wingate would compromise two-thirds of his force to test the security of his code. O'Day's story concluded:

> On the tarmac mechanics stand under the bellies of Spitfires, installing crude racks to convert the famous fighter into a bomber for one mission. Everything having to do with the Chindits is thus—specialized, *ad hoc*, improvised.

> Fourteenth Army HQ has a peculiar air at the moment as news is awaited from Pinlebu. Though Wingate, Slim's subordinate, is about to attack, the officers most concerned seem more curious than apprehensive. There is none of the preattack tension, the clenching of fists, the pats on the back to stir the juices as one sees in war to remind

one of the minutes before a rugby match. We correspondents remark to one another about the peculiar detached attitude here. One fellow identified it this way: "It's as if the Japs are about to attack us rather than the other way around."

Forty-seven hours after they departed, Wingate's party returned from their reconnaissance. Kane's face dissolved in relief as the five commanders lurched into the flicker of the campfire. They were back safe and undiscovered, an occasion for a double ration of rum and total relaxation; yet their carriage did not change from a weary alertness. Neither did they give way to the excited jabbering of men who had passed through peril with a worthwhile result. All were grave, and even Wingate seemed more concerned than confident as he put on his pith helmet.

"Well?" Kane asked as they sat themselves on a log.

"Swarming with Japs," said Giddings, the mortar commander.

With very few words they explained how impossible it had been to work close enough to study the Japanese dispositions. However, they'd learned the trail to Homalin was heavily traveled. Wingate's guess that a corduroy road had been carved back to Wuntho was correct. It seemed certain that the deception supply drop would bring the Japanese in a rush, possibly with a light tank or two—the Burma Rifles had seen tread marks around the road. The only positive developments were the discovery of good ambush positions to cover the fake withdrawal to the south and a remote, unused ford over the Tinda for the real getaway to the north.

"Can we harbor the mules over the ford?" Kane asked, a most critical factor in the plan.

Hollins, the mule commander, did not look up. Wingate answered for him. "At night, if it's done right. They'll cross the Mu with the mortars."

"Helluva lot of traffic on that trail," said Giddings. From his tone Kane realized he had argued long and unsuccessfully with Wingate.

The enormous risk Wingate was taking became apparent to Kane. Central Force would split four ways: Briggs's small ambush at the deception drop, the succession of ambushes to lead the Japanese south after the attack, the main attack itself, and the mortars with the mules slipping north of the Tinda.

Wingate gave his two column commanders parting instructions before they briefed their men: "We didn't see your objectives but we're not out to seize them. Tell your fellows we'll shoot and scoot."

The Chindits began lightening their packs to only ammunition and grenades. Bedrolls and rations went onto the already laden mules.

The men were somber, grumbling about the separation from the essentials carried on their backs. When the Chindits learned the mules would be in as much danger as themselves, they began speaking of Wingate in terms Johns and Arden used.

"If the Japs catch the mules there's nothing to eat this side of India except our bullets," said a sergeant from the Kings, "and we won't have many of them left either."

Wingate noted the situation in a scribbled entry to Lorna:

The men are troubled and anxious. I expected them to be. The outcome of this attack will result in either mutiny or unshakable confidence that will steel them for the rest of the expedition. We will be attempting a most difficult maneuver as our first test in combat. In the eyes of the men, Pinlebu will mark me as either insane or invincible. So be it. After victory they will follow me to hell.

61

Stripped down to their assault packs, Central Force slipped warily into the jungle. In loose-fitting tunics, large pockets extending below the hips, they sealed their sleeves and cuffs against leeches. In their soft-brimmed hats the Chindits resembled South African troops. Their uniforms, made of cotton and poplin material, held together for about a month, though the crotch ripped apart much sooner from clambering through the jungle.

Briggs's company had already left to cover the deception drop. He was a veteran of the Bush Warfare School, "the dean of the faculty," Dalton called him.

"Briggs thrives on harrowing missions," Wingate wrote, "the way a master musician hones his talent performing compositions too difficult for other professionals."

Led by the BIA impersonators, Central Force filed down the trails as the first light of dawn seeped into the jungle. Each man carried two "shoe" mines, the insidious device which had taken Atkins's leg at Safartak. When huge quantities of the mines were captured from the Germans in North Africa, Wingate had Wavell ship thousands to Saugor. The mines were Briggs's protection and his principal means of delaying reinforcements from Wuntho, for a shoe mine could blow off a tire as easily as a man's foot.

At the same trail junction where the mines were distributed, the mule train and the mortars split from the infantry. They would have to cross both the well-used Homalin trail and the Mu without detection—four hundred men, two hundred beasts slipping by the Japanese at intimate distances.

The mule train tiptoed north during the day and prepared for their night crossings. A late-rising half moon would provide illumination for the attack while the preceding darkness gave cover for the passage of the mule train.

The five hundred remaining Chindits crept into the jungle single-file to deploy in a line from the Mu to the Tinda, thus trapping the garrison between the rivers; then, when moonlight revealed the village, they would inch forward to grenade range. Two snatch teams would dart in from the flanks to raise havoc in the camp and seek out the prize Wingate highly sought—a Japanese officer, who would be the first to be captured in the Far East since the war began.

A fisherman dawdling with his nets stopped the movement to the Mu; barking dogs froze the point squad making its way toward the Tinda. The sultry morning passed to the tempo of languid birdcalls and the hum of meandering insects. Long halts, facedown in the brush, meant the thread of men was winding ever more slowly between the rivers.

When the Chindits came within a mile of Pinlebu, the jungle thinned into clumps interspersed with cultivation. They could get no closer by day. Wingate pulled his men back to the edge of solid jungle away from any stray villagers strolling out to tend their fields.

Four cart-wide trails converged on Pinlebu through the Chindit line; wide gaps were left for them as a few woodcutters had already returned to the village, and more could be expected when twilight ended their day's work. The greatest hazard was by the Wuntho trail. Wingate had to deploy a hundred men between it and the Tinda, yet hardly an hour went by that a squad of Japanese did not march down the trail into Pinlebu. Major Bradshaw watched them go by for most of the afternoon before darting his first squad across.

Jungle muffled the sound of the engine—the truck was almost upon him before Bradshaw heard it rumbling down the trail. As the tarp flapped in rhythm to the bumps, Bradshaw could see the cargo—bags of rice for the Fort Hertz expedition.

Wingate worked himself up into a tree, parted the branches, and studied Pinlebu through his binoculars. He saw low bamboo and thatch buildings nestled in broad-bladed foliage, separated by paths growing hard after the recent rains. Because of superlative camouflage, the Japanese-built structures were not apparent even to binoculars. They were low bunkers with thatch-roof disguises, further concealed by quick-growing foliage. Not even Wingate's mortars could do them damage; the best he could hope for was to keep their entrances covered by fire.

Wingate watched the captured British truck roll in. A soldier walked to what looked like a hedge and opened a high gate—except it was not a hedge but an overgrown barbwire compound. The soldier leveled his rifle, and ten bedraggled Kachins trudged out. He prodded one with his bayonet, hurrying the others. The Kachins shouldered sacks of rice and filed out of sight through the village. When they reappeared, it was at the edge of the Mu. Wingate's eyes widened as a dozen more Kachins pushed out into the surging water.

They struggled for footing, found familiar rocks, then plodded two by two at armpit's depth to the opposite bank. The Japanese positioned them with shouted instructions until a long bamboo mat appeared from the Pinlebu shore, linked in sections by vine hinges. Each pair of Kachins in the river passed the sections forward to the next pair; then a dozen more took intermediate positions until there was a temporary footbridge on their shoulders. On this the rice carriers crossed and disappeared up the Homalin trail.

There was little other sign of the Japanese except a network of trenches and bomb shelters around the village. As the day lengthened, bullocks plodded back across the fields to the village guided by little boys sitting atop the haunches. A Japanese scurried out of one of the bunkers. His speed and sense of purpose were familiar in any army: he was a messenger from someone important inside. Wingate studied the roof more closely.

There among the shadows of the fronds he found the drooping line of a wire forming a Y, the sign of a dipole antenna, the clue to a major radio inside.

From the orientation of the dipole it seemed Pinlebu was in communications with Bhamo, the headquarters of the Eighteenth Division a hundred miles away. Wingate took an azimuth on the radio bunker; it would be the first target of his machine guns. He slithered down the tree. There would be little sleep that night; so he curled up in some tall grass with his pith helmet for a pillow.

62

He felt a nudge and came fully alert. It was dark; the signal for the Chindits to crawl forward into the fields. In two hours a radio signal was due from the mule train. They had five hours until moonrise. The southern ambushes were already in place, as was Briggs, waiting for the deception drop timed for the middle of the attack.

Wingate positioned himself near the Wuntho trail and concentrated on the silence. Fire from far down the Wuntho trail meant Briggs was prematurely engaged. Fire from across the Tinda meant bad luck for the mules and mortars. Fire from the village meant discovery of the crawling Chindits, so the sound of success was silence.

Not that the night was quiet. Flights of mosquitoes, risen from the recent rains, whined at twilight. There was the barking of dogs. Wingate listened closely, hoping to hear them often and at random. The village dogs would surely sense the approach of five hundred alien odors. It was best if their barking was already a familiar sound in the night.

Wingate swept the darkened village with his binoculars and thought back to earlier attacks, to Ethiopia, to Palestine. No high cause propelled him into battle tonight, no kingdom to restore, no race to protect, but rather his personal creation taking identity as the luminous metronome circled the dark face of his watch.

He had thought through all the possibilities: Japanese reinforcement from the north, from the south; counterattack from the village; even a Japanese air strike. Platt, Enright, Johns, Arden. He could imagine them standing close by as if only concealed by the darkness, their eyes on his watch.

Wingate watched and listened. He was in control of surprise—he would unleash it. He knew that made him at least the temporary ruler of the battlefield.

"Sir!" It was Kane. "The mules are across the trail."

"Good."

Much better than good. The Homalin trail was probably a more hazardous crossing than the Mu. Now only that stream remained before the mules and mortars were in relative safety on the north bank of the Tinda.

He swung his binoculars toward the distant rustle of water. The mules would cross far beyond his vision, but the magnified view seemed to project his presence nearer them. He imagined Hollins as he approached the western bank, five senses ultra alert, a sixth gauging the depth and force of the water.

Minutes, hours—the usual divisions of time distorted into that psychological time which governs vigils and insomnia. Like divers disoriented in the darkness of the depths, Wingate and Kane consulted their watches for contact with external reality.

Incidents of the night now seemed separated by gulfs rather than spans of time. Memory was blank tape until a burst of barking broke the night's absorption with itself.

It seemed to be a little dog, a young one. It yapped peevishly as if arguing with a silent intruder.

"Hush...I'll give you a Jap leg bone," Kane whispered.

Five hundred men looked toward the sound, willing silence to return. A new night spirit awoke as the dog went on in solitary fury. Then a deeper bark from elsewhere, a slower tentative bark of an older dog disturbed from sleep and undecided whether there was something out there worth investigating.

The barking went on with tireless repetition. Somewhere in the village a lamp was lit; in twenty minutes it went out. Gradually the hills emerged in outline as the cloudy sky glowed in a pearl pastel. Hollins had not reported; moonrise was approaching.

A shot from upstream—a British rifle. A single shot, almost an inquiry—either an accident with the mule train or discovery by a BIA patrol.

Then two quick shots and an answer by Bren guns. Wingate waited for a reaction from Pinlebu. He waited for Japanese attention to turn north for a moment. His binoculars detected movement by the bunkers. He blew a whistle. The Chindit line crackled with fire.

"Sustained rate," Wingate shouted. The machine guns spurted out sporadic bursts over a background of rifles.

Muzzle flashes spurted hesitantly from the bunkers. The Japanese were unprepared. Thatch began to burn, jabbing long shadows into the fields. The Chindits closed to within a quarter mile but as they did the Japanese were able to slip into the trenches; their weapons began to stutter as loudly as those of the British.

The half moon emerged to illuminate the little siege at Pinlebu. Within the next hour Hollins reported all across with the loss of four mules and a Gurkha. As Wingate had suspected, Hollins had run into a BIA patrol. In the next hour Giddings reported the mortars in place; an hour later the mules were harbored on the getaway trail.

By then the firefight had developed into vigorous sniping. The Chindits conserved ammunition while the Japanese reaction seemed uncertain. Before he broke off under the cover of the dawn air strike, Wingate would try to induce the Japanese into a display of "heroic panic," as Dalton called a quirk of their fighting spirit.

This was a reaction to the unexpected, the Japanese antidote to surprise and embarrassment. It demonstrated their aggressiveness and courage when those qualities seemed the only means to restore face. The fact that he had been caught unaware was already a humiliation

for the Pinlebu commander. He could redeem himself only by sweeping the Chindits from his doorstep, an act Wingate hoped would be
one of heroic panic.

It was almost their military habit, Wingate had learned, for the Japanese to attack at dawn. The Chindits were to let their fire peter out as
that hour and the British air strike approached. Wingate's mortars would
also be silent until then. Meanwhile, he awaited the deception drop and
Briggs's action on the Wuntho trail: 3:33 A.M. was drop time. Through
the drawn-out din of the firefight, Wingate strained his ears for the slow
throb of C47 engines.

They never came. The first news from Briggs was at 4:05. His
voice on the radio was steady, but bullets snapped in the background.
Was the drop aborted? he demanded. He had already collided with
the Japanese from Wuntho. They'd pushed back his outposts and were
coming on like a freight train—a company so far, more in support.
They had just hit his main trail block. Artillery was zeroing in on
him.

"I want to get going now!"

"We need another ninety minutes here," said Wingate.

"Can't. We're out of mines."

"We've got 'em pinned down so don't worry about this direction."

"I've taken everyone off that side already..." Static interrupted Briggs.
"They're working through the woods. They'll have me flanked."

"Use your fallback."

"Listen—everybody's engaged right *now*. No one to set up a fallback. Whoops—there it is." Through the static Wingate heard a crash
and a boom. "That was hello from the tank corps. We'll talk about
this, you know where." Briggs went off the air.

Now there could be no luring the garrison out at dawn; no chance
to induce a heroic panic. The Japanese commander knew reinforcements were on the way from Wuntho. The Pinlebu attack had to be
broken off at once.

"Kane, pour in the mortars. I want them down to ten rounds in an
hour. Then pack 'em off. Everyone else over the ford. Any dead to be
planted south."

Which meant that while Central Force sped north under the cover
of mortars, the dead were dragged to the southern ambushes to feign
retreat in that direction. This bogus rear guard was led by Lieutenant
Ingersoll of the faculty. He would draw the Japanese south like a mi-

rage constantly receding with the horizon, until many miles away it evaporated in the jungle.

There was no plan for them to rejoin Central Force. Ingersoll could try to link up with South Force, but otherwise he was to take his men back seventy trackless miles to India, subsisting only on rations they carried.

By moonlight on the slopes north of the Tinda the mortarmen watched their projectiles fall on Pinlebu. Erupting dirt and splintering bamboo muted the fire of the defenders. In a crouching run the Chindits thinned their line and slipped toward the ford where Wingate waited.

He was in high spirits. "Good work, fellows.... Fine job.... This is a night they'll remember.... Take care of that shoulder.... Good shooting, lads.... *Gurkhali prom!* ... Nice work, nice work.... Any extra mines we'll use right here."

Then it was time for the mortars to back away.

"Kane, they must be up that trail in ten minutes."

"Yes, sir."

"Ten minutes. No more."

"Yes, sir."

"I know they enjoy the shoot but it's time to go."

"Yes, sir."

"Hollins is to gallop those beasts if he has to! Two hours' lead on the Japs is *minimum.*"

It was tempting to remain for the air strike, but the Wuntho force had to be respected. The last Chindits to withdraw were the machine gunners, who crisscrossed the shattered village in the predawn. Wingate waited for Ingersoll to take up fire from the south; it started right on schedule. When the machine gunners reached the ford, it was past time for Wingate to depart. A squad of Burma Rifles fidgeted impatiently; it was their job to remove traces of the Chindits from the trail.

He took a last look at smoldering Pinlebu. For the Chindits, six dead, four seriously wounded, and a dozen lesser wounds was the cost for his audacity. He had probed the hornet's nest and left them buzzing in futile ferocity.

"How many do you think we killed?" he asked Au Thang.

"Many Kachin."

Wingate stopped and looked back, trying to place where in the smoke the Kachin stockade had stood. The human bridge—it would cross the Mu no more.

"Yes, Pinlebu was a village, wasn't it?"

63

Pinlebu was more than a village for Slim and the correspondents: it was a battle with no known outcome. The RAF had struck at dawn, hugging the hills, swooping out of the rising sun. They'd laid their bombs along the trench line without direction from the ground, for the Chindits did not answer the radio. Japanese had been seen coming off the Wuntho trail; more seemed to be in action south of the village. The Spitfires came around for their machine gun runs with good effect, but on the third pass Zeros were spotted winging from Indaw. Short of ammunition, the RAF outran pursuit to India.

This was all that was known of the battle except that Pinlebu was shredded.

Why hadn't Wingate received his deception drop? the correspondents asked. A critical shortage of artillery ammunition developed in the Arakan was the answer; besides, risking precious aircraft to deliver shells to the Japanese had never overjoyed the supply people.

"When will you hear from Wingate?" was the next question.

"As you know," Colonel Johns answered patiently, "there is a scheduled time each night. Central Force is apparently putting distance between itself and the Japs. Wingate will probably not stop long enough for a report until he feels it is safe to do so."

"Has he scheduled a drop?"

"Not yet."

"Doesn't he need one?"

"It would seem he would. However, North Force is well supplied and they may be linking up soon."

"Do you think the attack succeeded?"

"No way of knowing."

"Is South Force involved?"

"Not directly."

"Anything new from them?"

"Nothing since Dalton reported reaching the Mu in the vicinity of the Menlo."

"Were you surprised Wingate was able to attack Pinlebu at all?"

Johns paused reflectively. "Without knowing what he did about the garrison, I can hardly speculate. He apparently found the Japs to be fewer or less formidable than originally supposed."

"Then you're not surprised."

"If you had told me a week ago that Wingate could attack Pinlebu, I would have been surprised. Now that he has, I'm not surprised. Don't ask me to explain—that's just one of the paradoxes of this expedition."

"Is it succeeding?"

"As the Americans say, so far, so good—except we don't know anything about his losses."

"How long can he carry his wounded?"

"As long as they're alive."

The handful of wounded were not Wingate's major problem. Only two required mule litters. There was one medic per company and one doctor per column. They could stabilize the condition of the seriously wounded, but ultimately an airstrip must be found for a light plane or these men would die. The best hope for them was with Fox-Boynton, who had ample time to reconnoiter the watershed east of Namza.

It was toward Fox-Boynton that Central Force marched day and night. They had broken away cleanly from the Tinda with light packs and easy loads on the mules. The southern ambushes had drawn off most of the Wuntho force. Briggs managed to slip away as well; he made radio contact and estimated he could join Wingate in about three days.

Wingate could have hardly hoped for a better outcome—it was the first significant battle in which the British had beaten the Japanese. Suddenly Wingate was commanding a veteran force, confident in themselves and in him; yet the Chindits were wary and soldierly now—no more cigarette wrappers on the trail and careless fires at night.

But there was no time for fires: Wingate pushed his columns north for thirty-six hours before letting them sleep. He knew his getaway was not secure unless he put at least six hours on any pursuers. Inevitably the Japanese would scout to the north; inevitably they would find the Chindit trail, but they would also find many others, and the Burma Rifles' trail disguises were superb. At one junction they might strew a few shoe mines; at another they might put a sniper to draw a patrol off the scent. At a third, the sniper might protect the real route. These rear guards carried bags of trail litter for further deception. The overall effect was for the web of jungle trails to diffuse Japanese patrols until the pursuit force scattered down every possible route. The jungle could absorb the searchers like water sprayed on the desert.

Despite a good head start, dangers remained for Central Force. From time to time hunters and woodcutters were encountered. The Chindits' fate could depend on their reliability, which was a judgment for the Burma Rifles. Where possible the natives were observed in hiding while they crossed the Chindits' trail and went on their way, but if they were traveling the same direction they were blindfolded and taken along, later to be removed to other trails and told to keep walking without looking back.

Such accidental encounters were not a problem during the escape from Pinlebu. Most of the natives despised the Japanese for their cruelty and arrogance; others lived in such isolation that they were unaware of the war.

Once a day Wingate doubled back through the column primarily to visit the wounded, secondarily to impart vigor and vigilance to the men, who would look up to see him in helmet and beard, striding to the thrusts of a long staff, sometimes with Kane but more often alone.

At a gap between columns, Wingate sat down on a log for a moment. He took off his helmet, closed his eyes, mopped his brow; when he reopened them he was under the stare of four aborigines from the stone age.

A man, a woman, a child, and a hunter—the young family of a woodcutter, perhaps, accompanying the hunter who knew the trails. The family gaped at him with mixed awe and fear. The hunter regarded him with wary approval. They ignored another marcher whom Wingate sent to fetch Au Thang.

Wingate and the aborigines were left in silent communion. The boy tugged his mother's hand—there was nothing more about Wingate he wished to see. The parents seemed to look behind his head. Whatever they saw alarmed them. The hunter swiveled his head from side to side as if to peer around Wingate at something hidden behind him.

"Are they Naga?" Wingate whispered when Au Thang arrived. He jabbered something in the Naga tongue. Uncomprehending, the aborigines stared at the Burmese, who tried several other dialects to no response.

"Never seen any like them, sir."

"Blacker than Ethiopians."

"Live here long, long time I think."

"I suppose we can trust them."

Au Thang shrugged. The safe thing to do was turn them back into the jungle before they saw any more Chindits.

"There's no trail behind them. Not even a trace. They appeared out of thin air. What do you make of them?"

"Tree spirits maybe," Au Thang laughed. Most of the natives of north Burma were animists.

Wingate rose, raised his helmet in farewell. In the moment he replaced it the four were gone with barely a rustle in the foliage, a disappearance that left even Au Thang pop-eyed.

Lorna, the impression from these four apparitions remains vivid and returns at unexpected times as though I were reliving some motor accident. There in the middle of modern war was this glimpse of human life predating our most remote history. I stared, searching for some link between us which could cross the ages. But there was none. The hair still rises on my neck when I think of them.

I must say I was more glad to see Fox-Boynton than he was to see me. With candor that I much value he termed the Pinlebu raid "reckless" though he agreed my strategic purpose was worthy. It remains to be seen if it was worthwhile. My purpose to excite the Japs about the security of Pinlebu seems to have been fulfilled; from aerial photographs, Cochran has advised us that a labor battalion is now at work on field fortifications between the Mu and Tinda and that a couple of tanks may be stationed there now. These are Japs who might otherwise be out looking for us. This development does not satisfy Fox-Boynton, who is convinced Kawabe has troops to spare and all we've done is stir them up—much the same point Wavell made in proposing cancellation of the expedition. This issue is for historians to resolve.

If we here in the jungle are uncertain about Pinlebu, the same must be doubly true in Imphal. I simply reported that Central Force "sideswiped" Pinlebu; Arden & Co. can put that in any light they choose—I'm sure it will be the most unfavorable to me.

Meanwhile, completion of the first phase of the expedition is at hand. Our principal difficulty now is not so much from the enemy as from impossible terrain. The jungled ramparts between us and the railway have scarcely been explored. Even the Burma Rifles are little help in such wilderness. To better our chances of penetrating to the east I've split the Chindits here into four groups rather than two. Each is probing into the hills; when one finds a way the rest will gather behind it.

64

"Trackless jungle" was a term misused by correspondents in the Far East, many of whom had seen very little jungle except from the air. In most valleys there were plentiful tracks and trails. Only in the hills away from natural corridors was there truly trackless jungle, and it was in such terrain the Chindits were forcing their way east through rain forests rarely seen by humans.

The jumbled hills held the pathfinders at bay. Dense scrub matted the lower slopes with softwood trees crisscrossing out of the spongy soil. Here the jungle was its most oppressive and depressing: musty with fungus and leaf mold, sour enough to set men coughing. Higher timber twisted into the dark earth like giant augers. In the crumbling deadfall, arm-thick vines diffused sunlight as if through stained glass.

A day of hacking and climbing brought patrols to a summit and often a glade shaded by towering treetops. Here they radioed their reports: "Too thick for mules. Continuing search." Then crashing downhill, their exertions muffled by the pulpy woods and haggard vines. No trail, no track, no sign that men had ever crossed these wilds.

Before the next climb, a stream. A stream was a welcome signpost: it was going somewhere, and after the first range of hills, all the streams meandered toward the Meza. But Wingate would not follow streambeds; not for long anyway, for they would be the routes for any Japanese patrols.

"Crash on, step over, stoop down, part the filmy leaves, push back drooping vines, brush away grains of punk falling on the back of the neck. Watch out for ferocious ants erupting from the deadfall...."

Where a stream opened the jungle there was a glimpse of the sky. Torn uniforms sagged with sweat while canteens dipped into water as clear as the stratosphere.

"We must first be searching fingers," said Wingate of the groping exploration, "then close like a fist to strike the railway."

At about the middle knuckle he marched with Bradshaw's column. It moved like an accordian: its patrols fanning out until the balance of the column closed up on the best route discovered.

The best routes led only deeper into mountain thickets. Each night brought the same dejected reports from the other columns: no way to the east, no sign of Casten's Trace.

From the time Central and North forces united, Casten's Trace had been like the proverbial Northwest Passage—a route rumored to lead from the Mu to the Meza somewhere through the pristine jungle. It was named for Richard Casten, a forestry official in Burma who had partially explored the region before the war. His "trace" showed on Wingate's maps as a wavy dotted line and meant only that Casten had left intermittent markings en route to the Bonchaung Gorge, now the target for Wingate's plan to bury Kawabe's railroad.

After a week of exhausting discouragement, the Chindit officers no longer believed in Casten's Trace. Fox-Boynton now called it the Prestor John Trail. Though under Wingate's orders to press on with the search to the exclusion of all else, Fox-Boynton instructed his columns to find a clearing for a supply drop. If the other commanders were not as disobedient, they were as needy.

A promising clearing was discovered on a steep hillside. Wingate acquiesced to a drop only during the next moonless night, which meant a two-day wait while the Chindits went on quarter rations. "I'd rather starve than be discovered," was his reply to Fox-Boynton's protest.

In a hilltop glade Wingate slept with Au Thang, Kane, and the radio crew sprawled around him. His stomach woke him. This would be the last night with a moon; soon there would be K rations, but distributing the supply drop would take two days, two days lost from the trek, two more days for the Japanese to patrol, two more days for them to tighten the pressure on South Force. Dalton was the best in the business for eluding pursuit, but given enough time and troops the Japanese would be onto him.

"I would have to say," Wingate wrote, "the expedition at this point is failing...." He looked up at the bleared light of the orange moon falling through the boughs a hundred feet overhead. He scratched out what he had written and began again: "Tonight I look up in a marvelous cathedral. Perhaps I awoke to be reminded that great beauty and suffering are often partners."

A pale violet mist reached down through the vaults of space between the soaring trunks. As if all his men had fallen asleep under some magic potion, silence pervaded the stand of giant kanyin trees. The sound of his pen seemed too loud for the scene; he laid it down.

His eyes drifted closed, then reopened, only to close again till the alternation went on unnoticed. Palestine, Ethiopia, the Chindwin, Pinlebu—a collage of war was balanced for the moment by nature's ethereal peace.

From which side of his consciousness the hunter appeared, Wingate did not know. His hand went to his pistol; his mouth opened in a faint cry that couldn't leave his lips. It seemed to be the same aboriginal hunter. But it couldn't be—not seven days and fifty miles deeper into the wilderness.

The hunter held a lance as Wingate usually held his staff. Wingate raised himself to his elbows. The hunter looked at him with placid curiosity, then moved as if to conclude the visit. His direction seemed to be east. Wingate pointed that way; the hunter nodded and made ready to leave.

"Au Thang," said Wingate softly. His interpreter came awake with a gasp. "Don't frighten him."

Au Thang tried all the dialects he knew. The hunter listened patiently then indicated he would like some water. By now Kane was awake and embarrassed by the lapse in security. The hunter was quickly given a canteen.

"I think he may be going our way," Wingate mused.

"We could send a patrol with him," Kane whispered.

"Yes. Yes."

Au Thang mimicked men marching while he pointed east. The hunter nodded. "Banmauk?" Au Thang asked.

"Banmauk," the hunter answered with his first and last word.

"Banmauk!" Wingate and Kane exclaimed together.

Rations were quickly pooled so a company could follow the hunter without waiting for the resupply drop. They were gone with the dawn. By late the next afternoon they reported that more than machetes were needed if mules were to follow. That was a small discouragement because they had seen blazes on the trees; they were following Casten's Trace.

65

The trace became known as "Casten's Tunnel." North and Central forces were strung out in single file, two thousand men slipping sideways between constraining brush and branches. Each night with heavy axes the trace was widened to squeeze the mules forward. The foliage was so dense that flashlights were used freely. "A creeping cage," Fox-Boynton called the route, for the Chindits could have been exterminated by two Japanese machine guns, one blocking each end of the column.

The mysterious hunter silently guided the lead squad as they hacked until their arms wore out and another squad relieved them. Saplings sprang back at them with the strength of catapults. The foliage closed in so thickly that men flung themselves upon it to create a penetration, then backed off to charge again. For miles the undergrowth was so matted the Chindits stepped into it without their feet reaching the ground.

The contours of the hills and ravines were deeply drowned by vegetation. It took several days before Wingate realized they were working their way along a jagged watershed. Casten was extolled and cursed as one of the world's great explorers for keeping an orientation on such terrain.

When the foliage thinned a bit the terrain became rougher. "Steep as a hard-on," Fox-Boynton described it, but it more resembled the teeth of a ripsaw. The mules, heavily laden from the resupply drop, took the short ascents on the run, using momentum gained in the preceding descent. Many were so badly galled by sharp stalks and branches they had to be shot. Then their carcasses created huge problems blocking the trail. Axes went to work to dismember them.

On Casten's Trace four of the wounded died. There was neither time nor place to bury them so they were laid aloft in cradles formed by large branches. One of the Kings went mad when he came upon a dead man's arm dangling through the leaves. Nothing could be done for him except heavy morphine injections.

The Chindits were in the tunnel for six days while covering some thirty miles. They broke out into lighter jungle like escapees from a dungeon, their uniforms in tatters, their skins like boiled fish.

"Where's our leader?" Wingate asked after savoring the fresh air of the Meza valley. Kane looked at him blankly. "The aborigine, George, our guide."

"Haven't the foggiest." And no one had the energy to find him. "Went back to the stone age, I suppose."

The Chindits emerged with the bulk of the Japanese army scattered in outposts and small garrisons behind them. No forces large enough to trouble him lay between Wingate and where the Bonchaung Gorge cradled the railroad less than twenty miles away. Ahead the jungle was broken with clearings; drop zones were plentiful though he dare not use any until he cut the railroad.

It was time to describe the situation to Slim, learn what was going on with South Force and whatever Japanese countermoves had been detected since Wingate disappeared into Casten's Tunnel.

He learned the Japanese were most active south of Pinlebu. To Kawabe, the Chindits seemed to be the advance guard for a larger force to follow. He was reacting as if the expedition were an effort to take pressure off the Arakan front by advancing to the Mu on a broad front between the Tinda and the Menlo. Consequently the Japanese were reinforcing that area and the railroad by concentrating their security forces between Wuntho and Kyaikthin.

All this meant that the Pinlebu raid had been almost too successful in diverting attention to the south. Japanese outnumbering South
Force ten to one were converging from all directions. Soon Kawabe's
patrols would crisscross the jungle between the Mu and the Z Range,
leaving Dalton without enough real estate in which to hide. Arden
recommended that he turn around and make for the Chindwin before
the ring drew any tighter. Scoones could possibly send a relief force if
Dalton hurried to meet it.

"Then Johns could say he 'saved' the Chindits," Wingate snorted.

"Maybe he should," Fox-Boynton replied.

"I'll let Dalton decide."

Dalton's decision was to cross the Mu and slip through the advancing
Japanese, then harbor in the Bambwe Taung Hills and make ready to
support Wingate's raid on the railroad. The principal difficulty in this
plan was resupply in such a relatively small area now teeming with enemy
patrols. But Dalton had a plan as bold as any Wingate ever devised. If
Fox-Boynton could swing south and hit the tracks in the vicinity of
Nankan, the Wuntho garrison would react in that direction away from
Dalton, who could then take a major resupply in the Bambwe Taung
Hills with only the Pinlebu garrison to worry about.

Wingate approved the idea, adding that he would hit the Bonchaung Gorge concurrent with both Fox-Boynton's attack and Dalton's
drop. This became the new plan for the Chindits. Arden could forget
about assisting them.

Arden could scarcely overrule a plan which followed uninterrupted
successes to date. The RAF promised Dalton maximum support, which
Slim reinforced with a personal message to Wingate: "You have shown
us you are masters of the jungle. Soon you will be masters of the
Japanese."

66

That was the way Wingate was thinking as well: the railroad dangled like a necklace before him while the Japs were looking the other way. He was impatient to muster his men for the decisive thrust to their objective, anxious to get them on the move during the enemy's distraction. But the Chindits were reeling from exhaustion.

The column commanders unanimously protested that without a resupply drop the approach to the railroad would become a death march. Their bodies were "deeply in sleep debt," as Fox-Boynton put it—hardly anyone had been able to lie down on Casten's Trace. They were reduced to half rations; every man needed vitamins and sulfa for cuts and jungle sores; rusting weapons and rotting webbing should be thoroughly cleaned and dried. The men needed to soak up some life-giving sun—and the mules were worse off then they. Above all the expedition had to have food.

Wingate listened to all the reports, his eyes stoking fire. Delay was as impossible as resupply he said; the Chindits must strike before hunger further sapped their energy.

"These aren't Chindits right now, Orde," Fox-Boynton fumed, removing his monocle. "You're not looking at soldiers—only the shells!"

"The worst is behind us. It's easy marching from here. Only inertia holds us back, and inertia increases with every hour. History is at the end of that trail, Adrian!"

"The war won't end when we cut the tracks. Japs will be here like cavalry. Then what? What then, Orde? The rail ties will make fine crosses for our graves."

"Did I forget that detail or weren't you listening? We receive drops at the same time we cut the tracks; indeed our strikes will cover those drops."

"I thought they'd cover Dalton's."

"His as well."

"That's better but it doesn't help us now. Food is an emergency. The men are spent. They're dry batteries."

"Efficient or not we must *move!* This is the time for exalted leadership, my fellows," he said to the circle of column commanders. "You must find it within you to pull the last measure from your men!"

His exhortation was met with downcast eyes, vacant stares, and shaking heads.

"Give us two days, sir. Just two days and a small drop," said a column commander as others nodded.

"We can do it then," said Bradshaw.

"The spirit is willing," said Kane, "but the flesh is..."

"*Never* too weak!" Wingate snapped. "Nothing is too weak except your own resolve. It's time to ask yourselves if you are worthy of the men you command. I see no objection in the Burma Rifles. Au Thang: ask your compatriots if they will accompany me to the railroad." Au Thang regarded him warily. "Ask them, I say."

"This is no time for posturing, Orde," said Fox-Boynton.

"Posturing? Mark me, gentlemen: you will return to your columns and ask for volunteers to accompany me to the railroad *tonight.* Kane, get me the four healthiest mules in the train. Load them with demolitions till their backs bend.

"Now once you hear the explosions—and you will—wait for a resupply and join me...when you've finished tea, of course.

"Volunteers report to me here at 1500. Now get off your arses and let the *men* come forth from your columns. On your feet!" Wingate drove his staff into the ground like a javelin.

His commanders struggled to their feet. Some departed in a rage, some crestfallen. Fox-Boynton remained.

"I want your men too, Adrian. Get moving."

"You'll get them," Fox-Boynton moved closer. "But you're doing great damage, greater than you realize."

"I'm here to do damage, Colonel. Have you forgotten that? Any sensibilities I wound are collateral and insignificant."

"Do you think Bradshaw and the others *want* to fall short? Don't you think all of us are trying as hard as you? We're all in this jungle together, you know."

"*Trying* is not doing. We British seem to lose sight of this most obvious truth. Victory and defeat seem equally acceptable to us provided the effort is admirable. Now get me Briggs. I need doers."

"You have two thousand doers here. It's just that we're not all Briggs and Wingates."

"Briggs and Wingates will hit the gorge. The rest of you poltroons..."

Fox-Boynton kicked Wingate's staff to the ground. "Yes! What will become of the rest of us after you gloriously kill yourself? History lies down that trail—your place in history, that's certain. That means success for you, doesn't it? The expedition can be annihilated and you still succeed if you bury the gorge. LRP is proven! The Chindits will take their place in history beside the Light Brigade!"

Chindits stood aghast at the confrontation, but neither Wingate nor Fox-Boynton paid them any notice.

"Are you provoking me? Do you want to be relieved?" Wingate's voice dropped several scales in intensity.

"No."

Wingate bent over and retrieved his staff. "I'm glad you did that, Adrian. Gave me time to think." He drew Fox-Boynton over to the map. "Now what do we need to go on?"

"Rest and rations."

"Two tons enough?"

"That would barely get us to the railroad."

"All right. Don't know why I didn't think of this sooner. I could be tired myself." He seemed to collect himself. "Cochran—he's a doer. He'll bring us six B25s. Three carry bombs and strike Indaw. The other three carry rations—free-fall them into us, then carry on to Indaw like they were real bombers."

"Tonight?"

"If possible. There are your rations. Get your rest till they arrive. You with me?"

"I'm with you."

Wingate spit out orders and instructions as if nothing had happened. As the Chindits slowly heaved themselves into motion, Fox-Boynton collapsed on a log. "Orde," he said as his commander strode by, "would you have really gone on to the gorge?"

"Depends on how many volunteers went with me. Somehow I got the feeling there wouldn't be many."

67

Like dazed survivors of a great flood the Chindits shambled on. Gauging their slow movement, Wingate had the bombers pass directly over his columns in the moonlight. The bomb bays opened as signal fires flickered briefly. Long, dark objects arched toward a swampy clearing, striking with splashes, burying themselves until the clearing resembled a cemetery of dilapidated tombstones. The planes flew on to their bombing targets while the Chindits scrambled over the crates of rations; then they trudged on for another two hours before daybreak when Wingate let them pull into the jungle and eat.

They ate, slept, and recovered all the next day. With double rations in their stomachs they would still need a full drop in a matter of days; so the raid into the Bonchaung Gorge could last no longer than a single night.

It would be a night by the Meza. Already scouts had gone ahead to reconnoiter both entrances to the gorge while Wingate checked the firing wires and detonators. He prowled the Chindit camp for most of the day, encouraging, extolling, exhorting—except he found few men awake to hear his speeches.

The scouts returned by midafternoon to report the target was less than ten miles away. As fanfare for that news, the long toot of a locomotive sounded faintly through the jungle.

At one end of the gorge the scouts discovered a log blockhouse, probably used as a telegraph station. The Meza flowed noisily a quarter mile away and jungle grew to within a hundred yards of the blockhouse. Once it was captured the mules could pass with their loads of dynamite. Bradshaw decided to take the blockhouse by stealth—no supporting fire unless the attack was discovered.

That was the situation with Wingate. After the bomber resupply,

Fox-Boynton split off with North Force to cut the railroad some fifteen miles farther south. Dalton, if he were able to dodge his pursuers, would hit the rails another fifteen miles beyond Fox-Boynton. All
three forces scheduled major drops to coincide with their attacks. In
so doing, distant Japanese garrisons might think the railroad had been
attacked by air.

As twilight fell, a platoon of Gurkhas surrounded the blockhouse.
Behind them the dynamite-laden mule train stood ready. The attack
opened with the snipping of the telegraph line.

The Gurkhas had crept so close to the blockhouse they heard the
clatter of the transmitter stop and the Japanese cursing within. Four
Gurkhas with grenades were ready for the door to open. It remained
closed as they heard the Japanese arguing. Then the lights went out
inside. The Gurkhas heard the door creak.

Fox-Boynton and Dalton, miles apart, had tapped the telegraph
line. When it went dead they fell upon their targets. The three-pronged
attack, devised the year before in India, now struck the railroad like a
trident.

Grenades clattered on the floor; the blockhouse vented gray smoke,
the explosions muffled by thick log walls. Gurkhas surged from the
jungle, trotting their mules into the gorge. On the roof of the blockhouse, they saw the unmistakable silhouette of Wingate in his pith
helmet raising his staff.

"This is the hour! The training, the crossing, the trek—all have
led to *now*...."

The men stopped for a moment. Some laughed, some shouted
huzzahs—all were quickened from their fatigue—then they went on
like a crowd passing an evangelist in Hyde Park.

"Major Bradshaw, join me."

"Yes, sir."

"Here atop this bunker I shall detonate the charges."

"Yes, sir." Bradshaw gave quick instructions for the box plunger
to be passed up to the roof. Spools of wire spun out behind the mules.
In the darkness men rappeled down the steep cliff above the railroad,
planting charges as they descended.

When Bradshaw climbed on the roof, he realized Wingate was not
there just for theatrics: it was a vantage point at the mouth of the
gorge. He could see winks of light to the south, followed in a few
seconds by the sound of gunfire from the North Force attack.

Fox-Boynton's principal targets were a railway and a road bridge side by side over a deep culvert. His charges were in place, but demolition was interrupted by a truck loaded with off-duty Japanese headed toward the village of Nankan. There was a quick slaughter; then Fox-Boynton's charges were the first to announce the Chindits' success.

Farther south the rumbling earth aroused the Wuntho garrison. Dalton watched headlights come on, the beams probing the darkness as the trucks pulled forward and back, troops scrambling around them.

During the day South Force had exchanged fire with the Japanese on the Pinlebu trail. Dalton's men slithered between their patrols en route to the railroad. It was too strongly protected for him to get near. His contribution now was to engage the Wuntho garrison before it turned north against Fox-Boynton; then Dalton could do no more than protect his own supply drop.

"Mortars, please," he said, beginning bombardment of the trucks.

Flashes from the fighting on the ground greeted the C47s as they searched for the Chindits' signal fires. The pilots were pleased, knowing the battles below would mask the sound of aircraft engines. Wingate's signal fires went on, but the gorge remained dark beside the twinkling ribbon of the Meza.

Nervous as burglars, Central Force waited restlessly for Wingate to lean on the plunger. He in turn waited for the aircraft to approach the gorge; they would be his witness to its destruction, his witness for Slim, Arden, Johns—for every doubter west of the Chindwin.

"My hands grip the plunger," he shouted to his audience below. "Hands from the shadows join mine, as do yours—every one of you who toiled in this great and noble mission—while the souls of our fallen comrades watch from the jungle.

"Hear me now, you ghosts of the brave! Press with the hand of Jehovah...and let the hills hear His *thunder!*"

The exploding hillside burst into daylight colors, a giant flashbulb for a picture of men crouching, scattering, recoiling.

A wave of compressed air jolted the leading aircraft. "I saw the Irrawaddy from Katha to Inywa," said the pilot, "like a reverse eclipse."

Mules reared and kicked as the cliff convulsed in a thundering downfall. The surging rumble perpetuated itself, rolling as though from a timpani between the hills, down the valleys and back. The ground shock shook even the solid blockhouse and set lamps swaying in Wuntho thirty miles away.

Clods of earth thudded down on the roof. Wingate pulled back the plunger and held it overhead like a cross in benediction.

"It is done," he said as dirt and debris pattered down on him. The earth subsided into the gorge like a newly filled grave.

The morning after the gorge was buried, a small transport flew Colonel Tenaka, commander of the Indaw garrison, to General Kawabe's headquarters near Mandalay. Kawabe and his staff sat stonily as Tenaka erected a map board for their view. His briefing was brief:

"General. Between Wuntho and Pinlebu, Eighteenth Division patrols fell upon a British force of approximately a thousand men withdrawing to the northwest. We inflicted losses and took sixteen prisoners. We have learned that this force is led by a Colonel Dalton. He is under the command of a brigadier general named Wingate who led guerrillas against the Italians in Ethiopia. Wingate's force in Burma is called the Chindits. Their mission was to cut our supply line to Myittkyina. Last night they succeeded. This disgrace is my responsibility."

Tenaka took up the short sword he had placed on the empty table in front of him. With a short, lateral thrust he slashed deeply between the hipbones. Barely grimacing, he sat down, then toppled forward onto the table as if in a permanent bow to Kawabe, who took no notice of the suicide. He walked slowly to the map and drew three arrows converging on the bend of the Irrawaddy. His staff scribbled notes as his words and Tenaka's blood flowed.

"The gorge will be cleared if you have to eat the soil. A train shall pass through it in three days. And this disgrace to the imperial army shall be *avenged!*" He pushed back Tenaka's torso and ripped out a handful of viscera. "Now bring me Wingate's guts." He flung down Tenaka's, which splattered on the floor. "Or be hanged with your own."

68

The correspondents clustered around the aerial photo still damp from the dark room.

"That's a pretty pile of dirt."

"Looks like the tracks came up to the mountain but the Japs forgot to build a tunnel!"

Arden smiled faintly amid the jubilant laughter.

"General Arden."

"Yes."

"There's no secret any more, is there?"

"Very much so. The size of the force, their route into Burma, means of resupply..."

"But I mean the Japs know that somebody buried their railroad. Can we say it was the Chindits?"

"I suppose...if you say no more than that."

"Commanded by Orde Wingate?"

"I don't suppose he'd mind. Use your judgment, gentlemen."

"Is General Slim pleased?"

"Immensely."

"What's Wingate's next move?"

"That's up to him—and as usual he has not advised us."

"Can he get out if he wants to?"

"If he hurries I think he can."

"What's the hurry?"

"The Eighteenth Division principally. With the Chinese in hibernation they have nothing to do except track down the Chindits. The Fifth Division is also closing in the vicinity of Mandalay; I'm sure they're available for the hunt as well."

"Two divisions against one brigade?"

"And more. Don't forget these fellows." Arden pointed to the patrols west of the Z Range.

"Can't Fourteenth Army create a diversion somewhere?"

"We are fully committed in the Arakan. That's more than a diversion, gentlemen; that is the principal front in this theater—a fact you sometimes forget."

"What would you do if you were Wingate?"

"Break out to the north. Up the Meza Valley. If he hurries he can get out before the ring closes."

"Do you expect to learn his plans soon?"

"Yes."

Wingate was already devising them, but for once he was vacillating. North and Central forces (now geographically reversed) pulled off to the northwest. It would be a simple if arduous matter for them to slip back through Casten's Trace to reappear in the Mu Valley, further bewildering the Japanese. Indeed, once back at the Mu, Wingate could make himself appear as a new force from India with the apparent mission of following up the attack on the railroad. This he termed the "Campfires" Plan, a reference to his favorite biblical deception by which David created the impression of a much larger force.

The trouble with Campfires was that it left Dalton in the lurch. South Force had seen the most action, the pressure and strain on it had been greatest, and it needed relief even more than the rest of the Chindits. It was now in a vise between Wuntho and Pinlebu. The best alternative for Dalton to join Campfires was for him to sideslip and cut straight north, paralleling Wingate's route after the Pinlebu raid. If Dalton were hard-pressed, Wingate could reinforce him through the Pambu Valley.

Between the headwaters of the Pambu and the Tinda was a jungled plateau that had long interested Wingate. If the entire brigade were drawn around its perimeter, he would have the defensive bastion he sought to complement LRP. His full theory, dating back to the Tibesti Plan, called for the "strategic offensive with tactical defensive," that is, penetrating to a vulnerable area in the enemy rear and there choosing strong ground where he could oblige his foe to attack him. In such a defense his force would in effect be multiplied numerically because, as he was fond of expounding, it would take three attackers to dislodge one defender.

The odds were much longer against him in his present situation, but the plateau had many drop zones, a few capable of improvement to where C47s could land with reinforcements and supplies. All three forces could converge on the plateau without serious interference by the Japanese. In every respect the Plateau Plan seemed an excellent one, particularly since it meant the men could take off their packs, dig in, recover their strength, and evacuate the wounded.

The third plan was so radical that Dalton and Fox-Boynton were shocked even to hear it described. This was the Irrawaddy Plan, whereby the three forces would march toward the great bend of that river, cross it, and traverse the Indaung Forest to the Kachin Hills, where friendly tribesmen would provide strongholds and succor for the Chindits. After a few weeks of recuperation, Wingate would commence raids to the south.

From the Kachin Hills, he might also join hands with the Chinese. Aerial resupply would have to come from airfields in China because the Kachin Hills were beyond the range of loaded C47s flying from India. Thus, Wingate's transports would have to fly a triangular pattern, India-China-Burma, then back to India. This was particularly inefficient use of the previous C47s; so the Irrawaddy Plan, whatever its other disadvantages, had never been seriously considered before the expedition.

At the moment it had one overriding advantage: it sent the Chindits where the Japanese least expected them to go—east, deeper into enemy territory.

The last plan, called Buckshot, had always been a contingency for catastrophe: namely, to break up the three forces into their component columns and disperse, each taking an individual route back to India. Each column was purposely self-contained with the radio capability to call in its own drops. Now, with the railroad cut and the expedition a success, Buckshot was probably the safest plan in terms of preventing further loss of life for the beleagured columns.

The decision at hand was of such importance that Wingate called a council of war, the first and only such meeting of his career. The council would be only himself, Fox-Boynton, and Dalton, but Dalton was very much occupied in shaking off pursuit in the Bambwe Taung Hills.

Nothing Wingate ever asked of him was more difficult, but Dalton was equal to the summons. His incomparable understanding of jungle and Japanese made South Force practically vanish like the tree spirits of the sheltering forest. Instead of seeking security in dispersion, he brought all his patrols in, closed up his columns, and marched them into the most difficult jungle he could find.

There nearly a thousand men occupied a perimeter only a few hundred yards in diameter, a space of molecular size in the jungle cosmos. Though the odds of discovery were reduced from the hundred trails they had been marching to a single, static location, that one in a hundred possibility remained. To reduce it to insignificance, Dalton put out signs on the approaches to his position.

The signs were in Japanese warning of mines on the trails, warnings issued by "the Authority of General Kawabe." The Japanese search parties had become a hodgepodge of units from Pinlebu, Wuntho, Indaw, and even as far away as Bhamo. Overall command was uncertain, but everyone knew at the top of the pyramid was General Kawabe, an authority above all others to remain unquestioned.

Dalton's outposts surveilled the signs from nearby trees. Only three Japanese patrols were observed; all turned away when they saw the signs. One patrol leader marched up to the sign and bowed deeply before withdrawing.

Even the successful coiling of his columns did not solve Dalton's problems. He judged they would be safe for only a few days, and it would take him longer than that to navigate cross-country for his meeting with Wingate and return. He could only keep his appointment if he found faster transportation; this he did by comandeering a Japanese truck on the Wuntho-Nankan road.

With a squad of Burma Rifles disguised as BIA, he hailed passing vehicles until one pulled over. The Good Samaritan was soon dead in the jungle. Dalton was able to drive to within fifteen miles of Wingate's harbor, where the truck was hidden in the brush for the return trip.

69

Dalton's arrival was the capstone to the Chindits' cresting morale. They had not merely bested the invincible Japanese; they seemed to be humiliating them. Light observation planes now cruised over the hills to aid the search parties. To the Chindits snoozing under the leafy canopies, the drone above them signaled the futility of the once dreaded enemy.

The Japanese began dropping "wanted" leaflets from the planes. Burma Rifles were sent out in civilian garb to obtain some and returned giggling: Wingate's picture was from a newspaper showing him with Selassie outside the palace.

"What does it say?" Wingate asked Au Thang.

"It says you are wanted for murder and...vandalism!"

Laughter crackled through the Chindit camp as they learned of their commander's crimes. Wingate was so amused he changed his radio call sign to "vandal."

"Confusion to the enemies of the crown," said Fox-Boynton, raising a toast with his bamboo mug. Their libation was an insidious Burmese distillation of sugar called *pinta*. The setting resembled the last night near Imphal, though the view now was only the walls of a jungle glade. Wingate had ordered a double ration of *pinta* for all ranks to celebrate Dalton's miraculous arrival.

"Aren't you celebrating, Bruce?" Wingate noticed that Dalton had only sipped his toast.

"Yes, this is all very nice here."

"Then drink up," Fox-Boynton urged. "Chin-chin."

"I feel like I'm having cocktails in the eye of a hurricane."

"Lots of activity out there?" Wingate asked blithely. "Well, we're

301

here with our cocktails anyway. Do you remember our last night in Imphal?"

"Certainly do."

"An odd lot we were, plotting to go after the dreaded Japs: the patrician Fox-Boynton, the saturnine Dalton, and the renegade Wingate. Here's to us, I say!"

"Hear, hear. An odd lot we are. What say you, Bruce?"

Dalton quaffed his *pinta*. "We're not three the academies would have recommended, are we?"

"Bugger the academies!" said Wingate. The three bashed their mugs together.

"I brought you here for some business actually."

"Oh, I thought this was someone's birthday."

"Probably is, but what I wanted to talk with you about is the *Bismarck*."

"Is she chasing us, too?"

"You've been in the jungle too long, Adrian. The *Bismarck* was sunk by our gallant navy."

"Well here's to the sailors! Which reminds me of our interesting discussion last. Remember how we distinguished sailor's and airman's courage, Orde? Seems pertinent to review matters in the light of your interesting theory and our current experience."

"Presently. But first, the *Bismarck*. Our situation now is much like hers, I'd say, when she broke into the open ocean after sinking the *Hood*, much to the surprise of all." Dalton nodded agreement. "There she was, the most dreaded dreadnought on the seas, having punished our navy in an astonishing manner. Consider her captain's options at that point. They seem to have been three: first, to return to Norway where her devastating potential would force our fleet to double its guard against another raid. *Bismarck* at that point would have stripped our convoys of every capital ship, leaving them naked to the U-boats— and all she had to do was return to port."

"Quite, quite," Fox-Boynton agreed.

"A bolder course, however, was to disappear into the mist and lurk for a time around the convoys, slipping in for a raid if the opportunity arose, while taking care to keep an escape route open. That involved some risk, but she sailed with the momentum of victory, an intangible factor which seems to beget further success.

"Her last option was to exploit her initial victory and humiliate the Royal Navy by sailing around them to France. We know now that her captain chose that option. If you're following my analogy, I propose to do the same."

Dalton and Fox-Boynton smiled. Wingate was once again presenting outrageous propositions in order to provoke counterarguments.

"Well, if you want to be captain of the *Bismarck*," said Dalton, "let me have my lifeboat and I'll go home." Fox-Boynton chuckled as Dalton's elbow nudged him.

"So Bruce, you favor return to the Mu Valley?" Wingate inquired.

"Yes, I'm for Campfires. I think Plateau could also work, but I wouldn't try it unless Slim guarantees a battalion to come in by air."

"Frankly, I don't think Slim could deny you at least a battalion at this point," said Fox-Boynton. "He has always been one to reinforce success. And if we set up on that plateau, he can't just leave us out there. Besides, Sir Archie wouldn't allow it."

"So you favor Plateau?" Wingate asked.

"No. I'm for taking the ship and all her crew back to Norway for the very reasons you've sketched so well." He leaned forward and removed his monocle. "Nothing we can do here will have nearly the significance of what the Japs think we *might* be able to do. They are certain to exaggerate our capabilities unless we show them otherwise. I'm for packing up and heading north, all the Chindits together; exit at Homalin. Let the Eighteenth Division follow us if they can. We'll bloody them with ambushes all along the way."

"Bruce?"

"I like that too. I like it as well as Campfires."

"But I propose to take the Chindits across the Irrawaddy."

"Sure, just wait for it to freeze and have Cochran drop in some ice skates."

"No, better than that. It seems a "river festival" or something is about to begin—so Au Thang tells me. The Burmese are presently cruising the Irrawaddy with every vessel that floats—a tribute to the river deity. We shall requisition their boats, reward them with some mules, and return the boats when we have crossed."

"No more *pinta* for you tonight," said Fox-Boynton.

"Or me either," said Dalton. "I want to get back to the road before dark."

"No, we musn't delay you. Gentlemen, here are the photos of the most promising crossing sites. While the Japs are looking up here, we will have a few peaceful days at the river. Bruce, I think that south of Tagaung would be best for you..."

"Orde, your humor becomes macabre," said Fox-Boynton, lowering his voice.

"Sorry. I wasn't trying to be funny. I plan to send you across between Inywa and Satsa."

"You aren't joking, are you!"

"No. And I'd rather not have another scene."

"What the hell to you expect to gain by crossing the 'Waddy?" Dalton asked coldly.

"I expect to leave Kawabe looking for us on this side."

"And when we get across—if we do—what then?" Fox-Boynton fumed. "We'd be out of Cochran's range. Elephant grass is a monotonous diet. Please, Orde, tell us you're not serious. It's been such a pleasant afternoon."

"The C47s can still reach us, only with lighter loads. They won't have to come by way of China. Lighter loads just mean more frequent drops."

"Who says we'll get more drops?" Dalton asked.

"Even if we got them, Orde, they couldn't sustain the men, much less the mules."

"And why not?"

"The direction is *wrong,* that's why. The men are rejuvenated now because the worst is over—the mission's accomplished. There are perils ahead but they're headed for home. Don't you realize what a difference that makes?"

"I expect our friends in the Kachin Hills will offer us haven. We are closer to them than to India."

"What have you heard from the Kachins?" Dalton asked.

"Their patrols are ready to guide us once we're east of the Shweli."

"That's all?"

"I feel that's enough."

"Why won't they go into the Indaung Forest?"

"I'm not sure."

"Well I agree completely with Adrian. We've got enough strength to do Campfires. With support, we can give Plateau a try. The Irrawaddy's crazy."

Wingate looked down into his mug. "What sort of 'strength' do you mean?"

"What Adrian was talking about. 'Sailors' courage or whatever you were calling it. The well's running dry for these fellows. They may not show it but they're petering out."

"We hardly know what South Force has been through," said Fox-Boynton. Wingate nodded slowly.

"It's a difficult decision. The most difficult I've ever had to make."

Neither colonel wished to end the pause that they hoped meant Wingate was reconsidering. Fox-Boynton stirred the leaves with a stick: "It's going to take everything we've got just to get home. That's why I have doubts about Plateau: help might not get here soon enough. But to march deeper into unknown enemy territory is really quite beyond my imagination."

"My imagination... sees what others can't. The typhoon stills every breeze."

"I admire your imagination as much as anyone," said Dalton. "I have from the time I met you at the Bush School. But there's a gap in it. You know what I mean?"

"Tell me."

"I'm not sure if I can. Your imagination's not so good when it comes to your own men."

"Exactly," said Fox-Boynton. "You can anticipate the Japs' moves, but when it comes to us there's this blind spot. Your imagination becomes imaginings."

Long seconds passed. Wingate rose. "If by that you mean I see in you what you do not see yourselves..." he quaffed his drink, "you're right! If the reach of my mind exceeds the grasp of yours, that's why I am the commander!"

70

Divided once again into three forces, the Chindits approached the railroad for the second time. The observation planes were behind them, searching to the northwest; as Wingate predicted, the Japanese were looking for him everywhere except in the direction he was going.

Resisting their destructive impulses, the Chindits crossed the railroad as if it were only another opening in the jungle. Then came lesser rivers before they reached the mile-wide Irrawaddy.

There, between sandbars and low islands, the Royal Navy entered the Burma war. His ruminations on the *Bismarck* inspired Wingate to request that a long-range seaplane be detached from antisubmarine duty in the Bay of Bengal. A bold naval aviator volunteered for the mission. Loaded with outboard motors, the amphibian flew to a night rendezvous on the Irrawaddy to pick up the Chindit sick and wounded.

The Wingate magic was at work once more. With the outboards, which would soon become property of cooperative Burmese fishermen, the Chindits put themselves across in a single night.

"I consulted an atlas today, General Slim."

"Did you, Sir Archie?"

"I wanted to see how the Irrawaddy compared with other rivers of the world. It's not the longest. That's the Amazon, of course. Not the widest either. Ranks third, though, in the volume of water it carries. And you know what else, Bill? The Irrawaddy has never been forced."

"Never? Not even in ancient wars?"

"I had Montague check. So far as he knows, no army in war has ever crossed the Irrawaddy. And here Wingate has done it practically on the spur of the moment."

Slim shook his head. "He's sticking his head in a noose. I can't believe he doesn't see it. I want him to countermarch, sir. I need your support. I must send him an order in both our names. Otherwise I don't believe he will obey without an appeal to you."

"You propose that we jointly overrule the genius of the jungle?"

"I certainly do. And I'll take the jibes from the press and all of Wingate's fury when he gets back. The Chindits are too valuable to expend in Wingate's folly; you know that as well as I. They should be brought back by the most direct, safest route; then they should be dispersed as a training cadre for the rest of Fourteenth Army. We need their experience, their confidence."

Wavell smiled. "I wouldn't send those plans to him over the air. We might never see Orde again."

"We may never see the Chindits again if we let them drift away toward China. He's taking himself nearly out of transport range you know. Putting himself in such an obvious trap! The Irrawaddy at his back, the Shweli in front of him. Japs moving up from the south...." Slim struck the table with his fist. "I really think he's cracked, sir. Like a diamond he is both brilliant and brittle."

"I remember Platt once telling me much the same. The fact is, Bill, Wingate consistently defies all predictions. He keeps winning. Embarrassing sometimes, isn't it?"

"Imagine we were both drunk at Brighton, aye? I persuade you to give me a month's pay, which I promptly place on a roulette number. I win, you win, we win.... We're gloriously intoxicated. Then much to your alarm, I take the whole pile and lay it on another number..."

"My heart's in my throat..."

"Yes, quite... but we win again. Even greater rejoicing, aye?"

"Right you are."

"Then for the third time, I carry the bushel to the roulette table.... Need I go on? You wouldn't let me keep playing for such stakes, would you, even if my winning streak was the wonder of the casino?"

"There's more to Wingate than luck."

"All the more reason to bring him back. Confidentially. I acknowledge his genius. I would support a second expedition. But he's of no use to us dead in the Indaung Forest."

"If things start to go badly, the Chindits can always disperse; infiltrate back here in small groups."

"That's his Buckshot theory. To me it sounds like a jungle Dunkirk."

"They'd dribble out, wouldn't they—like Burma Corps in '41?"

"Yes, and do you remember how the press assumed the whole corps was lost?"

"Vividly."

"This command could hardly withstand another shock like that. That may be the nub of it. May I ask how I could present the loss of the Chindits to the press? 'Sorry, gentlemen, we lost three thousand fine fellows out there near China. Please realize they were commanded by a most compelling brigadier who pretty much acted on his own impulses. I watched and worried for him, but, you see, Orde Wingate simply calls upon his personal gods to lead him. Yes, yes. I know I'm a lieutenant general and he was only an acting brigadier, but you have to understand the late, great Wingate to appreciate my predicament.' How's that, Sir Archie?"

"Much better than I could put it. But I've never had a way with the press."

"If Wingate goes on as he plans, I should request to be relieved."

"Your request is denied in advance."

"You shall have to act on my request again when this tragedy unfolds."

"If you think he's cracked, why not relieve him yourself?"

"That authority is yours alone. The Chindits are mine only for operational coordination."

"Are you recommending that I relieve him?"

"You should have told him to get on that seaplane—told him to come back to confer with you. We could have observed him. Parachuted him back in if he's OK. From here we can't tell the degree of strain he's been under. I think if I could talk with him I could gauge the man."

"Bringing in the seaplane shows me he still has his wits about him."

"Did you talk to any of the wounded who came out?"

"Not yet. What did they say?"

"If he's in any way as bad off as they are, the expedition should be canceled immediately. Mentally those men were right on the brink; and it didn't take a psychiatrist to see it."

"What did they say of Wingate?"

"Nothing very complimentary."

"What did they say?"

"Some thought him mad. Some thought him inspired. The rest thought he was both."

Wavell sighed deeply. "Maybe I should, but I can't relieve him now. He may confound us again; and consider, Bill, if he is confounding us, what he must be doing to the Japanese."

The Japanese knew too little about the Chindits to be confused. Two days after the crossing, they received vague reports of trans-Irrawaddy movements. Colonel Yakamura, the regional commander for the search, thought the reports unreliable; nevertheless, with no other Chindit sightings, he set about to investigate.

Most of his men were now patrolling the railroad, but with no threats from any other quarter Yakamura had troops to spare. This was the very contingency of which Wavell had warned in proposing cancellation of Mercury; it was the new reality which Wingate faced as he entered the Indaung Forest.

Soon it became clear why the Kachin guerrillas would not cross the Shweli to join him. To do so they would be leaving the protection of the jungle, as there was no jungle in the loop formed by the Irrawaddy and the Shweli—there was only "forest" in the European sense of the word—trees growing in order, mostly teak, crisscrossed with logging trails and access roads.

Ten miles into the Indaung Forest, Wingate knew he had made an enormous mistake. The Chindits, in effect, were crossing an open field thirty miles wide. The forest protected them only from the Japanese air force. It was this unbroken canopy which had deceived Wingate in the aerial photos: from the air everything looked like dense, pristine jungle.

On the ground, however, the forest vistas were long, wide, and unobstructed by secondary foliage. The ground was horizontal; the trees vertical and widely spaced, giving the impression of a cage.

Within the cage, Wingate's obsession was for speed. Scuffling boots raised faint dust clouds and crackled through the teak leaves till the march sounded like a swarm of crickets. The sacrifice to speed was thirst; for the expedition was now well into the dry season. At night the Chindits dug for surface water, rarely drawing enough for two canteens per man. The mules began to collapse.

Marching with Kane, Wingate played the part of a man betrayed.

"I can't believe Dalton didn't know about this. What the hell did Bush Warfare School do up here, anyway? And the Kachins—Christ—

what kind of allies are they not telling us about this plantation? Do you realize the Japs could practically *drive* right up to us?"

Kane glanced over at his glowering commander. The moment didn't seem right to ask the question on every Chindit's mind: resupply—when, where, what mix? What the Chindits needed most was water, but to deliver it by air was ludicrous both for its weight and for the other essentials it would replace.

Or could there be resupply at all in the forest? Kane wondered. The first drop east of the Irrawaddy might be the last, for it would draw the Japanese like filings to a magnet.

71

"No drop till the Shweli" was Wingate's decision; it was radioed to Fox-Boynton and Dalton, where it was ill-received. The Indaung Forest was shortest where Central Force was crossing it. On Fox-Boynton's route the forest was half again as wide and double for Dalton who had gone forty-eight hours without food and almost without drink.

Fox-Boynton signaled, "Psalms 22." The applicable verse read, "I may tell all my bones: they look and stare upon me." Not to be outdone for grim humor, Wingate referred him to the Gospel of St. John: "Consider that it is expedient that one man die for the people, that the whole nation perish not."

Dalton had no opportunity to enter the biblical conversation. At dawn he collided with a strong patrol moving north into his march route. He attacked aggressively, driving the Japanese back, but the patrol was the advance guard of a motorized battalion. South Force suffered its first defeat. Sluggish, inefficient from hunger and dehydration, they split up and fell back.

Dalton reported they would be lucky to reassemble by nightfall. When he got them back together, South Force must have a resupply including medical bundles, for he had many wounded. He would contact Cochran himself. He also needed more mines, as he would use all he had to break away from the Japanese.

Dalton's misfortune was the diversion Wingate needed to resupply Central and North forces. However, resupplying all the Chindits at one time was never contemplated in Plan Mercury. The radios chirped constantly between Kane and Cochran: not enough aircraft, and they'd be operating at almost maximum range. Who was to have priority among the forces? Wingate decided it would be himself.

"Dalton may lose most of his drop if he's in contact with the Japs," he explained. "And if they get around him they could hit Fox-Boynton tonight. We have the safest location."

"So how do you want the percentages, sir?" said Kane in a clipped voice.

"Half for us. A quarter for each of them."

That night, for the first time, two transports were shot down. The motorized forces had antiaircraft guns, weapons not previously encountered by the Chindits. Without any word from their commanders, every man realized the expedition had reached its easternmost limit. Wingate turned the Chindits around. Once more they faced the Irrawaddy; this time it was not a barrier to be crossed but the jaw of a trap to be forced open.

Once more the search planes droned overhead. They seemed to be hovering, unsure of their quarry below but certain the Chindits were in the Indaung Forest.

The rasp returned to Wingate's voice. He no longer doubled back along the columns, encouraging his men. He kept Au Thang and Kane close beside him. Would the fishermen help him at the river again? Au Thang did not know. If Japanese were patrolling the far shore, he did not think any boats would venture into a possible cross fire.

Without boats, the mules must be left behind. Without mules, there was only one alternative left for the expedition: Buckshot—dispersal and exfiltration to India.

"Why isn't the radio loaded?" Wingate demanded as Central Force broke camp for the Irrawaddy. Kane had the radio ready; expecting Wingate to give the Buckshot order to Dalton and Fox-Boynton.

The jungle floor rumbled slightly—Japanese artillery, a sound previously unheard. "Never get through that canopy," Wingate said loudly for the Chindits' benefit. "Hard on the monkeys, that's all. Now get that radio mule-borne." The radio began to chirp. It was Dalton's call sign. "We'll hear about it tonight.... Get moving."

Wingate would look no one in the eye as they marched. All ears were cocked to the south. If they heard North Force's guns, a division of Japanese could be only fifteen miles away. At twilight, as Wingate's advance guard came up on the Irrawaddy, the pursuers collided with Fox-Boynton, in a furious firefight.

The code for his reaction was "SFB"—shoot and fall back—a standard maneuver; the Chindits had frequently rehearsed in Saugor for the possibility of one column being attacked in the vicinity of another. The force under attack was to shoot and fall back through the "covering" force, which lay in ambush for the attackers. Fox-Boynton announced he would SFB at once.

Wingate ordered him to hold instead. Not enough light for the maneuver; great risk of confusion as North Force pulled back through Central, he said—high probability of firefights between the Chindits.

Fox-Boynton pushed his radio operator aside. In the background the thump of mortars emphasized his predicament. He had to fall back before the fire reached the center of his position, where the mules were tethered.

"We're leaving the taxis [mules] anyway," Wingate replied. "Drive them to Surrey [east]." Wingate was recommending that since the mules would be left by the Irrawaddy, North Force should now stampede them to the east, giving the impression the Chindits were continuing into the Indaung Forest. This advice was the first inkling for Fox-Boynton that the Chindits would disperse.

"Vandal, is this Buckshot?" Fox-Boynton asked numbly.

"Negative. Stand by for next." North Force was to await instructions.

Au Thang was scouting the river for boats. Before departing into the Indaung he arranged for the fishermen who had received the outboards to meet him if they saw a certain signal from the eastern shore. Their commitments were vague. It had seemed a small matter for Wingate at the time, but now these casual arrangements might be the only way to save the Chindits. Au Thang hoped that with their new outboards the fishermen would require the fuel he had buried on the bank.

The signal fires were lit. The great question was whether the boats would venture into that stretch of river if they heard Fox-Boynton's battle in progress.

"Tell Cochran we've got to have some fighters."

Kane looked up from the radio where he had been monitoring South Force's frequency. "Dalton has eight P47s this afternoon. The Americans are going to try some new flame weapon called napalm."

"Divert the strike to Adrian."

"Sir!"

"All right. I'll tell him myself. Put Bruce on."

"Vandal for Satan. Vandal for Satan."

The static crackled as Kane watched Wingate's shoulders tighten.

"Satan for Vandal," Dalton's weary voice replied. Kane had been following South Force's situation as they broke contact with the Japanese and pulled back into some low hills closer to the river. There the Japanese in their trucks had rediscovered him, but through clever ambushes and sharp counterattacks, Dalton kept them at bay and his own exits open. He had called for the fighter strike in hopes of knocking out the trucks.

"This is Vandal. Must have Flip for Cyclops. Genesis 19. Over."

As brief as the message, it told Dalton everything. The air strike would go to North rather than South Force. The reference to Genesis was, "Return not whence ye came. Seek salvation in the mountains." Rather than turning west for India, Dalton was to continue on for the Kachin Hills—continue through the widest expanse of the Indaung Forest.

Kane lit one of his last remaining cigarettes. He could imagine Dalton as the import of Wingate's message set in. The pith helmet shaded his eyes as Kane's widened. Dalton's reply broke through the static.

"Roger."

"Bedlam," Wingate answered, the code word for shutting down the brigade radio net, a precaution against Japanese aircraft tracking the signals. This was the first time he had called for Bedlam; to Kane it seemed the oddest of times when the three forces badly needed to coordinate their escape efforts.

"Tell Adrian to Bedlam; then tell him to come up on our internal frequency."

Kane was left to mull these strange developments: Wingate had

taken the forces out of three-way communications; he would talk with
Fox-Boynton but without Dalton listening. Wingate clambered down
to the riverbank in search of Au Thang. Kane slipped behind a tree so
the radio crew could not see how he trembled.

72

Scattered through the Irrawaddy in front of North Force was a chain of
low islands which echeloned toward the opposite shore. Optimistical-
ly, Fox-Boynton called them "stepping-stones." During the night he
sent three of his best swimmers into the river. But they were not to
swim, they were to let the flood carry them from island to island, each
stop closer to the west bank. When they reached as far as they could
go under these conditions, they would signal; if the signal was from
the west bank, North Force had a chance to recross.

But would the Japanese be waiting for them? No roads reached the
west bank as they did in the accursed Indaung Forest, but from the
circling of Japanese observation planes, the hunt seemed to be up on
both sides of the river.

The fighter strike took the pressure off for the moment. The Japanese had never seen the jellied fire called napalm; it seared their heroism and exploded two trucks. Nor were the P47s finished. They shot
down an observation plane and became Wingate's observers until their
fuel ran low and Zeros appeared from the south.

The Americans sighted considerable enemy activity around Inywa
from where Wingate hoped the fishermen would send down their boats.
That explained why none had responded to the signal fires. Wingate
was left to stare at the open river and the faint outlines of the islands.

Obedient to Wingate's orders, Dalton slipped east into the dry river-
bed of the Salin Chaung. His escape left the Japanese free to move
their trucks and guns north near the settlement of Satsa. There the
Burma Rifles, once again impersonating BIA, located an artillery bat-

tery which could devastate the islands if the Chindits were discovered on them.

Fox-Boynton meanwhile was discovering some defensive advantages in the Indaung Forest. Well-sited machine guns covered a great deal of ground, as their fires could interlock. The machine guns were too heavy to take back over the Irrawaddy, so Fox-Boynton used them extravagantly to check the Japanese in a series of fallback positions.

With boats no longer a possibility, Wingate moved south to join Fox-Boynton near the islands. While the rest of Central Force constructed rafts, Wingate took the two healthiest companies, commanded by Captains Briggs and Lynch, and swung back into the forest to come around on the Japanese artillery near Satsa.

For Kane and Fox-Boynton, this was the first move they approved since Wingate buried the railroad. They met at the North Force command post opposite the stepping-stones, as they called the islands. Fox-Boynton regarded Kane wanly, motioned for him to meet behind a tree.

"What's going on, George?"

"I've never seen him act like this."

"Why didn't he put out Buckshot?"

"He wants... I think he wants Dalton to go on. I—I may be wrong."

"No, you're right. South Force is his sacrifice. That cold-blooded..."

"He sent them two drops," Kane said in defense.

"Of course. He wants all the activity down there, all the attention."

"He'll be saving most of the Chindits."

"Will he! All the channel swimmers anyway. Those islands aren't an escape route, George, they're a necklace in a noose. Listen to me: if we get a thousand men back across the Irrawaddy it'll be through prayer. Then where are we? No mules, no radios, no mortars, no machine guns, maybe fifty rounds per rifle—and only with the strong swimmers. Take a look around, George; this is the last you'll see of the Chindits."

Kane sank to the ground.

"Are you all right?"

"Adrian..."

"Sorry, but you must be aware how desperate these hours are. How many wounded do you have?"

"Twenty-two who will never leave this shore."

"I have double that many."

"Would a resupply do any good?"

"Once we get across we must have one—if only to give the men some hope. I don't care what *he* thinks." Kane nodded. "We've got to arrange it now before he dumps the radios."

"Where?"

"Fox-Boynton pulled out a rumpled map. "Here." He pointed to where the Meza split before its confluence with the Irrawaddy. "Anyone who gets across can find the Meza. If he follows it upstream he'll find the drop. Rations and ammo."

"Free-fall?"

"Yes. Like last time—Cochran will have to use bombers. They can find that river fork without our marking it."

"You don't want to tell him?"

"I'm asking you not to."

"We'll have to tell everyone."

"We'll tell every man who reaches the last island—and hope Wingate isn't one of them."

"Adrian!"

"You still believe? I should have plugged up my ears instead of listening to him. He's a siren who's drawing us to destruction!"

"I have to believe in him. We need another miracle."

"It's a tragic miracle we've stayed with him. I was so stupid, so seduced with his theories and visions. Damn him!"

"Adrian..."

"Why shouldn't the men hear the truth? He may not be back. Have you thought of that? Haven't you wondered why he's gone off into the woods leading an attack that should be the job of some captain?"

"You think he's going to *cross?*"

"He may. He just may. Takes two of the best companies. They'll be his personal bodyguard back to India."

"You'd be in command."

"He took no radios?"

"No."

"We're crossing tomorrow night. With or without him."

The four clearings were so small the guns pointed vertically to clear the treetops. In the twilight, the artillery looked well tended. There was little ammunition to be seen, and apart from some perfunctory cleaning the Japanese seemed idle, waiting for trucks to bring up more shells.

The trucks could arrive at any time. Wingate had to move fast, but his little command had not been responsive. Their march was more a shuffle even with light loads. Men were coughing, constantly coughing; Wingate had to send a dozen back to the river. And these men were in the best shape of all the Chindits.

"This is all going to be very simple," Wingate explained when his force found the artillery. "Lynch blocks the roads while Briggs walks through the batteries. No shooting unless fired upon. Drop one grenade down each tube, then assemble on Lynch's flashlight. Head for the river. Leave tracks going south, then get in the river and wade upstream to North Force. Questions?" There were none. The two captains moved back to pass on the plan to their platoon leaders.

His legs felt like a blend of lead and rubber. He slumped against a tree, looking back at the direction from which the Chindits would be coming. His head bobbed wearily. He fought sleep but then gave in—certain someone would wake him as the attack line formed. Wingate's last thought was that there might be some rice in the Japanese camp.

He was sprawled on the ground, his clothes stiff with sweat. Exhaustion and discomfort competed for his consciousness. An oily film of grime smothered his pores; his toes and crotch itched to a burn.

He came awake dully, reluctantly, struggling for orientation. Trees above him like an English park. Luminous pinpoints rose out of the darkness—2:18 A.M.

"My God!"

The attack! He had briefed Lynch and Briggs around 11:00 P.M. For a moment he imagined they had left him.

A gravelly snore both reassured and infuriated him. The Chindits had literally fallen in their tracks. The attack line was asleep, every captain, sergeant, and private, all within fifty yards of the Japanese. They had slept through H hour and two hours more.

Through his rage, he had to smile. He laughed silently, imagining a great oil painting in the Imperial War Museum, a polished brass plaque identifying "The Attack at Satsa," showing the Chindits in heroic sleep.

Wingate crawled down the line nudging the soldiers more gently than he felt. Under such conditions a man could awake with a cry if he were jolted into consciousness. The squad leaders apologized. Lynch and Briggs were contrite, and the Chindits seemed ready to go back to war.

Utter peace had pervaded the forest while they and the artillerymen slept, a peace which also lulled the Japanese sentries and numbed the moonless night. The clearings were patches of lighter darkness in the black of the forest. Until the Chindits crept closer they could not make out the outlines of the guns.

Leading the attack were the stealth killers, two men ahead of each platoon with a blackjack in one hand, commando knife in the other. They would pick off a sentry if they could, one man stunning with his blackjack, his partner stabbing with his knife.

A dog proved to be the best Japanese sentry. His sudden bark triggered a sheet of fire that caroomed off the cannons and filled the night with sparks and metallic ringing.

Two, three muffled explosions as the grenades blasted the cannons' bores. Finally the fourth—the job was done. Wingate searched for Lynch's signal light. It appeared, but the Chindits seemed to ignore it. The firing had stopped, the Japanese were cut down, but the Chindits were rooting through their camp like boars.

"Move on! Move on, you louts. This isn't a cafeteria!"

Men rallied on the flashlight, carrying handfuls of rice like snowballs.

Two Chindits dead; four wounded, one hopelessly with a bullet in his lung. His squad strapped together a litter with rifles and slings.

A compass azimuth was set for the river. A half hour of fast marching before they heard the deep-throated murmur of the river. On its bank the force turned south, leaving plenty of boot prints, then out into the water for the first quarter mile north.

For a moment the wading stopped. The man with the lung wound had died. Standing in the water his squad untied the slings, converting the litter to weapons again. As if in farewell the body lingered awash in the waves, then drifted away as his squad splashed on against the stream.

73

"What's going on out there, gentlemen?"

Wavell had called for a full briefing on the Chindits before he met the press. Slim and his staff were drawn up before him but they had little to tell. Blue symbols locating the three Chindit forces on the map were half the story; the rest was the cluster of Japanese flags around them.

"South Force is continuing east," Brigadier Arden stated, "while North and Central seem to have returned to the river. Based on Kane's request for an uncontrolled drop on the Meza, we suppose they plan to recross."

"Uncontrolled?" Wavell asked.

"Yes, sir. A bomber free-fall again. No signal fire."

"Can you get that for him?"

"We never contemplated Wingate employing bombers as transports," said Arden. "We are very reluctant to use them in that way. Cochran is willing but we need every B25 to drop bombs in the Arakan, sir, not rations in north Burma."

"I don't think Kane would ask for them if they weren't in serious trouble. Bill, I hope you can find a way."

"We shall, sir."

"Now what do you make of Dalton? He was the most seriously engaged; now he's merrily marching east while the rest are slinking back to the river."

"We've requested a clarification of intentions, sir," said Arden, "but we haven't heard from any of them in twenty-four hours."

"Doesn't sound good."

"Personally I think Orde's about to be pushed into the river. I'll admit Dalton's movements confuse me."

"Does Orde still have the boat engines we sent him?" asked Wavell.

"We don't know," said Johns. "He rarely advises us of such details."

"Now, the last two drops—they went to Dalton?"

"Yes, sir. Only one was a resupply, the other a deception drop well to the south."

"I hope Kawabe is as confused as I am. Gentlemen..." Wavell groped for the right words, "up to now the only good news I've been able to report from this theater have been the exploits of the Chindits. I've not exaggerated them but nonetheless they've captured Churchill's imagination. As you're well aware; the press interest is also intense. To be perfectly frank, the Mercury operations have diverted attention from our flounderings in the Arakan. For this I believe we can all be grateful. Bill, I think we must contemplate some sort of relief effort if our worst fears come to pass. I realize we can't mount an expedition to penetrate hundreds of miles of jungle, but I want some plans, some evidence that we are more than remote spectators. I also realize how precious our air assets are at the moment, but I can't exaggerate the importance of the Chindits either."

"We very much share your concern, sir," Slim replied. "At the moment transports don't seem to be what the Chindits need."

"General Wavell," said Arden, consulting his figures, "of thirty-five aerial requests received from the Chindits, thirty-four have been provided. The one exception was a drop of 105 shells at Pinlebu that would have fallen into Japanese hands."

"I very much appreciate your support to date. Don't let your efforts flag for a moment. Innovate. Please innovate. We simply can't leave the Chindits out on a limb."

"Colonel Johns had a suggestion, sir," said Slim. "Allen."

"Sir Archie, the Chindits are really an experimental unit as we all appreciate. As such, we don't know if we've been giving them all the monitoring they deserve. That is, we've not yet sent in anyone to look them over, see what sort of shape they're in. I imagine they're much more tired than Orde would admit."

"Drop someone in with a resupply, you mean?"

"Perhaps one to each force."

"Anyone in particular?"

"I would suggest three colonels from your headquarters, sir. They'd carry more weight—with Wingate anyway."

"That could be awkward. How would they report their findings?"

"Code perhaps."

"Work up the details."

"I hope there's time," said Slim.

"How do you mean?"

"If things are as bad as they might be, Wingate may Buckshot the Chindits in the next twenty-four hours." Wavell arched his brows. "Disperse them, that is: every man for himself."

"Wouldn't we have some forewarning?"

"Not necessarily. Not from Wingate."

"In such an eventuality—Buckshot, if you will—I don't want the press to know of it. I realize the mutual confidence you have with the correspondents here, but I cannot have any word of potential disaster leaking to London. Tell them the Chindits are embarking on a new phase in the expedition that is of utmost secrecy. Drop the curtain. If they don't appreciate it, too bad."

"Understood, General Wavell."

"Well now, I very much hope we're being alarmists about this. Dalton seems to be making good progress."

"I might point out, sir, that he's marching right out of range of the transports," said Arden.

Wavell caught Slim's eye. "I never liked that part of the plan." Slim nodded. "Now if Wingate were to Buckshot, would that turn Dalton around?"

"Buckshot is really a contingency tactic," said Johns, "rather than a detailed plan. The three forces, I'm sure, would consult on the specifics. South Force might well return as a unit rather than in small groups. Things like that Wingate, F-B, and Dalton would work out on the brigade net."

"Which we can't monitor...I suppose."

"No, sir."

Wavell leaned forward in his chair, his chin on his knuckles. "Bill, if Buckshot comes to pass, I'd like you to send an inspector out as Johns suggests—drop him in on Dalton. I must have at least one of the forces come back relatively intact. Now let's hope Wingate is just up to another of his surprises. I felt much this way before Pinlebu."

Wavell rose. Slim and his staff came to their feet and saluted. As Sir Archie went on to meet the press, Slim touched Johns's arm.

"You're the inspector," said Slim. Johns stiffened as the color left his face.

74

Two hours behind schedule, the Satsa force marched toward the thump of Fox-Boynton's mortars, hurrying to beat the dawn.

Since midnight mortar shells had been dropping on two impact areas where the Japanese positions were a half mile apart. Wingate was orienting his force to pass between the two, using the mortar shellings as boundaries. He was in high spirits. The Satsa attack had been just what he needed: a cause for renewed self-confidence and a boost for Chindit morale. His own conduct in the Indaung had almost shocked him. Using his own standards as those of others, he was certain he had lost stature.

Now, as he gave his company commanders their last instructions, he felt and appeared like the Wingate of Pinlebu.

"I remind you this is a unique little exercise: we're breaking through from the Japanese rear to regain our own lines. There are three principal hazards. First, we must avoid contact until we reach the impact areas. We expect the Japs there to have their heads down. Remember, the mortars fire for five minutes at fifteen-minute intervals. When they stop you go between them. Second, we must clear as wide as swath as possible. Once we head for Fox-Boynton, our backs are to the Japs, so we must *clear* the area between the two impact areas. The third hazard is Fox-Boynton's fire. They're expecting us, but for God's sake be sure to pop your signal flares when you head in. I'll stay with Lynch. Questions?"

"When North Force hears us open up," said Briggs, "won't they stop the mortars?"

"I'm sorry. Yes, that's quite right."

"We do have more than fifteen minutes then?"

"Yes."

"I'm ready."

"So am I," said Lynch.

"Surprise will get us through, gentlemen. Take everything with a rush."

The Satsa force was a mile from each of the two impact areas when Lynch and Briggs split. Through the ghostly haze of predawn the men slinked from tree to tree like American Indians about to attack a fort.

Wingate stayed with the right flank of Lynch's company, which would swing like a gate when the attack began, as would Briggs's left flank. Wingate would be at the center, where he could prevent a gap forming between them.

The Chindits moved fast during the five-minute mortar barrages, returning to high stealth during the silence. The shelling was in quantity, reassuring quantity. Fox-Boynton was not husbanding shells for mortars that would never recross the Irrawaddy.

The Chindit shadows suddenly merged with the trees. Wingate strained his ears. He could hear nothing, yet the Gurkha riflemen beside him seemed to follow with his eyes something his ears were tracking. It was off to the left but coming closer.

Three cracks of a rifle in close succession. The clattering tin of a Japanese food kit. A low whistle, and the Chindits moved on in a running crouch.

A bullet snapped through the trees from Briggs's direction. "Jap!" said the Gurkha. Wingate nodded. That wasn't good. They had apparently seen Briggs before he had seen them. But then silence.

When the mortaring resumed, he could see the dark outlines of the treetops shake. It was the signal for a flurry of fire from his right, then to his front, then rippling to his left across Lynch's line. Japanese and British weapons stuttered at each other.

He heard the faraway drum of a Vickers, the heaviest machine gun in North Force, a strategem by Fox-Boynton to make the Japanese think they were being attacked from the front.

Lynch's men broke into a run, converging on the Japanese fire. Wingate waved his men toward the center, but he could get no one's attention as the Gurkhas filled the forest with their war cries.

Briggs's men had converged like bees on a pair of machine gun nests. Wingate could see nothing of them, though dawn had imperceptibly settled under the trees. They had run into more than expected and maybe more than Briggs could handle.

A yellow flare arched into the trees from Lynch's side and hung
smoldering in the branches. The success signal was corroborated by
waning battle sounds from Lynch's attack. It appeared his company
would soon link up with North Force.

The two Gurkha squads with Wingate belonged to Lynch but were
now fighting the Japanese from Briggs's sector. Wingate slipped away
to find Lynch and have him bring his whole company over.

Unarmed as always, Wingate moved from tree to tree as bullets slugged
into the trunks. His pith helmet spun to the ground, a hot black crease
across the visor. He dodged to the next tree. He looked revived, he felt
renewed, as if the deflected bullet had signaled the return of divine favor.

The battle was silently intensifying on Briggs's side. North Force could
hear the fire subside as British and Japanese stalked each other; then
even the rifles went quiet as both sides fought with grenades.

The boom of grenades still sounded intermittently when Wingate
reached a North Force outpost. The Chindits hailed him nonchalantly,
as if their commander regularly appeared out of the forest with a bullet crease in his visor. He drank half a canteen as he waited for a guide
to take him to Fox-Boynton.

"Where the hell have you been?" was Fox-Boynton's greeting.

"Detained. What's happened with Briggs?"

"I think he hit the Japs as they were about to attack me."

"You may be right. Try the trumpet."

"Damn! Should have thought of that."

A bugler was summoned. Stories from the Burma Corps in 1941
related that the Japanese often attacked to a bugle call. Each Chindit
column had trained a bugler to imitate Japanese calls such as "charge"
and "withdraw."

"Which command should we give them?" Fox-Boynton asked.

"Well if they've planned to attack, it was probably to take your
Vickers. I suppose we should sound "withdraw" unless you're ready
for them."

"We're ready."

A former trombone player from Liverpool was given his instructions; armed only with a Japanese bugle, he followed a squad of bodyguards toward the battle. A half hour passed while the Japanese seemed

to be gaining the upper hand; then martial notes like a teutonic hunting call quavered in the forest.

It was followed by a short pause; then the Japanese guns went silent.

A slow minute passed; then the call went up again, repeating as it
drew toward North Force. Suddenly scattered shouts supported the bugle; the ground seemed to sprout Japanese.

The charge was on. North Force awaited it, but the Japanese were
almost upon them before the Vickers roared in chorus. Their fire crisscrossed the front but the charge appeared immortal.

They came from trenches and pits so exquisitely camouflaged that
the earth seemed to eject them. They came with bayonets, waving
swords, and battle flags. They came on and they fell as if on a wheel
that revolved them back into life. Wingate and Fox-Boynton shared
the protection of a thick trunk which began to shred. A Japanese grenade set Wingate's ears ringing. "More than we could have hoped for!"

"Much more!"

"Bloody good luck, Adrian, coming on their attack that way. They'll
pull off when this is done. We'll cross the Irrawaddy as if it were the
Serpentine."

75

Amid piles of smoking cartridges the Vickers ruled the forest. There
were still Japanese to be killed but the slaughter was over. A hundred
and fifty of their dead spread like high water traces on a beach. Scattered among them were twenty-four British bodies like flotsam left by
the tide.

One of them was not a Chindit. A white man, probably a prisoner
from Burma Corps, was found with his hands tied among a heap of
Japanese around their command post. It was easy to guess why he
was there. The Japanese apparently planned to have him cry out in the

At the Irrawaddy. (*Courtesy Imperial War Museum.*)

night like a wounded Chindit. When his plea was answered by North Force, Japanese grenadiers would follow him into the British lines.

This man was not a volunteer for his captors. His ears had been sliced into strips that hung down like locks of hair. The Japanese had started on his nose when they were interrupted by Briggs's attack.

Briggs would lead no others. Four men brought him back, each holding a corner of a Japanese ground sheet. His company fell in behind the cortege, oblivious to the rifle fire that still cracked behind them, while the men of North Force watched numbly. Wingate joined the procession as it moved back to the Irrawaddy.

The riverbank that had resounded with saws and axes became silent. Wingate nodded to the carpenters: work on the rafts had to continue, for the crossing must begin that night while the Japanese recoiled from their defeat.

In his story of the expedition, Kane recalled the remainder of the day:

We were submerged in contradictory emotions. There was the early satisfied babble of men who had won in a difficult and daring way, dampened as always by the cost of the victory. Briggs's loss was like no other. It represented a vanished *capability* for the Chindits, something as valuable and a loss as great as if our aerial resupplies had been canceled; something which could not be replaced by bravery or fortitude. Briggs was more than a man, more than a leader. He was an assurance that nothing was impossible if he were involved with it.

The results from Satsa could not long be savored. "Dispersal groups" were formed to internally balance our strengths and weaknesses so that each group would have equal chance of surviving the ordeal ahead. This meant parceling out the Burma Rifles, the wounded, the top swimmers, officers, and NCOs in equal measure. Consequently, units which had trained, marched, and fought together for months were broken up and reassembled into dispersal groups averaging fifty men. This resulted in some extreme personal dislocations, and were we not all Chindits, brothers by the name we shared, there might have been rebellion, but each of us knew that every man who had come this far was a worthy companion for the rest of the journey....

With a permanent pain in my heart masked by whatever confidence I could feign, I presided over the devolution of the expedition. First there was the destruction of equipment we could not take on our backs. Mortars, radios, machine guns which had been our crushing burdens over Casten's Trace disappeared into the Irrawaddy. Then came the task of destroying our companions. Beasts they are called and we had called them worse at the Chindwin, but they had come to be treasured friends in the jungle.

The mules were dispatched with a single shot to the forehead. This was done privately as if by some unspoken convention, each muleteer leading his animal into the forest for a solitary farewell. Many returned weeping. From that moment I think some lost heart and hence their lives in the privations to come....

Amid such depressing and disheartening activity, Wingate was severely taxed to spark our spirits. There are two indelible recollections
of him from that last day on the eastern shore. One was the service he
recited over the dead as they lay shrouded with fronds. Briggs was
before him on a makeshift bier as he recited the Psalms. He took the
DSO from his own tunic and pinned it on Briggs. Wingate, Fox-
Boynton, Bradshaw, and myself then carried the body to the river as
others brought the remaining dead.

The other unforgettable memory was even more wrenching. This was
Wingate's call for the terminally wounded. When they were assembled he explained their fate. Not that they didn't know what was to
become of them—that was all too clear from the circumstances. He
asked that they have their mail ready in an hour; then he read a message he would leave with Lieutenant Kincaid, the ranking officer
among them. It was addressed to the Japanese commander. In simple and soldierly terms Wingate stated that these wounded had fought
for their king and country just as the Japanese were doing. He expressed his admiration for the code of Bushido, which requires that
the wounded be treated with respect.

It was a message of moving dignity but its reception was mixed.
Some men asked for grenades to take some Japs with them. Others
were emotionally unhinged. Several cried for lethal injections but
morphine had to be rationed for other men and for the days ahead.

I remember thinking how private an experience is death, that there
can be no consensus, no agreed way or common route for the passage. We die as we have lived, in our personal way, expressing
the personality we have developed. . . .

Stunned, nearly disarmed, unprovisioned, and weakened, we waited
for our commander's last message to us as a group. He did not speak
of desperate retreat, though that was what we were commencing. He
did not dwell on the perils, though no unit in our condition ever
attempted such a perilous crossing. He did not mention the hardships ahead or the destination of all our hopes. He spoke as if the last
phase of his plan were unfolding on schedule and as anticipated. I
quote his words as I wrote them down in the dusk:

"From the beginning our plans included the probability that the
expedition might exfiltrate after having done its work. This work

we have accomplished in greater measure than anyone, even myself, expected. We have succeeded collectively because each of you individually has overcome the fears and doubts that daunt lesser men. The qualities you have demonstrated will shortly be tested by new challenges, but just as you crossed the Chindwin, just as you ruptured the railroad, just as you passed through impassable jungle and over one of the world's great rivers, you will surpass yourself in the weeks ahead.

"This last phase of our expedition is indeed the final proof of its concept. At Imphal, when Mercury was about to be canceled, I told Field Marshal Wavell that if need be we could become lightly armed guerrillas, and like guerrillas skip back to our base in India. We have planned for this contingency, we have trained for it, we are prepared for it through our months in the jungle, so now we say 'we are ready' and ready we are.

"'Embark then with me upon the waters.'"

There remained one major piece of equipment to be dumped into the water—the brigade radio. Kane assumed Wingate would send a final message to Slim and Dalton. He did: a single-word message, "Buckshot." The ciphers were then burned, the crystals smashed, and the heavy set heaved over the waves to vanish in a plunging splash.

"A little late to be telling Dalton, don't you think?" Fox-Boynton asked.

"Do you think so?"

"Now he has to recross the Indaung."

"Not necessarily. He can pick any route he likes."

"Except west."

"He's close enough to the Kachins now. They can help him, especially with guides."

"He'll never get out of this forest and you know it!"

"Don't underestimate Dalton."

"I don't. My mistake has been in overestimating you."

"I can understand why you would say that. I'd simply ask you to reserve judgment till we're back in India."

"Yes, judgment will come in India. Be ready for yours."

"Good luck, Adrian. Hope to see you on the other side."

"I don't know what I hope for you. Your greatest service to us might be to miss one of the islands. I believe in *De mortius nil nisi bonum.*"

"No, you owe it to both the record and the future of the Chindits to state your opinion of my tactics, whether I be dead or alive. If I erred, let the truth be known that it was my tactical error in the field, not a flaw in the concept of LRP."

"What concept provides for betraying Dalton?"

"Adrian, we both have too little energy to waste in acrimony. Say what you will, when you will, and let Dalton do likewise. I fear no judgment except Jehovah's."

76

The bend of the Irrawaddy appeared as a loop of silk on dark felt. The only lights in the night were the exhaust jets of the C47. Over the left engine Johns peered down at the junction of the Shweli and the Irrawaddy. The huge peninsula they formed were the boundaries of the Indaung Forest, a synonym for the noose into which Wingate had thrust the expedition. Now Johns was about to join the most exposed of all the Chindits: South Force, which had reported continuous combat almost from the time they entered the Indaung.

It was Wingate's Buckshot which put Johns into the parachute straps that cut into his new jungle uniform. Somehow he was to help South Force get out in one piece.

Small help he expected to be. If anyone in the Far East could extricate South Force, it was the man leading them now. Dalton was not thinking in terms of Wingate's "dispersal groups"; South Force was keeping its columns together, falling back, fighting, even digging in when necessary, and demanding heavy equipment for the new warfare of the open forest.

First Dalton called for five hundred shovels and bigger mortars. Now he wanted howitzers and antitank guns to go after Japanese trucks.

He had determined that the 412th Japanese Brigade was in the forest with him. They had two motorized battalions and two on foot, one of which Wingate had mauled at Satsa. That left the odds against Dalton at three to one; before the Japanese pushed reinforcements into the Indaung, Dalton thought he could pick off the trucks in a baited ambush. If he could wreck his pursuers' vehicles before he broke out of the forest, he could take any direction and melt into the jungles beyond the Shweli.

Johns peered down into the darkness. Three minutes to drop, the pilot announced; yet there were no signal fires below. Then five of them, forming a T, flickered on. Johns looked for red flashes of gunfire but the forest seemed at peace.

The plane lurched forward as the tow line detached. Parachute bundles slithered toward the tail; the nose tipped up as Johns groped down the bulkhead toward the rushing wind. The suction caught him; a step into space and he was gone in the propeller blast. It flung him upside down before his 'chute jolted into its dome. He saw the T for an instant; then his feet crashed through the treetops.

"Well, of all the things I needed, you weren't one of them," was Dalton's greeting. "I could have had three cases of K's for your weight."

"Sorry, Bruce. Just trying to help."

"I hope you brought some rum."

"With the compliments of Bill Slim."

Johns in fact brought Dalton four bottles, knowing he was less than welcome, not just for the scarce food he replaced but because of their earlier acquaintance in Burma Corps. In Mandalay Dalton openly expressed his contempt for Johns after the "Pagoda spotter" incident.

Dalton took all four bottles, gave them to his wounded, and left Johns to fend for himself the rest of the night as South Force distributed the supplies. The plentiful noise and shouting, the casual use of flashlights, surprised the visitor, who assumed the Chindits lived like hunted fugitives.

His first night on a ground sheet left Johns stiff and sore. He awoke to the steady sounds of digging. Now and then an azimuth was called out into the forest, sending a surveyor scurrying left or right as the new artillery was sited. Johns wandered about gathering impressions while taking care not to disturb anyone in their work.

But another colonel joining South Force was not overlooked by the Chindits. Sleepy eyes popped open to see his epaulets and fresh uniform. Without being told, the men sensed he was among them to gauge their esprit, so he was offered many chipper greetings and parade ground salutes. It was easy for him to ask questions. His first was, where were the Japanese? No one seemed much concerned, though preparations for their arrival was the sole activity.

Feeling like a bewildered cadet, Johns sneaked off by a tree to try his first K rations—brick-sized chunks of concentrated nutrition provided by the Americans to "promote Allied cooperation and constipation," as Fox-Boynton once described the rock-hard rations. Among the Chindits, one K had to stretch over twenty-four hours, though sometimes there was local rice to supplement it.

Zachary, Dalton's sergeant major, could see that Johns was being treated like an untrusted stranger rather than an important guest. Before Johns broke open his meal, Zachary approached him.

"Ah, there you are, sir. Won't you join the officers for breakfast?"

"Thank you very much, Sergeant Major," said Johns, as if he had been invited to tea with the duke of Kent.

Dalton, his two column commanders, and his operations officer were sitting on the bank of a newly excavated bunker that seemed to be the South Force command post.

"Sleep well?" Dalton asked, barely noticing his arrival.

"Quite well, thank you. Gentlemen."

"You know Oxley, York, Driscoll?"

"Sir, if you'd like to shave," said Sergeant Major Zachary, "the medical station is beyond about two hundred yards. Water's boiled for the surgical instruments."

"I see. Thank you, but beards seem to be the fashion in the Indaung Forest."

"One canteen per day. Use it any way you like," said Dalton.

"Your men seem extremely fit and alert for the circumstances."

"They're not. One of the reasons we're digging in is because we're marched out."

"So this shall be South Force's last stand, so to speak?" The chocolate bar nearly cracked his teeth. Johns looked around to throw it away.

"Don't want that?" York exclaimed.

"Why...no. I'm afraid I've bitten into it."

York took it from him eagerly and rewrapped it.

"Yes," Dalton answered as if there had been no interruption, "this will be our last stand, win or lose. Those 105s you brought along—they're a surprise for Yakamura. I hope Slim understands."

"You'll spike the guns, of course, when you pull out."

Dalton nodded. "We expect the Japs to arrive sometime tomorrow night. They'll probe us a bit, then attack at dawn. We get them or they get us."

"What's keeping them back?"

"Nash and Pettigrew."

"Two companies?" Dalton nodded. "They'll lead Yakamura into your ambush I suppose."

"Not just into it but through it," Oxley replied. "We must get the trucks, you see, or Yakamura can chase us forever." He drew a large U on the ground with a stick. "We must allow them to break out of the bottom here like it was another fallback position. When their infantry goes on in pursuit, their trucks will follow and we'll get them from both sides."

"Then we'll need a major drop," said Dalton, "about ten miles north."

"You plan to cross the Shweli?"

"Near Hinlo."

"That puts you out of resupply range."

"That's why I said our next drop will be a *major* one. I don't expect another for maybe two weeks. You can get busy right now on the cipher pad. You're my acting supply officer. I need hay—a lot of hay—I know it's bulky but there's no forage this side of the Shweli."

"What do you know about the other side?"

"Not much. That's why I need the Kachins. Are they waiting for us?"

Johns's face drained. "I haven't a clue."

"What?"

"You've never asked about the Kachins."

"From the time we crossed the Irrawaddy the plan was always to link up with the fuckin' Kachins."

"That was Wingate's plan." Johns looked around as if he would prefer to continue the discussion privately. Dalton ignored his signal.

"Yes," he said, "and we're proceeding with his plan. You'd better talk with Evans. Tell him to put us in touch with the Kachins or jump in here and do it himself."

"Bruce, the plan is now Buckshot—head for home."

"I am heading for home. It's just that the rude Japanese are blocking my preferred route."

"Where do you expect to cross the Irrawaddy?"

"Where the Kachins recommend. They're going to guide us, dear fellow. That's what they do best."

"I think it'll be Zissel Island," said York. "I did some work up there with the school."

"My God, the Japs are thick as flies around Katha," Johns protested.

"They're pretty thick around here," said Oxley.

"You expect to go forty, sixty miles—maybe more—on one drop?"

"That's why we need the Kachins, Allen. Glad we've got you now. You're just the man to work this out," said Dalton, scooping the last grain of rice from his tin.

"After we chuck Yakamura," said Oxley, "we were going to send a patrol straight into the Kachin Hills."

"Would you like a go at that, Allen?" Dalton asked.

"Let me get on the radio to Evans. Anything else I should know about your plans?"

Oxley answered, "If we go out over Zissel Island, we'd take the next resupply in the Tri Range. And Bruce is giving some thought to recutting the railroad on the way to the Meza. That's about as far ahead as we're looking."

"Of course, we're ready to coordinate with Wingate as he withdraws," Dalton added.

Johns looked at the four officers. "Don't you know what he's doing?"

"Buckshot—same as us, right?" said Driscoll, matter-of-factly.

"Hardly! His buckshot is to break up both forces. Break up into bands of fugitives." To Johns's amazement, the officers laughed. "Frankly, fellows, he's leaving you here in the lurch. Coordinate with Wingate? I think by now his radios are at the bottom of the Irrawaddy."

Dalton rose and brushed the dirt off his rump. "I suppose he'll go down the Menlo Valley. He'll be in the lurch as much as us."

77

The dispersal groups were to embark a mile above the first stepping-stone. While the current swept them downstream, they would swim laterally a quarter mile to make landfall on the first island. Lesser lateral distances separated the remaining stepping-stones until the last, which was another quarter mile from the western bank.

For the crossing each ten-man group had five tabletop-sized rafts lashed together with vines. On these went the rifles and uniforms, leaving the men like ten tugs pulling five barges. A good swimmer with each "flotilla," as Wingate called them, controlled the last raft to prevent a broadside turn in the stream.

The best swimmers had gone ahead to man flashlights on each island. To demonstrate his confidence in the whole endeavor, Wingate's flotilla went first. Au Thang smiled bravely as he clutched the vine. He had crossed the Chindwin on an elephant and he felt much more at home there. The Gurkhas too had little swimming experience from the Himalayas.

A pinpoint of light appeared almost on the wavetops, the beacon for the first island. "There 'tis," said Wingate. He splashed in to knee depth, then raised his pith helmet to those ashore. His gesture was returned by some applause, laughter, and whistles at his nakedness.

"Full ahead starboard," were the last words many were to hear him say.

"Looks like they're tangled already," Kane muttered as the bobbing heads and rafts swirled into the darkness. He would see off all the remaining hundred flotillas. They launched themselves quickly.

With the strap tightly around his chin, Wingate's pith helmet guided his swimmers. "All right back there?" he shouted. "Count off." Each man repeated his number to the swimmer ahead of him till Wingate heard "two!"

He kicked and pulled on the vine; it seemed to go nowhere except downstream. The light grew no closer, and in the waves he frequently lost it. Only the receding shoreline gave any feeling of progress.

There would be no moon for five hours, then only a quarter. By then everyone should be on the last island, weakened by the long immersion, and with no calories to replace what they shivered away. There were only six K rations per raft. The Chindits would be like wet, naked infants coming into the world needing immediate protection and nourishment, but there would be little.

Instead there would be jungle and Japanese. That was the promise of the narrow, dark border of the opposite shore.

"All right back there? Count off!"

Ten, nine, eight, seven...multiplied by a hundred flotillas. Each life a number, each number a life following the pith helmet. A thread of humanity pulled by a needle, the needle pulled by a magnet...of what? The question came upon him as a mass of tangled branches loomed ahead. Like such flotsam, the question was prickly, half-submerged, and much to be avoided.

"Swimming far offshore brings me questions I never would think of otherwise." Wingate recalled Lorna's words from her last letter, the one that arrived on the seaplane carrying the outboards for the Chindits to cross the Irrawaddy. To cross the Irrawaddy—how confidently he had considered the question, how totally he had relied on his genius.

"Swimming far offshore..." was how Lorna prefaced her thoughts on what she would do if he were lost in the war. "If I imagine it now, I feel I'll be better prepared if it happens. Do you find that morbid?" No he didn't; not at all, not in the flood of the Irrawaddy.

"Sir...sir! Dawa..."

A shaven head glistening...a Gurkha...a hand...gone.

Something bobbed once far ahead. The river rolled on through the night.

"Count off."

"Ten,..., eight, seven, six..." The missing man was indeed one of the two Gurkhas. There was hope. The first island was close enough to see the silhouette of the guide behind his flashlight. The flotilla was dead on course for the spit where he stood.

Wingate's feet searched for the bottom; it was steep and felt like clay. He shouted for the guide to sweep his light over the racing water. What happened? he asked the number-ten man.

"Think his feet tangled! Underwater debris."

The light coned out on the river, revealing its muddy color and the shapes of wooden matter floating swiftly by like icebergs. A figure ran down the beach. It was the lost Gurkha's companion.

"He's from Dawa's village, sir."

"Wrap up in the grass and get warm. When you're ready start searching the beach."

"Can we look for Dawa now, sir?"

"All right, but don't get lost. Take a count every ten minutes. "And don't go back in the water for anyone. Look for a long branch to..."

"Flotilla, sir!" the guide called out.

Writhing like some great water snake, five rafts bore down on the spit. "Right, pull right!" the guide shouted. Hands splashed in the water, then clutched for shore. The rafts and vines curled around the spit; before the flotilla was ashore the next came under the light.

The scene began to resemble an amphibious invasion. Rafts were jerked out of the way of oncoming flotillas. Vines became safety lines flung to rafts drifting wide of the island. Groups formed to sweep the beaches, others to tow their flotillas to the opposite end of the island for the next launching.

"Looks like a seagull rookery," said Fox-Boynton as he came ashore; when his flotilla landed, the island was a nocturnal study in teeming white. Fox-Boynton looked for the pith helmet but learned Wingate had gone on to the next island. The reason seemed clear when the sergeant major gave him the report: out of fifty flotillas, all had arrived except numbers sixteen, nineteen, and thirty-four.

"He said for you to take command till Major Kane arrives, sir."

Fox-Boynton nodded. Thirty men lost not counting individuals pulled off their rafts. He remembered asking Wingate how many he expected to lose. "Can't guess. No experience factor," had been the reply. "I suppose we'll do well with five percent."

Five percent: one man from every other flotilla, one rifle unclaimed on a raft, one less division of the rations. Fox-Boynton could see the ruthless logistics of Buckshot developing. He could imagine Wingate lecturing at Woolwich about "Military Darwinism in Exfiltration" or some such grand concept that would entrance his audience. Wingate would demonstrate rationality while Fox-Boynton remembered the naked Gurkha scouring the shoreline like a dog that had lost its master.

"So I'm in command on bare-arse island, am I?" said Fox-Boynton, as if to no one.

The sergeant major looked at him quizzically. "Why yes, sir. Those were his instructions."

"When does he want the final count from here?"

"Don't know that he does, sir. Was that in the plan?"

Fox-Boynton shook his head. "I wish I could do what he does."

"What's that, sir?"

"Not count the casualties till the campaign is over."

78

As Dalton predicted, the main Japanese attack came at dawn, though the battle approached South Force all the previous day as two of his companies retreated toward the ambush. There they held, only to be broken when the full weight of Yakamura's force caught up and pounced upon them like hounds on a fox. From the bunker Johns could hear the famous "banzai" of the attackers, the answering sputter of the Chindits' rifles, the duel of grenades.

Before the British and Japanese became too entangled, Dalton struck with the weight of his new artillery. It thundered down on friend and foe alike, but the defenders were protected by the emplacements dug for them by South Force. The 105s shook and splintered the trees as the Chindits cheered for more.

Smoky dust settled on the shattered attack as gloom settled on the Chindit commanders: no trucks had been lured into the artillery ambush. Yakamura could replace his dead, and when they were mounted again the chase would be on once more.

Rifles still punctuated the morning with single shots as each fallen Japanese soldier was drilled through the head. No one noticed Johns leaving the bunker as Dalton huddled with his commanders over new plans.

Johns strolled toward the base of the ambush. He started to cross through the shattered trees when Sergeant Major Zachary called after him.

"Wait a bit, sir. Let me give you an escort. Some Japs die pretty hard, you know."

"Much obliged."

A silent Gurkha and a gaunt Liverpooler joined Johns. They soon came upon smoldering Japanese bodies. The two Chindits took turns on watch as the other frisked the dead for rice.

"Now here's some luck!" said the Liverpooler. "This bloke must have been carrying rice for the whole squad. You want a third, sir?"

"No thank you. Please split my...share."

"Much obliged indeed." They came upon another fragmentary corpse. Whatever hit him had blasted his rice around like confetti. "Looks like a ruddy wedding, aye, sir?" Johns smiled faintly. "Looks like they *all* had a couple 'a pounds apiece. They were ready for a long march—that's my guess."

"Artillery make big mess," the Gurkha grumbled, picking the dirt from a fistful of rice.

"Would you mind taking these grenades, sir? We'll give them back to the Japs in due course."

"Gladly." They walked on searching for rice and grenades.

"Were either of you in Burma Corps?"

"No sir."

"This is most remarkable."

"What's that, sir?"

"The Japs were terrifying."

"They still haven't been to Sunday school, sir."

"No, but here we are—here *you* are—picking through them like carcasses in a slaughterhouse. You Chindits have very much broken a spell, do you know that?"

"We kill Japs," said the Gurkha.

"You certainly do. In the Arakan I don't know that we've killed this many in a month."

"You need some Chindits down there," said the Liverpooler.

"Yes, if we ever get you out."

The two Chindits fell silent. When Johns reached the bottom of the U, which the Japanese had nearly overrun, he saw what the greatest difficulty would be in getting the Chindits out—the wounded.

The two column physicians were working among them with professional desperation. Johns recognized their procedure as triage, a sort-
ing of injuries according to three degrees of severity, which in
nonmedical terms were hopeless, possible recovery, and probable recovery. What jarred Johns was that the attention seemed to be nearly
exclusively on the "probables."

The hopeless were deeply sedated, hardly able to recognize the chaplain who crouched over them.

"Religion?" he asked. Depending on the answer, the chaplain drew
one of three cards from his pocket and read the appropriate service.

"Colonel Johns." It was a voice among the "possibles," one of thirty
who made up the largest triage group. Johns looked among them. "Sergeant Vance, sir." He recognized the name of a man who had worked
in his section in India; he recognized the voice but it was weak, and
no one in the emaciated rows on the ground resembled the Vance he
remembered. "Over here. To your left, sir."

Vance was a shriveled figure with one leg ending at the knee. Johns
shuddered as he had when he saw his first mutilated beggar in Calcutta.

"Harry," he murmured, squatting down beside Vance, who was
propped against a tree. He smiled, slowly showing teeth that had gone
brown from neglect.

"Wouldn't have a fag, would you, sir?"

"Certainly." Johns lit a cigarette for him. "Anything else?" He
put his hand to his canteen. Vance nodded. Water was too scarce to
advertise; all the wounded were thirsty. Vance drank deeply.

"Wasn't expectin' to see you again, sir." Johns searched for a reply
but none came. "What brings you out to the legion of the lost?"

"Slim's doing his best to get you out."

"Give him my regards, won't you, sir?"

"I promise."

Vance inhaled deeply. "Doc says I shouldn't smoke. Circulation. I
got gangrene. Don't matter now. I won't be leavin' Burma."

"When were you...hit?"

"Back down the trail. Three days ago I think, maybe four. With
Pettigrew. Me mates here carried me the whole way, God bless 'em."

"We'll carry you on."

"Not likely. I'm in the wrong group now, y'see. I thought I'd be
with them"—he nodded toward the "probables" where the doctors were
working relentlessly—"but I guess the infection's got the best of me.

Not much left a' me is there, Colonel?" Their eyes met; Vance could see Johns had no words. "I'd appreciate it if y'ever get a chance to see my Jenny."

"Harry, you're not in...*that* group." He motioned toward the silent rows of the hopeless.

"I don't need morphine. That's the difference. I want to thank you, sir, for approving my transfer."

"When you volunteered for the Chindits?"

Vance nodded. "We're like no one else in the world."

"The world will soon know that."

"How do you mean, sir?"

"There are newspapermen crawling over Imphal. All they want to hear about is the Chindits." Several of the possibles turned their heads. It was gratifying for Johns to exploit the subject. "Men, I'm Colonel Johns from Fourteenth Army Operations. I've come to realize—I don't know why it took so long—that you brave lads have no idea of the admiration you've attracted to this expedition. The newspeople are under censorship regarding the Chindits till you return, but then you will be undoubtedly the most famous brigade in the army. I don't mean Fourteenth Army—I mean the entire British army. There's not a formation in the desert, on the home isles, or anywhere which approaches the reputation you have earned for yourselves."

A feeble cheer went up, even among the hopeless. In that moment Johns discovered a mission for himself, one easy to perform and rich in personal reward: he had only to tell the Chindits how amazing they were. His face flushed with emotion; he bent down again for some private words with Vance, who was smiling introspectively.

"Nice to hear you leadin' cheers for the Chindits, sir."

Johns smiled at the irony. When Vance worked for him in India, Johns and Wingate were fiercely opposed. "I think the men could use some appreciation."

"That we could. Keep it up, sir."

"Believe me, Harry, the pleasure is mine. Your wife's address—it'll be at HQ, won't it?"

Vance nodded. "If you don't have a chance to see her, a note will do, sir."

"I shall see her, Harry, face to face."

The tears he had held back took their course as he gripped Vance's hand in both of his.

*   *   *

Johns wandered among the South Force positions for the rest of the morning. His praise, which he put in the names of Slim and Wavell, seemed to impart a sourceless energy. When he returned to the bunker, he found the news he had spread preceded him.

The same four officers with whom he had his first breakfast were about to leave the bunker. Driscoll patted him on the shoulder as he went by. York stopped to shake his hand.

"There's no Catholic like a convert," said Oxley. "See you later, Colonel Johns."

"What did he mean by that?" Johns asked Dalton.

"Well, you haven't always been a Chindit booster, Allen."

Johns removed his hat and sat down. "Bruce, that's an enormous misinterpretation. Though on reflection I shouldn't be surprised. You probably believe that I, and perhaps the rest of the staff, are prejudiced against the Chindits. That maybe even Slim is."

"No, you shouldn't be surprised—because it's true."

"But it's not."

"No? Have you forgotten Shakedown?"

Johns nodded thoughtfully. "I see what you mean. Yes, I accept a rebuke for our attitude during Shakedown, and perchance some instances thereafter."

"And before."

"All right—and before. I quite forgot those frictions as something almost prewar. On my word, Bruce, all that was forgotten once the Chindits took the field. You are in our thoughts constantly, not just as a part of our work but the very reason for it."

"I'd have to say our support has been all right out here—though I give most of the credit to Cochran and the Americans."

"Which they justly deserve. For the rest of us, I must ask you to consider how difficult it's been working with Wingate."

"Is that why you scrubbed his drop at Pinlebu?"

"There was just not enough 105 ammunition to give away to the Japs, Bruce. Shouldn't surprise me if some of your barrage today wasn't shells we saved by denying Wingate at Pinlebu."

"What did you mean he's left us in the lurch?"

"He marched you farther east into the Indaung."

"Yes?"

"Well, isn't it obvious to you? He maneuvered South Force to cover his own escape."

"This is a grim little war out here, as you saw for yourself. Sometimes a limb must be sacrificed to save the body."

"You are his right arm. South Force has had more combat and more success than he. Blowing the gorge was a showpiece he reserved for himself."

"I did the same thing with Nash and Pettigrew. They drew the Japs while we got away."

"They were a temporary decoy. At the decisive moment you saved them—and you planned to all the while. They weren't just tossed out like scraps of meat to throw Yakamura off the trail."

"You think that's what Wingate's done with us?"

"What other conclusion is there? What was his message: 'seek ye shelter in the mountains'? Wasn't that telling you to keep going for the Kachin Hills? Is that what you would have done otherwise?"

"No. He made a mistake there. He should have pulled the whole expedition out. But once he continued we all had to go for mutual support."

"Bruce, on my honor as an officer, I'm telling you that North and Central forces did *not* continue into the Indaung. They turned around almost immediately."

"I know how you feel about Orde. Don't try to turn me against him."

"When you get back, God willing, look at the resupply request for the night of the fifteenth. Cochran will have it. It asks for a blind free-fall on the Meza. Rations and ammo only. Can you imagine such a request for any other purpose except to support Buckshot? On the *fifteenth*, Bruce, within hours of telling you to 'seek shelter in the mountains.'"

"Why are you telling me this?"

"To give credit where it's due. It was a revelation to me this morning."

"What was?"

"That your feats—the feats of South Force—are sacrifices to Wingate."

79

From the last stepping-stone Wingate could make out a speckle of lights on the opposite shore: the tiny village of Tigyaing a few miles north of the mouths of the Meza. Beyond, the quarter moon hung low over the Sheba Hills.

"Au Thang."

"Yes, sir."

"Why are there many lights so late at night?"

"Maybe fishing with lights."

"The Japs do that too, don't they?"

"Yes. Fish more than Burmese."

"Well let's hope their catch doesn't include us. Rafferty, are you ready?"

From another flotilla, Wingate had pulled Sergeant Rafferty, a member of the faculty, to replace the lost Gurkha. Lieutenant Underwood, the instructor in jungle survival at Saugor, was also added to Wingate's party in place of the other Gurkha. This was done before Anderson or Fox-Boynton reached the last island.

"The moon waits for no one," said Wingate. "Let's get under way."

This time there were no cheers to mark the launching. The remaining Chindits watched Wingate's drift closely, for in this final bend before the Irrawaddy widened the current was the swiftest.

Wingate gave one glance back at the island. The glistening nakedness of the huddled Chindits showed bones in stark relief and skins leprously white until the water's chop curtained his last look at the expedition.

The view of the western shore rose and fell as the flotilla bobbed in the river's surge. There was no landing target, no guide or marker toward which to steer. Any landfall would do to begin the trek to India. Though it meant a longer time in the water, Wingate hoped to ride the river to a large island close against the shore. A landing there would put him the farthest west.

He expected the rest of the expedition to strew out along the shore. The pulsing current would disperse them, and it was dispersion which would foil the Japanese: the Chindits were to wriggle back through the jungle like a shoal of minnows.

Though the water was warm, his teeth were chattering. "Count off," he commanded twice more before he heard the rustle of elephant grass in the breeze.

Flung against a steep-sloping beach, Flotilla One scrambled onto a flat boomerang-shaped island covered with towering elephant grass with blades as sharp as sabers. Wading along the narrow beach, rafts in tow, the ten men searched for a place to cross the remaining hundred yards of water. In the moon's shadows there was nothing to see of the waiting jungle except its skyline. A dip in the treetops indicated a backwater of the river.

"Might try there, sir," Underwood whispered.

The flotilla launched once more. This time Rafferty led, followed by Corporal Turpin, probably the best marksmen in Central Force. Next came Corporal Hudspeth, another crack shot and one of the trail-blazers on Casten's Trace, followed by Sergeant Myers, a medic; then Wingate and Au Thang. Behind the rafts were An Nu, a superb scout for the Burma Rifles, Quillan, an expert in jungle ambushes, Jarrett, a former foreign legionnaire in equatorial Africa, and Underwood. Flotilla One was a handpicked band with survival talent exceeding that of any other on the river, a fact which left many Chindits muttering.

The current was sluggish for their last immersion in the Irrawaddy. They reached the backwater and passed under a shadowy arch as claustrophobic as Casten's Trace. The flotilla breast-stroked through still water as deadfall and underwater tangles thickened and reached for them.

Gradually the canopy drooped closer to the water. The men could hear their labored breathing. They tried to stand but the bottom was a jumble of drowned branches. Finally, in the darkness, Rafferty felt a giant log angling into the water.

He decided to pull everything into the brush till daylight. In the black thicket the men tried to sort out boots and uniforms but then gave up, and despite the prickle of twigs they were soon snoring.

* * *

Morning would not have roused them were it not for their hunger. Whatever obstacles lay ahead, whatever patrols and ambushes the Japanese had waiting for them, whatever natural accidents, injuries, and sickness might befall them, the primary enemy of the escaping Chindits was hunger. Already their exertions had depleted their energy where no amount of rest would restore it.

Three K rations per day were barely enough to fuel ten hours of jungle hacking; they would eat but one per day and thereby stretch their entire food supply over three days. With luck—a lot of luck, Wingate realized—in three days they might reach the Menlo Valley. From there survival depended on what they could extract from the jungle.

Time was the ally of hunger. As they left the Irrawaddy, they were as strong as they ever would be. As hunger gnawed down their stamina, they would weaken: fewer meals per day, less alertness at danger points, more vulnerability to accident and illness. Time, therefore, was the essence of survival, and time depended on the route.

The route to the Menlo Valley required an immediate decision. Marching would probably be fastest northeast of the Sheba Hills; however, they would be traveling in a natural corridor between the hills and the Meza close to the village of Tawma, which was surely a patrol base for the Japanese.

The jungle wrapped the flotilla in brambles. Underwood crashed into the brush in search of edible tubers while Wingate, Rafferty, and Au Thang debated the route.

"We'd be the first to pass through," Wingate mused. "If the Japs don't know we're on the west bank, we could probably slip right by. Think we could get any rice at Tawma?"

"I don't know, sir," Au Thang answered. "Japanese are very cruel if they find Burmese helping us."

"I just have the feeling we should head straight into the hills."

"More chance of game up there," said Rafferty. "Better shooting where there's less underbrush."

"Couldn't be more brush than here," said Turpin. He was to cut trail for the first leg of the trek.

"Au Thang, could we shoot something to eat around Tawma? Bullock maybe?"

"Maybe, sir. I never see Tawma before."

"Damn it, I told Underwood to be back by now."

Underwood did return, but empty-handed, drawing a scowl from Wingate. Nervously the party struck off for Tawma.

Hudspeth directed Turpin with the only compass. The lowlands were worse than Casten's Trace, the heat worse than the Indaung Forest. In single file the ten men crowded in back of each other like cattle in a chute. No thought was given to the Japanese unless the Chindits crossed a trail. A trail would be welcome in spite of the danger.

The tasks of leading and wielding the machetes were rotated. When his turn came, Wingate slashed into the branches as if he were hacking through a burning house.

"Damn thing's dull already," he gasped when his turn was over. He presented the machete to Rafferty, who broke trail with even, methodical strokes.

"We'll never get to Tawma at this rate," Wingate snapped.

Rafferty did not look back. His progress was as good as Wingate's. "Sir, we learned something at Saugor: if you want to move fast in the jungle, go slow."

"You're certainly going slow enough."

The bottomland gave way to a slight slope with trees a little wider spaced. Beads of sun dribbled through the canopy.

Jarrett stopped in midstride. An Nu froze like a dog honoring another's point. Wingate craned his neck to see the cause. The jungle was just as thick, no evidence of a trail, only a patch of light on filmy leaves.

Jarrett and An Nu were looking down; then the Burmese backed away and ducked his head as Jarrett's machete flashed. A writhing coil bounced off a log; a headless snake became a Chindit meal.

They did not stop to eat. With the second machete, Myers skinned and gutted the three-foot reptile while the march continued.

"What was it?" Wingate asked.

"Cobra, sir," said Jarrett as he thrashed on.

80

The appearance of leeches suggested nearby cultivation. The foliage showed bursts of bright green where young trees grew over ancient plots. Animal trails furrowed the matted jungle floor. Finally they came upon a woodcutter's trail: a tiny track leading somewhere.

It was shoulder-wide and overgrown and diagonally intersected Wingate's azimuth. Without asking anyone's opinion, he gestured for Quillan to follow it.

The speed of march tripled, but the trail bent to the east where the ground became swampy. Hudspeth tapped Wingate's shoulder.

"Sergeant Rafferty wants a halt, sir."

"This is no holiday outing," he grumbled, but passed up the signal to halt. Rafferty crashed up behind him.

"This is taking us to the Meza," he said.

"Glad you have an atlas. You need a rest?"

"No, sir." There had been no rest for eight hours. Wingate signaled to continue the march.

The woodcutter's trail eased north again, then wavered to the east where it lost identity in bamboo thickets. The Chindits skirted the bamboo until they came upon a stream. Here they drank deeply and ate the cobra, which yielded a shrimp-sized piece of meat for each man.

Underwood passed around handfuls of fern leaves. "Too bad they're not younger, but they'll still give you some iron and bulk. Chew thoroughly."

"If that trail wasn't going to Tawma, where was it coming from?" Turpin asked. Au Tang shrugged.

"I think we'd better double back on it," Rafferty said quietly.

"The hell we will!"

"Just a half mile, sir. Remember that little ridge?"

The men glanced sidelong at Wingate, whose glare lit the jungle. "No, I don't remember a ridge. What about it?"

"I think it would put us closer to Tawma."

"Closer than *what?*"

"Closer than the way we're going."

"What do you think, Hudspeth?"

"I think I know where he means."

"*Well?*"

"It'll be hard bashin' if this bamboo gets any thicker, sir."

"Sergeant Hudspeth, I'm asking if you favor this 'ridge' to our present route."

"Yes, sir."

"An Nu?"

"Me too."

"Underwood?"

"The ridge, sir."

"All right, Rafferty: lead on and you'd better be right."

The march reversed. In twenty minutes it halted as Rafferty cut into the jungle. Slow hacking continued for another three hours. Just before dark they came upon another trail, this one heading on a promising azimuth. Wingate would have raced on to see where it led but the consensus was against him. Too weary to assert himself, he joined the others for a K ration.

"We'll scout out Tawma tomorrow when we're fresh, sir," said Underwood in the darkness.

"He's asleep," Rafferty replied. "Help me with his boots."

They were unlaced, and the sergeants began to pull them off when Wingate revived for a moment. "Huh! What...what're you doing?"

"Shouldn't sleep in your boots, sir," said Myers patiently.

"Take care of your feet, General," said Rafferty, suppressing a chuckle that Wingate did not hear for he was back asleep.

A cigarette glowed in the darkness. "After dinner smoke, gentlemen?" Quillan invited. Like a firefly, the cigarette went around the four men accompanied by praise for Quillan's waterproof condom.

"What do you think, Lieutenant?"

"We should find Tawma tomorrow."

"Aye," said Rafferty.

"What do you think we should do?" asked Myers.

"Have An Nu look around."

"Aye."

"Suppose it's Jap?" Quillan asked.

"Might hit it anyway," said Rafferty.

"How's that?"

"A squad of Japs we could handle."

"Have to be one Jap, one bullet, mate."

"I'd like to have a Jap rifle for the rest of the trip. Then every one we kill is an ammo resupply."

"There's something to that."

"Think he'll go along?"

"I don't know him."

"Me either."

"A bit testy today."

"Rafferty, I want to tell you something," Underwood lowered his voice. "Whenever I think you're right, I'm going to back you up."

"And I," said Quillan.

"Thanks, mates. I might need your help."

Wingate awoke in the semidawn. He had dreamed of Lodolf, where from a headland he could see the sea and his far-off castle. His horse nuzzled his neck; he reached to touch the wet spot... and felt a leech swollen to the size of a snail. He tried to remember the method of extraction. He tapped Myers into consciousness.

"A little alcohol, sir," he said sleepily, and handed him the first-aid kit.

The leech slowly backed out. Wingate seized its slimy toughness; some blood oozed from its suction cup. As though it were a tube of toothpaste, he squeezed the leech and drank his own blood.

Myers went back to sleep and no one else was awake. Wingate took a rifle and a machete, and slipped down the trail.

Tawma was barely a clearing in the lesser jungle a half mile from where the Chindits slept. Only the cocks were awake. A cat with her litter lay in the single path dividing six thatch huts. A drooping corral enclosed a bullock and some scrawny pigs. Where was the cultivation?

Wingate wondered. He could see traces of what might have been paddy dikes, broken, ruined. No garden patches.

A Burmese woman emerged from one of the doorless huts to scamper down the trail away from Wingate. She descended into the jungle and presently returned with a gourd of water. A Japanese emerged, yawned, squatted by the gourd, and began his morning ablutions.

The woman made five such trips, and soon the village "street" was full of Japanese washing, praying, and stretching.

"What do you think, sir? Knock 'em off?"

"No. They're a visiting patrol. Probably coming down the trail now."

"Japs travel with rice."

"They don't when they're on a circuit."

"Tawma's a station?"

"Could be. I sort of doubt it though. Nothing growing around there."

"I look," said An Nu.

"Go ahead. But be back in an hour. I think we're going on."

Nothing more was said till An Nu departed. As he gathered some bark for breakfast, Underwood asked, "Did you say go on, sir?"

"Yes."

"Just drop in on the village when the Japs pull out?" said Jarrett expectantly. Wingate's shrug was negative.

"We can scoop up the chickens. Maybe the pigs," Myers suggested.

"I don't want the Japs to know we've been here at all."

"Chrissake, General! We hacked all day to get to Tawma. That was the big hurry yesterday—remember?"

"Now you men listen to me: you don't realize how valuable we are. There are no men like us in the army. None. We are veterans of LRP. Our experience cannot be replaced. Without us there will not be another expedition. It is our duty—my duty as commander—to ensure our escape."

"We bloody well won't escape without some food!"

"There might be three days of food in that village. Probably less. Tomorrow, the next day at the latest, other groups are going to reach Tamwa. They're going to run into Japs. Yakamura will bring in reinforcements. They're going to hunt between the Meza and the hills.

They'll be looking south and probably sweep toward the Irrawaddy. We'll be behind them heading west. Understood?"

"You're going to let the others bash with the Japs?" .

"I am." The men were silent. "Till we're on safer ground, we'll just tighten our belts and live like the monkeys. They don't starve. Let me try some of that bark."

81

On the last stepping-stone, Fox-Boynton decided that half the flotillas should steer for the confluence of the Meza, the other half head straight over the Sheba Hills. The prize for the Meza landings was the hidden supply cache dropped by Cochran, but with the prize went the peril of Japanese patrols around Tawma. The route through the Sheba Hills was safest from detection but lacked any provisions except what could be extracted from the jungle.

As the Meza group was most likely to fight, Fox-Boynton elected to lead it with Anderson as his second in command. Grayson and Burchfield had the same relationship for the Sheba group. The Meza group, roughly defined, was the old North Force, while the Sheba group consisted mainly of the old Central Force. There was a grim safeguard in this organizational turbulence: if captured, a man might reveal his unit to be North Force, Central Force, Sheba group, Meza group, Seventeenth Flotilla, Seventy-seventh Indian Brigade, Kings—combinations of units that would set a Japanese intelligence officer's head swirling.

Adding to Yakamura's confusion was the scattering of the flotillas. Six more were lost between the last stepping-stone and the western shore. Two were swept back to the eastern shore near Tagaung, where the Burmese fed and concealed them until news of a Japanese patrol reached the village chief. Rather than bring repercussions on the village, the nineteen Chindits slipped into the hills. When the Japanese left, the village chief offered boats for the Chindits' use, but their leader, a corporal from the Kings, told his comrades they could make a contribution to the expedition by continuing a Chindit presence on the eastern shore; that by a little raiding and ambushing they would confuse the Japanese and divert resources from the main search.

Sniping and waylaying, the little force slowly rearmed itself. This done, they became such a nuisance for Yakamura that he sent a motorized company after them and off Dalton's trail. Seventeen of the "east shore" Chindits were tracked down and killed; two survived the war concealed under the huts of friendly Burmese.

Another flotilla was swept miles south of the Sheba Hills, where six men reached the western shore. Led by a sergeant of the Burma Rifles, four of them reached the railroad south of Kyaikthin. Starving and at the end of their strength, they also decided on sacrifice to deceive the Japanese. For days they camped by the rails, eating nothing but leaves. Finally a small troop train bringing reinforcements north puffed through the jungle. The Chindits fired on the locomotive, stopping the train. They saved one round apiece to prevent capture.

Even the drowned flotillas added to the Chindits' deception. The Japanese found corpses washed ashore as far south as Male; indeed, Yakamura looked at evidence of Chindits scattered over a thousand square miles, though soon his interest focused principally near two places: Hinlo, where South Force prepared to break out of the Indaung Forest, and Tawma, where Fox-Boynton was about to break into the Menlo Valley.

What puzzled Yakamura to distraction was that these two drives were in opposite directions: one due east, one due west. The campaign had bewildered him from the start, and at this point he was ready to believe his wildest imaginings. Extermination of the Chindits remained his preeminent mission, but he had an overriding fear of another humiliation like Pinlebu or, worse still, the Bonchaung Gorge.

He found it possible to believe that the two diverging thrusts were part of a new Chindit offensive. From this premise it was conceivable that South Force was headed toward a linkup with the Kachin guerrillas, whose size Yakamura was predisposed to exaggerate. Following the linkup, he conjectured, the combined forces might even strike toward Bhamo, the headquarters of Eighteenth Division. Of all the dreads that troubled him, the embarrassment of uncovering Bhamo was perhaps the greatest.

Even more unacceptable was another attack on the railroad between the gorge and Kyaikthin. He had sworn with his life that the rails would never be cut again, and he knew Kawabe was ready to redeem his pledge. For the Chindits to debouch in strength into the Menlo Valley meant certain exposure of the railroad.

Of the two horns of his dilemma, the safety of the railroad loomed foremost. There were seventy miles and the Kachin Hills between South Force and Bhamo; moreover, Yakamura had contact with the eastern thrust of the Chindits, though Dalton was roughly handling the 412th Brigade in the Indaung Forest. On the Meza, the situation was far less clear, with scattered engagements, unreliable reports, and no roads between the railroad and the river by which Yakamura could move his reserves.

Swallowing his pride, he requested reinforcements of Kawabe. It was one of these trains which the four starving Chindits ambushed. The report of this pathetic little skirmish did not mention the emaciated state in which the bodies were found, nor the apparent lack of ammunition or the suicides (Japanese customarily killed themselves to avoid capture, so they found it unremarkable for the Chindits to do likewise).

The skirmish on the railroad set the priorities for Yakamura's next plan. Its central feature was to patrol every mile of track between the gorge and Kyaikthin. The secondary effort was to plug the gap between the Meza River and the Sheba Hills. No additional forces would be sent into the Indaung. South Force would be followed and their crossing of the Shweli prevented if possible, but Yakamura was no longer confident of encircling and crushing them.

Thanks to the fog of war which the Chindits created for Yakamura, his plan untethered South Force as Wingate's sacrificial lamb of the expedition. They were still slogging on foot while the Japanese trucks threatened their flanks like cavalry, but Dalton was able to receive a major supply drop; daily his eastern progress brought him closer to the Shweli and the end of the open forest.

The Shweli turned from northwest to northeast near Hinlo. The Japanese in their trucks reached this bend before him but were obliged to split their force to cover Dalton's possible crossings. He called in a deception drop to the southeast while arranging for Kachins to secure a crossing to the north, leaving the Japanese to guess which direction he was heading. He did neither, instead crossing at the most unlikely point at the very bend in the river.

The Japanese reacted swiftly, almost closing a circle around Dalton on the west bank. All the mortars, many of the mules, and the wounded were abandoned, but South Force finally came out of the forest, crossed the river, and entered jungle where no truck could follow. The Chindits crawled away to revive while the Kachins scouted the east bank to warn when the Japanese crossed.

Still mystified about whether South Force would head north or south, Yakamura hesitated in choosing a crossing for his own forces. Dalton was also uncertain about his next move. His tactical sense urged him to entice the Japanese into ambush as they went astride the river. He could then remove Japanese interference with his freedom of movement once and for all.

But South Force simply lacked the energy to carry out the maneuver. Their muster had shrunk from a thousand to little over six hundred, and of this number barely a third were fit for combat. Dalton had to recognize their condition and resorted to stealth rather than strength to shake the Japanese. South Force melted east into the jungle, leaving the Kachins to delay Yakamura's pursuit for three days.

Giving Dalton a few excellent guides, the Kachins withdrew back into the hills. Their service to South Force was now reciprocated: Yakamura hadn't the forces to mount both a punitive expedition into the Kachin Hills and a reconnaissance to pick up Dalton's cold trail, which now headed north. Taking Dalton's most seriously sick and wounded with them, the guerrillas slipped back into their wilderness strongholds, where they lived out the war in relative peace. Their brief but decisive association with the Chindits culminated in a permanent link for some of the wounded, who married into the tribe and made the Kachin Hills their lifelong home.

Like the Israelites after crossing the Red Sea, South Force was nearly free from their pursuers but still menaced by the wilderness. Dalton drove them on like Moses, squeezing arduous marches out of legs that could hardly shuffle. He dared not risk a supply drop unless he was absolutely certain it would be undetected. Finally, halfway between the Shweli and Zissel Island, South Force collapsed. A night drop was arranged and delivered, but even with full rations, new boots, and medicine, South Force could not move on.

There was no sign the Japanese had located him, so Dalton took a break from the war as if it were a maneuver at Saugor. Stragglers were collected. A second resupply brought in fresh uniforms, vitamins, mail, congratulatory messages from Slim and Wavell, and triple rations of rum. Dalton pulled South Force into a tight laager as he had in the Bambwe Taung Hills, then took a three-day holiday around a stream where the men bathed, picnicked, and slept.

Someone remembered the Prince of Wales's birthday, so before the march resumed Dalton formed up the troops in their new uniforms and held a little parade through the trees to the beat of a stick on a hollow log and the piping of a Kachin flute.

The "stand-down," as this bizarre interlude was called, put South Force in remission from terminal exhaustion. Ahead was the Irrawaddy; the next resupply would be in the Tri Range twenty miles beyond.

Abashed by South Force's escape from the Indaung, Yakamura was doubly intent to contain North Force at the Tawma Gap, as the funnel of jungle between the Meza and the Sheba Hills came to be called.

82

Fox-Boynton personally searched the fork of the Meza for the free-fall drop. The jungle was thick but the heavy wooden boxes had crashed through, strewing the ground with boards, nails, bullets, and rations. When everything that could be found was recovered, North Force still had only one rifle for two men but nearly a hundred rounds per rifle and six days of rations, which could be stretched into twelve.

Realizing speed was the key to escape, they immediately turned west—and squarely into the blocking force Yakamura had rushed to Tawma. With survival in their own hands, North Force fought to break through. The Japanese, led by officers with samurai swords unsheathed, were equally enflamed.

Each day increased the Japanese strength, so Fox-Boynton probed for weak sectors before the Japanese could reinforce them. With no radios to control his lieutenants, he could only influence the battle with general instructions; these were to push and pry ahead by day, everyone attacking at dawn without letup until dark, then continuing the advance by infiltration at night. It was much the same tactic by which the Japanese had routed Burma Corps.

It was costly in men and, what seemed more important, in ammunition. The wounded lay where they fell; a man's life was worth less than the few bullets he carried. To kill a Japanese soldier was to both reduce their number and add a weapon to the Chindits, but even without a weapon each Chindit found a combat role to play.

It came about without orders from the officers: a man without a weapon paired himself with a rifleman. The weaponless man became a decoy, drawing Japanese fire while his partner maneuvered for a kill. Too often the decoy had to rush the Japanese before they would reveal themselves.

Even suicidal courage could not force an opening. Dodging along the front, Fox-Boynton pulled out two composite companies of the best-armed men. It was a triage of the unwounded: those left in the line were nearly defenseless, their purpose only to occupy the Japanese in front of them by bluff and grenades. Meanwhile Fox-Boynton assembled his strike force where the Japanese flank touched the hills. At night grenadiers probed the Japanese, trying to draw fire from their machine guns. At dawn the strike force crashed forward in the British equivalent of a banzai charge.

In his account, Kane related how he awaited the result:

The sound of fire from the left reached me like two distant and widely separated peals of thunder. From F-B's plan I knew it would be thus—first the attack springing from the jungle at dawn; the answering volleys from the surprised Japanese, followed by a lull after the ranks of our brave men shattered. Then the second assault by the follow-up company when they found the weapons of the dead.

The fire faded in the jungle. The men in front of me shouted and moved about in the foliage as if they in turn were about to assault the enemy, who were only fifty yards away. I was left to consider my impotence as I awaited the message from F-B. The messenger had to crawl the last yards to my position. His eyes imparted shock from which I inferred futile disaster, but he said, "We turned them sir." Then he sobbed, "You're in command."

I looked at him dumbly. Thirty hours without sleep. My perceptions were incoherent. We'd turned the flank—victory. But I was in command? As incredible as it seems I would have preferred defeat to the loss of Adrian Fox-Boynton....

Like so many, so very many in the green caldron of the Tawma Gap, his remains were never recovered. Two men saw him cut in half by a long burst of machine gun fire. He had raised himself, bidding the gun to speak, calling for his own death to save the lives of those he led. His name, his example, will forever glisten the eyes of Chindits. It was another man who gave us our name, but it was Adrian who gave us his life and our honor.

The west flank was open but in hours the Japanese would counterattack. Through a patter of fire Kane dodged down the line, all the way to the Meza. His shouted commands were brief—move left, wait for nothing, break out toward the Menlo.

Unsaid was the necessity to abandon the wounded, unstated was the need for individuals to volunteer to cover the evacuation. "Stay behind" was a self-pronounced death sentence spoken by scores of volunteers who would never be seen again.

The breakout lasted for less than twelve hours. Kane's rear guard fought stubbornly, strengthened by captured machine guns. Yakamura reported the success of his counterattack as a great victory; yet he again was faced with troubling uncertainty. To him Fox-Boynton's attack seemed like the opening of a general offensive. For all Yakamura knew, thousands of well-armed Chindits were massing to overrun the gap. The force which had broken out toward the Menlo concerned him, but back on the railroad he had his second and strongest line of defense. Yakamura thus saved North Force by sending no one to pursue them until he probed the abandoned Chindit positions in the Tawma Gap.

His patrols found two hundred Chindits dead and dying. Single shots cracked in the jungle until the defenders' ammunition expired. Those Chindits who did not save a bullet for themselves met death under bayonets or the battering of rifle butts.

They were disemboweled and decapitated, their heads and guts brought back to headquarters—the reward for Wingate's parts had been doubled since the time his face appeared on the leaflets. But the bounty seekers faced a problem: how could Wingate be identified? To the Japanese, all British looked alike, especially in death. Consequently, a few wounded Chindits were temporarily spared for a unique torture.

At Tawma they were tied to chairs in the sun without water, beaten according to the Japanese mood, and their wounds used for urinals while the gruesome trophies were carried in from the jungle. The contorted face of a comrade was thrust in front of them. "Wingate? Wingate?" they were asked.

"No...No..." was the answer from swollen lips; another severed head was tossed aside, and the viscera to the rooting pigs.

Two of the tortured decided they might protect their commander if the Japanese believed him to be dead. When the head of a man of Wingate's age was presented to one of them, he nodded. The glee of a Japanese sergeant turned to rage when a second "Wingate" was identified. The Japanese pursuit of truth involved bamboo slivers under fingernails until one of the men retracted.

But while the "genuine" head and intestines were being wrapped for presentation to Yakamura, an officer cautioned that the second Chindit might not be honest but merely more stubborn. Indeed, after crushing his testicles, the man was found to be lying. The two deceivers were bound together, doused with gasoline, and burned as an example to the other prisoners. Wingate remained officially at large.

83

The martyrdom of North Force let Central Force slip away from the Irrawaddy without a fight. Grayson thought he heard the battle of the break out as they wound into the Sheba Hills. There the terrain was rugged, but the jungle penetrable. Dehydration was the principal torment until they found streams on the western slopes; then nutrition became the equivalent of survival.

Living off the jungle was impossible for so large a band of men. Sooner rather than later Grayson had to risk contact with the Burmese to seek their rice. Positioning his force for a quick getaway in case the village belonged to the Japanese, he sent some Burma Rifles into Hintha.

They were welcomed; the village's experience was another chapter in the history of Japan's atrocity: Yakamura's troops had carried away the village girls to the railroad, where they were chained in a boxcar and raped by the garrisons between Kyaikthin and Wuntho. The village chief's protests had left him impaled on a stake where he lay dying for three days before the eyes of his villagers.

For the Chindits, the Burmese emptied their granaries. In the name of George VI, Grayson wrote them an IOU for redemption at whatever price obtained at the end of the war. Almost as valuable as the rice was the villagers' familiarity with routes leading west. South of Kyaikthin, the railroad could be crossed without detection. On hidden trails, progress was speedy as far as the Mu, the boundary of the villagers' knowledge.

In two more days, Grayson had Central Force west of the railroad, but with his good fortune he did not forget the rest of the expedition. With no demolitions to damage the rails, he used two of the villagers' elephants to drag up a quarter mile of ties. This sabotage was done over the protest of Burchfield, who argued that cutting the rails would be like a burglar alarm for Yamakura.

It was, and also his death knell. When he received the news, Yamakura did not wait to be relieved of his command. Without a word to his staff, who braced for his suicide, he removed his badges of rank and decorations as if in preparation for the ritual of hari-kari. Instead, looking like an overage private, he departed for Grayson's rail cut. There, as his aide stood at stiff attention, Yakamura marched alone into the jungle, his ancestral sword in hand. He never found the Chindits and was never found himself.

Kawabe replaced him with Colonel Isano, his best regimental commander from the Arakan front. In addition to the ten thousand troops already hunting the Chindits, Isano deployed his three battalions at Pinlebu, Kyaikthin, and Ywatha. Within this triangle he flooded the jungle with patrols. He was satisfied with the security of the railroad now thickly picketed between Kyaikthin and Indaw.

He was confident no significant number of Chindits could elude him to the south, for there a motorized division had recently arrived from Rangoon. North of the triangle, the aborted Fort Hertz expedition was withdrawing from Homalin to Pinlebu. Kawabe ordered this force to halt and defend that line against the Chindits or an attack from India.

Thus the Japanese defenses were set. Isano expected the bulk of the Chindits to withdraw down the Menlo Valley, then through the gap between north and south Zibyutaung ranges, where they might link up with a British relief force crossing the Chindwin from Auktaung. Isano believed Dalton's troops had dispersed into the Kachin Hills, where later they could be handled like guerrillas. Only in misjudging the location and intentions of South Force was Isano wrong.

After the stand-down, South Force made good progress to the Irrawaddy opposite Zissel Island, which parted the river into two narrow channels. The flat island was covered with elephant grass; both shores were unpopulated and unpatrolled. The crossing was easily accomplished in a night with no losses.

Once more on the western shore, South Force broke trail toward the Tri Range and their next supply drop. Their Kachin guides had turned back for their homes in the hills. Dalton was once more on his own, his six hundred men gradually regaining their stamina.

It was Johns who could detect that even in their recovery the Chindits were only shadows of the men who had crossed the Chindwin. They marched half as fast; simple orders took twice as long to carry out. Their movements were almost languid: from prying open cans to cleaning rifles, they went about their tasks like arthritics.

Using their rifles as canes, they clambered up the slopes, panting as if the air were thin. The supply drop was postponed because they were too slow to prepare for it.

"The spirit is willing," said Johns.

"Now you're sounding just like Orde," Dalton replied, sweat streaming from his face. "I know the flesh is weak. Mine is too. We're about a month overdue in India. That's really the only problem: we've been out here too long."

In the valley to the west the toot of a lonely locomotive drifted up into the hills. The two colonels glanced at each other; the sound re-

minded them of their first profound disagreement. Dalton had ordered
a ton of TNT in his supply drop: he intended to cut the Indaw-
Myitkyina railway before taking South Force out of Burma.

North and Central forces' radios were at the bottom of the Irrawaddy. Dalton was the last of the Chindits able to communicate with India, the only element left in the expedition which could call for resupply
drops. He could also receive intelligence reports on Japanese activity.
From these he knew Isano had no inkling of his whereabouts. Johns
pleaded with him not to change the fortunate situation.

"South Force is in no condition to fight, Bruce." Dalton's silence
showed he accepted that opinion. "You would be jeopardizing every
man here if you cut the railroad." Johns detected a nod. Dalton was
seated on a log, the men of his headquarters slumped against trees
twenty yards away. His glance told Johns to keep his voice low. "And
to what end, Bruce? The Japs can repair the line in less than a week.
The Bonchaung Gorge is clear already."

"We didn't come out here for a walk in the woods."

"You've already kicked Kawabe's arse. Get away before he tram-
ples you."

"You know why I'm gonna' cut it."

Johns squatted down in front of him. "It won't help! There are
just too many Japs out there. You know that better than I do. There's
nothing we can do for the others, Bruce. You *know* that!"

"I owe it to 'em. They're Chindits."

"What do you owe to *these* men?" Johns swept his arm around the
hillside. "They deserve the chance to survive as much as anyone with
Wingate. Would you send your son back into a burning house to get
his brother? I don't want to use the word, Bruce, but as the commander here you can't be sentimental."

"Then don't use it. And don't try to command South Force."

"How many Japs do you think you'd draw away from Wingate?"

"We've been over that."

"You know how many, and you know I'm right: too many to let
you get away but too few to really help."

"I know the Japs better than you do. When we cut the rail they'll
run around and jerk off."

"Balls!"

"Look, Allen, when we get back you can write a nice appreciation
of my decision. You can show Slim how right you were; how your eyes

were clear while mine were clouded with sentiment. How I took unnecessary chances and losses. You'll probably be a general someday but
you'll never be a Chindit."

"Chindit or not, I have a job to do out here."

Dalton swigged from his canteen. "You never told me why Slim
sent you to us. The real reason."

"Simple: to get South Force out in one piece."

"To make sure I did?"

"If necessary. I've not spoken in the name of Slim, but I will if I
must."

"Oh, will you?" Dalton sneered. "You know, I was just getting a
little used to you, Johns. You did nice work with the Kachins; I should
have told you so. But you're still a crafty careerist—still got a ramrod
up your arse, still trying to torpedo Wingate. His success burns you
like acid, doesn't it?"

"I don't know which amazes me more: his perfidy or your loyalty."

"Listen, when it comes to perfidy, you could give him lessons."

Johns rose as Sergeant Major Zachary approached. He had been
supervising the collection of the bundles dropped the night before. He
was ready with an accounting.

"Sixteen bundles requested; twelve received, sir. All broken down
and disturbed. DZ's clear. Column's ready to move."

"What the hell? What's missing?" Dalton asked.

"The TNT, sir."

"Thank you, Sergeant Major. We'll move out in twenty minutes.
Johns," Dalton hissed as Zachary walked away, "if you had anything
to do with this..."

"How could I? You've never let me near the radio."

Which was true. Yet Johns realized what had happened in Imphal:
Arden had surmised what the TNT was for and the likely consequences
for South Force. Dalton could fume on the radio but Arden would not
let him draw the Japanese to his escape route. Dalton guessed as much.
As the column struggled down the hillside, he gestured for Johns to
march beside him.

"Remember the cut south of Kyaikthin?" Dalton asked. Johns nodded. "Why was it allowed?"

"That's easy: no explosives—Imphal wasn't involved. Don't forget, only South Force still has radios. Arden can't prevent sacrifices
elsewhere." Dalton grunted, then fell into silence. "Mind if I ask you

something, Bruce? Do you believe yet that Orde abandoned you in
the Indaung?"

"Abandoned? No. He used me. He uses everyone. But where he's
different from you is that he doesn't use people to further himself. He
does it for...I was going to say LRP, but it's something more I don't
understand. Do you?"

Johns spit out the bit of sap he was chewing. "At Woolwich he
was forever playing Wagner on his gramophone. I'd listen with him
sometimes. Listen and polish my leather, but he never stirred. Totally
absorbed, you know. Never gave a thought to his leather."

"And I bet yours was the brightest in the term."

"Rapturous music. 'Full of crouching energy,' I remember him saying. Always argumentative, Orde was, and I didn't mind baiting him.
I think he rather liked me for that. He likes to grapple; even more
than fighting he likes to grapple. Know what I mean?" Dalton nodded. "At the end of *Götterdämmerung* I wondered aloud how such stupendous music could emanate from so vile a character as Wagner."

"Wagner used people, didn't he?"

"Abominably. I enjoyed making that point with Orde, then hailing
my own favorite, Mendelsohn, a composer whose high virtue matched his
high talent."

"But Orde preferred Wagner, aye?"

"Yes, even while conceding my point. And, as you well know,
Orde rarely concedes anything. He would have liked for Wagner to
have been a better man; it bothered him that he wasn't, but he wouldn't
dwell on the paradox. 'Genius,' he would say..." Dalton interrupted
with a chuckle of recollection. "You've heard his opinion?"

"Yes: 'genius is its own excuse and explanation.'"

84

For a moment memory overcame his hunger. The creature crouched high in the boughs was Bathsheba nursing. The ten men gazed up from the underbrush; Wingate passed the rifle to Turpin, who quietly found a branch to support his aim.

They'd heard the baboons crashing in the distance, at first mistaking them for a careless Japanese patrol or a band of fleeing Chindits. Then Underwood perceived the noise was above them. The herd skirted them at thirty yards' distance, then stopped, their caution overcome by curiosity.

The shot snapped through the twigs. Baboons screamed as they vanished in frenzied leaps while Bathsheba toppled like a duck from flight. She crashed against large branches in her fall; her infant detached and hit the ground squalling. The Chindits scrambled forward to prevent its escape, but it sought its mother's body and quickly joined her in death.

Except for bark and leaves, the baboons provided the first food for the group since they slipped around Tawma. They had reached the Menlo River near its headwaters, where it resembled a trout stream overhung by jungle. They waded through its shallows and skirted its pools, and were debating whether to use their only grenade to kill fish when the baboons appeared.

They consumed the carcasses like piranha, cutting the fur into insoles for their deteriorating boots. Little thought was given to Japanese patrols, which might have heard the shot. They had crossed no trails, and the jungle remained silently solitary. With few words they continued downstream.

They knew nothing of the breakout from Tawma Gap, for they were well into the jungle when Fox-Boynton battled for the Japanese

flank. It was a private expedition for the ten men, who counted themselves lucky as they headed toward the first certain peril, the railroad.

They all knew the "right" way to cross the tracks: they should sur-
veil it first in daylight to locate any trip flares or mines. At night,
scouts should cross first, then guide the rest to safety. Boot tracks must
be carefully erased, and the site should be well away from the Menlo
bridge, which was sure to be heavily guarded.

This is how the crossing would have been done at Saugor, but every day—almost every hour—was vital for Wingate's band as they lost
ground to malnutrition and exhaustion. Mentally listless, they were
unable to plan for a problem like the railroad.

After three hours of wading, the river deepened. Wingate commanded a halt. "Was that an eighth moon last night?" He was uncertain of his own memory.

"Believe so, sir," said Underwood.

"Then it'll be black tonight. What do you say we float from here?
Soon as it gets dark."

"How far, sir?" Rafferty asked.

"Far as we can get. To the Mu if possible."

"Under the *bridge?*" Wingate nodded; Rafferty shook his head. "Won't
be fifteen feet high."

"There's probably wire across the water. Floodlights too," Underwood added. "Japs are sure to be touchy about that bridge."

Wingate looked at the sand tapering into the river's depth. He
knew they were right; they should start breaking trail back into the
jungle now, but here was this effortless transportation gurgling around
them, moving toward salvation. His head felt light, as if malaria were
returning.

"All right," he sighed. "What do you say we lay up here, drift
down, and take a look tonight?"

Rafferty and Underwood glanced at each other and acquiesced. What
Wingate proposed gave them a couple of extra hours' rest; provided
they went ashore well upstream of the bridge, security need not be
compromised. There were questions of whether they should strip or
float in uniform, whether to wear the boots around their necks or on
their feet, and how to carry the five rifles. For Wingate, these matters
seemed as abstract as theology; he was feeling woozy and running afever.
As he curled up in the leaves, Myers gave him one of the last anti-
malarial tablets.

*   *   *

Connected to one another by vines, they slipped into the water clothed, boots around the neck. The rifle slings were woven around branches for flotation. While there was light the flotilla drifted in the shoreline shadows; with total darkness they steered into midstream.

They could hear the current quicken where the Menlo narrowed. Branches reached down at the bends as if to grasp them. Later, the river widened to nearly fifty yards and grew sluggish. To progress, the men began to swim, but the warm, sinuous drift of the water left them listless.

They took another bend; a vague dome of light seeped through the jungle. Jarrett, the best swimmer, was leading. He began stroking for the shore, followed by the rest of the flotilla. Underwood had been right: the Japanese had floodlights on the bridge.

The vine writhed in the quickening current. Jarrett reached for an overhanging branch; it broke in his hand. The vine reversed. Hudspeth, the last man on it, was then closest to shore. He reached for the foliage; it slipped through his grasp. Twenty arms splashed like paddles but the vine drifted out toward the approaching light.

"Buckshot!" Wingate slashed the vine.

Seven men swirled toward the bridge. Wingate and two others struggled to shore. Gasping, they looked back on the river. They saw the vine separate; two heads bobbed together, making headway to the opposite shore; the other five drifted toward a dark island outlined by the penumbra from the bridge.

Wingate, Au Thang, and Jarrett scrambled through the grass. As they came upon a narrow trail, they heard a machine gun roar from the bridge. The trail led toward the railroad where every Jap was alert; still Wingate crashed on, the jungle battering his shoulders. A British rifle cracked from the river—once, twice—the floodlights went out.

A figure blocked the path. Wingate leaped upon it, thrusting his knife in an uppercut. Jarrett finished him with the butt of his rifle. Au Thang grabbed the soldiers carbine and pushed by Wingate. Voices ahead. Au Thang stammered something in pidgin Japanese. Wingate was pushed aside by the patrol charging in the opposite direction.

The trail rose steeply, then flattened. Rocks, metal—the tracks. Firing from the right, whistles from the left. The three hurled themselves over the bank and rolled headlong into the jungle.

They lay wheezing for a moment, then crawled farther into the trees. Above them flashlight beams swung down the rails. They heard a Japanese command repeated in shouts. A British rifle cracked in reply.

"They say 'capture him!'" Au Thang whispered.

Uncertain of directions, Wingate found himself on the river again. The underbrush stirred on the other shore, a desperate thrashing of fugitives.

"Myers?"

"And Quillan," came a gasping reply. "He's hit."

"Tow him. Meet you downstream."

Wingate watched the shadows move. Myers backed into the water, dragging Quillan under the armpits. He mumbled wildly as the current caught them.

The five met at midstream and drifted together for the rest of the night, taking turns supporting Quillan even after he died.

Morning found them fifteen miles downstream, where the Menlo made a hairpin turn to the north. There they went ashore like shipwrecks. As Au Thang looked for fruit, the men stripped to dry their clothes. They removed Quillan's as well; everything he wore could be used in the days ahead. Jarrett found faded family pictures in his pocket and a copy of Wingate's order of the day when the expedition had crossed the Chindwin.

"Long time since the Chindwin," Jarrett murmured as he looked at the sodden paper. "Thought a lot of you, Quillan did."

"Myers," Wingate asked, "how long will he remain...?" He could not finish the question. Myers looked down at the corpse, stiff and hard as a drowned board."

"I'd rather starve, sir."

85

In a letter flown out on the seaplane Wingate had written:

The casualty list revealed a name I hoped never to see. Corporal Colin Parnell lost his life fighting with South Force. He was the son of the esteemed doctor who ministered to me aboard Llandovery Castle. You'll remember me saying how Manfred was nothing less than my savior. Without his recommendation I would not have been returned to full duty or been eligible for the command which is now crowned in triumph on the banks of the Irrawaddy.

Colin's fate is a most bitter irony. Anything you could do to ease Manfred's anguish will be a comfort for me as well. I haven't his address, but with Africa winding down it's likely he may be back in London. I'm sure you'll find him and express the depth of my grief for his brave boy....

Dr. Parnell's townhouse was on Chesham Place, one of the marble-curbed streets in Belgravia where no one ever seems to be outside. Its wrought-iron tidiness defied even the blitz.

Lorna spoke to Mrs. Parnell on the phone; an early visit was arranged.

A soft chime rang when Lorna pushed the polished brass button.

Mrs. Parnell seemed older than her husband, who took Lorna's hand at the threshold. "I can see why he was swept off his feet," he said.

"Orde told me how kind you were. Mrs. Parnell, I hope you didn't prepare anything."

"This is our hour for tea. Manfred's schedule is so irregular. I have some lemon."

"I'd love some. Thank you very much."

Over the silver tea service was the picture of a twenty-year-old looking out at the future with confidence in the verities represented by his
uniform. Lorna sat down to study him while his parents stood silently. Lorna was the first to take out a handkerchief.

"Colin will never age," said Dr. Parnell. "That's almost like never
dying."

"A most noble expression," said Lorna, her chin trembling. "Orde...
might have the words to fit yours. . . . I'm afraid I do not." She nodded
thanks as Mrs. Parnell poured tea.

"Where did he die?" asked his mother. "We were told it was secret."

"In Burma."

"He was a Chindit?" his father asked. The press was featuring the
existence of the expedition without providing any details.

"Yes. He surely was."

"We knew he volunteered for something. His address was an Indian brigade."

"Orde was personally and deeply grieved. You know he owes his
command to you. . . . This must be such a bitter irony."

"Manfred is incapable of bitterness. I. . . I'm afraid that I'm wasted
by it." Mrs. Parnell began to sob.

"Evelyn."

"I'm sorry. I'm very sorry, Mrs. Wingate."

"I urge her to express the grief, Lorna. 'The soul would have no
rainbow had the eyes no tears.'"

Lorna added her own as the doctor gazed at his son. "Have you
other children?" she asked. He shook his head. "Sometimes I think
final victory will be hollow. Perhaps I shouldn't say this, but what
will be left? What can peace mean when so many. . . so very many of
our best. . . "

"When last we spoke, Orde hoped to be a parent with you."

"Not yet."

"I'm sure he told you about the soothsayer."

"Yes."

"No doubt he's right."

"We very much hope so. Doctor. . . "

"I'm Manfred, please."

"Thank you. Orde owes you his command. My debt is much greater—
I owe you his health."

"I was nothing more than a scribe recording his recovery. Orde generates his own health, his own strength, indeed his own future."

"And he's capable of generating his own destruction. Forgive me—I don't want to revive his case."

"We have lost our son, Lorna." Parnell caressed his wife's shoulder. "It would be doubly painful if you lost your husband. So let us speak of the possibility: you're quite right—Orde can destroy himself."

"And others with him," said Mrs. Parnell hoarsely. "I'm sorry. I don't mean to be intimate."

"Please.... How could we be anything but intimate?"

"Presumption is no part of Evelyn's character. I hope you see that."

"I do. Certainly."

"When Orde is a father he may find the missing ingredient. I'm all the more sure of that now—for the ingredient has vanished from me...."

Dr. Parnell gave himself to weeping so convulsive that Lorna silently excused herself.

86

There were signs of the Japanese everywhere. Even beyond the Mu, where Wingate expected patrols to be few, there were fresh tracks by the streams, crushed twigs on the trails. Approaching the gap between the Z ranges, the four men rested by day and moved by moonlight.

They had seen the gap as a deep notch on the jungle horizon; it was a major gorge ahead, a funnel for any movement through the hills, and surely a site for Japanese ambush.

They climbed slowly through stacks of deadfall; each man peering into the darkness to place his feet. When Jarrett paused to look again up the gorge, the moon cast a narrow shadow across it. Below him an invisible stream gurgled over rocks exposed by the dry season.

The shadow could have been a mass of vines hanging across the stream. A second possibility stopped Jarrett as he swung his leg astride a massive log. The Chindits froze, supressing heavy breathing. Jarrett had to have a closer look. He sidled toward the stream.

It was a rope bridge hanging inert in the moonlight; a tunnel-like trail opened the jungle at both ends. Jarrett reached back to beckon the others forward: this gorge must be given a wide bypass.

Myers and Au Thang slid over the massive log, stripping its rotted bark as they did, leaving Wingate a treacherous slippery surface. He fell heavily, his rifle clattered against the log.

Jarrett waited for the background sounds to return, but the jungle seemed to be holding its breath. He turned to retrace his steps. The four men backed away from the sagging rope as if it were a giant serpent.

After weeks of patrolling, the Japanese had heard weapons fall in the jungle. The sound is unmistakable. They knew men were out there, the question was only who and how many. A large group could not have approached without making more noise, so the platoon leader withheld his machine gun. Twelve carbines shredded the jungle with saturation fire till the platoon leader's whistle stopped them like the stroke of a conductor's baton.

Two Japanese stepped over the cartridges they'd fired, moving as stealthily as the Chindits. At the massive log gouged by bullets they found Jarrett. They dragged him by the arms through the snags and branches as if to add an additional punishment to death.

He was the first Chindit to be killed by this platoon from the Ywatha patrol base, indeed the first encounter in the gap between the Z ranges. Jarrett was duly decapitated as a possible Wingate, but at Ywatha a glance at his red hair brought disappointment. The price remained on Wingate's head while Jarrett's joined a pile from Central Force.

The hillside was impossibly steep and overgrown. Leaves slapped against their mouths till they could taste the jungle. They were struggling up, up where there was no water in the gullies and the sun's heat sifted through dry, haggard foliage. All night and through the next day they had struggled up the ridge, which seemed to have no crest.

Though beyond there were ridges equally smothered and forbidding, Wingate had to reach the top of this first one or else, like a mountain climber halted beneath the summit, he would perish on the steep slopes where rest was impossible. He was at the end of his strength, but Myers was worse: a ricochet had lodged in the back of his neck. He had not lost much blood, but the wound was bursting with infection.

By dark they reached the crest and collapsed in a grove of mahogany. As the night cooled they awoke to lick condensation from the bark.

"I'm staying here, sir," Myers said wheezing.

"No you're not. Let me see it." Wingate raised himself to touch the wound. "Can I take the bandage off?"

"Last one, sir."

"Use mine," said Au Thang. A great white patch covered his eye where a branch had jabbed it.

"You'll need it, mate."

"I get water in next valley. Bring it up here."

"This is my last night. Take my word for it."

"Hang on a bit, Myers. There'll be water downhill."

"No, my mates are waiting for me."

When Wingate awoke in the predawn, he heard only one man breathing. Myers lay on his back, his hands by his side, eyes open, lips drawn back in the rictus of death. They could take no chance of his being found; his body plunged down the steep slope he had climbed the day before to be caught by vines that enshrouded it forever.

The next valley was a ravine. At the bottom a stream trickled through undergrowth so dense and matted Wingate had to dip the canteens without ever seeing the water. The following climb took the remainder of the long day.

They were somewhere in the South Z Range struggling west. The two men said nothing, though Au Thang could sometimes see Wingate's lips move. The ridges kept rising over them like combers on the open sea.

Once they came upon three eggs of an unknown bird; once they ate a small lizard after stalking it for an hour. There were berries and roots which they ate without asking; there were hard-shelled beetles and grubs. If they were trapped, they were not lost, for they pressed on to the west, west into the afternoon light, west against the grain of the ridges.

Stumbling, crashing, they took another descent. The inevitable stream slaked their thirst at the bottom; then the wall of trees confronted them once again. Once more they prepared to climb but found themselves walking. The forest was thick but seemed to be separating. There was a vague familiarity in the pattern of growth; it seemed they had traversed such a jungle years before when they were young and strong.

Weaving through the trees, staggering erratically, they entered a dell where the underbrush thickened. Over the next hour they began to recognize a western slope. The shallow valley eventually turned to the south; they moved away from it, but the drain of the land had suggested itself: they were at last somewhere in the watershed of the Chindwin.

A distant trumpeting carried through the jungle. Wingate believed he was hallucinating; he had already experienced some malarial delirium. He tapped Au Thang, who was leading.

"Did you hear?"

"Elephants."

"Wild?"

Au Thang nodded. In time they came upon trails bulldozed through the jungle zigzagging between patches of the elephants' favorite vegetation. They came upon dung the size of burlap bags, which they picked through for edible grains.

In the second day out of the Z Range they crossed the first man-made trail. It ran north-south, probably for woodcutters, but it looked too heavily traveled for peaceful use.

In two more hours they came to another trail that seemed on an intersecting course with the first; this suggested a settlement to the north where the trails met. A settlement would probably mean Japanese.

No risk could override their need for rice: they decided to turn north. Au Thang led; he would approach the settlement to see if the Burmese were alone. Wingate followed twenty yards behind, just close enough to keep him in sight. Au Thang carried the Japanese carbine to impersonate a BIA soldier.

Wingate watched Au Thang lurch down the trail. His pants were held up by one loop around the moldy belt. Long tears showed skin the color of parchment. The soles of his boots flapped like sandals. Wingate glanced down to realize he looked much the same.

He limped forward quickly so as not to lose sight of Au Thang, for the trail began to bend. His vision blurred as his mind drifted like a radio tuned between overlapping stations: the trail became a road and then a trail again. Au Thang was another man, or the figures may have merged. Then the road was back, the road from the gorge, the gorge at Safartak. Au Thang walked on but then he was Atkins, Atkins approaching the truck...turning to say,

"You win. I lose. Winners go on..."

"Au Thang!"

He looked back. The bullets hit and spun him toward Wingate. Figures rushed toward them. Au Thang screamed under the bayonet. Wingate bolted into the jungle.

87

By day the jungle is a place of fleeting motion. Birds on the wing dart warily beneath the branches and often alight to reset their bearings. Below there is even less movement. The predators are nocturnal, so by day the jungle floor is ruled by the elephant, and even it does not much disturb the habitat. Though its passage is ponderous and destructive, the foliage rises from under its weight almost as the sea reclaims the wake of ships.

For all its strength the elephant respects the jungle and the contours of the land. Though invulnerable, the elephant watches more than it moves. It seems to know that the message of the jungle is to wait—to watch and wait—for something is always about to happen, or something may.

Wingate's motions were neither fleeting nor respectful of the contours he was crossing. He fought the jungle in long spasms, resting to

pant and suck his sweat, then crashed on, glancing at the treetops
where dappled sunlight filtered down to him. The general glow of the
afternoon was his only guide, for but one direction concerned him—
west.

He may have heard the pursuit behind him: there was no way he
could be sure. Sometimes it seemed to be approaching, sometimes falling back. And it began not to matter. The foliage took on ethereal
shades like double images of their natural colors. Birds he perhaps had
heard but had never seen during the long escape now flit among the
branches. River birds he imagined; like shorebirds sighted on an endless voyage, they might be harbingers of his destination.

This was tropical magnificence he had not appreciated, not even
seen. Nightfalls and daybreaks in wilderness splendor. Mighty columns
of mahogany giving way to teak with its carpet of leaves crunching
underfoot. Then bamboo—bamboo of the kind around major water.
Small clumps at first, then whole islands in the jungle. Daylight led
him west but west led him into heavier stands of bamboo. Till it became a wall.

He peered into darkness while the midday sun flowed around him.
The bamboo stalks crowded each other to unseen depths. He wandered
from side to side seeking an entrance. The bamboo grove curved before him like the coastline of an undiscovered continent, sinuously,
intriguingly—as if to beckon him ashore. He entered a grassy bay.
Within it he found a narrow opening into the interior.

The opening tapered to the width of his body. He squeezed through
to another passage. If he was lost, he was also safe, for no pursuit could
follow. But now there was no further progress. The bamboo enclosed
him. What light there was gave no direction. A tent-shaped opening,
no higher than his knee, was the last parting of the solid wall. It was
as dark as a rat hole; yet he crawled in.

In this animal trail were things unseen. He heard them scuffle and
slither to make room. A serpent hissed before his face; his cry sent it
on to even smaller passages.

The slimy tunnel deflected from a huge banyan tree, its convo-
luted trunks merging into its roots. He climbed, leaving blood and
skin on the bark. Breathing with open mouth, he pulled himself up.

There were thick branches, plenty of support. He climbed higher
as the sun expanded on a green panorama. From above the bamboo
tops he inched out on a limb and parted the leaves. In all directions

a great wash of sprouting bamboo grew like a lawn almost as high as the limbs of isolated trees like his. There was no going back, no going forward. There was no farther to go; this was the end of the expedition.

His head fell on his hand as he realized it. First one ankle, then the other unanchored from the limb. In a minute his consciousness wavered, his body rolled.

There was young bamboo where he fell; it crushed under his weight. He felt an inch of water running under his body, then he passed out again.

It was twilight, when the eyes adjust to seeing in darkness.

Wingate watched the bayonet tip descend to the point of his chin. The blade was stuck through a "Wanted" leaflet. A hulking aborigine, draped in hides, appeared to confront him. He tapped the bayonet point on Wingate's beard.

"Who are you?" Wingate asked, easing himself to a sitting position. The answer registered in his mind, bypassing the auditory medium.

"A hermit."

"From God?"

"From you. From us."

"I don't understand." He focused on the bayonet. "I can't think while death is so near."

The hermit looked down on Wingate with growing distaste. *"That's when you think best. Because death is the source of your spell."*

"What spell?"

"It wraps around you like those vines holding up the rotted tree. I remove myself so you may study it." The hermit tucked the bayonet under his hides. Wingate thought he would disappear as the aborigines had vanished before.

"Where is the river?"

"I am not here to be used. Understand that."

"Do you hate me?"

"You rob souls of their chosen time in this world."

"But what is most precious in this world? I say it's freedom!"

"It is time. *In the mortal world what is most precious is time."*

"I fight those who devote their time to destruction."

"You fight yourself."

"No, the Japanese."

"You will see their creed and yours as only different shades of illusion. To see that will be the punishment for you both."

"I pay for my sins by fighting evil." It seemed the hermit responded with laughter. "My faith is my confidence."

"Your faith was created by creeds you accepted as coming from God." Wingate shook his head, closed his eyes, gripped his forehead, and plunged into memory. *"Take no blame for your first ignorance. It was in Lodolf."*

"Lodolf!"

"Have you forgotten?"

"Hermit, can you also see ahead?"

"All is here to see."

"I never studied mysteries."

"What you call the future is veiled to preserve the present. Like Ishmael, I can tell you that two paths lead from here, two future lines traced from your past. The first moves sideward. The second branches before the horizon: to the left, darkness before the next plane; to the right, clouds."

"I will draw it."

Wingate raised himself uncertainly, took the bayonet and carved the sand, but confusion overcame him and the hermit's picture faded.

"Do you still want to see?"

"Yes!"

"Watch what I draw." The hermit traced on the sand a Y-shaped rune, with a right-angle turn before the fork of the Y.

"On this rising line your life has cut a channel not easily turned. We are here where the angle is sharp. It turns you to me."

"How?"

"You are lost in the jungle. Like many of your followers you will never be found. You can start a second life from here and even leap through the next plane."

"But my wife."

"Let us look." He stirred the silt to swirl away in the silent current. *"Lorna shall have your son. There is a second life for her and reunion in another age. You have shared with her little more than what you craved."*

"No!"

"If the past is too much, you must wait for the future."

"I have no feeling to travel with you, hermit."

"You feel no need."

"No."

"Then let others state the need. Look again at the water. Look long."

The hermit slashed a cross in the flooded sand. The grains spurted into a rivulet that became a flaxen surge streaming into the current; and from this flow rose the nether scenes of Wingate's wars, the starvings, the drownings, the wounds of gunshot, bayonet, and torture. Like photos on a carousel, the hermit held each scene before the mind's eye and imparted the man's name.

"George Sexton...William York...Colin Parnell...John Tuttle... Miles Kincaid...Nigel Briggs..."

"Stop!..."

"Bugasi Vishnarama...Dawa Sherpa...Ronald Jeffers...James Underwood...Richard Jarrett...Thomas Myers...Au Thang..."

"Stop it!"

"I've just begun." He jabbed again at the sand. *"Look back at the water."*

"Take them away!"

"As many lives as grains of sand. Look—I command you!" The hermit hurled the bayonet where it stuck in the roiling flow. *"Would that every general be brought to these sands."*

Wingate sobbed. "Hermit, must I face this?"

"And more. You must meet the Arab, Italian, Ethiopian, the Kachin, Burmese, and Japanese. And there are animals, creatures God put on earth for purposes other than slaughter."

"Have I no higher purpose?"

"To make art of war. That has been the highest purpose you set for yourself. It is your spell. You must break it, on this plane or the next."

"I would shatter."

"On this plane I would guide you. On the next there will be other guides. Some might be men you sent to their death."

"I will shatter."

"Do you think yourself whole now?"

Wingate shot a glance at the bayonet, then at his toes awash in the shallow current. "For all you have shown me, I cannot go with you."

"Your countrymen hold you high. You can have that memory if you take the path with me."

"But if I go on to the last fork?"

"It branches as you can see. Both directions lead to "glory," as your deceiving language calls it. You may have to see this. Look back at the waters—I'll show you deaths to come."

"No!" Wingate turned his face away.

"Then I'll speak certain words. Glory. Rank. Power. Think as these meanings revive in you. Glory, rank, power. Now to the water—look, I say!" Slowly, furtively, Wingate's eyes returned to the sands still writhing in images. *"Glory. Rank. Power."* The horrors dissolved like scraps of paper drawn into fire. *"The blinders of conscience: glory, rank, power. The smoke that closes the inner eye. Glory, rank, and power can even erase these moments in the stream."*

"They have never been my masters."

"That you can test."

Wingate staggered to the banyan tree and slumped against it. "Would it be well for me to die?"

"Churchill will answer you."

"I could lie down here."

"You stand in the Chindwin's water. The far shore can be reached under today's sun."

"But I could remain here beneath this tree and die."

"That is beyond my control. To me it is better than the left fork; that leads to Israel, a land which shall have war enough without you."

"I...I..."

"Serve life for once! Serve war no more when this one is over."

"I would serve Zion if it called me."

"It will."

"I'm like this stream. I cannot stop myself."

"Then take the other branch."

"Where does it go?"

"It is opportunity for quick escape, yet with time for reflection."

"Early death?"

"So it will seem."

"Must I deliberately...like Cairo?"

"No. Choose that branch and I will bring you to it."

"Can you do that?"

"Only if you ask."

"Do it."

"Look at me. What do you see?"

"A silhouette."

"My head. What do you see?"

"Your hair drapes it like a hood."

"Yes. As a hood I shall appear again. When you see it you will join me. Steep yourself in life till then."

"When?"

"After rewards tumble upon you like a torrent. You have served a worthy cause by your own standards and you may be part of a higher purpose not given for me to understand. That is my feeling, so now I seal the message of the sands. Look at me once more, Orde Charles. A new life will bud next time we meet."

The boughs dropped where the hermit vanished.

88

Early morning mist seeped up the hillside, tugging insubstantially at drooping vines rising from the valley where the mist enclosed the river like a cocoon. It was unusually cool for the dry season—cool and damp—a condition which kept Scoones's outpost under their blankets after daybreak when they should have been alert for stand-to.

One man roused himself. A match scratched into flame; soon bacon sizzled on the campfire, its odor drifting with the natural vapors. A battered kettle began to whistle faintly. Men stirred under their blankets, yawning in contemplation of another monotonous day. No one heard the foliage part.

*   *   *

"How do you know?" General Scoones's aide barked into the field phone.

The wire through the jungle was miles long, the answer faint but excited: "He *says* he is! And he's got that helmet..."

"How does he look?"

"Not too spry."

"Get the strip ready for an L-1."

The trees rushed at him as if he were falling in an avalanche. His stomach rocked back against the seat till he felt he would vomit. Then sky filled the windscreen; blue, cloud-dotted sky—more sky than he'd seen in three months.

The light plane leveled off close to the treetops. He couldn't remember the geography, though somewhere beyond the ranges was their destination, Imphal. The jungle had finally released him; looking down he felt the plane skim over it like a motorboat.

The American pilot looked over at him. An acrid stench filled the cockpit as if a corpse were strapped into the copilot's seat. The pilot smiled as he thought of the reception ahead: a red-coated band playing for this man who looked and smelled like an Indian beggar.

He had to be helped down the short ladder and steered toward the greeting party, which advanced toward the plane when they saw him so feeble. Suddenly Slim hovered over him. Wingate saluted him with a Japanese bayonet.

"Well, Arden," Slim said over his shoulder, "the planning for this ceremony overlooked an important contingency." The greeting party laughed, as Wingate's tunic was too tattered to receive his third DSO.

The press could hardly be held back as he was led to an ambulance. He appeared dumbfounded by their shouted questions. A photographer who asked him to raise his helmet got only the picture of a dazed stare.

"How did he look?" Wavell asked, calling from New Delhi.

"A mix of Gandhi and Rip Van Winkle—with a little Rasputin."

"What did he say?"

"A word of thanks."

"What?"

"Yes—and to Arden. It quite took him aback. Something about the excellent support we provided throughout the expedition."

"Zounds!"

"He's in a bad way. All these chaps are in much worse shape than Dalton's."

"Where are you keeping him?"

"Same tea plantation as Dalton."

"How's Bruce's arm?"

"They think they can save it."

"You don't expect any trouble between them, do you? All this may be a little too much even for Orde. Don't let the comparison with Rip Van Winkle go beyond his appearance."

"Not to worry. They are both under the charge of a marvelous nurse, Matron MacGeary."

"How soon do you think he can travel?"

"That's up to the doctors. You want him in Delhi?"

"Winston wants him in London."

Slim suspected their connection had garbled. "Who did you say?"

"The PM, Bill. Let me read you a little letter from Churchill to Ismay; quote: 'See how these difficulties are mounting up and what a vast expenditure of force is required for trumpery gains.' He's talking about the Arakan, Bill."

"Oh..."

"'All the commanders on the spot seem to be competing with one another to magnify their demands and the obstacles they must overcome.' That's you and me, I suppose. 'All this shows how necessary it is to decide on a commander. I still consider he should be a determined and competent soldier...' He's talking about someone to take my job. Now yours: '*Wingate should command the army against Burma. He is a man of genius and audacity, rightly discerned by all eyes as a figure quite above the ordinary. There is no doubt that, in the welter of inefficiency and lassitude which have characterized our operations on the India front, this man, his force and his achievements, stand out; no mere question of seniority must obstruct the advance of real personalities to their proper stations in war. He should come home for discussions at an early date.*'...Bill, are you there?"

"Yes....Sorry, sir. I'm quite dumbstruck."

"So was I. Needless to say, I feel Wingate is far too erratic to command an army."

"Then maybe the best approach is to let Churchill see that for himself."

"Pack him straight off for London?"

"I'll speak to the doctors."

"Give this a second thought. Orde can charm the fangs from a cobra."

Twilight had only begun to cool the veranda but Wingate was already bundled in a blanket. Matron MacGeary had studied him closely before allowing him to watch the sunset from a deck chair. He was clearly having a recurrence of malaria and should be in bed if not in the hospital. She had dismissed Slim's inquiry regarding Wingate's ability to travel. Out of the question, she said; he was to have total rest for a week before even receiving visitors.

Dalton was not a visitor but rather the only other patient recuperating at the tea plantation overlooking the Imphal Plateau. Near Homalin his arm had been shattered during South Force's last action in Burma. It was an unnecessary engagement, a hasty attack ordered by Dalton as a swan song to the expedition.

His footsteps squeaked on the veranda; he expected Wingate to turn, but the frail, bundled figure in the deck chair continued to tap a Japanese bayonet against his stomach.

"Nice to have this view again, aye, Skipper?"

"Oh!...Bruce! Had no idea..." The bayonet clattered to the floor where he shoved it under the chair.

"Mac said not to disturb you."

"You're not. Please, won't you pull up a..."

Dalton had already rolled a deck chair. "You need to be disturbed so screw Mac."

"What's wrong with your arm?"

"Bullet. A memento from Isano."

"Who?"

"Your Japanese counterpart. When did they find you—yesterday?"

"I don't remember."

"So you haven't been briefed or...no, I guess not. Mac wouldn't let anyone near you. Well, let me tell you what happened to Mercury." Wingate stiffened. "Just some highlights: F-B took most of North Force through the Tawma Gap. Since you abdicated command, he sent Central Force through the Sheba Hills, Grayson in command. They swung around to the south—had some tough fighting in the South Range. About eighty percent of them got through." Dalton looked at Wingate for a reaction but saw none. "To make a long story short, South Force came out the Uyu Valley without much trouble, six hundred strong—or weak I should say. North Force fell into hell. Less than a hundred got through so far. Don't think there'll be many more."

"F-B?"

"Killed at Tawma. There's a chance Kane's alive: he was seen west of the Mu. Forty percent of the Chindits are unaccounted for. Forty percent." Wingate drew the blanket tighter. "You know what's worse? The papers are calling you a hero, a genius, a military miracle man. Congratulations, you butcher."

"I'm worse than that."

"Yes. Visit the hospitals and you'll hear better descriptions."

"The men hate me."

"The ones who know enough."

"Like you."

"'Seek ye shelter in the hills'—you didn't have the goddamn guts to tell me to Buckshot—give us a chance to fight our way out. All you had to say was hold 'em, Bruce, till we get the rest of the expedition back across the 'Waddy."

"I sacrificed you."

"I could accept *that,* Orde. All you had to do was tell me you needed the sacrifice. I had to sacrifice companies. I don't feel good about it, but at least I told..."

"What are you officers doing?" Matron MacGeary's formidable shadow fell across them.

"Arguing," said Dalton. "It's a sign of returning health."

"I forbid it! Colonel Dalton, return to your room at once. Brigadier Wingate, you've been up long enough. And if I hear any further contention it's off to the hospital for you both. I will *not* have my leniency abused."

"You've been very kind," said Wingate contritely. "Please forgive us."

"Miss Mac does not forgive easily," Dalton grumbled.

"For good reason in your case. What's that in your kit?"

"I was going to share a libation with my long lost commander."

"I warned you, Colonel."

"No, please..."

"Give me that bottle."

"Matron MacGeary, that's dark Jamaican..."

"Give it to me, I say."

Dalton surrendered the rum with a pitiful sigh. She drew the cork as if it were Excalibur. "You might as well return your commander to the jungle. Alcohol will undo his medications just as surely—to say nothing of spreading the infection in your arm." She began to pour the rum onto the grass. "A libation did you say, Colonel Dalton?"

"Yes, yes! Only a small one..."

"Sealing your reconciliation?"

Dalton hesitated. The brown fluid gurgled toward the bottom. "Yes," he blurted.

She snapped the bottle to horizontal. "A tot then for that purpose—but no more."

89

The Lancaster reminded him of Platt's bomber. This time it was Wavell's, equally sumptuous, equally private. Wingate was accompanied only by a nurse as the plane took off from Delhi for Karachi on the first leg to London. The similarity with his flight from Addis Ababa to Cairo seemed strangely irrelevant to him: Ethiopia belonged to a different lifetime.

How much different became evident when he landed in Cairo for refueling. A brigadier (Enright's successor) representing the commanding general, Middle East command, was there with champagne and a request: could Wingate pause long enough to address the officers at GHQ?

With a smile which he hoped did not appear ironic, Wingate had to refuse. His orders provided him no leeway whatever—he was to proceed to London as fast as the plane could fly, and there report directly to Sir Alan Brooke, Chief of the Imperial General Staff, the head of the whole army—the British army—the highest-ranking general of all.

The Lancaster's next refueling was Gibraltar. It flew peacefully over the North African coast, now free of the enemy, as was the southern half of the Mediterranean. The Allies were now fighting on Sicily, from whence they would jump onto the toe of Italy and drive that nation out of the war.

This was the summer of 1943, the pivotal year of the war when the Axis was thrown back on all fronts: the Mediterranean, Russia, and in the Pacific. The historic battles of Alamein, Stalingrad, and Midway marked a permanent turn of the tide, for though D Day in Normandy was still a year away, everywhere the Allies were on the march. Everywhere except in Burma, the only stagnant theater.

China, Burma, and India had been lumped into SEAC—Southeast Asia Command—also known as the Supreme Example of Allied Confusion. The Chinese of Chiang Kai-shek were fighting the Chinese of Mao Tse-tung with far more intensity than either fought the Japanese. However, the Americans never relented from Roosevelt's dream of arming and training Chiang's hordes to take Japan from the west while MacArthur and Nimitz closed in from the east.

Consequently, the American presence in SEAC was devoted to supply and air support to keep Chiang fighting until Slim reopened the Burma Road. American transports, temporarily diverted from Chiang's service, had provided the drops for Wingate's expedition.

It was the job of the British, as the Americans saw it, to punch through to Bhamo, the western terminus of the Burma Road. If Wingate's paltry force nearly reached the Kachin Hills, why couldn't Slim's army drive on to Bhamo? This question was an embarrassment for the British in the highest Allied military councils. In order to retain American supplies and cooperation in the all-important European theater, they had to acquiesce to the "China strategy" in SEAC.

But the British (wisely it turned out) never thought Chiang worth the trouble. Instead they had their own sub-rosa agenda for SEAC: rather than attack in strength across north Burma, they put their emphasis along the coast, hoping to leapfrog with short amphibious landings down to Rangoon and beyond to Malaya and ultimately Singapore. Such planning and requests for precious landing craft raised suspicions

among the Americans that Britain's foremost priority was to regain its
prewar empire. For this purpose the Americans were unwilling to expend their resources and blood.

Command of SEAC thus required the attributes of a keen strate-
gist and a deft diplomat. As if to assure consistent incongruity in this
mainland theater, command was awarded to an admiral. He was an
extraordinary one, a cousin of the British royal family, a man almost
as unconventional as Wingate himself: Lord Louis Mountbatten.

He became known as the "Supremo," a position above Wavell in
the British hierarchy, and as Allied commander he directed the American efforts as well. With the Chinese he also dealt with an American,
the irascible "Vinegar Joe" Stilwell, a man of many hats.

As chief of staff to Chiang, he represented them with the Supremo.
Stilwell was also commander of the American supply troops in India
except for the aviators. He was an infantry general, a fighting general,
but with an ambivalent attitude toward Wingate.

He admired the Chindits' spirit and Wingate's willingness to go
after the Japanese in the jungle, but after the expedition Stilwell called
him an exhibitionist whose erratic tactics had cost him a third of his
force (that was the final percentage when the last Chindits straggled
back). Nevertheless Stilwell recognised that LRP was an innovation in
warfare nearly as significant as Billy Mitchell's discovery that bombers
could sweep navies from the seas. Therefore Stilwell wanted his own,
an American, LRP force to lead his Chinese into north Burma. A regiment of volunteers was assembling in India for that purpose; like the
Chindits they adopted a colorful name—Merrill's Marauders.

It was to meet Mountbatten and discuss the coordination of the
Chindits with the Marauders that Wingate supposed he was being summoned to London. Naturally he hoped the Marauders would be placed
under his command for a second expedition; he had always found the
Americans easier to deal with than his own army. Most of the Marauders were jungle veterans from the Pacific, where MacArthur was
pushing the Japanese off New Guinea. Their commander, Merrill,
would therefore not be a junior partner. Wingate assumed Stilwell
would not give him operational control of the Marauders unless the
Chindit contribution to the expedition were at least double that of the
Americans. To that end, Wingate needed a second brigade. Mountbatten was the man to give it to him and appropriate rank to fit the
enlarged command.

Staring down on the Atlantic, his thoughts seemed as tossed as the waves. Unlimited ambitions crowded his mind while anticipation of reunion spun them away. His visit to London was highly secret, so much so that he had not been permitted to inform Lorna he was coming. He wondered how the excitement of the surprise, the private joys ahead of him, would compete with the intense maneuvering he must accomplish in London.

He was whisked away to the War Office without time for a phone call; there he closeted with Sir Alan Brooke for most of an afternoon. As Brooke wrote in his memoirs, Wingate pretty much had his way:

I was very interested in meeting Wingate.... [He had] turned out a great success and originated long-range penetration forces which worked right into Japanese-held territory. In the discussion I had with him he explained that he considered what he had done on a small scale could be run with much larger forces. He required, however, for these forces the cream of everything, the best men, the best NCOs, the best officers, the best equipment, and a large air lift. I considered that the results of his form of attacks were certainly worth backing within reason. I provided him with all the contacts in England to obtain what he wanted, and told him that on my return from Canada I would go into the whole matter with him to see he obtained what he wanted.

With ease which amazed him, Wingate's hands were placed on the levers of power—nearly unrestricted power. Brooke left him with only one caveat: Wingate was under no circumstances to reveal himself to the press. Glorification of the expedition had become a staple of the feature writers; if they learned the chief Chindit was in town, he would have less success eluding them than he had the Japanese.

"Don't make yourself conspicuous," said Brooke, his hand on Wingate's shoulder. "Better get into some civilian clothes as soon as you can. And could I ask you a favor?"

"Certainly, sir."

"Could you possibly shave your beard?" Wingate's hand went to his throat. "I know it's a personal matter, but, you see, in your pictures in the papers you are bearded. Less chance of recognition without it."

"Of course. It shall be done."

"Fine. The only other thing: please let 10 Downing know of your whereabouts. I believe Winston might like to meet you before we depart for Quebec."

"Quebec, sir?"

"It's the supreme state secret of the hour, Wingate—Churchill, Roosevelt, and the Combined Chiefs of Staff for both countries are to confer for the first time since Casablanca. We embark on the *Queen Mary* early in the morning. Don't breathe a word of it, not even to your wife."

90

His mind immersed in opportunities, Wingate left the War Office on a long, aimless walk. In jungle dress and pith helmet he drew many stares, none of which he noticed. Only when he passed phone booths did his attention turn from his new bounties, but for the moment his mind was in too rapid ferment to respond to Lorna's voice.

A policeman appeared ahead. He was standing at the middle of the block like a sentinel. The architecture behind him looked familiar. Wingate glanced at the sign: Downing Street. Why not? he asked himself. Rather than phone Churchill's secretary, Wingate would leave Lorna's phone number with the butler or whoever was home.

In his history of World War II, Churchill described what happened when Wingate came to the door:

> I had heard much of all this [the Chindit expedition], and also how the Zionists had sought him as a future commander-in-chief of any Israelite army that might be formed. I had him summoned home in order that I might have a look at him before I left for Quebec.
>
> I was about to dine alone on the night of August 4th at Downing when the news that he had arrived by air and was actually in the

In England, August 1943.

house was brought to me. I immediately asked him to join me at dinner.

We had not talked for half an hour before I felt myself in the presence of a man of the highest quality. He plunged into his theme of how the Japanese could be mastered in jungle warfare by long range penetration groups landed by air behind enemy lines. This interested me greatly....

I decided at once to take him with me on the voyage. I told him our train would leave at ten. It was nearly nine. Wingate had arrived just as he was after three days' flight from the actual front, and with no clothes but what he stood up in. He was of course quite ready to go, but expressed regret that he would not be able to see his wife.... [T]he resources of my Private Office were equal to the occasion.

"Mr. Prime Minister," Wingate said almost reverentially.

"I imagined you to be a larger fellow. Are you feeling well?"

"I feel like a Catholic before the Pope."

"Remember it's the Catholics who make the Pope."

"But the faithful remain so only if he shows flashes from the godhead."

"If I do, it is the reflected fire of the British spirit. Come, we've time for several drinks before dinner. Brandy?"

"Whiskey, please. I had no idea I'd be meeting you."

"The best meetings are happenstance. Sit down by the fire and let me have a better look at you. Hmmm. Much as I expected: you carry the aura of battle about you."

"And you the stamp of ultimate victory. You, of all others, sir, make us proud to be Englishmen."

"It's heady stuff being a symbol. Pride and accomplishments are like water on both sides of a lock. Sometimes the two levels are even, but more often not. Such is your case, sir. Your rank is not level with you accomplishments. I shall take steps to equalize them. Here's to the Chindits and their fascinating commander."

Churchill removed his cigar and raised his glass. Wingate drank half of his before setting it down.

"Your excellent whiskey shall be my excuse to speak more freely than etiquette might allow."

"By all means."

"Then I must tell you in candor that I've come to question my ability to command."

"Nonsense. You only need rest."

"My vision for long-range penetration is clearer than ever. However, I've begun to shrink before the prospect of so many lives entrusted to the man I become in the field. If you think less of me, Sir Winston, for this admission it is because I am less."

Churchill touched him on the knee. "Contrawise, my dear Wingate: I think all the more of you. Your admission is indeed startling, not for its content but for prejudice to your personal advancement. Here you are telling the man who could give you an army that you hesitate to receive it. You put the welfare of the army before your own ambitions; I know of no other general who would sincerely do so. May I shake your hand."

"I feel much better."

"And so do I. My commanders rarely reveal themselves as you have. Nay, they never do, not when our mission in this war turns us numb to the ghastly responsibilities we treat as routine. I've thought of men dying for my inadequacy. You've seen them."

"That, I'm afraid, is a source of my anguish: I've scarcely seen them even when they fell all around me."

"But from what you say, you've felt them die—felt them like a deep puncture which leaves little evidence on the surface. A tiny scar. A tough one. Believe me, we could not send men to die, you and I, if it weren't for the denseness of our scars."

"I will mull on your insights."

"You cannot mull with an empty glass." Churchill gestured to the decanter beside Wingate. "I expected to be enthralled by your plan to expel the Japanese, but you have drawn us into even more interesting topics."

"There was something you once said—in a speech, I suppose."

"Almost everything I say now is in a speech."

"Yes," Wingate laughed.

"Which one?"

"Not so famous. Not 'blood and sweat.'"

"Thank goodness."

"You spoke of dying on an occasion. That this—this war—was a time..."

"When it is equally good to live or to die."

"Yes. And you're quite right."

"Not for you, my boy. Life is your element! It is about to give you its resources. I've rarely seen Brooke so enthusiastic as he is for your strategy. Was he accommodating?"

"Completely."

"He's usually a miser. I've seen Montgomery leave his office in a rage. Put your penitence behind you, Orde. The world is turning to smile on you."

"I'm beginning to notice that."

"We've much to talk about. But first your immediate plans: we sail tomorrow at dawn."

"Sail?"

"To Quebec. My third conference with Roosevelt. There'll be major decisions for Burma. This is utterly secret, of course. Is there anything to prevent you from accompanying me?"

"You are my prime minister, but Lorna is my wife."

"Nearsighted of me. Just a moment." He picked up a phone. "Clive, Brigadier and Mrs. Wingate are going with us. Yes, do. I'll consider it done. Now then," he said, turning to Wingate, "how did the sensibilities of a humanist become fused with the attributes of a commando? I've heard you kill Japs with your bare hands. Or did you use that bayonet? The butler wanted to disarm you, didn't he?"

"I'm much better prepared to discuss strategy than biography, Sir Winston."

"Then do. You will make a marvelous impression on the Americans. You are the one man who can dispel the notion that the British army is reluctant to fight the war of the jungle. How did you accomplish what you have? And how will you carry long-range penetration to final victory?"

"Aerial strongholds, sir. This time we shall fly in. There are dozens of potential airstrips in northern Burma which, with some work by lightly equipped engineers, could handle C47s. We shall land fresh and saucy at remote sites so the Japs cannot reach us for several days. They'll find us dug in, supported with artillery, and ready to fight. The Japs will dash themselves against our strongholds; then we'll sally out to cut their roads and rails. Our strongholds will be permanent patrol bases, protected areas from where we can evacuate the wounded..."

"Go on."

"The wounded, sir, will never be abandoned again."

91

Her phone rang at midnight. It was Churchill's private secretary. No, nothing had happened to Orde; she was asked to excuse the hour and prepare for a "trip" of several weeks' duration—her obvious questions would be answered within hours.

Through the night the train retraced the journey of her first wartime reunion. Though the destination was unknown to her she was headed for Glasgow and a familiar quayside. Lorna was checked through two security barricades; when she emerged from the second she could make out the looming outline of the famous ocean liner. Tiny at the foot of the gangplank was another now famous silhouette—the man in the pith helmet.

He spun her with her feet off the ground.

"We're the last to board."

"Let me look at you!"

"Come. We shall do little else."

Churchill's party numbered two hundred, a tenth of the *Queen Mary's* peacetime capacity, but with all its prewar luxuries preserved and now reserved for the supremely important. The Wingates were among them, almost one of them, Lorna realized as she gazed from her porthole at the summer sea.

Wingate drowsed nude on the spacious bed behind her. In his semisleep he felt for her, asked for her in the aftermath of morning love.

"Close by you, dear," she said, and slipped down beside him. "Shall I ring for tea?"

"What a thought." He watched her with a drowsy smile.

"What a dream."

"Aren't you afraid this idyll will spoil you for the rest of the war?"

"'Live today,' didn't someone say?"

"Churchill had a similar recommendation for me, did I tell you?"

"About life beginning to reward you?"

"Yes. And so suddenly."

"Like winning the lottery."

"Winners go to the next round."

"Why did you say that?"

"Winners?...Yes, that's Atkins again, isn't it? Wonder where he is."

"Why wouldn't you let me trace him?"

"Faces go by like riders on a carousel. I can't stop to focus."

"After the war."

"Yes, I very much want to see him. And Manfred if I can endure it. This ship reminds me of our talks."

"And what about the *Cathay?*"

"Yes, of course. At least as romantic, wouldn't you say?"

"I should hope so—without mother here."

"What did she think of me?" Wingate pulled the sash for room service.

"More impressed than I."

"Nonsense. I devastated you."

"I can only recall one kiss."

"Then you turned to leave me forever."

"So young, yet so wise."

"Regrets?"

"Only when you're far away. And fear for you, Orde. You'll never know my fear."

"There's more war behind than ahead of us now, Lorna. The end is in sight. At Quebec they'll be planning the beginning of the end."

Foremost on the Quebec agenda was the shape and size of Overlord, the cross-channel invasion of France. In this Wingate had a professional but not a personal interest. On the grand stage of the world war, he had but a supporting part: Burma was still a sideshow but an important one in terms of overall Allied comity.

From the British view, Burma was the area in which they could accede to American demands in order to extract concessions for more important theaters. To this end Wingate found himself in the unique position of being a point of agreement between the Allies: The Americans wanted a decisive drive across upper Burma and so did he. The British high command wished to skip down the coast toward Singapore. If the Americans were satisfied with the size and vigor of a second Chindit expedition, the rest of Mountbatten's forces might be available for amphibious ambitions.

"So you'll be working for Lord Mountbatten? How exciting!" Little had been less than exciting from the moment the phone in London had sprung her from sleep. Now she was enjoying the transformation of her husband from an army brigadier to a naval officer, for such was the only uniform available on the ship. She laughed as he buttoned the double-breasted tunic.

"You'd rather have me in jungle dress?"

"Heavens no. You're strikingly handsome in blue. Is it too late to transfer to the navy?"

"With Churchill all things are possible. Though I would prefer to miss these formal dinners."

"The admiral of the jungle seas."

"They almost drowned me," he said, studying his new appearance. He wore no rank on his naval uniform, only the ribbon for his three DSOs. Once again he was clean-shaven.

"I want to hear about it tonight."

He unbuttoned the tunic. "Then let's take dinner here."

"We can't just be absent from a seated dinner."

"I think we can. We're small fish in this ocean."

"Orde, I borrowed this gown from Lady Ismay. She'll be looking for us."

He nodded glumly. "You're enjoying all this, aren't you, dear?"

"Aren't you?"

"Yes. Of course. I should be more grateful. It's just so much, so fast. Such luxuries should be spaced through one's life, not consumed in a single orgy."

"Take your orgies when you can, darling. Like Selassie's palace."

"Maybe that's what inhibits me—the debacle after the palace."

"There is no Platt here to shanghai you."

"No, the Platts are in India now."

"And you're quite safely out of their reach."

"You're right, my dearest, as you usually are. I must teach myself to relax."

"Let me pour you a whiskey."

"Ever attentive; ever loving. What a world it would be without womankind." He opened the porthole and sipped the drink she handed him. "Your love seems to come almost from another species—or at least a breed different than mine."

"The sexes are complementary." She poured herself wine. "Do you remember us speaking of that?"

"In Sheffield I think." Breeze wafted through the porthole like a spirit. "Lorna, if the war were to claim me, do you think you would remarry?"

"What?"

"I just felt like asking."

"What a brutal question."

"Sorry."

"It's very painful to even think of it. You are irreplaceable. I would wish to die. Is that what you want to hear?"

"No, no: the last thing I want to hear."

"Remember how we closed the discussion of your suicide? Let's do the same with the subject of remarriage. Or should I ask you the same question?"

"Selfish of me. Here," he said brightly, "let's go out among the beribboned statesmen. They are a cast for your enjoyment. You've had less to enjoy from this war than I. This is a holiday you well deserve."

"You've found things to enjoy in this war? To hear that makes me feel you *are* from another species."

"Yes, it's the ultimate male vice."

"Incomprehensible."

"Can you understand everything I feel?"

"I want to."

He rebuttoned his tunic. "Let me put it—illustrate it—this way: every Chindit, dead or alive, would not begrudge me these hours, for I paid for them in full."

"That's enjoying war?"

"That's enjoying what war brings. Without anticipating it, without requiring it. Only deserving it." Glenn Miller music drifted down the decks from the ballroom. "Shall we dance? No, we should go, shouldn't we?"

"Oh I hope my dinner partner isn't dull. I'm very much spoiled being with you."

"Eat an onion. Perhaps he shall surrender you to me."

They searched among the outlying tables but couldn't find their names. At the center of the ballroom a tall, elegant admiral gestured for their attention.

"Orde, isn't that...?"

"Yes. Lord Louis."

"I think he wants us over there. She's frightfully attractive."

"If you're seated by Mountbatten, he has the better trade."

Lord Mountbatten, great grandson of Queen Victoria, could have been a creation from Lodolf. His lineage reached back to Charlemagne, with subsequent blood relations among the czars and kaisers as well as close kinship to the House of Windsor. It was said of his family that the wars of Europe were family squabbles. The Prince of Wales was his best man at his wedding to the beautiful heiress, Edwina Ashley.

"But he's no playboy," Wingate whispered as they crossed the ballroom.

Hardly. At the opening of the war, Mountbatten commanded the destroyer *Kelly,* escorting endangered convoys through the English Channel, hunting U-boats in the North Sea, and evacuating commandos from Norway. Bombed and torpedoed, the *Kelly* was ordered scuttled, but, adrift on the hulk with eighteen volunteers, Mountbatten brought her home under tow. A year later off Crete he finally abandoned ship after taking a bomb in the magazine. Adrift once more, this time on flaming oil, Mountbatten's raft was strafed by German planes.

He was awarded a much deserved DSO, then given the tasks of developing the Allied headquarters and technology for the invasion of France. His imagination was a match for Wingate's; among his proposals was an "unsinkable airfield" composed of frozen seawater and wood pulp, a laughable fantasy, but similar in innovation to two of his ideas which became realities. One was PLUTO, or petroleum line under the ocean, a pipe which fed fuel directly from England to the beaches of Normandy; also his idea were the giant pontoons towed across the channel and sunk with the hulks of ships to form artificial harbors.

He became Supremo at the age of forty-three, an admiral whose talents had surpassed his element. Many considered him the greatest military generalist produced by World War II. As Supremo, he had only one counterpart: Eisenhower. Lorna could not help but be dazzled.

"And how did he dance?" Wingate asked with mock gruffness. It was late; they were strolling the deck alone.

"Superbly no doubt; I only remember what he said."

"Tell me in spite of my jealousy."

"He said I glided before him like a summoning spirit."

"Oh."

"And Lady Mountbatten?"

"No similar comment."

Their kiss sputtered with laughter.

92

At high speed, protected by even faster destroyers, *Queen Mary* "drove on through the waves" in Churchill's words, while "we lived in the utmost comfort on board her with a diet of pre-war times. As usual on these voyages, we worked all day long." As a last-minute addition to the party Wingate had less to do and abundant time to prepare his presentation to the Americans, whose air support, even more than the Marauders, was vital to his plans.

Early in the voyage Churchill summoned him to give what amounted to a dress rehearsal for Quebec. Field Marshal Brooke attended as devil's advocate, interrupting with the sort of objections the Americans were likely to raise. Both he and the prime minister and the chief of the imperial staff found the same fault in Wingate's proposals, a fault which followers of his life could least imagine.

"They said I wasn't 'thinking big,'" said the bemused Chindit.

"I don't understand the expression," Lorna replied.

"It's an Americanism—means I'm not asking for enough."

"Well, my dear, go down to your wishing well."

"I've asked for three brigades—the equivalent of a division. They don't think the Americans will take us seriously unless we're planning for eight or so brigades; that's practically a corps."

"Could you use all those troops?"

"Could I! I'd sweep north Burma like a cyclone. From at least three directions as well as by air. This is stupendous."

"Well don't spend all your time now poring over those maps."

"Just the rest of the day."

"Orde, aren't you afraid with so many troops they'll put someone over you?"

"What do you mean?" He was already circling potential strongholds around Lake Indawagyi.

"Well a corps calls for a lieutenant general."

"I forgot to mention: I'll have a second star before we land. If a Chindit corps is approved, there'll be a third by the end of the month."

"Orde! How can you be so casual? Is there no end to this glory, this rank, this power? I'm utterly flabber...What's wrong?"

"What did you say?" He'd sat down to stare at her.

"I was about to say I'm utterly flabbergasted by your soaring fortunes. Aren't you? Not that I'm not confident or thrilled or..."

"No. What was it about glory?"

"Well, there's been that already. Why don't you read those clippings I gave you about the Chindits? Sometimes you hardly seem interested in their fame—*your* fame."

"And power."

"I hope it's not more than you can handle."

"It shan't be."

"Not with appropriate rank it won't. And now that is being bestowed in full measure."

"I can't explain it, but it seems I was awarded this recognition previously and only now is it manifesting."

She sat down beside him. "The soothsayer made no such prediction, did he?"

"Not to me. Most of his findings were for Selassie's ears."

"I was in such a rush that night I forgot to bring his telegram. He sent you the warmest congratulations."

"Who?"

"Selassie, of course."

"For what?"

"The Chindits, my love. When we're back in London there's a whole scrapbook of articles on your exploits. Why didn't you give anyone an interview?"

"Didn't I?"

"There's not a single quote from you."

"Well, I answered some questions as I recall. Publicity, I've found, arouses jealousy."

"I sensed that in Allen Johns's comments. *He* wasn't reluctant to speak his mind."

"What did he have to say?"

"Mostly about Colonel Dalton and how he did so much better than your force."

"There's something to that."

"'Dauntless Dalton,' the article called him."

Wingate laughed. "That he is. What else?"

"Only that American general, 'Vinegar Joe,' had anything less than complimentary to say. He seems well named."

"I respect him."

"Will he be at Quebec?"

"Not likely. He's a great pal of Marshall's, however."

"I forgot who the important Americans are."

"Most important is Marshall. If he's with me, it's beer and skittles the rest of the way. Arnold's the other one—head of the AAF. I must couple his planes with my brains. The rest are courtiers."

"Roosevelt?"

"The king. Indeed, now the king of the alliance. The American weight has tipped the scales. Europe will be largely their show."

"But not Burma."

"No, this is the only theater where we provide most of the infantry. That's the reason I may have a call on the Marauders. Stilwell permitting."

"From what you've said it doesn't sound as if he will be eager to reward you with American forces."

"Yes, I'll probably have to take a bigger slice out of Slim. Eight brigades is nearly half his army."

"Will Sir Archie help you?"

"I doubt it. His vision of the Chindits is much more circumscribed than mine. He might have supported a three-brigade force but certainly not eight. I found him almost distant the last we talked. Johns has probably poisoned the well since he moved up to Sir Archie's staff. Fancies himself as some expert in LRP now."

"Well, he went with Dalton, didn't he? That's what the papers said."

"As an observer," Wingate snorted, "halfway through the campaign. Poked around like an inspector general. Wouldn't let Bruce cut the railroad again."

"Will Johns be a nuisance for you now?"

"I'd like to put his name on one of those leaflets and drop him in the Indaung."

"What leaflets?"

"Didn't I tell you? The Japs had 'wanted' leaflets all over the jungle. With my name and picture on them. Picture of me and Selassie— I must write and tell him about it. I was worth about fifty quid."

"I hope you saved one."

Wingate pressed his eyes. "I had this terrifying dream at the end. On my belly was one of the leaflets..."

"Orde, sit down!" He had risen suddenly. The blood drained from his face. "Now do what the doctor said." She scurried to fetch his pills. "You look a fright," she said from the bathroom.

"I'm all right," he stammered.

"He said you must expect some relapses. Now lie down and take this."

He took the medication but sat on the edge of the bed staring at the rug. "I've got to tell you this. The bayonet you asked about. Someone gave it to me—I think. I believe. I don't know. This will sound..." He clenched her hand.

"Orde, I'm here. Tell me."

"I was at the Chindwin but I didn't know it...." His words babbled out. "A native—an aborigine—found me. He called himself a hermit of God....He hated me for all I'd done!" Wingate pressed his temples.

"It was a *dream*, darling. You were hallucinating."

"Then how did I get *this!*" Scrambling to the closet he brandished the Japanese bayonet.

93

The doctor called it a recurrence of malaria; Wingate was committed to his stateroom under Lorna's care. Much against his wishes he was excused from the last plenary session of the chiefs of staff where he was to have put forth his detailed propositions for Avalanche, the code name for his second expedition. Mountbatten looked in on him over the next two days. He assured Wingate that Avalanche was so well conceived that Brooke's staff was already satisfied with their understanding of it and had every confidence in its acceptance by the Americans. Wingate was enjoined to rest; that would be the best preparation for his moment on center stage in Quebec.

The idle hours weighed heavily on him. He took to roaming the decks, Lorna by his side. They reminisced about their courtship on the *Cathay* and he told her more of his voyage on *Llandovery Castle* with Dr. Parnell. Not knowing what new upset it might cause, she did not return to the episode of the bayonet. She concealed it in the closet; to her it represented evil and ill health, a specter from the jungle which should be exorcised from his memory. She planned to fling it overboard. It seemed like the scars on his throat, evidence of mutant forces within him, unpredictable and involuntary as an epileptic seizure.

Ahead of them was a rocky coast. The destroyers fell away, giving *Queen Mary* a straight passage into the harbor of Halifax. Thanks and farewells blinked between the warships and the luxury liner.

From Halifax Churchill's party boarded a special train for Quebec. They arrived three days before the Americans. Wingate's vigor seemed restored; he rehearsed and polished his presentation till he almost wea-

ried of the subject. Meanwhile Lorna deserted him for Canada's cor-
nucopia of commodities unseen during the war years in Britain.

She was shopping when he concluded his piece on center stage:

MAJOR GENERAL WINGATE: Every Chindit requires a larger measure
of support than a soldier fighting on the Fourteenth Army front. You
who allocate the resources of war best realize the Chindit must therefore be more productive. He is. During the first expedition he, in ten
weeks engaged more Japanese than his Fourteenth Army counterpart
did in ten months. Nevertheless, what is given to the Burma army
must be taken from Europe or the Pacific. We in Burma realize we are
the least important theater. Should we forget, we've only to look at
our shortages! (Laughter.) But within our scarcities we still have the
means if they are applied with vision. The vision found in the concept
of long-range penetration has been tested and demonstrated to be sound,
not just in my first expedition but with MacArthur's army as well. For
what is his leapfrogging campaign but a form of long-range penetration? He eschews frontal attack and deposits his forces by ship against
supply installations well to the rear of the Japs' fighting troops; these
he leaves to wither on the vine. In a trifling way, the first Chindit
expedition imitated these imminently successful long-range penetrations by General MacArthur.

Now what shall the second expedition be? Where the first was hit
and run, the second will be land and stay. The details are before you,
gentlemen. May I now respond to your questions? There must be many.

PRESIDENT ROOSEVELT: Bravo. Long-range penetration: a seductive
expression, Winston. Is it yours or did you hear it from Stalin?

PRIME MINISTER CHURCHILL: We are both too old. Our penetrations
are either short or not at all.

GENERAL MARSHALL: General Wingate, who will secure those landing strips for you?

MAJOR GENERAL WINGATE: No one, sir. There are innumerable landing fields in this vast area. The Japs couldn't possibly cover them all
even if they knew we were coming.

GENERAL MARSHALL: Nonetheless, one Jap with a machine gun could
deny you an entire landing field.

GENERAL BROOKE: Moreover, the aircraft you require would seriously cut into the transports supplying the Chinese.

MAJOR GENERAL WINGATE: The relative worth of my war effort compared with Chiang Kai-shek's is a matter for you gentlemen to determine.

PRIME MINISTER CHURCHILL: I wouldn't give a pinch of snuff for Chiang's whole army.

PRESIDENT ROOSEVELT: Now Winston. Hap, can we support Wingate's grand designs?

GENERAL ARNOLD: We'll have to rob Peter to pay Paul—but I think we can.

GENERAL BROOKE: Like any field commander you've padded your aircraft requirements considerably.

MAJOR GENERAL WINGATE: But I haven't.

GENERAL BROOKE: Defend then, please, this number for "medical evacuation." Throughout your expedition you call for five transports on constant call even before you've prepared the permanent landing strips. How could you use aircraft when there's no place for them to land?

MAJOR GENERAL WINGATE: Through a technique suggested to me by Colonel Cochran called "body snatching."

PRESIDENT ROOSEVELT: Body snatching! Winston, you've surpassed yourself.

PRIME MINISTER CHURCHILL: On my word: I cannot claim authorship.

GENERAL BROOKE: How's that?

GENERAL ARNOLD: Phil thinks we can pull gliders off the ground without having to land. The C47 flies low with this skyhook. The glider strings his two cable perpendicular to the flight path; he hooks and is jerked off.

GENERAL BROOKE: Jerked off. Really?

PRESIDENT ROOSEVELT: That reminds me of how de Gaulle said he first...Remember?

PRIME MINISTER CHURCHILL: Quite. I remember. He used a charming French term for it...

GENERAL MARSHALL: If the skyhook works you'll need those C47s. If it doesn't, you won't.

MAJOR GENERAL WINGATE: I will not abandon my wounded. I've simply lost that capability. I, personally, cannot send my men back into the jungle again unless I can promise them a way out if they're wounded.

GENERAL BROOKE: You're not up to it?

MAJOR GENERAL WINGATE: No, sir.

PRIME MINISTER CHURCHILL: I don't believe there's another general in the war who's faced this sort of thing. We certainly appreciate what a searing experience it's been for you, Wingate. There must be a humane side of war. I'm glad you're insisting that it be made a tangible reality.

PRESIDENT ROOSEVELT: So say we all.

Wingate's proposals were quickly translated into directives to Wavell, who in another upper-level shuffle, was now the SEAC ground forces commander and Mountbatten's principal army lieutenant. A telegram was flashed requiring him to designate the eight brigades (some twenty-five thousand men) to comprise the Avalanche expedition. He was not to concern himself with aircraft; these would come from new American assets provided by General Arnold.

The timing of the wire was perfect for Wingate. The Quebec conference would conclude in two days; Wavell would have to respond in twenty-four hours, leaving no time for Slim, Arden, and Johns to sway him. Wingate seemed to be in an unassailable position supported from the summit and soon to be reinforced by the Supremo, who, from Quebec, would fly to Ceylon to set up the new SEAC headquarters.

The answering wire from India was a marvel in extemporaneous opposition. Wavell began with a new item: the worst monsoon in eighty years was devastating the Ganges delta, wreaking havoc with the army's supplies and overloading them with humanitarian concerns (the entire city of Calcutta was facing mass starvation). Then there were the military arguments: Avalanche made auxiliaries out of the Fourteenth Army—a role reversal with the Chindits. Heretofore, a second expedition was to be an aid, not a substitute for a general advance by Fourteenth Army. Now Avalanche stripped Slim of the units necessary for such an advance, causing an imbalance that could leave the Chindits once again deep in enemy territory with no significant supporting attacks from other fronts.

Moreover, there was no time to train twenty thousand men in Chinditry; neither was there sufficient acreage at Saugor, Wingate's original training ground. Furthermore, eight independent brigades meant breaking up the newly formed West African Division with consequent colonial political repercussions.

All Wavell's remonstrances brought snickers or scoffs from Wingate until he reached the last one: the matter of command for Avalanche. Though Johns's and Arden's hands were evident in the argument, it wounded him to read it put forth by Wavell. Citing Stilwell's low opinion of Wingate, Wavell suggested that if the expedition were bifurcated, Stilwell could probably be convinced to place the Marauders under Dalton, with whom he'd had "productive discussions," whereas Stilwell balked at entrusting his American infantry to Wingate. Not aware of Wingate's new second star, Wavell went on to propose that Dalton be promoted to brigadier and thus coequal with Wingate. The wire from New Delhi ended with a knife twist, all the more painful for Wingate because the hand which held it was Wavell's.

While not endorsing its implication, it is illustrative of the situation here to repeat Stilwell's sentiment when we approached him with the prospect of Avalanche as outlined by the Combined Chiefs of Staff. Said V. J., "If Wingate lost a third of his boys in the first expedition it'll only take two more to wipe out the Chindits." This is the opinion of the man who would lead the vital Yokeforce (Chinese) offensive to exploit Avalanche from the east. Noteworthy too is the attitude of the Mercury veterans whom we have canvassed. Of the two thousand who returned, I guess that fewer than half would volunteer again for LRP operations. We believe the grapevine of the army is spreading this reputation beyond the Chindits. Where the term "Wingate's Raiders" was a term of pride, "Wingate's Kamikazes" is now gaining currency among the units selected for participation in Avalanche.

In Quebec Wavell's misgivings were disregarded as petty and spiteful. Wingate magnanimously withdrew his request for the Marauders who could attempt their own long-range penetration from Ledo toward Myitkyina. Though denied an Allied command, Wingate was enthroned as king of the Burmese jungle; his crown would be evident when he returned to India and his detractors.

With these confirmatory matters settled, little remained of the Quebec conference except ceremonies. Wingate flew down to Washington for a day to consult with the American air transport specialists on his forthcoming needs. He returned jubilant and confident that Avalanche would be the best equipped and supplied operation ever undertaken in the Far East.

He dressed for the last time in his borrowed naval uniform. The next day he would fly back to London for a conference at the War Office; Lorna would return on the *Queen Mary*. She staggered into their hotel room laden with packages.

"Need some help?"

"Orde, you won't believe the things I've found. There are four *pounds* of coffee in that bag."

"What's this one?"

"Coffee beans. For that old grinder we haven't used since '39. This is more sugar than I've seen since the blitz, and these are *nylons.*"

"I need them for my parachutes."

"You'll like the way I use them. Oh, but I'm late! When's the dinner?"

It was the most formal and grand of all the affairs. With only the inner circle dining in the main ballroom, there were still a hundred guests. As only a junior major general, Wingate sat with Lorna at an outer table. The six courses concluded with interminable toasts during which they whispered their parting thoughts. It was past eleven o'clock when the other guests at their table suddenly turned to them— for Churchill had as well. His gravelly thunder rolled across the ballroom.

"Mr. President, having toasted what seems to be the entire free world, and even our Communist allies, I offer a parting glass—and from my seat if I may be permitted—to the newest general in this room and to his lady most recently reunited. Mr. President, during our passage of the Atlantic I was enchanted to observe that romance can steal even into the grim councils of war. To them: Orde and Lorna Wingate, who remind us that close on our Allied victory will be the young rushing from the ends of the earth to one another's arms."

94

They prepared for bed, a sparkling vista of Quebec centered in their window.

"Orde, I'm still thrilled to my toes."

"The man has a gift for toasts."

"That was such a personal thing he said about us. Just look at the lights. It's as if the war were over."

"Far from it. Wear nothing tonight. Save your new nighties for solitary occasions."

"Of course. How could you have supposed anything else? I feel like dancing nude on the rooftops. Come, Admiral, out of your uniform."

"With all haste."

"Can you keep it?"

"Property of the Royal Navy, I'm afraid."

"Keep it anyway. It shall always remind me of this enchanted interlude."

"It's been that, hasn't it?"

"As if you came out of the sky waving a magic wand over our lives. Is there anything more in the world you could want?"

"Not after you undress."

They coiled and explored, locked and separated with unhurried urgency. The elements of life combined in a moment of ultimate oneness. They rearranged themselves for further pleasure, blurring the boundaries of their bodies.

"If we could only keep this!" she exclaimed.

"What do you mean?"

She pressed the sheet on the sweat of his forehead. "Just wishing," she said. They lay tangent through the length of their bodies. She tossed the sheet; it floated down on them. They semislumbered.

"Did you feel it, Orde?"

"What?"

"Our hearts. For a few seconds—they synchronized."

"Just before."

"Yes."

She awoke hours ahead of the dawn. Lorna drew a robe around her, went to the window and opened it. Where Quebec had been a lattice of lights, there were long black tracts. For minutes she stood in the silence of the room.

"'Sweet memory, wafted by thy gentle gale...'"

"Orde. When did you wake?"

"'Now up the stream of time I turn my sail,'" came his voice from the bed.

"Why do you think of those lines?"

"Your silhouette at the window. No, stay there a moment."

"Come beside me. The city's sleeping like a baby in its crib."

"Let me be only a voice as I study you." She saw the sheet turn back as he rose on an elbow. "When shall I see such perfection again? When we are together forever. Not just these years but when time unites beyond its beginnings."

"Your inspirations are beautiful. You seem to have come back from the war. There can be gentle years ahead, Orde, if you value them."

"I will—as much as I've neglected them. I'll study war no more."

"We'll be hermits together. I'd gladly pack away the rank and tinsel."

"Yes. That's possible."

"Another year of war, perhaps? No more than two?"

"We look at time as if it were a coin forgetting that the circle is but a special ellipse: one peculiar form among an infinitude."

"I want these hours to creep—and the days thereafter to fly. Come back to me soon, Orde!" She hurried to bed, dropped her robe, slid in beside him. He was on his back; his body jumped as he awoke.

* * *

Later the phone announced the morning but they drifted back to sleep. Then they had to pack hurriedly. He was back in his jungle dress, his kit bag sealed. He looked at her with some confusion.

"Where is it?" he asked blankly.

"It's gone."

"Where?"

"At the bottom of the Atlantic."

The phone rang again. "Wingate. Yes, I'll be down in a minute." He hung up. "Let us part here—where there are no others." Their arms enfolded.

"Come back in full health. My love will grow as it waits."

He was only a step from the elevator when Churchill's aide hailed him: Wingate was to report to the prime minister's suite before leaving. The elevator hurtled him to the top of the hotel.

Churchill was in bed reading from sheafs of paper strewn across an enormous bed. Peering over bifocals he welcomed Wingate with chuckling recognition of his jungle garb.

"I shan't delay you."

"I remain at your disposal, sir."

"Just some parting counsel: remember, it's Kawabe I want brought down, not Slim."

"I'm eager to cooperate."

"It's a delicate position you're in: you have my support but his opposition. It's a position calling for a diplomat, whereas diplomacy is not foremost among your conspicuous qualities. That said, don't let anyone obstruct Avalanche. Contact me directly if it's serious."

"As a last resort."

"I'm uncertain whether Sir Archie will be a hindrance for you. On that possibility I've appointed him viceroy. Kicking him upstairs, as the Americans say. I've known Archie for decades. That's how much a Burma victory means to me."

"I owe Sir Archie a great deal as well."

"Practically your military godfather I've learned. He's my close friend and will continue to be. He'll understand even if he doesn't agree. I've cleared the decks for you, Orde, as much as I can. All I want in return is for you to go full speed ahead."

"With my recent naval experience I shall do just that."

Churchill's cigar bobbed with laughter. "Quite. You and Mountbatten make a pair: an admiral of the army and a general of the navy. One other thing: you'll be greeted at Heathrow. It may seem premature to involve you in postwar matters but the future has already marked you. Listen to his message." Churchill relit his cigar. "Wherever your ultimate loyalties lead you, I rely on the bond I feel between us. Godspeed then." He extended his hand. "Strike hard into Burma and bring us victories."

The transport droned across the Atlantic. Wingate had little doubt as to the nationality of the man who would meet him at Heathrow; he only wondered which of the Jewish leaders it would be, and what message he would bring. It surprised him that his mind was more on Burma; it was as if his first love had come back to him while he was heavily involved with another. Indeed, Weizmann had foretold it: the great battles of civilization were now distant thunder beyond the horizons of the Middle East.

The war had turned at sea. The iron-colored Atlantic below him was no longer the domain of the U-boat. Britain had preserved her lifeline by winning the Battle of the Atlantic. Japan, meanwhile, had lost the Battle of the Pacific to U.S. submarines. Neither troops nor raw materials could travel through her sprawling maritime empire. Everywhere Japan fought with no more than what she had on the ground.

For Burma this meant the Allies need not concern themselves with reinforcements for Kawabe. Wherever and whatever the battles, he would join them with his 150,000 men and no more. Slim's strength now equaled Kawabe's. This numerical standoff would promote stalemate if neither side felt strong enough for a general offensive. However, the allies now ruled the air: Kawabe's air force had been stripped to defend the Pacific islands. With the departure of the Zeros, Cochran could fly over Burma like an airline, land wherever the Chindits carved out strips. There would be quick salvation for the wounded. Wingate was content and quickly fell asleep.

To foil the press, Weizmann remained in the car, a bucket of ice at his feet.

"*Laheim!*" Wingate toasted with champagne to which only a trickle of bubbles remained.

"It was good of you to stop. Now on to London?"

"I must do much in only three days. I'm very glad for this talk."

"Israel will be waiting for you, my friend."

"Just remember there are others as capable."

"None with your drive, your abilities, your mastery of modern war. Could there have been another Moses?"

"Don't blaspheme."

"Orde, I could almost say you seem reluctant."

"Only unprepared."

"But Churchill certainly implied that after the war..."

"Yes, he'd approve."

"Are you pledged to Selassie?"

Wingate shook his head. "I served Ethiopia, I fight for Britain, but I belong to Israel. Will you remember that if I need an epitaph?"

"You must come back safely to us."

"To war again."

"If the Arabs will it."

"There is always someone ready to fight."

"We can never again be unready. The stories seeping out of the continent are horrible beyond words. We know there are camps now— vast camps designed for the torture and extermination of Jews. The dead will number in the millions. Israel must be a monument to them. It is the great sin of this century that only the dead see the end of war."

"Yes, only the dead. I must leave you, Chaim."

"Till a time of peace, dear friend. May God watch over you and fulfill His purpose."

95

All the doors of the War Office opened to him. Wingate's only concern was that he might forget some lesser of his fancies. Radios, jeeps, ration supplements, flame throwers, state-of-the-art grenades—some items so new Wingate was unfamiliar with them, like a shoulder-fired antivehicle weapon (the bazooka) and ingenious mines. Wingate's shopping list kept four colonels scurrying for weeks after he left. Everything had to be in Saugor within thirty days; the monsoon would clear sixty days later. As it left Burma, Avalanche would arrive.

Dalton was training the new command. The original Chindits were his leaven as the "faculty" had been for the first expedition. Kane was his second in command at Saugor but refused to serve under Wingate again. This was one of the clouds which adumbrated his return as he flew into the receding monsoon.

He bypassed New Delhi, where Wavell was now the viceroy of India, refuelled in Calcutta, where he radioed ahead of his arrival in Imphal, the headquarters of now Field Marshal Slim. Wingate strode through it under the silent stares of the Fourteenth Army staff; they exchanged glances as the door to Slim's office closed behind him.

"Hello, Bill."

"Ah, Orde—you're back."

"Yes."

"Meant to get out to the airfield but things are jumping around here as you can see. Upshot of Quebec, of course. You must have put on quite a show."

"Nothing like the one we'll put on for Kawabe."

"Yes, indeed. Best of luck and all that. It's the cast of your show that I suppose you're here to see me about."

"The Seventieth Division, please. I'd like them right away."

"Regrettably, Stilwell has not seen fit to release Merrill's Marauders to your care. Nothing I can do about that."

"It's the Seventieth I'm asking about. Who's commanding?"

"Arden. Major General Arden it is now. Congratulations for your second star by the way."

"The same for your field marshal's baton. I return Arden to you; I'll need only his troops. Who's his chief of staff?"

"Johns."

"Keep him too. When do I get the Seventieth Bill? They should be in Saugor right now."

"No one has told me that you get them."

"You're not reading your mail."

"I suppose you refer to the Quebec wires. With Sir Archie gone, they're for Mountbatten to implement. He seems to be getting settled in Colombo. We should hear from him shortly."

"As shortly as it takes me to call him. May I use your phone?" Wingate reached for it.

"No."

"A little common courtesy, Bill."

"That would change the atmosphere. Could we talk civilly?"

"Just don't try to sidetrack me, sir. And if you'd like a less controversial subject, what did Stilwell have to say?"

"Little more than an eloquent 'no.'"

"You talked to him?"

"No."

"Nothing in my behalf? Couldn't you have sent Dalton up there?"

"Vinegar Joe did not request either my counsel or your representative."

"And you did not offer either."

"I would have gone out of bounds to do so."

"Far be it from Field Marshal Slim to do *that*."

"Quite right. I respect the hierarchy of which I am a part. Of which you are a part, a most important part now, General Wingate."

"A little honey with Vinegar Joe might have saved you some of the Seventieth. Now the Marauders have to be replaced by Fourteenth Army."

"Wrong. They will be replaced—if they are at all—by the source of all your resources, from your benefactor, the prime minister."

"You're going to lose, Bill. You're going to lose your first battle as a field marshal."

"Perhaps we can be cobelligerents if not allies." Slim walked over to the wall map of Burma. "Tell me if I comprehend your bold new plan. Your selling point is 'strongholds,' I believe—strongholds and a private air force courtesy of the Americans. These are your proposed landing sites, are they not?" He pointed to locations near the Shweli, the Meza, and the Irrawaddy, terrifying names from the first expedition, now Japanese vulnerabilities for the second. "You have convinced Cochran to land unarmed transports on undefended jungle strips. Amazing."

"I'm sure you did your best to convince him otherwise."

"If I have no duty to the Americans, I certainly do to the British troops who would be so recklessly exposed. But I did not prevail. You have powerful patrons."

"They'll get me the Seventieth Division, Bill. All you can do is delay their training. Where is your concern for these British troops?"

"They'll not come from my army."

"They will unless the Russians join us. Why not accept it so we can get on with the war? You can dig your trenches in the Arakan while I take the offensive in Burma. A simple division of labor: you defend, I attack."

"Impertinence will get you nowhere."

"Neither will patience at this point! A division of Chindits are taking the field early next year—with or without your acquiescence!"

"Churchill cannot command Fourteenth Army from Downing Street! And I'm the only commander east of Italy who's worth his salt!"

"Don't bet your new baton on that!"

"I bet my career on it! If you want to play your trumps, I'll play mine."

"You doubt I hold the aces?"

"I hold the rest of the deck. Were I to leave, this headquarters would stage a sit-down strike!"

"Who'd notice a change?"

"They'd block every request you made. They'd keep you out of Burma till the monsoon came back. The contempt you heap on this headquarters is returned full force, Wingate. I think you know that. You also realize that I can be relieved but my headquarters cannot."

"You'd do that, wouldn't you?"

"My life is dedicated to the defeat of Great Britain's enemies. So is yours. Our confrontation is utterly distasteful to me."

"And to me. Believe it or not."

"Then we should not destroy each other."

"All I want to destroy is Kawabe. Can't we unite against him?"

"Yes. Let us cooperate. You want my men. I want your planes."

"Harken to the trader."

"Perceive: you need garrison troops."

"Don't twist words. I need fighters to garrison three strongholds—sally ports for my Chindits."

"The Third West African Brigade."

"For Christ's sake."

"Solid troops."

"Solid black."

"A surprising remark coming from the leader of the Ethiopians."

"Third Brigade comes with an artillery battalion."

"No! An unconscionable waste. How could you use artillery in dense jungle?"

"Do I get the West Africans complete with artillery?"

"You're galling me."

"Yes or no. I'll find a telephone somewhere, you know."

"All right," Slim sighed.

"In exchange for?"

"Cochran."

"Did you say *Cochran?*"

"Cochran—the First Air Commando—your private air force."

"March the West Africans up your arse."

"Cochran would still directly support the Chindits. I simply will assume overall command."

"Direct support means I, and no one else, gives Cochran his missions."

"Yes. I've been to the war college."

"Under no circumstances could you override me: isn't that what the book says?"

"Hopefully never. However, I would retain the authority to divert his planes in an emergency."

"And who defines an emergency?"

"I do."

"No. Only Mountbatten."

"I would not do so lightly. I give you my word."

"Your word is the only thing about you in which I have much confidence. Agreed."

"Do we need more than a handshake?"

"Not even that."

96

If Slim downplayed the significance of Chinditry, there was another commander in the theater who did not: General Kawabe. The size, supply system, objectives, and casualties of the first expedition were unknown to him, but as 1944 approached he was convinced the British had added a dimension to the war in which he could move himself. That is, if Wingate had struck from Assam into Burma with three brigades (the Japanese guess), Kawabe could use the same terrain for three divisions striking from Burma into Assam.

This bold maneuver had two objectives which Wingate would have admired had he known the Japanese plans. First, it would achieve surprise. Everywhere the war was running against Japan; they had not undertaken an offensive anywhere, except against the inept Chinese, for over a year. The last possibility the Allies were expecting was a thrust into India. Second, a successful thrust would put Kawabe in the defensive positions now held by Slim. Inevitably a great Allied offensive would be undertaken to reconquer Burma. Kawabe could best repel it from the hills of India rather than trying to hold the permeable lowlands of Burma. In the parlance of western war colleges, Kawabe's offensive was a "spoiling attack."

He went about his preparations as Wingate began his. If the second Chindit expedition had taken the same overland routes as the first, the Japanese and British spearheads would have collided near the Chindwin.

However, Avalanche called for only one overland brigade. The rest of the Chindits were to fly into five "airheads," all within a forty-mile radius of Zissel Island. During the next month small teams of scouts would infiltrate into Burma, cross the monsoon torrents of the Z Range, snake back along Casten's Trace, and disperse to the prospective airheads. There these pathfinders would radio information on the conditions they found and wait, perhaps as long as a month, for engineers to parachute in with the tools necessary to clear the strips for gliders. In the gliders would be more engineers with heavier equipment to develop the strips to handle transports.

From these strips, named for famous thoroughfares like Picadilly and Broadway, the Chindits were to march out to their strongholds. Strongholds were the theme of Avalanche. Indeed, Wingate began his training directive for the second expedition with an inscription from Zechariah: "Turn ye to the stronghold, ye prisoners of hope." Moving from the Bible to Burma, Wingate wrote,

> The ideal situation for a stronghold is the center of a circle of thirty miles' radius of closely wooded and very broken country passable only to pack transport owing to great natural obstacles. This center should ideally consist of a level upland with a cleared strip for Dakotas [C47s], a separate supply dropping area, taxiways to the stronghold, a neighboring friendly village or two, and an inexhaustible and uncontaminatable water supply within the stronghold.

> The motto of the stronghold is "No Surrender."

There were no such perfect locations—indeed none which were more than ten miles in radius. But quickly seizing the terrain for strongholds before the Japanese reacted gave the Chindits time to dig in and fly in artillery and stores of ammunition, food, and the other supplies necessary for a period of siege. For the Japanese would inevitably attack.

Their reaction would be slow but violent. In this Wingate understood his enemy and exploited his military vices just as he had with the Italians and their entirely different set of vices. The Japanese would come on and dash themselves against the strongholds. As they recoiled, Allied air power would work them over; then the Chindits would probe out from the strongholds against their weakened enemy.

Gaps would be found for large Chindit patrols that would then slip across the countryside raiding and ambushing as they had on the first expedition. They would radiate through Kawabe's rear areas for weeks, receiving their supplies by air. The wounded would be returned for aerial evacuation from the strongholds, which were permanently garrisoned.

The stronghold system realized Wingate's long-held belief that LRP could continue indefinitely in the enemy rear. As well provisioned, planned, and supported as Avalanche seemed to be, even Dalton was won over. He could not, however, persuade Kane to cross the Chindwin once more under Wingate's command. The two awaited him at the Saugor airstrip after his stormy conference with Slim.

The radio crackled in their jeep. "Pharoah," Wingate's new call sign, was due in five minutes. Kane had not seen him since he waded into the Irrawaddy.

Dalton put his hand on Kane's shoulder as Wingate's plane touched down. "You want him to sign it right here?" Dalton asked.

"I certainly do."

"Would you rather I . . ."

"No. Stay here."

Wingate was met by his aide and several batmen, but when he saw the waiting jeep he waved them aside.

"Notice what a shave does for him?" Kane muttered. "Dr. Jekyll and Mr. Hyde."

"He may have left Hyde in the Chindwin. At least talk to him." None of the three bothered to salute.

"Bruce . . . George." Wingate extended his hand. Only Dalton took it.

"Hello, Orde, and good-bye," Kane said quietly.

"I understand."

"Hop in," said Dalton. "Talk about it at camp."

"Not me," said Kane. "I'm getting on that plane."

"I need you, George. I can't ask you to forgive me, but I can ask you to stay with the Chindits. I need you because they need you."

"I haven't the stomach for your kind of warfare. You and the Japs are made for each other. Need I explain?"

"No. I'm told you've applied for transfer."

"Right here." Kane handed him the paper; Wingate glanced at it.

"6th Para.—they'd be lucky to get you."

"Just your signature, please."

"But they won't." Wingate scrawled "Disapproved" across the transfer and looked up coldly at Kane's wrath.

"All right. I'll take it to the IG."

"You can't leave and you should know it."

"I should have made that remark to you at the Irrawaddy!"

"You're as important—more important—to the Chindits than I am. Everyone knows how I reacted like a trapped fox—chewed off my leg to escape. But Bruce and Burchfield and Grayson—all the other officers who are able are going back with me, aren't they? Aren't they, George?"

"Much to my disgust."

"Your disgust is what makes you irreplaceable. You cannot accept what I did. For that I offer you belated tribute. For that I demand you bear witness to my conduct for the rest of the war."

"I no longer heed your demands. Your spell is broken. I've witnessed enough of your butchery. I'll not be your conscience!"

"The vacuum I had for a conscience has been filled—and overflowing with remorse."

"Indeed."

"Can't ask you to believe that, of course."

"No. Don't."

Wingate sighed. Both his officers sat with folded arms. "Did you happen to hear my new call sign?"

The two colonels looked at each other and smiled. "We suggested it," said Dalton.

"George, as builders the pharaohs were a stupendous success. As men they were slave drivers without mercy. But were it not for some Egyptian with a conscience like yours, how would we have learned the human cost of a pyramid? Such accounts were not written by those who admired the pharaoh. I'm surrounded by Chindits; most of them are my admirers. So most of them will look at the completed pyramid and say, 'I worked with Wingate. I helped him do it.'

"When this war is over I want you to remind Pharaoh's admirers that his pyramid was also the tombstone for thousands of workers. Workers who trusted him. Thousands."

"This may not be for me to say," said Dalton slowly, "but I think if F-B had heard Orde just now he would have stayed."

Kane climbed into the back seat; they roared up the mule path leading to the training camp.

His last picture, in a C47 for the second Chindit expedition. (*Courtesy Imperial War Museum.*)

97

Wingate's D day was set for early March. The months again began to blur.

There were seven times the number of men to train. Chindit levies and support drew in more nationalities than any other military force in the world. At the core were the English, Ulstermen, Welsh, and Scots; serving under First Air Commando were New Zealanders, New-foundlanders, Australians, South Africans. A battalion of tall, slender Kenyans; a brigade of heavy-set West Africans, their cheeks slashed to identify their tribe; Gurkhas, and the Burma Rifles now augmented by detachments of Chins, Kachins, and Karens; a company of Hong Kong Chinese. Americans ran the air show, the new railroads backing the front in Assam, the endless convoys of supply trucks. There were Indians this time—their infinite variety of caste, race, and religion. Steel helmets, turbans, berets, and shakos were all exchanged for the slouch hat of the Chindit.

Ten thousand men and sixteen hundred mules would go in by air, each load plan analyzed to the smallest detail, even the angle of the bullet with which to shoot a breakaway mule without puncturing the fuselage. Column commanders were flown out on bombing raids to examine Picadilly and Broadway. The pathfinders—the pick of the Chindits—were launched into the monsoon to stake out the landing fields. Their radio signals crept across the map of Burma.

In early February the Picadilly pathfinder team went silent. Soon the reason became clear: Kawabe was not waiting for the end of the monsoon. His columns were moving west through the jungle.

He struck first with a feint toward Chittagong. An Indian division was cut off. Slim quickly countered with reinforcements for which Wingate graciously "loaned" him some of First Air Commando. With Slim's strength diverted to the south, Kawabe struck his main blow between Kalewa and Homalin. His objective was suddenly apparent: Imphal, the linchpin and main supply base for the entire Fourteenth Army front. Slim had to rush his reserves back north again; again the aircraft were Cochran's.

He didn't begrudge them, Wingate told Mountbatten, just so his transports were available when Avalanche kicked off in March. The Supremo fully agreed.

For the third time in three years Wingate went into a private training camp to instruct thousands of men in his way of fighting. The new Japanese advance only increased the intensity of the training. In Khartoum he knew everything and the trainees nothing; in Saugor 1942 his cadre knew everything about jungle warfare, while he, like most of the original Chindits, knew very little. Now in Saugor 1943 he was heeded as the author of the book on Chinditry.

He instructed some of the most ancient and famous units of the British army: Lancashire Fusiliers, the Black Watch, the South Staffords, Cameronians—regiments with battle streamers from Waterloo and the Somme. Sir Alan Brooke had promised him the best and delivered. Even Wavell's son was serving with the Gurkhas.

With such professional manpower, the only major problem was dispersing the torrent of new equipment which poured onto the Saugor airstrip. Everything, even mules, came air express, top priority. Wingate was king of a rich and independent realm. He even modified the British uniform as he pleased. He came closer than any general in modern times to owning and running a private army complete with the luxury of an air auxiliary.

For all this, surprisingly little was expected of him and the vastly expanded Chindits. The strongholds were oriented on the railroad between the Bonchaung Gorge and the end of the line at Myitkyina. The overland brigade would ford the upper Chindwin a hundred miles north of the first expedition's crossing and slash through the northwest corner of Burma. SEAC gave the remaining twenty thousand Chindits the mission of "inflicting the maximum loss and confusion to enemy forces in north Burma." How this was done was up to Wingate.

His principal concern was in executing the largest tactical airlift in history. He had always been wary of aircraft; he knew little of how the transports should be loaded. He expected the men and equipment to land where he wanted them; his mind only began to engage when he pictured them on the ground where he could direct them like warships on the jungle seas.

Even so his tactical plan was sketchy. Once in the strongholds he would await the Japanese reaction. He would harass them and perforate Kawabe's supply lines, but the purpose of Avalanche was the premise of the full LRP theory—that the enemy would be forced to attack against terrain favorable to the defenders, thereby tripling the defenders' strength.

In December 1943 and January 1944 his principal purpose was keeping the entire Avalanche force intact despite the pleas and demands of Fourteenth Army for help against Kawabe's growing offensive. All such requests were referred to Mountbatten with the same note from Wingate: "The best response to a penetration is a counterpenetration. Avalanche goes on schedule at its present strength."

Amid such tensions his letters to Lorna seemed distracted.

21 January '44

Beloved, I have had three letters from you in a bunch—the most recent dated 22–12. It relieved me of some anxiety. I continue to enjoy excellent health. I have just completed a tour with Supremo. He is a splendid person! Apart from him and a few others my reception in British army circles is that of Pasteur at the hands of French medicos! . . .

I sometimes think my malaria has deprived me of my mental force— that although placid, fat, and happy, I have lost some of the intellectual acuteness and force that I enjoyed before the bug revived. However, I shall not worry too much about that. I spend much of my time in the air. My old dislike of flying is quite gone. . . .

My literary output of late has not been too good. War is, I suppose, a necessary evil—as a surgical operation. The drugging of one human being by another, the hideous mutilation by the knife, are in themselves an evil but become good through the motive. Can one fight in war with good motives? If not one ought not to fight. I believe one can. . . .

God bless you, my dear love, in 1944. I am very happy to be married to you. May we have many years together. I love you very much.

Orde

Lorna's letters caught up with him at odd times as he hopscotched about Assam where the Chindits were moving toward the starting line. The day after he wrote Lorna, Wingate decided to advance the departure of the overland brigade. So long as Avalanche continued to wait, the more difficulty he found preserving the plan in light of Slim's increasingly ominous situation. The overland brigade was also a gesture to Slim that, in spite of some contrary impressions, the Chindits would do what they could to take pressure off Fourteenth Army.

The main assistance from Avalanche would come in a month when the air-landed brigades swooped deep inside Burma. The pathfinders, except the vanished Picadilly team, were in position surveilling the landing sites. Meanwhile the overland brigade started from Ledo, Wingate there to see them off. As the *Queen's Own Regiment Journal* noted, the second expedition could not wait for the monsoon to subside.

We sat at Ledo doing nothing in the rain for several days.... The mules with their leaders meanwhile dispatched down the famous Ledo Road under construction by American engineers. They had a miserable walk for some seventy miles in ten to twenty inches of mud. The remainder of us were lucky to do the journey in an American convoy of huge lorries driven by Chinese. ...

The road was a jagged scar torn through dense jungles. Hairpin bends over mountain ranges up to five thousand feet, descents to semibuilt bridges over roaring torrents, and bulldozers and American negroes working everywhere were an unforgettable sight.

Another account picks up where the roadhead ended:

We began to clamber up a brown, muddy butter-slide;... to get up that first hill less than a mile in length, unimpeded by packs or weapons, took us a full hour. Two or three hundred of my men were working on it, building steps and traverses with bamboo and other wood felled by its side.... Later, when mules began to tackle the hill, they knocked the steps sideways in the violence of their struggles, so that they had to be rebuilt after every two or three animals had passed....

Far below and behind us in the valley, the roar of trucks on the road we had left continued while bulldozers pushed and pulled at the reluctant mountain. Deep blue smoke rose from wet fires of the Chinese labor camps. Sometimes for a few minutes the rain lifted, and one saw out across the valley to the towering mountain on the other side. . . . Wingate had seen all he wanted to see. He refused to be daunted by the obvious difficulties which lay ahead. "That's all right," he kept saying. "That's not too bad. You'll manage. . . ." Weeks later he confessed that he had in fact thought otherwise.

Those were weeks during which progress would be known only by radio. For the first time the Chindits were in the field without him. To the amusement of Dalton, Wingate raged at the overland brigade's failure to report as scheduled. Except for Dalton and Finley, the officers in his new headquarters regarded him as a bearded legend, a commando general—a man who killed with his hands, ate cobras, and scrubbed his hide till it bled. Feature articles had made much of his kinship with Lawrence of Arabia (with whom Wingate himself found no similarities whatever). In the soldiers' restless rumor mills, bizarre episodes and behavior in Lawrence's life were ascribed to Wingate.

Finley, his new chief of staff, wrote of the unexpected developments his reputation, real and imagined, caused in Chindit headquarters.

Some of the staff got really frightened of him during this period and I told him so. He frankly did not believe me but agreed to try to get to know them better. . . .

He had the most shattering effect on nervous officers; . . . he had no idea of the power of his personality over his juniors. One of our G3s was foolish enough to pass the general's door on the way to tea. The general had just read a letter which enraged him and he could not get hold of me. He called this officer in, made him read the offending letter, then told him to take it away and see that it did not occur again. The G3 came out feeling years older and gave up passing that dreaded door again. He was so frightened that he did not even dare say that the letter had nothing to do with his department.

Wingate mellowed when the overland brigade crossed the Chindwin like a brook in Somerset. The contrast between the two crossings, almost exactly a year apart, showed the difference between the maiden and mature expeditions: a column the size of Central Force went across in less than three hours.

Motorboats were flown in and flown out the same day. There was no fear of aerial detection as Zeros had long since been swept from the skies. As the commander of the overland brigade, a veteran of the first expedition, described the two crossings, the second was "a twentieth-century performance, whereas the first had been early Victorian."

Thousands of Chindits were once again in Burma. Avalanche was about to descend on the Japanese.

98

Wingate had always feared that the Japanese, surprised in 1943, would be waiting for the Chindits in 1944. He had nothing on which to base his suspicion, but it focused on the one landing site which the Chindits had not surveilled—Picadilly.

In order not to alert the Japanese, Wingate ordered no reconnaissance flights after February 1. This meant no aerial photos of the landing sites. This order was disobeyed the day before ten thousand Chindits boarded their planes for the first wave of the invasion.

The departure airfield was at Lalaghat. Slim and Wingate were there to see them off; Wingate would enter Burma when the first airstrip was secure. Slim described the scene:

On the morning of Sunday, 5 March, I circled the landing ground at Lalaghat. Below me at the end of the wide airstrip was parked a great flock of squat, clumsy gliders, their square wingtips almost touching; around the edges of the field stood the more graceful Dakotas [C47s] that were to lift them into the sky. Men swarmed about the aircraft, loading them, laying out tow ropes, leading mules, humping packs, and moving endlessly in dusty columns, for all the world like busy ants round captive moths.

Takeoff was set for 5:00 P.M. A half hour before, a jeep lurched to a stop where Wingate and Slim were standing. Cochran jumped out.

"You've got to see these," he blurted.

"What the hell?"

"Picadilly."

"What is it, Orde?" Slim asked.

"When was this?"

"Yesterday."

"Goddamn it, Cochran. You...you overflew!"

"Look—and you'll be glad I did."

The oval clearing was crisscrossed with what looked like matchsticks. On the ground they were twenty-foot teak logs.

"We've been betrayed," Wingate rasped. "No question about it. Bruce!"

It was Dalton's brigade which was to go into Picadilly. At best the photo was evidence of Japanese alertness; at worst a trap.

Wingate drew Dalton aside. "Shall we scrub it?"

Dalton thought for only a moment. "They've only blocked one. I'll go in on Chowringhee."

"No!"

"Well, we're watching the others."

"They could have artillery zeroed on them. Our pathfinders wouldn't know it."

"Want to ask Slim?"

"Hell no."

"It's up to you."

"I won't order you to go if I'm not going myself."

"Well I don't have room for your HQ."

"I'm not going to stick you out in the Indaung again."

"I can handle it, Orde. This time you're giving me a choice."

"I'm not going to stick our necks in a noose again..."

Slim noticed him pound his fist into his palm. The field marshal walked toward them, his hands clasped behind his back. Dalton glanced at him.

"Orde, make the decision or Slim will." Wingate remained silent. "Look, you're here, you're a major general. What do you think?"

"I feel it's all right. It won't be at first, but it'll be all right."

"Gentlemen?" Slim inquired. "Shall we slip takeoff and discuss this?"

"No need," said Wingate casually. "Bruce is going back into the Indaung."

"The responsibility is yours," said Slim, looking through his brows.

"Yes. Very much so."

Slim was to have returned to Imphal; the shock from Picadilly kept him in Lalaghat, where he appropriated the office of the base commander. Wingate could see Slim's light burning on the top floor, a reminder that his decision to go on with Avalanche would be studied with the widest interest.

Slim was not to be disturbed except for "the menu from the landing site," the initial report from the landing brigade, the same report which kept Wingate prowling through the headquarters all night. Dalton's report would be code phrases derived from ration items ranging from the favorite to the least liked. "Pork sausage" meant a satisfactory landing; "soya links" meant the opposite and to turn back subsequent transports.

There would be supplementary reports from Cochran's pilots; these began to attract a large audience in the control tent almost before the transports were out of sight. Wingate watched the C47s, each pulling two gliders, labor for altitude to cross the Naga Hills.

One of the small triangles in the darkening sky split apart. A red flare arched and descended as the drone of engines faded into the twilight. More red flares—the signal for failed towlines—lit the following hours. The struggle for quick altitude put too great a strain on the nylon ropes. Two gliders were one too many; in level flight the hardworking C47s could do the job but not in the steep climb immediately after takeoff.

Engines overheated. Fuel consumption, calculated to the gallon, quickly rose over projections. Delivery to the landing sites became an excruciating decision for each pilot in trouble: he could save his plane by cutting his gliders, leaving them to descend in the darkness into the trans-Chindwin jungle, or he could struggle on to the landing sites and face a forced landing himself in Japanese territory.

Of sixty-one gliders twenty-six had to be cut loose. The early aborts, like the one Wingate saw, were the lucky ones. The plane returned intact, the pair of gliders spiraled down in India. On the ground in the night, these Chindits didn't know where they were, as Slim related:

There was a brisk battle near Imphal between the Chindits of a crashed
glider, convinced they were behind enemy lines and determined to
sell their lives dearly, and our own troops rushing to their rescue.

Other gliders were strewn all across north Burma, never to be heard
of again except in the war journals of the Japanese. One came to earth
undamaged near the division HQ at Pinlebu on the very ground where
Central Force had attacked the year before. In the crash was a lieutenant who had been a sergeant on the Pinlebu raid. He sprinted out of
the wreckage to relive the most dangerous moments of his life. Before
the Japanese could investigate he had his men over the Tinda ford.
They disappeared into the jungle, never exchanging a shot with the
startled Japanese, and retraced the historic route over Casten's Trace.

For Kawabe it seemed that all Burma had become an enemy airstrip;
for Wingate, that he had once again lost a third of his force, this time in
the first hours of the expedition. "We should have tested them. We should
have tested them," he kept saying to no one in particular. He meant that
a two-glider tow should have been attempted over the Naga Hills before
the air movement plan based on the double tow was put into effect.

Finley bore witness to most of his self-recrimination. "I never got
involved. I just left that side of Avalanche to others," Wingate brooded.

"You delegated the problem to the experts, Orde. You can't do
everything when you're a major general."

"I should have ordered a test!"

"Cochran said it would work. You had to rely on him."

"Everyone is wrong one time or another. Even the experts. It was
for me to check."

"By morning things will look better."

"You know what they've been saying—Johns, Arden, those people—I'm out of my depth with this large a command. My abilities
stop at rifle range..."

"LRP was not conceived by a rifleman."

"My skills are at the extremes of warfare: I can plan an ambush or
a vast strategy, but in between my mind skips and stutters."

"That's what we're here for, your staff. If we haven't filled the gaps,
that's our fault. I most of all. I should be despairing, not you. And
I'm not. Wait till Bruce reports..."

*   *   *

Everyone who had a watch glanced at it constantly; those who didn't asked the time. 8:22 P.M.—the lead transports should be over Chowringhee, the first gliders nosing down toward a vaguely visible patch in the dark jungle. Wind whistling through the canvas fuselage, men braced for impact.... Wingate flinched as the second hand swept to vertical.

The hand revolved toward eternity. Clipped reports on the aircraft frequency but nothing from the ground. Forty minutes, an hour; still nothing but static. Eleven o'clock, midnight, 12:30; endless mugs of coffee for the Americans, tea for the British. The tent resembled a small airport in a large snowstorm. The pacing slowed. Some men read; others sprawled on the dusty floor. The light extinguished in Slim's temporary office.

Now all the aircraft were back. The pilots seemed shaken by the night. Some thought they saw fire on the ground; most weren't sure.

"Get me a Dakota and a parachute!"

Finley refused. "Relieve me outside!" he snarled. "You'll be enough of a spectacle out there."

Wingate burst onto the moonlit airstrip. "Now do as I say!" he shouted.

"I'll not!"

"Cochran will!" Slim's light went on as Wingate began to run toward the hangar. Finley tackled him in a stumbling bear hug. He swung an elbow that hit Finley's jaw with the sound of wood on wood.

"You beast..." Finley spit blood. "Wait. I'll do it."

"Get me that plane."

"You can't go in alone. I'll have to get some men from the security platoon."

"Get them!" Wingate turned back for the control tent. "I'm sorry, Malcolm."

"Will you wait another hour?" Finley held a handkerchief to his flowing mouth. A Chindit ran toward them. They stopped. Dalton's report was "soya links."

It was 4:00 A.M. Other signals followed close on. Broken, unclear, interrupted by roaring static, they began to sketch a picture of carnage and confusion on the ground in Burma. The morning flights into Chowringhee were canceled: the landing site was obstructed by crashed gliders.

The dead and dying were dragged to the edge of the strip. Among the gliders which had sheared off the treetops was the one with the AM radio. Wingate could only assess the situation with an overflight in the morning.

99

He took off at 4:30, an hour which would put him over Chowringhee at daybreak. Below him, Burma remained in shadows, its hills a rumpled rug.

This was his ninth crossing of the Chindwin, his seventh by air. Wingate no longer consulted his map; he knew the terrain as a neurosurgeon knows the cranial contours. The Mu, the Meza, the Menlo were no longer features of terrain but rather evocations of memory.

The Z Range folded gently at the gorge where Jarrett was killed. The departing night seemed to be his shroud. To the south the range wrinkled: one of the nameless ravines was Myers's crypt. A beautiful place to spend forever, Wingate had described it in a letter to the Myers family.

In an outpouring of penance he had written to all the families of the nine men who were lost in Flotilla One, letters which drew his mind away from the second expedition and back to the first. But he would write no more—not until after the war. Names and faces of the dead scattered his focus, distracted his attention. There would be a time for reflection and recollection, but the war must preside over the present.

The present seemed recessional to the last desperate weeks of Mercury: Avalanche had barely begun before he was faced with a postmortem. How had it happened? "Soya links"—the synonym for disaster. Had the Japanese somehow gotten wind of the landings? He had never thought much of security, never checked the means taken to foil Japanese spies. Like the double tow cables which failed, a vital detail had eluded his attention, another mark that his capabilities as a general fell short of his skills as a brigadier. Events seemed to be corroborating Wavell's opinion of Wingate, not Churchill's.

Wingate had never given a thought to the scores of Indians working for the Japanese around Imphal and Lalaghat. Gandhi's independence movement was encouraged by the Japanese; yet Wingate had been oblivious to the alliance, so caught up was he in strongholds and strike forces.

He still was. Now with the Chindits in battle on the ground, no treachery or espionage would further shape the outcome. Tiberias, Danghila, Pinlebu, Satsa—all had begun with portents of defeat until he swung into action. Now it was time again—he was approaching his element once more. Bonchaung lay before the pink-tinted cloud bank atop the Tri Range.

The American pilot banked north and searched the ground; Wingate followed his eyes. Ground shadows still obscured. The plane turned again.

"Two o'clock," said Lieutenant Hodges.

Wingate looked for flashes of gunfire. There were none; instead the clearing appeared as the aftermath of battle—but an air battle rather than land combat, for Chowringhee looked to be a glider graveyard. Some had splintered in the trees, their tails protruding as if permanently sinking into a verdant sea. Others had collided, wings and struts fused like dragonflies locked in death. But where was the fighting? It could only be over: the mute wreckage on the ground suggested annihilation.

Wingate adjusted his earphones and switched to Dalton's frequency. "Pharaoh to Satan," he broadcast, expecting silence in reply.

"'Morning, Pharaoh," Dalton answered jauntily. "You're up early."

"What's for breakfast?"

"A change in menu—'pork sausage.' Are you there, Pharaoh?"

"Pork sausage."

"Yes, I ordered breakfast late last night you know. Different situation this morning."

"Where are your hosts?"

"Haven't arrived."

"Then why the soya?"

"Checking in was messy."

"So I see."

"Need some body snatchers."

"Roger. Can you move?"

"Sure. Already started. I'm here waiting for the snatches."

"You've made my morning."

"Sorry to get you up."

"Clean up that mess and I'll join you for lunch."

There was a pause. Dalton could understand his anxiety, but Wingate would be out of place with Dalton's force as it trekked to its stronghold. It might be a week before an airstrip was ready. With five other brigades to be deployed, Wingate could hardly direct the campaign from under a tree.

"You're not Gideon any more," Dalton replied.

"Have dinner ready for me in three days."

"Till then."

Wingate switched to the intercom. "Get Lalaghat." Hodges nodded and twisted the frequency knob. Wingate heard nothing but crackle when he called.

"Need some more air under us," said Hodges. The B25 began to gain altitude. Wingate's spirits climbed with it into a brilliant rising sun.

One of the gliders loaded with ammunition probably burst into flames; this could have accounted for the "firing" the pilots reported seeing the previous night. No doubt "soya links" was an apt description of the landing, and from hundreds of miles away in India Chowringhee sounded even worse than it looked from one hundred feet overhead. Last night Wingate had gone through a general's worst experience: to have his master plan dashed by apparent disaster. Now he was about to experience a general's highest exhilaration: to send his command forward as his master plan unfolded into unexpected opportunity.

This he proceeded to do. His brigade poised for departure to Broadway had backtracked from Lalaghat when Dalton's report sounded doom. Now he wanted the second brigade airborne. All landings were to have been at night for maximum concealment, but the Japanese were off guard—Wingate sensed that in spite of the log obstructions on Picadilly. There was something peculiar about the logs that just didn't fit into warfare. He didn't know what it was, but he felt that Japanese hands had not felled the trees.

"Pharaoh to Vicar. Pork sausage. Scrub the latrines." This was the signal for the second brigade to take off. He could imagine the popping eyes at Lalaghat. "Advise Fat Man that Flip's dances are with me."

This meant the Chindits would use all Cochran's planes as planned. On the basis of "soya links" and the obstructions at Picadilly, Slim (Fat Man) had broadly hinted that Avalanche should be postponed if not canceled. Last night, Wingate had no counterargument. Mountbatten was also expected to side with Slim now that Kawabe's offensive was rising like a flood on the slopes of the Naga Hills. Slim needed Cochran's planes: last night it seemed he'd probably get them.

But no longer. Avalanche was to thunder down on the Japanese rear. In a week their last train would roll on the railroad; in two weeks the overland brigade would close on its stronghold; in three, Burma would be cut in half and the Chinese could finally move down to restore overland supply from India. Half the Allied ambitions at Quebec would be fulfilled—and it would be the Chindits who fulfilled them.

The B25 bore down on the Naga Hills. Wingate slid off his earphones to better concentrate on the plans ahead. The landing sites would be safer by day. No more gliders hurtling down in the darkness. . . . The bomber seemed to hit a bump. Black puffs in the sky, smoke sweeping by the windscreen. The plane rocked; the pilot hauled back on the yoke. The antiaircraft fire chased Hodges into the clouds. Wingate fumbled the earphones back into place.

"Christ, general, that's ack-ack!"

"Aren't we over India?"

"Sure are!"

Slim had not exaggerated. Wingate was finally impressed—Kawabe had hauled large antiaircraft guns across Burma and into the Naga Hills. His infantry would be even farther ahead, nearly upon the summits if not beyond. It was even conceivable they could interfere with the Chindit departure from Lalaghat.

Impatiently Wingate waited for the bomber to find its way through the clouds. Hodges veered far to the north.

"Vicar to Pharaoh."

"Pharaoh here."

"Request from Fat Man: divert to his tent."

"Fuck Fat Man," was Wingate's reply. It was obvious Slim wanted him in Imphal to tell him the war was lost unless Fourteenth Army got Cochran's transports. With all his men, equipment, heavy artillery, and air support Slim should be able to hold the Naga Hills with no more than his marshals baton. He had deployed his forces without Cochran so he could jolly well redeploy them. He'd had a month to do so after Kawabe's intentions became obvious. Now Slim could march his men through the jungle as the Chindits marched, as the Japanese marched. It was time Fourteenth Army showed it could match the Japanese as the Chindits had.

"Vicar, tell Fat Man you couldn't raise me." What had worked with Platt could work with Slim—silence.

"He has Spitfires aloft looking for you." It wouldn't work: Wingate's reputation was too well known.

He sighed. "Imphal," he said to Hodges.

100

Beloved, I write this in an American bomber headed for Lalaghat but now Slim has summoned me to Imphal to plead for my aircraft. He will probably blackmail me by withholding the West Africans he promised. I expect a disagreeable confrontation. Ah well, Imphal is where the mail first arrives so with luck I shall have one of your letters awaiting me.

Two staff officers were with Slim preparing charts, updating maps speckled with red symbols depicting the Japanese onslaught. Wingate ignored them as he advanced toward Slim's desk, grabbed a folding chair, reversed it, and sat down glaring.

"Haven't you more important missions for your Spitfires?"

"I wouldn't bring you here, Orde, were it not for these supplies you've requested for landings that are still problematic."

"My second brigade's in the air," he said offhandedly as he studied the supply papers Slim handed him.

"You're landing in broad daylight?"

Wingate nodded. "I'm not requesting these supplies. They've already been allocated to me. Right, Faircloth?"

The supply officer shifted his feet uncomfortably and looked to Slim for support.

"As army commander I must look at the overall situation. It is grave."

"It looks grave in India. In Burma we're on the attack. Kawabe will soon be as worried as you are."

"I am facing a *decisive* engagement. Kawabe is experiencing a raid."

"Then he too is facing a decisive engagement. But he's worse off than you are; at least your rear is secure."

"They're breaking through to Imphal, Orde. That *is* my rear."

"Turn Imphal into a stronghold then. Let 'em through and cut their supplies. You've got Kawabe where you want him, sir—crawling out on a limb. Let him through and saw it off."

"Thank you, but I didn't call you here for strategic advice."

"You'd be wise to take it anyway."

"When I take it you may have my baton."

"Thanks. Don't lose it to Kawabe first."

Slim reddened to his hairline. "Talbott, Faircloth: why don't you wait outside." They hurriedly exited.

"Bill, I hope we're not going to shout at each other."

"I've always admired your analogies to earlier warfare. Would you mind if I offered one?"

"I'd be grateful."

"It's from the American Civil War: I would compare your raid with that of Stuart when he rode around the Union Army at Gettysburg..."

"Wait a bit."

"Whereas I am Lee on the eve of battle at the turning point of the war."

"You never fail to call my offensive a raid. Well, I would liken it to Jackson's operations in the Shenandoah Valley. His actions were as decisive as the clash of the main armies."

"You don't care to be compared with Jeb Stuart? He was bold, rash, colorful, headstrong, and celebrated. I seem to remember that he wore distinctive headgear as well."

"Well, aren't we getting personal. No wonder you sent away witnesses."

"Generals should clash in private. You seem to forget that sometimes. But of course you haven't been a general for very long."

"Are you going to try to rape me of my supplies?"

"Present exigencies override the original plans."

"Meaning?"

"I'm detaching the Gurkhas from the Chindits. Your drops have to be cut by about a third. I've got to get a division up here from the Arakan."

"The Gurkhas are mine! The aircraft are mine! Mine exclusively. You *agreed!*"

"We also agreed that in an emergency..."

"You don't have an emergency! You have an *opportunity*..."

"Lower your voice."

"I'll raise it till Mountbatten can hear me in Ceylon!"

"I've fulfilled my bargain: you keep the West Africans."

"And lose my *Gurkhas?* Try and get them, Field Marshal Slim. We'll take on the British army as well as the Japs!"

"That's been your career. The orders have already been radioed to Lalaghat."

"Where they'll be carried out after my resignation."

"You might bluff Mountbatten but not me."

"We'll see who's bluffing."

"I never do. Bluffing is your style, isn't it? 'Campfires' and all that."

"I also believe in strongholds."

"Ten Downing Street, I suppose."

"If you force me there I'll use all its strength."

"You've never understood the soul of the army, have you?"

"I've understood the soul of war. The rest is mannerism."

"I'm surprised the Jews didn't show you how tradition is the bedrock of collective strength. Wars are not won by individuals but by organizations."

"Wars are also lost by organizations. They're won when the exceptional individual can shape the times."

"Like Hitler?"

"I'd love to discuss this further, but you're probably trying to detain me. Is that why you brought me here?"

"I never stab a man in the back."

"Just in the chest." They both had a short chuckle. "Well, I like it that way. Thanks."

"I want Mountbatten to see our arguments side by side. I'm willing to abide by his decision."

"I'm not—if it goes against me."

"You'll go over his head to Churchill, won't you?"

"As my American pilot says—'yup.' Tell me, sir, if you had my special access to Churchill, wouldn't you?"

"In all honesty, no."

"Why not? You believe in your position as strongly as I believe in mine."

"True. But we're different, you and I, as this discussion proves. In fact, you're different from all the rest of us. I hear the code of the officer: it says to present my views vigorously and honestly to my commander. Then when the commander makes his decision, I say no more. I hear that code clearly. I heed it—whether it works for me or against me."

Wingate rose as if the chair had become uncomfortable. "Yes, I've heard it too—till I'm bored. But a very honorable code. Praiseworthy." He put on his helmet. "Yet to follow your code you have to accept its underlying premise, don't you? It assumes that your commander is always right." He stopped at the door. "And something even more fundamental than that, Bill: your code was written by someone else." He strode out the door but stopped before he closed it. He was sweating. For a moment he thought it to be malaria. "Bill..."

"Yes, Orde."

"Let us shake hands."

"Gladly."

Wingate returned to the desk. Slim took his hand with a trace of bemusement.

"Farewell, sir."

"See you in Burma."

101

Slim's aide-de-camp rose as he went by. "General Wingate, I took the liberty...." He handed him a letter.

"Very thoughtful of you." He tore open the envelope as he went out. Before he could start reading, an American reporter was upon him.

"Where are you going, General?"

"Military secret," he said without breaking stride. The reporter
kept pace.

"Lalaghat?"

"The secret's out."

"Can I go?"

"Against Field Marshal Slim's policy."

"Can I go?"

"Sure."

The reporter rushed ahead to the plane. Word of Wingate's arrival
had just reached the press corps; now they scrambled to accompany
his departure. As he approached the B25 he saw them in a cluster. He
turned aside to scan Lorna's letter.

My dearest Orde,

*Truly God is great with bounty. Today Doctor Lampson confirmed a
most blessed secret I have suspected since a month from your departure.
I am to have your child. Your son, I'm sure. I feel Jonathan Orde
stirring within me. . . .*

"Hosannah!"

He flourished the letter. The reporters gaped.

"Hosannah! For unto us a child is born. To us a son is given!"

Like a boy he skipped toward the bomber. The reporters forgot
their questions as the crew produced a cigar which he lit, laughing
and coughing.

As if for the occasion, the sky opened in an array of sunbeams—
but quickly closed again—as the monsoon grudgingly retreated. Takeoff was delayed for an hour and then indefinitely, time for him to come
back to earth while he heard the progress of the Broadway landing.
Then he drifted away to be alone.

Around 5:00 P.M. the weather broke into roiling clouds. Lightning
flashed distantly but the worst of the rains had subsided. The bomber's two propellers threw a fan of spray as they sputtered into life. Five
Americans and four Britons clambered aboard.

As usual Wingate took the copilot's seat. He adjusted the earphones

with little interest in the instructions from the tower. Idly he watched
Hodges tap the altimeter, for it didn't seem to be registering. The
engines vibrated the plane as they roared to takeoff pitch. The B25
hurtled down the runway and departed the earth.

The sun had dipped behind the Indian hills, though its glow renewed as Hodges gained altitude. But zero remained on the altimeter.
He queried his crew chief. Wingate could not make out the reply. He
flicked on a tiny lamp illuminating the clipboard he placed on his thigh.
From his breast pocket he took out the folded paper and resumed his
letter:

My precious Lorna. . . .

Static crackled in his ears. From somewhere he heard what sounded
like a church service. *"Ask what questions you would wish unan-
swered if God loved you enough to let you create all your experience.
Only the future. . ."* The signal surged, then faded.

"What's that, Hodges?"

"What?"

"That service. Hear it?"

"No, sir. Were you on intercom?"

"Think so."

He began writing again:

*It's Sunday. From somewhere I hear this strange service broadcast in
English. I wish I could hear it better for it reminds me that like the
Indians I should never question the fate God holds out to me, for today
it delivered your most wonderful annunciation. A baby, a child, the
most precious gift of heaven to earth.*

". . . For what is heaven if not constant pleasure?" The voice sounded
like the hermit's. *"Should you be surprised if that's all to be found
there? . . ."*

"Come on, Hodges. Someone is playing with me."

"Say again, sir?"

"Someone back there is on intercom."

"Sir, I haven't heard a thing. You're picking up some other station."

"Who's preaching back there?" Wingate said over the intercom. "It's rather good."

He was answered by befuddled silence. Then the crew chief spoke up.

"We're just praying the altimeter's stuck, sir."

Wingate smiled. The voice in the service was vaguely familiar, so it seemed it must be one of the passengers. He returned to the letter as wispy clouds swirled by.

>...*with rank and power as my bulwark, I had quite a set to with Slim. I will win. Today I swelled at the title of general. This evening I am humble but so much more at peace with the title of father.*

"If you can dream all sensations, why can't all sensations be a dream?"

>*Yes, I too feel that Jonathan is within you. A son, Lorna, born of war, to live, we pray, in a world at peace. I have seen so much death, awake and in dreams, the end of so many lives. I have dreamed of them even while awake. But now there is this affirmation of life in your body.*

"...and all you take with you through death are your sensations, those of the mind rather than the body—just as you can hear music without it being played."

Flying beneath the ceiling was too dangerous with a faulty altimeter. Hodges pulled back on the yoke. The bomber, fighting drafts swirling from the hills, responded slowly, then lifted into the cloud layer.

"We'll try to get on top, sir."

The windshield was a blanket of gray. Wingate glanced at his surroundings for a moment before returning to his page:

>*To contemplate birth answers questions I've failed to ask.*

The amorphous gray seemed to condense at its base, then darkened to a single contour. The hill in silhouette was an onrushing hood. But he was looking at what he wrote:

>*Now I find that beginning is eternal, so there is no end*

In the instant Hodges cried out, Wingate placed the period.

Major General Wingate, alas, has paid a soldier's debt. There was a man of genius who might well have become also a man of destiny.

Winston Churchill

In a speech to the House of Commons, August 2, 1944

Epilogue

Area 12, Grave 288—an easy walk from the huge parking lot past the terminal for buses which regularly circle the cemetery's vast acreage to the accompaniment of amplified voices: "On the left is General Pershing, the first four-star general to..."

The path to the gravesite swings around a tall, theatrical portal which once marked the boundary of the cemetery before the wars of the twentieth century required expansion toward the river. On the portal's frieze are lines from "The Bivouac of the Dead" and other faintly archaic sentiments.

Metal medallions mark the corners of Area 12. Then the visitor looks for numbers on the backs of tombstones, for they face away from the path and toward the river. The numbers shrink from four to three digits as the visitor approaches the older, the original, section of Area 12.

This is a military cemetery, so individuality in memorials is slight. One thinks of Flanders Field and "row on row." In every direction rounded white tablets form perfect lines, perfect ranks, perfect order. The numbers descend through the hundreds with metronomic certainty—then there is one clear irregularity.

Even before the numbers point to his location, the search for Wingate is over. His tombstone is triple size in pale granite. The tingle of the search gives way to a smile, for he is here in death as he was in life—an exception, an anomaly, an irregularity.

It was not his rank which entitled him to his exceptional monument. Here in the egalitarianism of death generals lie beside corporals with wives and children interspersed. No, Wingate's monument is a consequence of the crash on March 24, 1944. He perished with the crew of the B25, and was consigned with them to a common grave.

The grave faces the Potomac. A freeway rushes between him and the Pentagon, while on the skyline gleams the white dome of Capitol

Hill. His life took him to many improbable locations; so, fittingly, did his death. Wingate spent only a few days on American soil but he rests beneath it forever in Arlington Cemetery.

If his tombstone is seen as permanent defiance of "processing," then his gravesite could be seen as an ultimate triumph for authority. His name appears with eight others, five of whom were Americans. What was interred was assumed to be the comingled remains of them all.

It was Allied policy that when common disaster obliterated victims beyond recognition, the remains were buried in the nation of the majority. Moreover, the nationality of the aircraft determined the place of burial when other factors were in doubt.

Thus, for Wingate, the question asked by Corinthians: "Oh grave, where is they victory?" was answered by policy. The crash left nothing of the bomber except its shadow scorched on the treetops. Forensic dentistry and other fragmentary identification had not been developed in 1944. The crash site was extremely remote; what was brought out as remains was largely guesswork.

Three countries appealed to President Truman for an exception to policy. Ben-Gurion, Selassie, and Churchill all wrote personally asking for reinterment at locations more associated with Wingate's life. All were diplomatically refused. Each country was then left to dedicate its own memorials.

Oddly, they all involved children though Wingate never knew a moment as a father. In England a tablet was dedicated at Charterhouse, where he had been an undistinguished schoolboy. In Addis Ababa he is commemorated by the Wingate School for Boys. In Israel a settlement for orphans was named Yemin Orde; fittingly it later became a training center for Ethiopian Jews who were rescued from the famine of 1984.

Burma never took much interest in the man who began its liberation. To India, the land of his birth and death, went his talisman and the emblem of his individualism; the only object at the crash site which could be positively identified with him was left for the jungle—his indestructible pith helmet.

At the lip of the crater was a slender stump resembling a rifle stuck into the ground by its bayonet. Somehow the helmet had landed atop the stump, forming the symbol of the fallen soldier of World War II. It was a scene the search party felt should not be disturbed. The aboriginal guides agreed though for a different reason: in their beliefs a headpiece on a stump marks the entry of a new resident in the jungle.

Author's Note

BORN OF WAR is not intended to be read as history for I have blurred fact and fiction just as reality and romanticism were blurred in Wingate's life. Conversation and his letters, except where here noted, are invented. So too are all communications and episodes involving Lorna, who is still living in the United Kingdom. Scenes depicting the marriage and its precedents are fictional.

Extracts from his real documents on pages 235, 255, 420, and 426 are edited. The names of general officers and historical figures have not been changed, nor have their descriptions of Wingate and his doings (e.g., those of Churchill and Cochran). Descriptions of Wingate by others are authentic though in most instances are attributed to fictional characters.

He was without doubt one of the most, and perhaps the most, original of all military practitioners in the twentieth century. His life therefore called for original treatment, which for me meant a "docu-drama" rather than a biography or even a conventional biographical novel. With only a little nurturing, the events and relations in his life (including even the encounter with a mysterious hermit during the escape in Burma) bloom into fiction.

Biblical quotations are from the King James version. In the public domain are lines from the following poems: "The Highwayman," by Alfred Noyes; "Tears," by John Cheney; "The Pleasures of Memory," by Samuel Rogers. Photographs except those identified as from the Imperial War Museum, London, are from *Orde Wingate,* by Christopher Sykes, as is the description of Wingate and his staff on page 428. Quotes from *Defeat into Victory,* by Sir William Slim, appear on pages 429 and 432.

Additionally the author gratefully acknowledges permission to in-

449

clude copyrighted passages from *The Turn of the Tide,* by Sir Arthur Bryant (Doubleday & Company), and *Closing the Ring,* by Sir Winston Churchill (Houghton Mifflin).

Maps are by Keith Jefferds. Major John Holmes of the British army provided cultural authenticity. Sara Oechsle produced manuscript from my cryptography; then Leslie Meredith tightened and heightened considerable portions with her editing. None of this would have begun or continued without the patience and support of my wife, Pamela.

Thomas H. Taylor
Berkeley, California

ABOUT THE AUTHOR

Thomas H. Taylor is a West Point graduate and colonel in the U.S. Army Reserves. His two previous novels, *A-18* and *A Piece of This Country,* are about Vietnam, where he won seven decorations, including the Silver Star, two Bronze Stars, and the Purple Heart with the 101st Airborne Division in 1965–66. After leaving the army in 1968, Taylor received a master's degree in sociology and juris doctor from the University of California. He practiced law in Berkeley and Saudi Arabia but now writes full-time and is a national long-distance triathlon champion. Rights to *Born of War* have been optioned by Nelson Films.